Humphrey's Book of...

Betty G. Birney worked at Disneyland and the Disney Studios, has written many children's television shows and is the author of over twenty-five books, including the bestselling *The World According to Humphrey*, which won the Richard and Judy Children's Book Club Award, *Friendship According to Humphrey*, *Trouble According to Humphrey*, *Surprises According to Humphrey*, *More Adventures According to Humphrey* and *Holidays According to Humphrey*. Her work has won many awards, including an Emmy and three Humanitas Prizes. She lives in America with her husband.

Praise for Humphrey:

'Humphrey, a delightful, irresistible character, is big-hearted, observant and creative, and his experiences . . . range from comedic to touching.' *Booklist*

'This is simply good-good-good.' *Kirkus Reviews*

'An effective exploration of the joys and pains of making and keeping friends, which will strike a chord with many children.' *Telegraph*

'Children fall for Humphrey, and you can't beat him for feelgood life lessons.' *Sunday Times*

Humphrey's Ho-Ho-Ho Book of Stories

Betty G. Birney

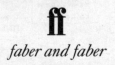

faber and faber

This omnibus first published in 2013
by Faber and Faber Limited
Bloomsbury House, 74–77
Great Russell Street, London WC1B 3DA

Typeset by Faber and Faber Ltd
Printed and bound by CPI Group (UK) Ltd, Croydon CR0 4YY

A CIP record for this book
is available from the British Library

ISBN 978–0–571–30757–9

2 4 6 8 10 9 7 5 3 1

Contents

School According to Humphrey

Contents

·ö·

The Worst First Day Begins

It was a quiet morning in Room 26, so quiet that all I could hear was the SCRATCH-SCRATCH-SCRATCH-ing of my pencil as I wrote in my little notebook.

'I'm writing a poem about the end of summer, Og,' I squeaked to my neighbour, the classroom frog. (I am Humphrey, the classroom hamster.) 'I'll read you what I have so far.'

> Summer, oh, summer,
> I hate to say goodbye
> Summer, oh, summer,
> Must you end . . . and why?

Og splashed gently in his tank as I continued.

> I loved summer days
> At Camp Happy Hollow.
> And now that they're over . . .

I stopped because there was nothing more to read.

'BOING?' Og twanged. Green frogs like him don't say 'Ribbit'. They make a sound like a broken guitar string. 'BOING-BOING!'

'I haven't finished it yet, Og,' I explained. 'I have to find a word that rhymes with Hollow. Wallow? Or Swallow?'

I stared down at the page again.

> I loved summer days
> At Camp Happy Hollow.
> And now that they're over,
> I can hardly swallow!

Og dived down deeply in his tank, splashing noisily.

'I don't think much of that line either,' I replied. 'I'll try again.'

Just then, our teacher, Mrs Brisbane, came bustling into the room, carrying a stack of papers. As usual, I quickly hid my notebook behind the mirror in my cage. As much as I love humans, some things are better kept private.

'After all my years of teaching, I should have known by now that on the first day of school, the line for the copy machine would be out of the door,' Mrs Brisbane said.

She stacked the papers on her desk and stared up at the blackboard and the noticeboards, which were bare, except for a list of rules in Mrs Brisbane's neat printing.

I'd copied those rules in my notebook while Mrs Brisbane was down at the office and I intended to memorize them as soon as possible.

Mrs Brisbane glanced up at the clock. 'School will start soon,' she said, turning towards the table by the window where Og and I spend most of our time. 'In case you two are interested.'

'I am!' I said and I meant it.

Even though I was sorry that summer was ending, I was GLAD-GLAD-GLAD to be back in good old Room 26 again. After the last camp session was over, my friend Ms Mac brought me back to the house where Mrs Brisbane and her husband, Bert, live. Og and I spent a few weeks with them.

I love to go to the Brisbanes' house, but it was so quiet there, I was looking forward to seeing my classmates again. Some of them had been at camp, like A.J., Garth, Miranda and Sayeh. But I hadn't seen some of the others for an unsqueakably long time!

The door swung open and in walked the head and Most Important Person at Longfellow School, Mr Morales. Mrs Brisbane is in charge of a whole class of students, but Mr Morales is in charge of the whole school.

As usual, he was wearing an interesting tie. This one had little books in many different colours.

'Morning, Sue,' he said to Mrs Brisbane. 'Ready to go?'

'As ready as I'll ever be,' she said.

He walked over to our table by the window. 'Guys, I hope you're all set to go back to work.'

'YES-YES-YES,' I answered, wishing that he could hear more than just the usual 'SQUEAK-

SQUEAK-SQUEAK' humans hear.

'BOING!' Og agreed.

'Good,' the head said, glancing up at the clock. 'I'd better be outside to meet the buses. Have a great one, Sue.'

'You too,' Mrs Brisbane said.

She hurried back to her desk and studied a piece of paper, then began muttering strange words like 'feebeeharrykelsey'.

Goodness, were we going to be learning a new language this year?

'Thomasrosiepaul.'

Did she say Paul? I knew that word. It was the name of a boy who had come into our class for maths last year.

I was about to point this out to Og when the bell rang as loud as ever. No matter how long I'm a student in Room 26, I'll never get used to that noisy bell.

Mrs Brisbane opened the classroom door and soon students started to come in.

I realized right away that something was wrong. *Terribly* wrong.

Mrs Brisbane smiled as the students entered.

'Take a seat,' she said. 'Any seat.'

I climbed up high in my cage to get a better look.

'Who are these kids, Og?' I asked my neighbour. 'I've never seen any of them before!'

'BOING!' he answered, splashing noisily.

More unfamiliar students came into the room. One of them was a girl who whizzed by in her wheelchair. Another was a boy who was really tall. He was as tall as our teacher – maybe taller!

'Just take a seat, children.' How could Mrs Brisbane sound so cheery, knowing these students didn't belong in Room 26?

As the classroom hamster, I felt I had to squeak up.

'You're in the wrong room!' I squeaked. 'This is not your room, go back!

'Welcome,' Mrs Brisbane told the students. 'Take a seat.'

'Wrong room!' I scrambled to the tippy-top of my cage. 'This is Room 26!'

Unfortunately, my voice is small and squeaky and I guess nobody heard me, because the students went ahead and sat down.

Mrs Brisbane kept on smiling and nobody

budged. Oh, how I wished I had a loud voice like my old friend, Lower-Your-Voice-A.J.

When the bell rang again, my heart sank. Mrs Brisbane is a GREAT-GREAT-GREAT teacher and pretty smart for a human. Why didn't she notice that her class was full of the wrong students?

'Og? What should we do?' I asked my froggy friend.

This time he didn't answer. I guess he was as confused as I was.

'Hey, Humphrey! It's me! Hi!' a familiar voice shouted.

Slow-Down-Simon raced up to my cage. He was the younger brother of Stop-Giggling-Gail Morgenstern, who *did* belong in Room 26. But she was nowhere in sight.

'Now *I'll* get to take you home some weekend,' Simon announced.

'Go back to your own room or you'll be late!' I warned him.

Mrs Brisbane told him to take a seat. Simon twirled around and rushed away, bumping right into a girl with bright red hair whose chair was sticking out in the aisle.

'You should be more careful, Kelsey,' he said.

'*You* ran into me!' The girl rubbed her arm. She probably got a big bruise. Ouch!

'What's happening just doesn't make sense!' I told Og. I don't think I was making a lot of sense, either. It was as if the world had just been turned all upside-down and Og and I were the only ones who noticed.

'Hi, Humphrey,' a soft voice said.

I looked up and there was Paul Fletcher, whom I thought of as Small Paul. He was the boy who came in for maths class every day last year because he was unsqueakably good with numbers.

Paul was smart. I knew he'd understand.

'Why are these students in the wrong room?' I asked him.

He pushed up his glasses, which had slid down his nose. 'This year I get to take you home,' he said. 'I can't wait!'

What was he talking about? Only students in Room 26 got to take me home for the week-end.

'Settle down, class,' Mrs Brisbane said. 'Please take your seats.'

Class? What was she talking about? This wasn't my class. Where were A.J. and Garth, Heidi and Mandy? Where were Gail and her giggles? Where were Richie, Art, Tabitha and Seth? Where were Kirk and his jokes? And where in the world was the almost-perfect Golden Miranda?

'Mrs Brisbane?' I squeaked. 'In case you haven't noticed, *this isn't our class*!'

Mrs Brisbane was too busy counting the students to hear me.

'We're short one student,' she said. 'But while we're waiting, let me welcome you all to Room 26!'

Crushed, I scrambled back down to the floor of my cage and scurried into my sleeping hut, where I could be alone and think.

I remembered that poem I'd just written about summer. Now I had an idea for a new verse:

> Summer, oh, summer,
> With days long and lazy,
> Now that you're over,
> Things are going crazy!

Humphrey's Rules of School

Before you take your seat in a classroom, it's always a good idea to make sure you're in the right room. This is important!

The Worst First Day Gets Worse

The final bell rang and everybody had taken a seat except the girl in a wheelchair, who was already sitting. There was still one empty chair left.

Mrs Brisbane went to the door and looked out into the hall.

'Oh, there you are,' she said.

She opened the door wider and a boy walked in.

'You must be the missing student,' Mrs Brisbane said.

'I'm not missing,' the boy answered. 'I'm right here.'

I thought he'd be in big trouble so I was surprised when Mrs Brisbane smiled and directed him to the empty chair. Then she stood in the front of the class.

'Good morning, class,' Mrs Brisbane said. 'Last year, I had one of the best classes ever. But I think this class will be even better!'

'Better?' I squeaked. 'That was the BEST-BEST-BEST class in the whole wide world!'

'BOING-BOING!' Og agreed.

I wasn't sure what I said was true. On the one paw, I couldn't imagine a better class than the one we'd had last year. On the other paw, it was the only class I'd ever been in. But where had my classmates gone?

'I'm going to rearrange the seating later in the day,' Mrs Brisbane said. 'But for now, I'll take attendance.'

'Are you listening, Og?' I asked my neighbour. I can never be sure, because he doesn't have any ears that I've ever seen. But he seems to understand me most of the time.

'Are we dreaming?' I wondered. So far, the morning felt like one of those dreams where everything seems almost the same as in real life but a lot weirder. For instance, I once had a dream where all of my human friends were rolling around in giant hamster balls. That was a very funny dream.

Once I dreamed that the class was being taught by Mrs Wright, the PE teacher. That wasn't a funny dream because she was always blowing on her very loud whistle, which is painful to the small, sensitive ears of a hamster.

Again, Og didn't answer me. Maybe frogs don't dream.

Then Mrs Brisbane began to call out the strange words she had been saying before. It turns out they were names.

'Kelsey Kirkpatrick?'

'Here,' the red-haired girl said, still rubbing her arm.

'Harry Ito?' Mrs Brisbane called out.

Harry was the boy who had been late to class.

She called on Simon, who answered, 'Present!'

Present? I didn't see any presents. Was it somebody's birthday?

'Rosie Rodriguez?' Mrs Brisbane said.

The girl in the wheelchair waved her hand and shouted out, 'Here!'

A boy named Thomas answered next, followed by a couple of girls, Phoebe and Holly.

'Are you paying attention, Og?' I asked my friend.

Og splashed a little but didn't answer.

And then something really odd happened.

'Paul?' Mrs Brisbane asked.

Right away, not one but two voices replied, 'Here.'

One of them was Small Paul from last year. The other Paul was the tall boy.

Mrs Brisbane smiled. 'I forgot. This year we have two Pauls in our class. Paul Fletcher and Paul Green. Now, how will we tell you apart?'

That was an easy question. One of them was SMALL-SMALL-SMALL and one of them was TALL-TALL-TALL.

Small Paul and Tall Paul eyed each other. Neither of them looked happy to have another Paul in the class.

'What did your teacher do last year?' she asked.

'He wasn't in my class,' Small Paul said.

'I went to another school,' Tall Paul added.

Mrs Brisbane nodded. 'I see. Do either of you have a nickname?'

Both boys shook their heads.

'Well, for now, let's say Paul F. and Paul G. Is that all right with you?' she asked.

Both boys nodded.

Then Mrs Brisbane called out one more name. 'Joseph?'

A boy with curly brown hair shifted in his chair a little but didn't answer.

Mrs Brisbane looked around at the class. 'Is Joseph here?'

The boy with curly brown hair nodded. 'Yes, ma'am,' he said. 'But it's not Joseph. It's Joey. Just Joey Jones.'

Mrs Brisbane smiled. 'All right, then. Just Joey it is. Now, class, I'm looking forward to getting to know you and you getting to know me. In case you don't know, I'm Mrs Brisbane.'

The teacher wrote her name on the board.

'There are two other members of the class you need to know,' she said.

Then she wrote my name on the board.

'Humphrey is our classroom hamster,' she said.

Everybody – and I mean everybody – turned to look at me.

Next, she wrote Og's name on the board. 'Og is our classroom frog. You'll get to know them both very well this year. You'll also have a chance to take Humphrey home for the weekend. I'll tell you more about that this afternoon,' she said.

The students all giggled and whispered and turned in their seats to look at us.

'Tell them they're in the wrong room!' I suggested and some of the students close to my cage giggled when they heard me go, 'SQUEAK-SQUEAK-SQUEAK.'

The teacher ignored me. 'First, let's get to know each other a little better. Would you take out your summer boxes.'

'Summer boxes?' I squeaked. 'What are they, Og?'

Summer was sunshine and campfires and unsqueakable fun. Summer wasn't something you could just put in a box.

I'm not sure Og could hear me since he was

splashing like crazy in his tank. But the strange students in class seemed to understand. They reached into their backpacks and pulled out boxes – all kinds of boxes – and put them on their desks.

'How did they know about the boxes?' I squeaked to Og. 'Why didn't we know?'

Og had no answer.

During the previous school year, I tried hard to keep up with my friends' homework, taking tests along with them, writing papers and even poems. Mrs Brisbane didn't know I did the work but I knew it, and that's what counts.

'All right, students. Let's share our summer experiences,' Mrs Brisbane said. 'That way, I'll learn a little bit about all of you. And you'll learn about me, because I brought a box, too.'

Mrs Brisbane took a box out of a drawer and placed it on her desk.

'I'll tell you about my summer first,' she said.

That got my attention. While I was at camp for the summer, Mrs Brisbane was doing something else, but I still wasn't really sure *what*.

'My son lives in Tokyo, Japan,' she said.

'He's a teacher there. This summer, he got married, so my husband and I went to Japan for the wedding.'

The smile on Mrs Brisbane's face let me know that she'd had a GREAT-GREAT-GREAT time.

'Weddings in Japan are very beautiful,' she said. 'The couple dresses in traditional Japanese kimonos.'

She held up a picture of a couple in very fancy clothes. 'That's my son, Jason, and his new wife, Miki.' Mrs Brisbane sounded very proud.

She passed around some Japanese money for the students to see. Next, she took out a red plastic ball she'd bought in Tokyo. I couldn't see it very well.

'Something's inside, Og!' I scampered up to the top of my cage to get a better look.

'BOING!' he replied. I guess he couldn't see either.

'I hope Humphrey won't be jealous,' Mrs Brisbane said. 'Meet Aki.'

She set the ball on the desk and the students howled with laughter as the ball started spinning wildly and coloured lights flashed.

'Rockin' Aki!' a strange, loud voice wailed. 'Rock 'n' roll rules!'

The ball looped and twirled unexpectedly as the lights kept flashing and the music blared.

'Where is Aki?' I shouted to Og, as if anyone could hear my squeaks over the noise. 'WHERE'S AKI?'

Mrs Brisbane shut the thing off.

'Show it to Humphrey,' Simon suggested.

'Yes, show Humphrey,' the other students begged.

So Mrs Brisbane brought the ball over to our table and set it down in front of my cage.

'I hope Aki doesn't scare you, Humphrey, but here goes.' She pressed a button on the ball and it all began again: the flashing lights, the looping and twirling and that song, 'Rockin' Aki! Rock 'n' roll rules!'

Now I could see what everyone was laughing at. Aki, a tiny toy hamster with wild, rainbow-striped fur, was rolling around in the hamster ball. Somehow, as the ball turned, he always remained upright as he danced.

I wasn't scared – not one bit. But I was quite impressed!

'Rockin' Aki!' I squeaked along. Of course, no one heard me. I couldn't even hear myself. 'Rock 'n' roll rules!'

I was truly sorry when Mrs Brisbane switched Aki off.

'I think that's enough rocking and rolling for today,' she said.

Some of the kids moaned and I agreed with them.

Mrs Brisbane returned the ball to her desk. 'So now you know what I did this summer. I also sent letters to all of your homes asking you to bring in a box with something that represents your summer. Who would like to share next?'

I just had to squeak up for myself. 'Hey, nobody sent me a letter!'

'BOING-BOING!' Og added.

Some hands went up in the air and Mrs Brisbane called on Simon. 'Say your name first,' she said.

Simon jumped up out of his chair, opened his box and took out a photo of a very familiar place.

'Simon Morgenstern. Here's where I went.

Camp Happy Hollow. They had a Howler and I was a Blue Jay and I burped the loudest and . . .'

Mrs Brisbane interrupted him. 'Slow-Down-Simon,' she said. 'Take your time.'

Simon tried to slow down and told the class about some of the adventures he'd had at Happy Hollow. I'd had adventures there, too, but of course, I didn't have a box because *no one told me to bring one*.

One by one, the other students shared their summer stories. Rosie had gone to a different camp. She held up a medal she won for winning a wheelchair race and a picture of her crossing the finish line. Boy, that Rosie could roll!

Harry held up a tee shirt that said 'I Survived the Blaster' and told about riding a REALLY-REALLY-REALLY fast rollercoaster. It sounded unsqueakably exciting to me!

Small Paul had taken a computer class and showed us a page of something he called 'code', but which looked like gibberish to me.

Tall Paul had a collection of pine cones from his family's camping trip in the mountains.

Holly held up an ear of corn she had grown herself when she visited her grandparents on a farm.

'I helped Grandma and Grandpa a lot,' she said. 'I fed the chickens and weeded the garden, picked the vegetables and took care of the dogs.'

'My word, that was helpful of you, Holly,' Mrs Brisbane agreed.

'And I rode a tractor and rode a horse and collected the eggs,' the girl went on.

'Thank you, Holly.'

Next, Mrs Brisbane called on a boy waving his hand impatiently.

'I'm Thomas T. True,' said a boy as he opened up a big box. 'And I went fishing with my grandpa and I caught a fish that was *huge*. It was bigger than I am!'

I was impressed and I guess the other students were, too, because they were all whispering.

'Quiet, students,' Mrs Brisbane told them. 'Go on, Thomas.'

'That fish was so big, it filled up the whole boat, so Grandpa and I had to swim to shore and pull the boat with us. Man, we ate fish for the rest of the summer!' Thomas's eyes sparkled.

'Do you have a picture of it?' Small Paul asked.

'Nope. We were too busy wrestling the fish to take a picture. So I brought Grandpa's favourite fly instead,' Thomas said, reaching in the box.

'BOING-BOING!' Og leaped with excitement when he heard the word 'fly'. After all, frogs think insects like flies are yummy. But the thing Thomas took out of the box wasn't even an insect. It was a goofy, feathery-looking thing.

'Grandpa ties his own flies. The fish think they're real flies,' he explained.

I hoped Og wasn't too disappointed that the flies were fake.

'About that big fish,' Mrs Brisbane said. 'How did you get it in the boat if it was bigger than you?'

Thomas shook his head. 'It wasn't easy, teacher. It sure wasn't easy.'

Mrs Brisbane told Thomas he could sit down and called on Kelsey.

My mind was racing with thoughts of a BIG-BIG-BIG fish that could probably eat a hamster *and* a frog if it wanted. But then I heard Kelsey say, 'Broken arm.'

A broken arm sounded painful so I listened carefully to her story. 'It was the last day of school. I was so happy it was the holidays, when I got off the bus, I raced home. But I tripped coming up the front walk and broke my arm.' She sighed. 'I was in a cast most of the summer. I couldn't go swimming even once!'

She opened her box and brought out a sling and a picture of her with a broken arm.

'The summer before that, I broke my leg!' Kelsey explained.

'I'm so sorry, Kelsey,' Mrs Brisbane said.

I was sorry, too.

'Who's left?' Mrs Brisbane asked. 'Joseph? I mean, Joey?'

Joey stood up, but he didn't look anxious to talk. 'I didn't do anything,' he said. 'I just stayed at home.'

'A stay-at-home holiday can be a lot of fun,' the teacher said.

Joey shrugged. 'It was okay. I played with my dog Skipper a lot.' He reached in his box and pulled out a Frisbee. 'He likes to catch this. He can leap way up and catch it in his teeth. He never misses. See? There are teeth marks all around the edge.'

I was starting to like Joey, but when I heard about Skipper's leaping and his teeth, I wasn't so sure. My experience with dogs has taught me that they are not especially friendly to hamsters and other small, furry creatures.

Mrs Brisbane glanced down at the class list. 'And who else is left? Phoebe Pratt?'

The girl called Phoebe didn't stand up. She just sat there, staring down at her table.

'I forgot,' she said.

'You mean you left your box at home?' Mrs Brisbane asked.

Phoebe shook her head.

'No. I forgot to make a box.' The girl looked miserable.

'Well, you can tell us what you did anyway.' It was nice of Mrs Brisbane not to be annoyed with Phoebe.

Slowly, the girl stood up. 'I had a stay-at-home holiday, too' she said. 'But I don't have a dog.'

'Can you think of anything fun that you did?' Mrs Brisbane asked.

Phoebe thought for a few seconds. 'I played games with my grandmother,' she said.

Mrs Brisbane asked questions about what kind of games Phoebe liked to play but I could tell that the girl was embarrassed that she didn't have a summer box.

So was I.

'Thanks for sharing, Phoebe. You may sit down now,' Mrs Brisbane said. 'It's almost time for break so please put your boxes away. But before you go outside, I need to find an assistant for Rosie.'

Not even one second went by before the girl named Holly waved her hand, shouting, 'Me! Me! Oh, please, I'll do it!'

'Very well, Holly,' Mrs Brisbane said. 'You and Rosie stay behind for a minute so I can tell you what to do.'

That annoying bell rang again and the students all left the room, except Holly and Rolling Rosie.

Mrs Brisbane explained that Holly would make sure the path was clear for Rosie's wheelchair, help her if she couldn't reach something, see that she got outside safely in an emergency and anything else that Rosie needed her to do.

'I'll do a good job,' Holly said.

'I'm sure you will.' Mrs Brisbane turned to Rolling Rosie. 'You'll have to make sure that Holly knows when you need help.'

'Don't worry about it,' Rosie said with a big smile. 'I don't need much help at all.'

Mrs Brisbane smiled back. 'Then I think it's time for you girls to go out to the playground.'

She watched as Holly swung the door wide open for Rosie's wheelchair and closed it again when they were in the hall.

Then she turned to Og and me. 'We have the whole year ahead of us to get to know these students.'

These strange students were *staying*? For the *rest* of the year?

Then she said, 'So far, so good.'

So far, I couldn't see anything good about the first day of school. I was too busy wondering what all my old friends from Room 26 were doing. And trying to figure out exactly where they were.

·ö· ·ö·   ·ö· ·ö·

Humphrey's Rules of School

If your teacher asks you to bring something to class, try not to forget. Of course, sometimes the teacher forgets to tell you what to bring, and that makes you feel BAD-BAD-BAD.

RULES-RULES-RULES

Usually I enjoy a nice morning nap. But there was so much going on that morning, I didn't have time to settle in for a doze until the strange students left for break. But my nap didn't last long, because when the students returned, I heard Mrs Brisbane talking and she sounded WORRIED-WORRIED-WORRIED.

'Harry didn't come back,' she said. 'Did anyone see him on the playground?'

'Sure,' Simon said. 'We shot some hoops.'

'What happened to him?' she asked.

Simon shrugged. 'I don't know.'

Mrs Brisbane frowned. 'I may have to send someone to look for him.'

'I'll find him!' said Holly, waving her hand.

'Send me.'

Just then, the door opened and Mrs Wright, the PE teacher, entered pulling Harry along with her.

'Mrs Brisbane, I believe Harry is your student,' she said. 'I found him on the playground, loitering.'

Loitering? That was a new word to me. I wished I had a dictionary in my cage. Then Mrs Wright added, 'When the bell rings, students should not dawdle.'

Dawdle? That was a funny word, too.

'I thought his teacher solved his problem last year,' Mrs Wright said. I noticed the silver whistle around her neck and crossed my paws that she wouldn't blow it. 'But I see she didn't.'

'Harry, why were you late?' Mrs Brisbane asked the boy. 'Did you hear the bell?'

Harry nodded.

'Did you see the other students lining up to come inside?' she continued.

Harry nodded again. 'Yes, and I was about to get in line when I noticed this cool anthill near my foot. I almost stepped on it! It was the biggest one I ever saw!'

'So you lost track of time?' Mrs Brisbane asked.

'Yes,' Harry said.

Mrs Wright shook her head. 'Dawdling.'

'Very well, take your seat,' Mrs Brisbane told Harry. 'Next time get right in line.'

'We do have rules, Mrs Brisbane,' Mrs Wright said. 'I hope your students obey them.'

Mrs Brisbane waited for Mrs Wright to leave. Then she said, 'Speaking of rules, I think it's time to go over the rules of this classroom.'

None too soon, I thought.

There was nothing too surprising about the rules Mrs Brisbane had printed on the board earlier that morning:

Follow directions as soon as they are given.

Raise your hand and wait to be called on before speaking.

Stay in your seat while the teacher is teaching.

Keep your hands, legs and other objects to yourself.

Walk inside the school and use your inside voice.

Treat people the way you'd like to be treated.

As I read the rules, I wondered how good I was at following them. I *try* to follow the teacher's directions. But what can I do if no one gives me directions? For example, what if no one tells me to bring a summer box to school?
Still, those rules got me thinking.

The rule about raising hands made me miss Raise-Your-Hand-Heidi, who sometimes forgot that rule last year, but I liked her anyway.

I can't stay in my seat because I don't actually have a seat. But I always try to stay in my cage while the teacher is teaching.

I try to keep my paws to myself, and I hope that dogs, cats and other large creatures will do the same.

I also try to remember to walk inside the

school. But I have to admit, sometimes I roll (in my hamster ball).

I always use my inside voice because even when I shout, it's not very loud.

And I treat people the way I'd like to be treated. At least I *mean* to.

Then Mrs Brisbane talked about the consequences of breaking the rules, which made my whiskers wiggle. A warning was bad enough and so was a time out. But a note home – eek! I thought that would be terrible until I realized that my home actually *was* Room 26. Next came a phone call home (but I don't have a phone). And finally, a student who broke the rules again would be sent to the head's office.

I liked Mr Morales a lot. But I didn't think I'd like to have to go to his office and tell him I'd broken a rule. He'd be unsqueakably disappointed in me.

I was imagining myself sitting in the head's office after breaking one of the rules when I suddenly heard Mrs Brisbane say, 'There is another rule in Room 26: all students must treat

Humphrey and Og with the greatest respect.'

My ears perked up.

'Did you hear that, Og?' I squeaked. 'She's talking about us!'

'BOING-BOING!' Og splashed around in his tank, which made the strange children laugh.

Mrs Brisbane explained that the students would get to take turns bringing me home for the weekend, but first they'd have to learn to take care of me. And while Og stayed in the classroom at weekends, because he didn't need to be fed as often as I did, they would learn to take care of him as well.

Then the teacher gathered the new group around my cage and put on some gloves, so she could show them how to clean my cage.

'Who wants to hold Humphrey?' she asked.

Not surprisingly, LOTS-LOTS-LOTS of the new students volunteered.

Mrs Brisbane slowly and gently picked me up.

'Never poke your finger in the cage,' she told the students. 'Give Humphrey time to get used to you.'

'Will he bite?' Phoebe asked nervously.

'No way!' I squeaked.

'Humphrey hasn't bitten anyone yet. But if someone poked a finger in his face, I wouldn't blame him,' Mrs Brisbane said.

'When I had a hamster, he bit my finger,' Joey said. 'But my mum said it was because he thought it was a carrot.'

Mrs Brisbane nodded. 'And if you don't wash your hands before handling a hamster, he might smell the food you've eaten and think you're something to eat, too.'

I don't like to disagree with the teacher, but first of all, many humans have hands that don't smell like anything I'd want to eat. And I'm smart enough to tell the difference between a carrot and a finger!

'Let's see. Why don't you take him, Kelsey?' she said.

Kelsey looked surprised.

I'm sure I did, too. Kelsey looked like a nice girl, but it did seem as if she could be more careful.

'Hold him in your hand, like this.' Mrs Brisbane transferred me to Kelsey's outstretched hand. 'Make him feel very safe. Cup your other hand over his head, like a little roof. I think he likes that.'

I do like that, as a matter of fact.

Kelsey was so excited to be holding me, her hand actually shook a little. I suddenly remembered about her broken arm and her broken leg and I hoped I wouldn't end up being a broken hamster.

'Don't worry, Humphrey. I'll be careful with you,' she whispered.

I relaxed and so did she. The shaking stopped.

'Can I pet him?' Simon asked.

'Gently,' Mrs Brisbane told him.

He stroked my back with his fingers. It felt unsqueakably nice.

Then Mrs Brisbane got busy cleaning my cage. She took everything out – even my water bottle – and put it all in a big bucket of soapy water. Luckily, my mirror is firmly attached to my cage and it stayed (as well as my notebook hiding behind it).

Next, she took a brush and BRUSHED-BRUSHED-BRUSHED everything clean.

After that, she took all the soft, papery bedding out of my cage.

'What's that?' Holly asked, pointing to a corner.

'That's Humphrey's bathroom area,' Mrs Brisbane replied. 'Those are his droppings.'

'His poo?' Thomas's eyes opened wide with surprise.

Mrs Brisbane nodded.

'Ewww – poo!' Thomas said.

Somebody giggled. Then all of the kids started chanting, 'Ewww-poo! Ewww-poo!' in a very rude way.

Mrs Brisbane shushed them. 'Come on. It's perfectly natural.'

'Perfectly natural!' I repeated. 'Besides, where else am I supposed to go?'

'May I hold Humphrey?' Rosie asked. 'I already know how to hold a guinea pig.'

Mrs Brisbane carefully moved me from Kelsey's palm to Rosie's. Her hand didn't shake one bit.

Next, the teacher scrubbed the bottom and sides of my cage until they were unsqueakably clean.

She let Helpful Holly and Just Joey put new bedding in my cage, while Phoebe filled my water bottle and Paul F. put fresh Nutri-Nibbles in my feeder. Yum.

Paul G. put my wheel back in and made sure it was spinning properly while Harry and Thomas put everything else back in place.

'It looks and smells a lot better now, Humphrey,' Mrs Brisbane said as she gently carried me from Rosie's hand back to the cage. 'Check it out.'

I hopped on that shiny clean wheel and gave it all I had.

'Look at Humphrey go!' Thomas T. True cried out. 'He must be going a million miles an hour!'

'He couldn't be going a million miles an hour. He'd break the sound barrier at 768 miles and I don't hear a sonic boom,' Small Paul said.

I was impressed. But I have to admit, I felt as if I was going a million miles an hour.

'I guess Thomas was just exaggerating a little,' Mrs Brisbane said.

'Thomas exaggerates a lot,' Small Paul said.

'Now, students, no bickering,' Mrs Brisbane told them. 'Let's go back to our places.'

I hopped off my wheel and settled down in that lovely fresh bedding.

Phoebe raised her hand and Mrs Brisbane called on her. 'Did you say we all get to take Humphrey home?'

'At one time or another, yes,' was the answer. Phoebe's face lit up.

'If you don't get a turn right away, don't worry,' the teacher continued. 'You'll get him eventually, as long as your parents sign a permission form. After all, families don't always have time for a hamster at the weekend.'

Phoebe's smile faded away but I think I was the only one who noticed.

I was the one smiling when Mrs Brisbane asked the students who'd like to take me home and every single hand went up.

Maybe these new humans weren't quite as strange as I thought.

·ö·

Later, Mrs Brisbane rearranged the seating in the classroom. First, she had everyone take their belongings to the sides of the room. Then she told each student where to sit. There were a few groans but mostly the kids settled down without complaint, until Mrs Brisbane went back to teaching and made some notes on the board.

Suddenly, a hand began waving. 'Teacher?'

Mrs Brisbane looked up. 'Please call me Mrs Brisbane,' she said. 'What is it, Kelsey?'

'I can't see with *him* there.' She pointed to Tall Paul, who was seated directly in front of her.

I could imagine it would be hard to see with Paul G. blocking her view.

'My mistake,' Mrs Brisbane said. 'I must have got the Pauls mixed up. Paul Green, could you switch places with Paul Fletcher?'

'Okay.' Tall Paul gathered his belongings and moved towards the side of the room.

Small Paul picked up his notebook and backpack and moved towards the front of the room. He wouldn't block anyone's view.

Somewhere in the middle, they almost walked right into each other.

'Watch out!' I squeaked.

Everybody laughed, except the two Pauls.

They carefully avoided walking into each other and I noticed that they also avoided looking at each other.

'Now can you see, Kelsey?' Mrs Brisbane asked.

'I can see fine,' Kelsey answered.

Mrs Brisbane continued with the lesson but I couldn't concentrate.

I was watching the two Pauls, staring down at their desks.

I was GLAD-GLAD-GLAD when the school bell rang at the end of the day and only Mrs Brisbane, Og and I were left in the room. Whew! It had been a tiring day. Like most hamsters, I sleep more during the day than at night, but with so much going on, I hadn't got much napping done. But there was no time to sleep now. I needed time to myself to try and figure things out.

I was deep in thought when I heard a familiar, friendly voice.

'I survived!' the voice said.

'Congratulations,' Mrs Brisbane replied.

I scampered up to a tree branch near the top

of my cage as one of my favourite humans, Ms Mac, entered the room.

Ms Mac was beautiful. Ms Mac was sweet. Ms Mac was amazing. If it hadn't been for Ms Mac, I would probably still be living at boring old Pet-O-Rama, hoping that someone would give me a real home. Ms Mac found me there and brought me to Room 26. Then she went to Brazil for a while and I had to learn to live with Mrs Brisbane. I wasn't too sure about her at first, but she turned out to be a great teacher.

Now Ms Mac was back. But where had she been all day?

She sank into a chair next to Mrs Brisbane's desk. 'I have a lot to learn,' she said.

'You'll be fine,' Mrs Brisbane assured her. 'But first grade isn't easy.'

So *that's* where Ms Mac was. She was teaching first grade at Longfellow School!

'It's exciting, but there's so much to teach them,' Ms Mac continued. 'I wish I had Humphrey and Og to help.'

She glanced over our way and waved. 'Hi, guys,' she said.

'Hi, Ms Mac! You'll be great at first grade –

mark my words!' I squeaked in encouragement while Og splashed loudly in his tank.

'How did your day go?' Ms Mac asked Mrs Brisbane.

'I think it will be a good year,' Mrs Brisbane said. 'Want to grab a cup of coffee?'

'Would I!' Ms Mac answered.

While Mrs Brisbane gathered up her things, Ms Mac came over to see Og and me. She leaned down close to my cage and I saw her big, happy smile and her sparkling eyes. She smelled of apples, 'Maybe I can borrow you once in a while,' she whispered.

'I hope so,' I whispered back. But unfortunately, I know all she heard was a very soft squeak.

Then Og and I were alone, left to think over the strange happenings of the first day of school.

'Thomas does exaggerate,' I said to my neighbour. 'I think that fish story was a tall tale.'

'BOING!' he answered.

'Phoebe is very forgetful, but Holly is VERY-VERY-VERY helpful,' I added.

'BOING!' he agreed again.

'I wonder why Harry can't hurry up,' I said after a little more thinking.

'BOING-BOING!' my friend replied.

'But I don't have time to worry about these strange students,' I continued. 'Because I'm busy worrying about what happened to my *real* friends from Room 26 – the ones from last year.'

I was silent for a few seconds, and then I squeaked what was really on my mind. 'Am I ever going to see them again?'

Humphrey's Rules of School

Treat hamsters the way you'd like to be treated, which includes telling them where their friends have gone!

Night School

When the room got dark, my thoughts got darker. Not only was I curious about where my old friends had gone, but I was also unsqueakably worried about what they would do without a helpful hamster to help them with their problems. I don't mean to brag, but I had lent a helping paw to all my classmates last year, even if they didn't always know it.

'No use sitting around and worrying,' I suddenly squeaked out loud. 'We need to do something!'

'BOING!' Og agreed.

Just then, the room was filled with bright light.

'Never fear, 'cause Aldo's here!' a friendly

voice boomed out.

'Aldo!' I shouted, happy to see Aldo Amato pull his cleaning trolley into the room. Aldo is the caretaker and he's also a wonderful friend. I'd seen him at camp over the summer but I hadn't seen him for the last few weeks.

He came up to the table and gazed down at me.

'You're a sight for sore eyes, Humphrey,' he said, reaching in his pocket. 'Here, have some sunflower seeds.'

Yum! I'm always happy to get my favourite treat.

Aldo found a jar of Froggy Food Sticks for Og and sprinkled some in his tank. 'Here you go, Og. Enjoy them in good health!'

Og swam around, gathering the little sticks in his huge mouth. I'm sorry he doesn't get tasty sunflower seeds like I do, but he doesn't seem to mind.

'So it's back to school for all of us,' he said. 'Back to work at night and back to college in the daytime for me.'

Aldo was going to college so he could be a teacher one day.

'I have some good courses this year,' Aldo continued. 'Including biology. That's where I'll learn about creatures like you.'

I chomped away on a sunflower seed, thinking that biology *must* be an interesting course.

'Look, I saw Richie after school. I think he's a little worried about his new teacher, Miss Becker.' I stopped mid-chomp. Repeat-It-Please-Richie Rinaldi was Aldo's nephew and a former classmate in Room 26.

'Miss Becker? Where is she? How can I find Richie?' I squeaked. 'Why is he worried?'

I guess Aldo didn't understand. 'I'll tell him you said hello,' he answered.

Suddenly, the sunflower seed didn't taste so good, because Richie was worried. Even if he wasn't in Room 26 any more, he was still my friend.

Then Aldo got to work cleaning Room 26. He was wonderful at his job. I thought he'd be an unsqueakably good teacher some day, but I knew that once he was teaching, Room 26 would never be quite as clean again.

Watching Aldo got my mind off my worries until he saw that red hamster ball sitting on

Mrs Brisbane's desk.

'Hey, who's this? Are they replacing you, Humphrey?' Aldo laughed, but I didn't think that was funny.

He turned the switch on and Aldo roared as the ball twirled and looped and flashed and the music blasted. 'Rockin' Aki! Rock 'n' roll rules!'

As Aldo watched, he did a little dance just like Aki.

After a while, he switched Aki off.

'That's funny,' he said. 'But don't worry. Nothing could replace you, Humphrey.'

'Thank you,' I squeaked.

'Richie would like one of those,' Aldo said.

I wish he hadn't reminded me of Richie. I didn't like to think about my old friend being worried.

After Aldo left and I saw his car pull out of the car park outside my window, I decided to investigate the school and find out where Richie and my other old friends had gone.

'Don't you think I should find out where this Miss Becker's classroom is, Og?' I asked.

'BOING-BOING!' Og is always encouraging, at least most of the time.

Of course, Longfellow School is a BIG-BIG-BIG place so I probably couldn't cover it all in one night. But I was at least going to try.

I pushed on my cage door. Thanks to my lock-that-doesn't-lock, the door swung wide open. To humans, that lock always looks tightly fastened. But I know that a little gentle pressure opens the door and I'm free to come and go as I please.

I climbed out, grabbed hold of the leg of our table and slid down. After I landed, I shook myself and scampered to the door.

'I'll be back to give you a full report, Og!' I told my friend. 'Wish me luck!'

'BOING-BOING!' he answered.

I crouched down and slid through the narrow space between the bottom of the door and the floor.

It was dark in the hallway except for some very faint lights which cast ghostly shadows on the walls. I shivered a little but nothing was going to keep me from my mission.

I took a left turn and skittered along until I reached the next doorway. I looked UP-UP-

UP and saw 'Room 28' on the door. I wasn't sure what had happened to Room 27 but I didn't want to waste time thinking about that.

After taking a deep breath, I slid under the door into Room 28. When I stood up, I was surprised to see that Room 28 looked almost exactly like Room 26 – except that everything was backwards! Well, not exactly everything. The blackboards and windows were on the same side as in Room 26, but the cloakroom, the teacher's desk and the clock were all in the wrong place.

'Eek!' I squeaked.

I scurried between the desks but since Aldo had just cleaned, there weren't many clues around to tell me who was in the room. I stopped to glance up at the blackboard. Luckily, the moonbeams coming through the windows hit at just the right angle and I saw 'Mr Michaels' written on the board.

This wasn't Miss Becker's room after all.

I didn't want to waste time in the wrong room, so I slid back under the door and continued up the dimly lit hallway to the next classroom on the left, Room 30.

'Here goes nothing,' I thought, as I pushed under the door.

Oddly enough, Room 30 looked more like Room 26 than Room 28. The cloakroom, the teacher's desk and the clock were in the same place as in Room 26.

But there were some differences. For one thing, the tables were placed in a great big circle. Mrs Brisbane had her tables lined up in rows.

Along one of the walls was a huge tree going all the way up to the ceiling. It was made of paper and each of the brightly coloured paper leaves had a name on it.

It was hard to read the names in the darkened room but I saw an Emma and a Margaret, a Christopher and a Ben. I didn't know any of those names, so this was probably the wrong room.

I escaped under the door and hurried to the room across the hall – Room 29.

It was unsqueakably dark in this room because the blinds were shut tightly. I could hardly even make out the shadowy shapes of tables and chairs. When I looked up, I let out an extra-loud 'Squeak!' because there were large round objects hanging from the ceiling, giving off an eerie glow. I felt shivery and quivery until I figured out that they were models of the planets in our solar system. Thank goodness Mrs Brisbane taught us about them last year, so I knew what they were.

I began to look for clues to find out if my friends had moved into this room. I darted to the front of the class near the teacher's desk. When I looked UP-UP-UP, I saw a sign sitting on top of the desk. 'Mrs Murch,' the sign read.

Wrong room again!

I hurried back out of Room 29 towards the next room. *There* was Room 27!

I took a deep breath and slipped under the door.

It was a little brighter in this room because the blinds had been left open and moonlight streamed through the windows. But a quick glance at the board told me I was in the wrong room again.

'Miss Loomis,' was written out in large letters.

But next to the teacher's name was a list of

students and some of them were very familiar.

Miranda, Garth, Seth, Sayeh, Art, Mandy. They'd all been in Room 26 last year. So some of the students had gone to Miss Becker's class and some of them had moved to Miss Loomis's class.

Then I remembered something.

'This is where Og came from!' I squeaked out loud.

It was true. Og had once lived in Miss Loomis's class. The day she brought him to Room 26 to stay was quite a shock to me, I can tell you that! But over time, I've got used to my funny green friend.

I was thinking about those early days with Og when suddenly a strange sound boomed out of the darkness.

'RUM-RUM. RUM-RUM.'

It was very loud and very deep – so deep, it made my ears twitch.

'RUM-RUM. RUM-RUM.'

The sound came from the corner and I could make out the shape of a tank sitting on a table.

'RUM-RUM! RUM-RUM!' the voice bellowed.

I cautiously edged my way towards the table. Yes, it was a tank, all right, and sitting in that tank was a huge frog, way bigger than Og! Instead of a pleasant smile, like Og's, he was leering. Or was he sneering?

'Hello, George!' I squeaked. 'I'm a friend of Og's. Remember him?'

RUM-RUM! RUM-RUM! George answered. He certainly didn't sound friendly. I recalled that Miss Loomis had got Og to keep George company, but George didn't like Og, so she'd brought him to Mrs Brisbane's class.

RUM-RUM-RUM-RUM! George was getting louder and louder. I guess he didn't like me either, so I ran away as fast as my small legs could carry me and slid under the door.

Whew! I could still hear George out in the hall. I was lucky to get away from him, but I was worried about my friends who were stuck in class with him every single day. They must be miserable!

I was tempted to race back to Room 26 so I could tell Og about my discovery, but the next door was marked Room 25. It was right across the hall from my classroom so I decided to check to see if that was Miss Becker's room.

For some reason, there was very little space between the bottom of this door and the floor so I had to flatten myself as much as I could and push myself through. The problem was, halfway through the door I just stopped.

I was stuck!

'Eek!' I squeaked. Not that it mattered. There was no one around to hear me.

I pushed again but I didn't budge. My head was in Room 25 and my tail was in the hallway!

My mind raced as I imagined spending the night under the door while Og worried about what had happened to me. Then I thought about morning, when someone would come to open the door. They might not even see me! I might get squashed as the door opened or stepped on by students. I might never ever see the inside of Room 26 again!

Then I remembered that at camp the counsellors always told us campers to stay calm in case of emergency.

'Stay CALM-CALM-CALM,' I told myself, although it's hard to be calm when you're stuck under a door.

After a few seconds, I felt relaxed enough to look at the room in front of me. I couldn't see much except a jumble of desks and the usual blackboard. I couldn't move my head but I could move my eyes so I looked all the way to the right and saw desks. Then I looked all the way to the left and saw the cloakroom. In front of the cloakroom wall was a large trolley filled with books. I had to squint to read the sign on it:

PROPERTY OF ROOM 25
MR MCCAULEY'S ROOM
DO NOT REMOVE!

So this wasn't Miss Becker's room. I didn't have to explore Room 25 after all. When I tried backing out from under the door, I didn't have a bit of trouble. If I'd stayed a little calmer, I might have realized sooner that although I couldn't slide forward, I could easily back out.

'Whew!' I sighed as I stopped in the dark hallway, listening to my heart pound. When my heart slowed down, I hurried across the hall to Room 26 and slid under the door.

'Og, I'm back!' I squeaked. 'I'm not stuck under the door!'

Og splashed wildly in his tank. 'BOING-BOING-BOING-BOING!' he called to me.

I dashed across the floor towards the table. It's unsqueakably difficult and dangerous for me to get back up to my cage but tonight, I wasted no time. I grabbed on to the long cord that dangles down from the blinds, held on tight and began swinging back and forth, pushing with all my might. The cord began to swing higher and higher until I was level with the tabletop. Then I let go of the cord and slid on to the table, zooming right past Og's tank.

Once I got my footing, I hurried into my cage and pulled the door behind me.

For the first time all evening, I felt safe. You have no idea how comforting it can be to have a nice cage for protection.

'Okay, Og,' I said when I could breathe again. 'Our friends are not in Rooms 28, 30 or 29. I didn't quite make it into Room 25 but I could see that it wasn't Miss Becker's class.'

'BOING!' Og seemed surprised.

'However, some of them are in Room 27. That's Miss Loomis's class – remember her?' I asked.

'BOING-BOING-BOING-BOING!' I guess Og remembered.

'George is still there and he's not a bit friendly!' I complained. 'Garth and Miranda and a whole bunch of students from the old class are there with him!'

Og took a giant dive into the water side of his tank and madly splashed around.

The more I thought about George, the happier I was that Og moved to Room 26. When Og stopped splashing, I told him more about my adventure – even the scary part where I got stuck under the door.

'BOING-BOING-BOING!' he said when I was finished.

I sighed and relaxed. I glanced around the room and saw that red hamster ball sitting on Mrs Brisbane's desk.

The thought of Aki singing and dancing made me laugh. I began humming – or at least my way of humming.

'Rockin' Aki! Rock 'n' roll rules!' I squeaked

as I hopped on to my wheel and gave it a good spin.

Then Og joined in. 'BOING-BOING!' he twanged. Then he dived into his water and did some unsqueakably wild splashing.

After a while, though, I stopped spinning and crawled into my sleeping hut to rest.

It turns out that investigating *and* rocking and rolling can make you VERY-VERY-VERY tired.

Humphrey's Rules of School

Whenever possible, try to walk through doors instead of under them.

A Friendly Face

Autumn, oh, autumn,
It comes when summer ends,
Autumn, oh, autumn,
What happened to my friends?

I was finishing a new poem in my notebook as the first bell rang the next morning and the strange students came streaming back into Room 26.

I was a little sleepy after my night of heart-pounding adventure, so I wasn't paying too much attention until a perky voice loudly said, 'Wait right there, Rosie! I'll get your backpack for you!'

It was Helpful Holly and she was doing a very good job of being Rolling Rosie's personal assistant.

'That's okay, Holly,' Rosie answered. 'I can handle it.'

Rosie did handle her backpack very well, moving it from the back of her wheelchair to the floor next to her table.

'I'll push you in,' Holly said.

'I can do it myself,' Rosie replied.

Holly suddenly didn't look very happy. 'I'm supposed to help you,' she said.

Rosie gave her a friendly smile. 'Thanks, Holly. If I need help, I'll let you know.'

'Okay,' Holly said. But she sounded RE-ALLY-REALLY-REALLY disappointed.

I was sorry for Holly because she was only trying to help. But I was glad to see that Rosie was so good at taking care of herself.

After she took attendance, Mrs Brisbane did something pretty surprising. (But then she's always surprising me.)

'Class,' she said. 'I asked you to bring in a list of three interesting facts about yourself in your summer box, remember?'

Most of the students nodded their heads.

I didn't nod because once again, nobody told *me* to bring in a list.

'Your answers were really interesting, so I've taken them and made a little get-to-know-you quiz,' she continued. 'We're going to take half an hour for you to ask each other questions and find out the answers. I've printed out sheets with the questions and places for your answers.'

After she gave them more instructions, the room got pretty noisy. While the students talked and wrote, Mrs Brisbane took snapshots of each one – although she forgot to take pictures of Og and me. It was too confusing to hear what everyone said, so I tried to think of three interesting facts about me.

Hamsters are pretty fascinating, I guess, because it was hard to narrow my list down to three. Here's what I came up with:

I am golden. (Which is true, because I'm a golden hamster. Last year, I wouldn't have been the only golden student in class because Miranda Golden – or Golden

Miranda as I called her – was in the room.)

I have a friend named Og. He is not golden. He is green.

I have a lock-that-doesn't-lock. (Which is true but I wouldn't put that on a list because it's a secret.)

I have a notebook hidden in my cage. (See above.)

I was brought to Room 26 by Ms Mac. (Whom I love.)

I am afraid of loud noises such as whistles.

I wish humans could understand me.

I miss my old friends.

You are all making so much noise I can't hear myself think!

I was still working on my list in my head when Mrs Brisbane announced it was time for the students to return to their seats. Then she asked questions from the sheets one by one and the students shared the answers they had written down. I wished I could write the answers in my notebook as well, but I didn't dare get it out because someone might see me and find out about it.

'Listen carefully, Og!' I squeaked to my neighbour.

Here are a few things I remember:

Hurry-Up-Harry likes table tennis. I don't know how you play tennis with a table but I guess Harry does.

Rosie has three older brothers. One of them has two guinea pigs. I think I'd like to meet them one day. The guinea pigs, I mean.

Slow-Down-Simon has a sister who was in Mrs Brisbane's class last year. (I already knew that. Her name is Stop-Giggling-Gail and I miss her!)

Helpful Holly wants to be a veterinarian and she volunteers at an animal shelter.

Tall Paul used to go to a school called

Golden Pines. He also collects remote control cars.

Be-Careful-Kelsey likes to climb trees. (Which sounds VERY-VERY-VERY dangerous.)

Small Paul Fletcher builds model planes.

Thomas T. True has a collection of shark teeth. *Great big* shark teeth.

Phoebe lives with her grandmother.

Just-Joey Jones likes strawberry ice cream. (Yum!)

While the students took turns reading for Mrs Brisbane, my mind drifted to the facts I'd heard.

Golden Pines was a beautiful name for Paul G.'s old school. If they had golden trees, maybe they had golden hamsters like me there.

I worried about Thomas's shark teeth. I hoped he didn't have the sharks to go with them, as I've seen pictures of them and they are unsqueakably scary creatures.

I also hoped Be-Careful-Kelsey was careful

when she climbed trees. She'd already broken her arm *and* her leg.

When the bell rang for break, the students raced out of the room.

'I'll hold the door for you, Rosie!' Holly said as she raced across the room.

'Okay,' Rosie answered as she rolled along next to her.

Thomas was just about through the door when Mrs Brisbane stopped him. 'Thomas, where's your jacket?'

'I don't need it, Mrs Brisbane. It's hot outside. It's about forty degrees,' he said.

'Thomas, please don't exaggerate. It's a little chilly and you have short sleeves. I want you to check the thermometer on the window and see what the temperature really is.' She pointed him in the direction of the window. Way past our table, there was a little thermometer stuck to the window that showed the outside temperature.

'What's it say?' she asked.

'Fourteen,' Thomas answered.

'Wear your sweatshirt,' Mrs Brisbane said. 'Or Mrs Wright will blow her whistle at you.'

Mrs Brisbane watched Thomas leave the room. She shook her head, then sat at her desk, sorting pictures of the students.

Suddenly, a voice called out, 'Hey, Humphrey Dumpty!'

I'd know that LOUD-LOUD-LOUD voice anywhere. It was Lower-Your-Voice-A.J. from my old class. I liked it when he called me Humphrey Dumpty.

'Hi, Mrs Brisbane,' he said.

'Hello, A.J. You know you're supposed to be outside at break,' she told him.

'Can I at least say hi to Humphrey?' he asked.

Mrs Brisbane smiled. 'Of course. But just for a moment.'

'Where have you been?' I squeaked as A.J. raced up to my cage.

'Hi, Humphrey! Hi, Og! I miss you guys,' he said, leaning in close. 'We don't have any classroom pets in Miss Becker's class. But we're working on her. She said she'd think about it.'

'But *I'm* your classroom pet,' I squeaked impatiently.

'Nice talking to you, too,' A.J. answered. If

only he could understand me!

'Can I take Humphrey home some week-end?' he asked Mrs Brisbane.

'My new students are awfully anxious to have him,' she answered. 'But maybe if there's a free weekend, I'll call on you. Now you go outside before Mrs Wright finds out you're in-side during break.'

A.J. raced out of the classroom and I don't blame him. I'd do anything to keep Mrs Wright from blowing her earsplitting whistle.

Later that afternoon, when I should have been listening to Mrs Brisbane talk about numbers, I thought about what A.J. had said. He and my other friends wanted a classroom pet. *Another* classroom pet. Maybe they'd rather have a guinea pig or a rabbit or a frog like Og. Or even *another hamster*.

My spirits sank down to my tiny toes.

Just before school was over for the day, as the students straightened up their desks, I heard Holly say, 'Simon, your backpack is too close to Rosie's wheelchair! What if she had to get out in a hurry?'

Holly *was* extremely helpful.

Simon picked up his backpack. 'Sorry, Rosie,' he said.

'There's nothing to be sorry about,' Rolling Rosie told him. 'It's not in my way.'

'It could have been a problem if —' Helpful Holly started.

'But it's not, Holly,' Rosie interrupted. 'Okay?' She glared at Holly and I thought Holly was going to cry.

'I'm just trying to help,' Helpful Holly said, blinking.

'Thanks,' Rolling Rosie answered.

I'm not sure she meant it. And I really didn't understand what was going on.

When the final bell rang, I overheard something else that was a little strange.

'Hey, Paul G., can you touch the top of the door?' Thomas T. True asked.

Tall Paul shrugged. 'I don't know.'

'Try it,' Thomas said.

'Yeah, let's see how far you can reach,' Simon added.

Tall Paul paused and reached way, way up.

When he got on his tiptoes, he could actually touch the top of the door frame.

'Man, you're a giant,' said Thomas. 'You must be a great basketball player.'

'Whatever,' Tall Paul mumbled on his way out.

Just then, Small Paul Fletcher approached the door.

'Did you see how high he could reach?' Thomas asked him.

'So what?' Small Paul mumbled, pushing his way past Thomas.

'Move along, folks, or you'll miss your buses,' Mrs Brisbane warned the new students. 'Better Hurry-Up-Harry.'

Harry was still at his table, slowly stuffing books and papers in his backpack.

'I don't take the bus,' he said. 'My mum picks me up.'

'Ah,' Mrs Brisbane said. 'Well, don't make her wait.'

'It's okay. She's always late,' Harry said.

After a few minutes, Harry left the room. Mrs Brisbane let out a big sigh and walked over to our table by the window.

'I always forget that it takes a while to get to know a new class,' she told Og and me. 'But it's an interesting group and I know you guys are going to be a big help.'

'I'll try!' I squeaked.

After all, I'm a classroom hamster and helping the teacher is my job.

But I still missed my old friends.

Humphrey's Rules of School

Follow the teacher's directions, even if your heart isn't always in it.

Shake, Wiggle and Spin

Mrs Brisbane left, and the room grew dark over time.

Then suddenly the door opened and the lights came on again.

'Hello, mammal! Hello, amphibian!' Aldo's voice boomed out as he rolled his cleaning trolley into the room.

'Hello, yourself,' I squeaked back, even though I didn't know what he was talking about. Last year he'd learned Spanish. Was he learning another language?

'Humphrey, you and I are mammals. But Og is an amphibian,' he explained as he started to sweep the room. 'I learned that in biology.'

I loved to watch Aldo sweep. He was so

graceful as he whirled the broom around the tables and under the chairs, straightening them as he went.

'See, humans and rodents like you, Humphrey, are mammals. We all have fur and ears that you can see and four legs. We're also warm-blooded,' he said.

'I knew we had a lot in common,' I said. I was unsqueakably glad that Aldo and I were both mammals. Most humans are not as furry as hamsters, but Aldo was an extra-furry human, especially with his great big moustache.

'Og, you're an amphibian,' he continued. 'You don't have any fur or hair and you've got webbed feet. Also, we can't see your ears.'

That was true. I'd been looking for Og's ears for as long as I'd known him but I still couldn't see them.

'You're also cold-blooded, Og.' Aldo got out his rag and started dusting the tables. 'Which means your body temperature goes up and down, while warm-blooded creatures like Humphrey and me have the same temperature no matter what the weather.'

Boy, Aldo is sure going to make a great teacher one day!

I was sort of sorry that Og and I didn't have much in common until Aldo said, 'I think amphibians are just as nice as mammals. Don't you, Humphrey?'

'YES-YES-YES!' I answered.

Og let out a giant 'BOING!'

A little later, Aldo stopped to eat his dinner and talk to us. He always gave us yummy treats. (Well, my treats were yummy but Og's didn't look too tasty to me. However, he's an amphibian and I'm not.)

While he ate his sandwich, Aldo told us something very interesting.

'Richie's still having trouble getting used to his new teacher.' Aldo paused to take a gulp of coffee from his thermos.

'He was sort of upset, because Miss Becker moved him away from Kirk. He should probably thank her for that because when he sits near Kirk, he usually gets in trouble,' Aldo said.

I knew Aldo was right. Kirk liked to tell jokes and Richie liked to laugh at them. None of the strange students told jokes. So far, anyway.

'She had to separate Gail and Heidi, too,' Aldo told us.

I could understand that because they were best friends. Gail was a great giggler and Heidi always giggled when she was around her. None of the strange students giggled like Gail. Not even her brother, Simon.

'Anyway, Richie will get used to her,' Aldo said. 'Just like you got used to Mrs Brisbane.'

It had taken me quite a while to get used to Mrs Brisbane, and she was just one human being.

How long would it take me to get used to a whole room full of strangers?

Aldo rose and started pushing his trolley towards the door.

'I think Richie's real problem is that they don't have a classroom pet in Room 18.' Aldo turned off the light. 'See you tomorrow night!'

I was a little disappointed when he walked right past Aki's red hamster ball on Mrs Brisbane's desk and didn't turn it on.

When the door was closed and my eyes got used to the darkness, I had an idea.

'Did he say Room 18, Og?' I asked my neighbour.

'BOING!' Og replied.

'That must be where the rest of our old friends are now. I'd sure like to see that room.' I was already pushing on the lock-that-doesn't-lock. 'I'll tell you all about it when I get back.'

Soon I was out in the hallway. I knew that Room 18 wasn't to the left of Room 26, so I turned right and scurried down the hall. It had those dim lights to guide me, but a school with no children in it is unsqueakably quiet.

It was hard to see the numbers on the doors from way down low but if I looked straight up, I could read them. Just like the night before, all the even numbers were on one side of the hallway and all the odd numbers were on the other. So I read them: 24, 23, 22, 21, 20. I ran out of hallway before I got to room 18, so I took a sharp left turn and the hallway continued. There was Room 19 and across from it: Room 18.

I was a little nervous about sliding under an

unfamiliar door after I'd got stuck, but this time the gap between the door and floor was nice and wide. Whew!

Room 18 didn't look all that different from Room 26. There were tables and chairs, blackboards and a teacher's desk. There was even a long table by the window, like the one where my cage and Og's tank sits. But instead of mammals and amphibians on the table, there was a neat row of boxes, each labelled with a name. I skittered across the floor to get a better look and saw the names of some of my good old friends from last year. Gail and Heidi, A.J. and Richie, Kirk and Tabitha – along with names I'd never seen before.

I stared at those boxes for a long time, remembering all the good times I'd had last year.

Then, suddenly lights began to flash. My insides did a flip-flop. Was someone in the building? Was it Aldo – or had someone broken in? Why were they flashing the lights?

BOOM! There was a loud crash. Someone was breaking in for sure!

There was a tremendous clatter – and my insides settled down a bit as I realized that it was raining outside. The flashing lights and crashing sounds were lightning and thunder! I hurried back out into the hallway and back to Room 26. Of course, *I* wasn't afraid, but I was worried that Og might be.

'Don't worry, Og. It's just a thunderstorm. It won't hurt you,' I assured my friend when I was safely back in my cage.

I told him about the boxes in Room 18 and the names on them. Maybe it made Og sad to think of his old friends so far away. He didn't make a sound, so for the rest of the night, I sat in my cage and listened to the rain.

It was still raining the next morning (but the lightning and thunder had stopped, thank goodness). The students arrived in Room 26 with an assortment of umbrellas, raincoats and hats, which were put in the cloakroom. I was glad to have a nice dry cage to stay in, especially since hamsters shouldn't ever get wet.

Just Joey rushed out of the cloakroom and hurried over to my cage.

'Hi, Humphrey,' he said. 'It's me, Joey.'

'I know you're Joey,' I squeaked.

He laughed. 'You answered me!'

'Of course,' I said. 'I'm a very polite hamster.'

I wished he could understand what I said.

'Humphrey, I had a hamster once. His name was Giggles, because he made little sounds that kind of sounded like giggles,' he said.

'What happened to him?' I asked.

'I don't have him any more,' Joey suddenly looked sad. 'He D-I-E-D.'

I guess he thought I couldn't spell, but I knew what D-I-E-D meant.

'I wanted another hamster but my parents got me a dog instead,' he explained. 'Skipper. I like Skipper – okay – I love him. But I still think about good old Giggles.'

'Of course you do. He was your friend,' I said. 'I'm unsqueakably sorry.'

'Now you're giggling, too!' Joey's face lit up. 'I like that!'

Well, I hadn't meant to giggle, but I was happy if I made Joey feel better.

When Joey ran off to join his friends, I told myself that whenever he was near my cage, I was going to giggle.

I climbed up my tree branch, all the way to the tippy-top of my cage.

More students came in, looking damp and drippy.

'Boy, that thunder last night was so loud, it shook the house and all our pictures fell down,' Thomas announced when he arrived. 'Even my teeth shook.'

'Thomas T. True, is that really true?' Mrs Brisbane asked.

Thomas shrugged. 'That's what it felt like, anyway.'

When Mrs Brisbane took attendance, Harry was missing again. She shook her head when she read his name, but he finally showed up in the middle of reading.

'Did you get an excuse from the office?' Mrs Brisbane asked. Harry reached into his pocket and pulled out a slip of paper.

'Dad drove me and we got caught in traffic,' he said.

I thought that made sense on a very wet day

and Mrs Brisbane didn't say anything. Harry went into the cloakroom to hang up his jacket. The other students kept on reading, but Harry didn't come out of the cloakroom, so Mrs Brisbane went back to check on him.

The cloakroom isn't really a room, but it's partially walled off from the rest of the room and I can't see inside from my spot by the window.

'Harry? What are you doing?' she asked.

'Just taking off my jacket,' I heard him answer.

'Well, Hurry-Up-Harry,' she said in a not-very-happy voice.

Harry came out with a grin on his face. 'Mrs Brisbane, did you know that eight of the jackets back there are blue? Much more than any other colour!'

Mrs Brisbane just said, 'Take your seat, Harry. We're in the middle of class.'

[.]ö[.]

The rain was still beating against the windows when the bell rang for break, so my friends had to stay inside.

Mrs Brisbane opened the closet and pulled

out a huge plastic tub.

'Here's my rainy day box,' she said. 'The things in here can only be used on days like this.'

She started taking out smaller boxes and lining them up on the desk. 'We've got board games and puzzles, art supplies and activity books. It's strictly first come, first served – no arguments. Now, first, let's get the wiggles out a little.'

Then the most amazing thing happened. Mrs Brisbane stretched her arms way up over her head and wiggled her fingers.

'Stretch . . . and wiggle!' she said.

Most of the students stood up. Rosie managed to stretch and wiggle right in her wheelchair.

I put my paws up on the side of my cage and stretched, too. I wiggled my whiskers at the same time. None of the other students could do that!

Next, Mrs Brisbane started rolling her head around.

'Wiggle your heads.'

The students did. They all looked pretty silly

but I tried it, too.

'Wiggle your shoulders,' she continued. 'Wiggle your arms.'

I wasn't sure about my shoulders and arms so I just wiggled everything.

'Wiggle your hips,' she said. 'Wiggle your knees.'

I'd never seen Mrs Brisbane act so unsqueakably silly before. The students were wiggling like crazy and they were giggling, too.

'Wiggle your toes and wiggle your nose.' Mrs Brisbane even giggled at that one.

I'm very good at wiggling my nose. I've had a lot of practice.

'And now shake.' Mrs Brisbane shook her whole body. 'Shake your problems away.'

The kids shook their bodies and laughed out loud.

'Okay, settle down,' Mrs Brisbane said. 'Now that the wiggles are over, you may come up and pick out a rainy day activity.'

The students all headed towards the desk, including Rosie.

'That's okay, Rosie,' Holly said, stopping her. 'I'll pick something out.'

'Thanks, but I'd like to choose my own,' Rosie said, rolling right past Holly.

Simon was the first one at the desk and he grabbed a board game. 'Who wants to play this with me?' he asked.

Small Paul and Tall Paul both came forward and said, 'Me!'

'Hey, Paul comes in two sizes: giant and miniature,' Simon joked.

The two Pauls didn't think it was funny. Neither did I. They both backed away.

'Never mind,' Small Paul said and he headed back to his table and took out a book.

'Og, did you see that?' I squeaked.

Og splashed around in his tank.

Thomas decided to play the game with Tall Paul and Simon. Rosie joined them and Holly raced up and said she'd like to play, too.

Simon checked out the box. 'Sorry, only four can play. First come, first served.'

Holly looked disappointed until Kelsey asked her to work on a puzzle with her.

Phoebe grabbed art supplies and was busy gluing things to bright pieces of paper and Joey joined her.

By the time Hurry-Up-Harry got up to the desk, there wasn't much left in the box.

'Are you feeling all right, Harry?' Mrs Brisbane asked him.

'I'm fine,' he said.

'You know,' she continued, 'if you could be on time at school for a whole week, maybe you could be the first student to take Humphrey home for the weekend. Would you like that?'

Harry nodded. 'Would I! Yes!'

'It's up to you to listen for the bell and return with the other students. I want you back in the room right after break.' She reached deep in the box and pulled out a smaller box. 'Now why don't you see if Paul F. would like to play this game with you?'

'Okay,' said Harry.

Soon all the students were busy with their activities and seemed to be having fun, which was a good thing.

But there were problems, too. I wondered if Harry could hurry up for a whole week. I could see there was a problem between Holly and Rosie, and between the two Pauls as well.

I hopped on my wheel for a spin because

that's where I do my best thinking.

If there's one thing that gets a classroom hamster thinking, it's a problem happening right in his own classroom.

Humphrey's Rules of School

It's easy to get your wiggles out but it's harder to shake your problems away.

A Visitor and a Visit

The next day was bright and sunny, which I normally like. Last night, I had wished for another rainy break so I could study the new students a little more. But the sunshine helped me think of another verse to write in my notebook:

> Autumn, oh, autumn,
> When the weather turns funny.
> One day it's cold and rainy,
> Next day it's warm and sunny.

I don't believe Mrs Brisbane thought it was funny when Hurry-Up-Harry arrived a few minutes after the bell rang. This time he brought his mum with him. She looked very worried as Mrs Brisbane greeted her.

'Mrs Brisbane, I'm so sorry. After your call last night, I promised myself I'd get Harry here on time, but then I had to stop for petrol,' she explained. 'Tomorrow, I'll get him here on time.'

'Thanks, Mrs Ito,' Mrs Brisbane answered politely.

Then she turned to Harry. 'Why don't you go to your seat and take out your language arts workbook?' she said.

'Og, did you hear that?' I squeaked to my neighbour when Mrs Ito had left and the students were all working. 'Mrs Brisbane called Harry's mum last night to talk to her about his being late.'

'BOING-BOING!' Og loudly replied, which made some of the kids laugh.

'That's serious,' I said. 'I hope he wasn't too upset.'

But when I looked over at Harry, he didn't seem upset at all.

The bell rang for break later in the morning

and the students rushed out of the room. I knew they'd be getting their wiggles out on the playground so I decided to try some of those exercises Mrs Brisbane had taught us the day before.

I wiggled my ears and my whiskers and I even jiggled my tail (something else humans could not do). Then I SHOOK-SHOOK-SHOOK my whole body, trying to shake my problems away.

'Rockin' Humphrey!' I squeaked.

I guess I looked a little silly but I felt good.

I felt even better when I heard a familiar voice say, 'Humphrey! What are you doing?'

I looked up and saw a wonderful sight. Golden Miranda and Speak-Up-Sayeh, two of my best friends from last year, were standing by my cage and smiling down on me.

'I think he's dancing,' Sayeh said in her beautiful, soft voice.

'We miss you so much, Humphrey,' Miranda said.

'I'm SORRY-SORRY-SORRY you have George in your classroom,' I squeaked. If only she could understand me!

'We miss you too, Og,' Sayeh added. 'George doesn't like you, but we do.'

'It's not the same without you two.' Miranda leaned in very close and whispered, 'I love you, Humphrey.'

I was a little worried that Og might feel left out, but Miranda leaned in close to his tank and said, 'You too, Og.'

My heart did a little somersault inside me. Golden Miranda still loved me. And I loved her back.

'Girls, Mrs Wright will be looking for you,' Mrs Brisbane said. 'She always knows when someone's missing from the playground.'

They laughed and promised to come and see me again.

The rest of the day, I tried very hard to concentrate on what the teacher said. But no matter what she said, I kept hearing Miranda's voice saying, 'I love you, Humphrey.'

Later, Mrs Brisbane made an announcement. 'Class, I'll be taking Humphrey home this weekend. Starting next Friday, he'll start going home with a different student each weekend.'

I was a little bit relieved not to be going home

with any of the new students, since I still didn't know them very well. However, I'm a very curious hamster, so I couldn't help wondering what weekends at their houses would be like.

Mrs Brisbane lived in a yellow house with her husband, Bert. After an accident last year, Bert was now in a wheelchair. He spent a lot of his time in his workshop making bird houses. (He made a big extension for my cage, too – thanks!) He also worked part-time at Maycrest Manor, a place where people get better after an accident or an illness. Sometimes he took me there to help.

It's pretty quiet at the Brisbanes' house, especially compared to some houses which are filled with kids and pets. Sometimes it's a little *too* quiet and I miss Og.

I dozed a lot that weekend. I napped while Mrs Brisbane tidied up the house. I slept while she went over students' papers. I snoozed while the Brisbanes went out on Sunday morning.

I was certainly rested when Mrs Brisbane opened my cage on Sunday afternoon and said,

'Humphrey, you must be bored to tears! I haven't paid a bit of attention to you this weekend but that's changing now.'

She scooped me up and put me into my yellow plastic hamster ball.

'How about a change of scenery?' she asked.

It sounded unsqueakably nice to me.

She carried me out to the garage where Mr Brisbane was hammering away at a piece of wood.

'I thought you might like some company,' Mrs Brisbane told her husband.

'Always do,' he said.

Mrs Brisbane sat in an old stuffed chair near the workbench and put my hamster ball on the ground. My hamster ball didn't have flashing lights or music, but I still liked it.

'Go and take a spin, Humphrey,' she said. 'You need the exercise.'

I started the ball rolling. Things look different from inside the ball and they sound different, too.

When the Brisbanes talked, they sounded as if they were underwater. But I could still hear what they were saying.

'Bert, may I ask you a personal question?' she said.

He chuckled. 'We've been married thirty years, Sue. I think you can ask anything you want.'

'Okay. What's the worst thing about being in a wheelchair?' she asked.

Bert thought for a few seconds. 'I can't reach that box of sweets you hid on the top shelf in the kitchen.'

Mrs Brisbane laughed. 'I put it up there so I can't reach it either.'

Then Bert got more serious. 'People are the worst part of being in a wheelchair.'

'Why?' Mrs Brisbane asked.

'Well, I don't like it when people treat me as if I'm different. I'm no different just because I'm sitting in a chair. I'm the same person I always was,' he explained.

His wife nodded. 'That's true.'

'And I don't like it when people try to help me when I don't need help,' Bert continued.

'But you can't blame people for wanting to help,' Mrs Brisbane said.

'I appreciate help when I need it and I know

I have to ask for help sometimes. But some people just won't leave me alone. Like Violet Rasmussen next door. If I'm outside for one minute, she runs over to see if she can help. She really gets my goat.'

Mrs Brisbane laughed quietly. 'You haven't changed a bit since you've been in that chair, Bert Brisbane! You're as stubborn as ever.'

'It's called independent,' he said, chuckling.

Bert began running a piece of sandpaper over a piece of wood. 'Why do you ask?'

'Oh, there's this girl in my new class. Rosie. She's in a wheelchair,' Mrs Brisbane said. 'She's very independent, too.'

'That's good,' Bert said.

'Yes, but she's not the problem. It's another girl.' Mrs Brisbane sighed.

'Something else, Bert,' she said. 'You know how when you were a boy, you were really short?'

Mr Brisbane smiled and nodded. 'Yep, until one year when I went from being the shortest boy in the class to the tallest boy in the class. It happened over the summer. Quite a change.'

'Which did you like better? Being short or

being tall?'

Mr Brisbane stopped sanding the wood. 'I guess there were problems, either way.'

'That's what I was thinking, too,' his wife said.

'Me, too!' I squeaked, rolling my ball closer to her chair.

'Oh, Humphrey, I almost forgot about you,' Mrs Brisbane laughed.

'No one could ever forget Humphrey,' Bert said.

'Humphrey won't be here next weekend,' Mrs Brisbane said. 'He'll be going home with a student from the new class.'

'Which one?' Mr Brisbane asked.

'Yes, which one?' I squeaked.

'I'm not sure yet,' Mrs Brisbane said.

We stayed out in the garage for a while, but the Brisbanes talked about other things, things I didn't understand. As I rolled around the garage, I tried to imagine Mr Brisbane as a little boy.

It was HARD-HARD-HARD. And when I tried to imagine Mrs Brisbane as a little girl, that didn't work either.

Maybe hamsters just don't have good imaginations.

Humphrey's Rules of School

Everybody has problems — not just you.

The Worst Class in the World

I was on edge on Monday morning before the first bell rang. Hurry-Up-Harry had promised to be on time every day. If he did, I'd be going home with him for the weekend. But I wasn't sure if his mum dropping him off late would count, since that wasn't really his fault.

Joey always came to class early and visited me before the bell rang so he could hear me 'giggle'.

On Monday, he was watching me spin on my wheel when Phoebe came and stood next to him.

'He's just like the hamster I used to have,' Joey said.

'I wish I had a hamster,' Phoebe said. 'My grandma says a pet would be too much work for her right now. But I asked her if I could bring Humphrey home one weekend. I thought she'd say no, but she said yes!' Phoebe looked so thrilled, I was thrilled, too.

'Slow-Down-Simon!' Mrs Brisbane called out as Simon dashed into the room, followed by Rolling Rosie and Helpful Holly. One by one, the students made their way to their tables until every place was filled . . . except one.

The hands of the clock inched towards the time of the final bell.

'Og, do you think Harry will make it?' I squeaked.

'BOING-BOING,' Og replied in a way that made me think he wasn't sure.

But just as the bell rang, Harry rushed into the room and headed straight to his chair.

'I made it, didn't I?' he asked breathlessly.

'Yes, and I'm glad,' Mrs Brisbane answered with a smile. 'But maybe tomorrow you could get here a few seconds earlier.'

Harry nodded and looked over at my cage. I'm no mind-reader, but I was pretty sure I knew what he was thinking. Maybe, just maybe, he'd get to take me home on Friday.

Last week, I'd noticed that Mrs Brisbane spent most of the time learning about these strange students: hearing about their lives, listening to them read, sharing ideas. But this week, she went back to the routine I remembered from last year in Room 26: teaching reading, social studies, maths, science.

While the strange students seemed quite bright, I was surprised to find out that I knew a lot more than they did about these subjects. At first, this was confusing to me, until I realized that I'd studied the exact same information last year. I felt unsqueakably smart! I was sure to get better scores on my vocabulary tests this year which made me HAPPY-HAPPY-HAPPY!

Maybe – just maybe – this school year wouldn't be as bad as I'd first thought!

But I changed my mind when two things happened right after morning break.

First, Mrs Wright came in with the students and marched up to Mrs Brisbane.

'There are several problems with your class,' she announced.

'Why don't we discuss them later?' Mrs Brisbane suggested. 'Alone.'

'I think immediate action is necessary,' Mrs Wright said firmly. 'Justice delayed is justice denied.'

Whoa. I didn't know what that meant but it sounded serious.

'Very well. What's the problem?' our teacher asked.

'*Problems*,' Mrs Wright said. 'First, I had to break up a fight between two of your students.'

'Eek!' I squeaked. 'Did you hear that, Og?'

Og splashed so hard, I was afraid he'd pop the top off his tank.

'Really?' asked Mrs Brisbane. 'Who?'

She looked around the classroom and I scrambled up to the tippy-top of my tree branch so I could look, too. I didn't see anyone bruised or bleeding, which was a good thing.

'Thomas,' she said, pointing directly at Thomas T. True. 'And that new boy. The tall one.'

Mrs Brisbane looked surprised. 'Paul Green?'

'Yes,' Mrs Wright replied, folding her arms

across her waist. 'The tall boy, Paul. He had Thomas in a headlock.'

Mrs Brisbane walked closer to Thomas's desk. 'Is this true, Thomas?'

'No, ma'am,' Thomas answered, glancing over at Tall Paul. 'We didn't fight.'

'Paul?' Mrs Brisbane turned towards him 'Did you have a fight?'

Paul hung his head and looked completely miserable. 'Not really,' he mumbled.

At this point Mrs Wright suddenly dropped her voice and whispered in Mrs Brisbane's ear. 'I saw . . .'

I couldn't hear a word she said! How can a classroom hamster help if that hamster doesn't know what's going on?

I must say, Mrs Brisbane looked surprised at whatever Mrs Wright said.

'I'll take care of this, Mrs Wright. Thank you.' Mrs Brisbane was always polite.

Mrs Wright's voice was suddenly loud again. 'And then, another one of your students did something *extremely dangerous*.' The way she said those words, '*extremely dangerous*', made my nose twitch.

Mrs Brisbane frowned. 'Which student?'

'Her!' Mrs Wright poked a long finger in the direction of Rosie Rodriguez. 'She was not using her chair properly.'

Suddenly, Holly leaped up from her chair. 'I tried to stop her! I told her it was dangerous,' she said.

Rosie glared at Holly. 'It wasn't dangerous. I do it all the time,' she said firmly.

'I think we can work this all out during the lunch break,' Mrs Brisbane said. She started walking towards the door. I'm pretty sure she was hoping Mrs Wright would also walk towards the door . . . and right through it. 'Thank you, Mrs Wright.'

'I think I should be in that meeting,' the PE teacher said. She backed towards the door. '*And* Mr Morales.'

'I'll let you know,' Mrs Brisbane said.

Mrs Wright was gone. I almost cheered at the way Mrs Brisbane took control. But I didn't feel like cheering when I looked around at the classroom and the unhappy faces of Tall Paul, Thomas T. True, Rolling Rosie and Helpful Holly. The other students all looked bewildered.

I probably looked bewildered, too.

On the worst first day of school, I'd been pretty sure this wasn't going to be the best class ever.

Now, I was beginning to think it was the *worst* class ever. And I was stuck with it!

It seemed like a LONG-LONG-LONG time until lunch and I think the other students had as much trouble concentrating on their spelling quiz as I did. Even though I'd learned the words last year, I got three answers wrong! When the bell rang for lunch, Mrs Brisbane asked Rosie, Paul G. and Thomas to stay for a moment.

'Shouldn't I stay with Rosie?' Helpful Holly asked.

'That won't be necessary,' Mrs Brisbane told her.

Holly looked very disappointed again.

As soon as the classroom was clear, Mrs Brisbane asked Rosie just what dangerous thing she'd done.

'I popped a wheelie,' she said, her eyes sparkling. 'I learned to do it at camp. You need to learn to do it to go up and down kerbs.'

Mrs Brisbane nodded. I'd never seen her husband pop a wheelie in his wheelchair but maybe he had.

'You just move the back wheels so the front wheels go up in the air, like this,' Rosie started to demonstrate.

'No need to show me,' Mrs Brisbane quickly said as she put her hand on Rosie's arm rest. 'I understand what it is. But it does seem a little dangerous.'

'Sure, if you don't know what you're doing,' Rosie explained. 'I practised and practised this summer. The camp counsellors were always there to catch us if we tipped over.'

'That's good,' Mrs Brisbane said. 'But there might not be anyone to catch you on the playground. Do me a favour, Rosie. Don't pop wheelies on the playground. You can do it at home if your parents say it's okay.'

Rosie looked disappointed.

'Is that a deal?' Mrs Brisbane asked.

Rosie nodded. 'Deal.'

'Now off to lunch,' the teacher said.

When Rolling Rosie was gone, Mrs Brisbane turned to the boys.

'So, tell me what happened,' she said.

'We were just fooling around,' Thomas said. 'That Mrs Wright, she's a busybody.'

I wasn't exactly sure what a busybody was. Perhaps it was a person with a whistle.

'Mrs Wright was just doing her job,' Mrs Brisbane said. 'She said Paul lifted you up off the ground and you were yelling.'

'Thomas told me to!' Paul burst out. His cheeks were flaming red.

'He told you to grab him and pick him up off the ground?' Mrs Brisbane asked.

'Yes,' Paul answered.

Mrs Brisbane pursed her lips and tapped her foot on the ground. 'Why did you do that, Thomas?'

Thomas shrugged. 'Just for fun, I guess.'

'Fun?' Mrs Brisbane looked surprised.

'Because he's always after me about being tall.' Paul looked completely miserable. 'He always wants me to do things. So he said, "I bet you can't pick me up." I didn't say anything, so he dared me. So I picked him up. That's it.'

'Is that true, Thomas?' Mrs Brisbane asked.

'Yes, ma'am. That's all it was,' he said.

Mrs Brisbane turned to Paul. 'Do you think it's a good idea to pick people up?' she asked.

'I guess not,' Paul answered.

Next, it was Thomas's turn. 'Do you think it's a good idea to dare people?' she asked.

'Maybe not,' Thomas said. 'We were just fooling around.'

'Don't fool around like that any more,' she said. 'If there's any more trouble like this, I'll have to call your parents. Do you understand?'

The boys nodded. Then she made them shake hands. But she didn't send them to the head's office – whew!

She sent Tall Paul off to lunch but had Thomas T. True stay for a minute.

'I don't think Paul likes you to talk about how tall he is all the time,' she said.

'It's pretty cool. He's practically a giant!' Thomas said.

'Please don't exaggerate, Thomas. Paul's just tall for his age. Remember the rule about treating people the way we'd like to be treated?' Mrs Brisbane asked.

'Yes, ma'am.'

'Try to be friends with Paul without talking

about his height. Is that a deal?' she said.

'Deal,' he said.

He and Mrs Brisbane shook hands and she sent him off to lunch.

After he left, Mrs Brisbane turned to Og and me. 'And now, maybe *I* can have lunch, too.'

But as she grabbed her lunch bag from her desk drawer, Mrs Wright came into the room.

'Where are the boys?' she asked.

'The matter's been taken care of,' Mrs Brisbane told her.

Mrs Wright didn't like that answer. 'Have they been punished?' she asked.

'It's all taken care of,' Mrs Brisbane said. 'I've got to eat now.'

She took her bag and walked past Mrs Wright and out of the door.

Mrs Wright stood alone in the room shaking her head. I was afraid she might blow her whistle, but instead she just left.

'Og, do you think Mrs Wright is a busybody?' I asked when my neighbour and I were alone again.

'BOING!' Og replied.

Then I hopped on my wheel to keep my

body busy while I thought about wheelies and dares and the strange students in the class.

Maybe this was the worst class in the world, after all.

🐾

Later, I worked on my poem for a while.

Autumn, oh, autumn,
When everybody's busy,
There are so many problems,
I'm feeling kind of dizzy!

🐾 🐾 Humphrey's Rules 🐾 🐾
of School

Keep your body busy but don't be a busybody.

The Worst Class Doesn't Get Better

Tardy.

It's not a word I'd heard very often. But I've figured out what it means: late.

If you're tardy, you have to go to the office and get a piece of paper that lets you back into class.

This year, I've heard the word *tardy* more often than I did all of last year. A few of my old friends were tardy from time to time, usually when the buses got in late.

But Hurry-Up-Harry was tardy a *lot*.

He got to school on time (barely) the first two days of the week but on Wednesday, he was so late, Mrs Brisbane had counted him as absent. When he finally arrived, he gave his slip of paper to Mrs Brisbane.

'Very well, Harry. Hurry-Up and get to your seat,' she said.

'It wasn't my fault,' he said. 'Here's a note from my mum. She tells you there that the alarm didn't go off.'

He pulled a letter out of his backpack and handed it to her. She read it quickly, thanked him and sent him to his seat.

He didn't go right away. 'We used to live almost next door to the school,' he said. 'Then I could walk. But now she has to drive me here and it takes longer.'

Mrs Brisbane looked at Harry as if she didn't know what to say. Which is pretty unusual for Mrs Brisbane.

'Does this mean I can't have Humphrey this weekend?' Harry asked.

'We'll talk about it later, Harry,' Mrs Brisbane said.

'It wasn't really his fault, was it, Og?' I asked my neighbour while my friends worked on maths problems. I should have been working on them, too, but I was thinking more about

Harry's problem then about number problems.

Og didn't answer. He just splashed lazily in the water. I wasn't sure what he thought about Hurry-Up-Harry.

·ö·

That night, when Aldo came, he went right to work, sweeping the room with long, graceful strokes of the broom.

'We're still learning more about you guys in biology,' he said. 'Amphibians and mammals.'

'What did you learn, Aldo?' I squeaked.

'Mammals are born from their mamas and amphibians hatch out of eggs,' he said.

I almost fell off my tree branch. 'Eek!' I squeaked.

Og came out of an *egg*? Like a *chicken*?

'Of course, after they hatch out of eggs, frogs are cute little tadpoles,' Aldo continued.

I wasn't sure what a tadpole was, but it was hard to picture Og being cute.

Aldo chuckled. 'Birds come out of eggs and so do some reptiles,' he said. 'But of course, birds have feathers. And fish have scales and gills.'

Suddenly my tummy felt a little funny. Gills and feathers, scales and eggs. I thought we were all just *animals*.

'In the end, we're all a lot alike,' Aldo said. He had finished sweeping and started straightening out the tables and chairs.

'Are we?' I asked.

My head was spinning. Og came out of an egg. He was cold-blooded and he didn't have any ears (that I could see). It seemed as if we had nothing in common.

'That's the great thing about biology,' Aldo said as he pulled a chair close to our table and pulled out his supper. 'We're all living things.'

He took a great, big, deep breath. 'And it's great to be alive, isn't it, Humphrey?'

'Squeak!' I answered. I couldn't argue with that.

Aldo pushed a little piece of lettuce through the bars of my cage but I wasn't particularly hungry.

'And great to have friends of all species,' Aldo added.

Suddenly, I remembered what Ms Mac had

said when she first brought me to Room 26: 'You can learn a lot about yourself by taking care of another species.'

I guess that meant amphibians, too.

'It's great!' I squeaked in agreement.

·ᵇ·

Tardy. Again.

That's what Harry was on Thursday. He got to school on time in the morning, but he came back from lunch after the bell had rung. He wasn't alone, though. Mr Morales brought him back.

'I found Harry staring at the trophy case,' he said. 'He said he didn't notice all the other kids going back to class.'

'I told him he'd be late,' Holly said. (She forgot to raise her hand first, which made me miss my old friend Raise-Your-Hand-Heidi Hopper.)

'Quiet, Holly,' Mrs Brisbane said. 'Harry, can you explain why you didn't come back on time?'

'Did you know Longfellow School won the All-District Basketball Championship five times?' he said. 'But they haven't won for six whole years.'

'No, Harry, I didn't,' she said. 'It's very interesting, but you promised me you'd get back to class on time after break and lunch.'

'I know,' said Harry, staring down at his feet.

Mr Morales told Mrs Brisbane he'd let her handle the problem. I thought Harry was LUCKY-LUCKY-LUCKY that he didn't have to sit in the head's office and hear how disappointed Mr Morales was.

I was a little disappointed in Harry. Why couldn't he learn to hurry up?

'Harry, can you tell the time?' Mrs Brisbane asked Hurry-Up-Harry when she kept him in during afternoon break.

Harry nodded. She asked him to tell her what time it was right then and he was correct.

'Have you had your hearing tested?' Mrs Brisbane said.

Harry nodded. 'I can hear just fine.'

'Then why are all the other students able to

hear the bell and get back to class on time and you aren't?' she asked.

It was the same question I would have asked if I had the chance.

'Just when the bell rang, I happened to be standing next to that trophy case. I'd never noticed it before,' he said. 'I'll be on time, tomorrow.'

'It seems as if you have two problems,' Mrs Brisbane said. 'One problem is that your parents have a little trouble getting you here on time.'

'I know,' Harry said. 'They lose track of time.'

Mrs Brisbane nodded. 'Yes. But *you* have a problem remembering to get in line and come back to class on time. You can't blame your parents for that.'

'I guess I lose track of time, too,' Harry said.

'I have an idea,' Mrs Brisbane said. 'Why don't you watch the clock in the morning and remind your parents when it's time to leave? It may not be your fault that you're late, but maybe you could try to help them.'

'Okay,' Harry said.

'Second, when you see your friends lining up, you line up, too. No matter how interesting the trophy case is or what size anthill you see. You need to take responsibility.'

I agreed with that!

'You won't have Humphrey this weekend, but if you can get back to class on time all of next week, you can take him home,' she said.

'Really?' Harry smiled from ear to ear. 'I can do it!'

Mrs Brisbane let him go out to break but after he left, she kept on talking. I'm not sure if she was talking to me or just to herself, but I listened. (I'm pretty sure Og did, too.)

'I've had problems with dawdlers before,' she said. 'But never quite like Harry.'

The next day, I waited anxiously for Mrs Brisbane to make a very important announcement. Luckily, I didn't have to wait long.

'Paul Fletcher will be taking Humphrey home for the weekend,' she said. 'I have the permission slip. Who is picking you up?' she asked.

'My dad,' Paul said.

I was happy to be going home with Small

Paul. He seemed happy, too. In fact, he looked a little taller for the rest of the afternoon as he sat up very straight and glanced over at my cage a lot.

'It won't be long now, Humphrey,' he told me after break.

Not everybody was happy, though. Harry looked embarrassed because he hadn't been on time all week as he'd promised.

Tall Paul seemed especially grumpy.

I know Helpful Holly was hoping to have me for the weekend, too.

But in the end, I thought Mrs Brisbane made a very good choice.

Small Paul's dad wore a suit when he picked me up. He had taken off from work early to get us. I have to admit, I felt unsqueakably important, but I did remember to say goodbye to Og as Mr Fletcher carried my cage out of the classroom.

'I'll tell you all about it Monday! Bye!' I said.

At their home, Mr Fletcher got me settled on a desk in Paul's room. 'Humphrey, I've been looking forward to meeting you for a long time,' he said.

'Thanks a lot!' I replied, which made Paul and his dad laugh, even though I'm pretty sure they didn't understand exactly what I'd said.

My weekend at Small Paul's house was pretty quiet, except for his little brother, Max. Every time he saw me, Max jumped up and down, flapped his arms and squealed. I think that meant he liked me. He was only two years old and much smaller than Paul. Sometimes Paul picked his brother up and carried him around.

To Max, Small Paul was extremely tall.

The Fletcher family did fun things like watch movies and play games and eat popcorn, like the other families I'd stayed with.

Paul, of course, did his homework, because he was a VERY-VERY-VERY good student.

On Sunday afternoon, Paul cleaned my cage while Max watched.

'Poopy!' Max said, flapping his arms up and down and squealing.

I was glad Paul didn't squeal.

Afterwards, Paul settled down at his desk and worked on his model planes. They had small wings and a small cockpit that were just about my size. I wondered how it would feel to fly. But then I remembered the unsqueakably dangerous boat ride I took once and tried not to think about it any more.

There were dozens and dozens of tiny parts to be glued together and the amazing thing was, Paul knew just where to put them.

While he worked, he talked to me. Luckily, I'm a very good listener.

'Just my bad luck, Humphrey, having another Paul in class,' he said as he carefully glued a wing in place.

He sighed a very large sigh. 'He *would* have to be tall.'

'He can't help that,' I squeaked, trying to be helpful.

'Have you noticed? He's always showing off how tall he is.' Paul carefully held the wing in place while the glue dried.

I was puzzled. Paul G. had never shown off, as far as I could see.

'I don't think he's a show-off,' I said.

'The big bragger,' Paul muttered.

Oh, if just once a human could understand my squeaks! Especially when I'm trying to be helpful.

'The worst day of my life was when he came to our school.' Paul let go of the wing and it stayed in place.

Small Paul was extremely smart but that didn't mean he was always right.

'Some day, I'm going to design, build and fly my own planes, Humphrey,' he said, looking down at his model with pride. 'Look at this. A Hornet. Mach Two. I guess you don't know what it is. But someday, maybe I'll take you for a ride.'

'Thanks,' I squeaked. 'I think.'

That night I had one of those weird dreams. This time, I was flying in one of Paul's little wooden planes. I was zooming high into the sky when suddenly a giant hand reached out and grabbed the plane.

I looked up at the face of the person holding the plane in his hand.

It was Paul Green. Tall Paul.

'Now you know what it feels like to be tall,' he said.

Then he raised his arm and let the plane go – UP-UP-UP into the clouds. I kept going and going until, thank goodness, I woke up.

Like I said, it was a weird dream.

॰

On Monday morning, Max gave a final squeal and I was on my way back to Room 26. Small Paul, as usual, got to class early.

Kelsey was right behind us and she bumped Paul's arm, which jiggled and joggled my cage like crazy.

'Be-Careful-Kelsey,' Paul snapped at her.

'Sorry!' she said. 'Is Humphrey okay?'

'Yes,' I squeaked weakly.

Kelsey seemed like a nice girl, but I wished she could pay a little more attention.

'How was your weekend with Humphrey?' Mrs Brisbane asked when Paul placed my cage back on the table by the window.

'Great!' Small Paul said.

'Maybe you can show Paul G. how to take care of Humphrey, now that you have experience,' she suggested.

Paul looked shocked. 'Do I have to?'

'Well, it would be nice,' Mrs Brisbane said. 'He's new to the school and he'd like to be included.'

'I'll think about it,' Small Paul answered.

I could see by the look on his face that he'd already made up his mind.

Just then, the final bell rang. Hurry-Up-Harry raced through the door while it was still clanging. He rushed to his seat and sat down, panting, but looking proud.

'I'm not tardy, am I?' he asked.

'No,' Mrs Brisbane said.

He looked pleased. But when I glanced at Small Paul he wasn't looking pleased at all.

'Og,' I squeaked to my neighbour. 'We really have our work cut out for us.'

'BOING!' he agreed.

Humphrey's Rules of School

NEVER-NEVER-NEVER be tardy and ALWAYS-ALWAYS-ALWAYS listen to the classroom pet (even if you have trouble understanding).

The Very Worst Day

That Monday was an unsqueakably difficult day. More difficult than any day we had last year in Room 26.

First, Thomas said that he'd seen a *wolf* while he was walking to school. But Mrs Brisbane got him to admit it might have been a big dog.

Mrs Brisbane reminded him not to exaggerate.

Worse yet, Phoebe had forgotten her spelling homework and burst into tears, which made me feel SAD-SAD-SAD.

Next, Mrs Brisbane asked Paul to come up to the board for some maths problems and both Small Paul and Tall Paul jumped out of their seats. When they got up to the board at the same time, they glared at each other.

The other students laughed.

'Sorry, guys. I meant Paul G.,' Mrs Brisbane explained.

Tall Paul turned red and Small Paul scowled as he returned to his seat.

Small Paul liked to do maths problems in front of the class. Tall Paul got the problem wrong and turned an even deeper shade of red.

As if that wasn't bad enough, Kelsey skinned her knee at break and had to go to the nurse's office.

Then, Mrs Brisbane had an excellent idea (as she often does). She decided to put me in my ball and let me roll up and down the aisles. She probably wanted to get her students' minds off their problems.

It would be very interesting if all humans could get a hamster's-eye view of their world at least once. If they did, they would probably clean their shoes more often – there really are unsqueakably *awful* things stuck to the bottoms of many shoes. Humans should pay more attention to their socks, too. On that day, both Thomas and Kelsey had on mismatched socks.

They'd also realize how much they tap their feet and move around in general, even when they think they're sitting still. As I spin around the classroom, I'm always GLAD-GLAD-GLAD I have that ball to protect me.

Despite the dangers, I kept rolling around lazily. The students were reading to themselves and after a while, didn't even seem to notice me.

As I approached Rosie's table, I decided it would be interesting to get a closer look at her wheelchair. I still hadn't figured out exactly how she would 'pop a wheelie'.

Rosie saw me coming closer and her eyes sparkled.

'Hi, Humphrey,' she whispered softly.

But when I got a little closer, Holly let out a yelp and grabbed my hamster ball, picking it up so quickly I was doing somersaults inside.

'Eek!' I squeaked.

'What is it, Holly?' the teacher asked.

'Humphrey could trip up Rosie's wheelchair! He got much too close,' she said, holding up the ball. 'But I've got him now.'

'He wasn't too close,' Rosie protested. 'I saw him there.'

'I think it's dangerous,' Holly said.

'The way you picked him up is dangerous,' Rosie replied. 'You could have hurt poor little Humphrey.'

I don't like to think of myself as 'poor little' anything, but she was right. I wasn't hurt, but I was definitely dizzy.

'You must remember to be gentle with Humphrey,' Mrs Brisbane said as she took the ball from Holly. She peered in through the yellow plastic. 'Are you all right?'

I squeaked, though it was a weaker squeak than usual.

Mrs Brisbane put me back in the cage, satisfied that I was okay.

I headed straight for my sleeping hut, which was the safest, quietest place I knew.

I crawled out a little while later when I heard Rolling Rosie ask if she could speak to Mrs Brisbane.

The room was empty because it was lunch time.

'You didn't pop a wheelie again, did you, Rosie?' the teacher asked.

'No,' Rosie answered. 'It's about my assistant.'

'Holly?' Mrs Brisbane said. 'Why don't you tell me what's on your mind.'

Rosie wheeled up close to the desk and she and Mrs Brisbane talked. Og and I were as silent as could be so we could hear every word they said.

'I don't think I need an assistant,' she explained. 'I can do almost everything myself. So could you tell Holly not to help me any more?'

Mrs Brisbane was silent for a moment. 'I could,' she finally said. 'But do you really want me to?'

'Yes!' Rosie answered. 'I know Holly wants to help but she helps much too much. She helps me when there's no problem at all. Sometimes, she gets in the way.'

'Have you told her that?' Mrs Brisbane asked.

Rolling Rosie nodded. 'I said she didn't need to help so much. It didn't work.'

Again, Mrs Brisbane was silent for a while. 'I can see you don't need much help, Rosie. But maybe Holly does,' she finally said.

'Holly?' Rosie sounded REALLY-REALLY-REALLY surprised.

'She likes to help,' Mrs Brisbane explained. 'I think she'd be pretty upset if I said you didn't need her any more.'

'Maybe she could help someone else,' Rosie suggested.

'Let's give her one more chance, Rosie,' Mrs Brisbane said. 'I'll have a word with her and see if things improve. Okay?'

Good old Mrs Brisbane. She really knew how to handle students. 'Now, we'd better eat. I'm going down to the lunchroom, too,' she said.

As they headed out of the classroom, I couldn't wait to talk to Og.

'Were you listening, Og?' I asked my neighbour. 'Helpful Holly will be upset if she gets fired.'

I knew that because I'd be unsqueakably upset if I got fired from my job as a classroom hamster.

'BOING-BOING-BOING!' Og agreed, splashing in his water.

I thought the day would never end but at last

the afternoon bell rang. As the students gathered up their backpacks, Mrs Brisbane took a sheet of orange paper and approached Phoebe.

'Phoebe, I have an idea to help you remember your homework,' she said. 'Each day, we'll put a big, colourful reminder in your backpack so you won't miss it. What do you think?'

'Okay,' Phoebe said.

'I've written your homework assignment on it. All you have to remember is to bring it back,' Mrs Brisbane continued.

Phoebe nodded. 'I will,' she promised.

'You can do it, Phoebe!' I squeaked. Then I hopped on my wheel and started spinning as fast as I could.

I think she was smiling when she left the room.

The day took a turn for the better after school when some of my old friends from last year came back to Room 26. There was Raise-Your-Hand-Heidi Hopper and her best friend, Stop-Giggling-Gail Morgenstern, along with Raise-Your-Hand-Richie Rinaldi.

I was spinning on my wheel when they came in and I was so glad to see them, I stopped suddenly and almost tumbled off. (Please don't make sudden stops when you're spinning on a wheel.)

'HI-HI-HI!' I squeaked. I'm not sure they could hear me over the loud splashing sounds Og was making.

'Humphrey! My favourite hamster!' Heidi said as she rushed up to my cage.

Gail giggled. 'Og! My favourite frog!' she said as she hurried to my friend's tank.

'And you're my favourite teacher,' Richie told Mrs Brisbane.

'Thank you, Richie,' she replied. 'But you have to give Miss Becker a chance. She's an excellent teacher.'

'I know,' Richie said. 'But she doesn't have any classroom pets.'

Heidi leaned in close to my cage. 'I'm doing pretty well raising my hand this year, Humphrey,' she told me. That was unsqueakably good news. Mrs Brisbane and I had worked hard to help her end her bad habit.

'BOING-BOING!' Og twanged, sending Gail into peals of laughter. I don't think Gail could ever stop giggling completely. At least I hoped not.

I was so glad to see my old friends from last year, I jumped on my wheel and started spinning fast, which made them *all* giggle.

'Go, Humphrey!' Richie said.

Then Og decided to dive into the water side of his tank and made an extra-big splash, which made them giggle even louder.

'Awesome, Og!' Heidi said.

'I think Og and Humphrey are glad to see you,' Mrs Brisbane said.

'Oh, Mrs Brisbane, we miss them so much,' Heidi said. 'We came to ask you something important.'

I slowed down the wheel.

'You say it, Richie,' Gail said.

'Okay.' Richie suddenly looked serious and he cleared his throat. 'Mrs Brisbane, we don't think it's fair that you have two classroom pets in Room 26 and we don't have any in Room 18. We were hoping you'd donate one of yours to Miss Becker.'

Thank goodness I'd hopped off my wheel or I'd have fallen over. I was REALLY-REALLY-

REALLY surprised – and so was Mrs Brisbane.

'Goodness! I don't think my students would like that,' she said. 'If Miss Becker wants a classroom pet, she can get her own. But I'm not sure she wants one.'

'She'd like Humphrey or Og! Everybody does,' Gail said.

'And Og came here from another classroom,' Heidi said.

'At least ask her. *Please*,' Richie begged.

Mrs Brisbane was unusually quiet. I was, too, and I didn't hear a BOING or a splash from Og.

'*Please*.' Gail looked so serious, I could hardly believe it was her speaking.

'*Please*,' Heidi added.

At last, Mrs Brisbane spoke. 'To tell you the truth, I can't imagine giving up either one of them. Don't you think they'd miss each other?'

Heidi and Gail glanced at each other.

'They weren't always together. Humphrey was alone in the beginning,' Richie said.

I had to squeak up for myself. 'But it was so lonely at night. Even scary!'

I'd almost forgotten how loud the clock

sounded in the empty room and how long the nights were without someone splashing nearby.

'BOING-BOING!' Og agreed. 'BOING-BOING-BOING!'

That made Gail giggle, of course.

Mrs Brisbane smiled. 'I'll tell you what. I'll think about it. And I'll talk to Miss Becker about classroom pets. But I'm just not sure it's a good idea to separate Humphrey and Og and take one of them away from my class.'

'Thanks, Mrs Brisbane. We really miss them,' Richie said.

They chatted with the teacher for a few more minutes and then it was time for them to go home.

After they left, Mrs Brisbane leaned in close to my cage and stared at me.

'To tell the truth, I can't imagine teaching without you and Og to help me,' she said. 'Am I just being selfish?'

'NO-NO-NO!' I squeaked at the top of my tiny lungs.

Mrs Brisbane chuckled. 'I don't think Arlene Becker wants any classroom pet – not even you,' she said. 'So don't worry.'

'Thanks,' I squeaked. 'I won't.'

But I did. I worried and worried and worried some more. And even though he hatched from an egg and was cold-blooded, I could tell that Og was worried, too.

Humphrey's Rules of School

It's actually possible to be too helpful.

Brisbane's Buddies

Worried? Did I say I was worried? It was worse than that. I was WORRIED-WORRIED-WORRIED and worried some more!

'Og!' I said when we were alone in the classroom. 'Do you understand what they were talking about?'

'BOING-BOING-BOING-BOING-BOING!'

Okay, so Og understood.

'I'm not sure it's a good idea,' I said. 'I mean, I miss our old friends.' I had a funny little pang in my heart every time I thought about them. 'And I'd like to see what they do during the day,' I continued.

'BOING!' Og replied. So he still agreed with me.

'But what about Mrs Brisbane? I'd miss her, too,' I said. 'And this Miss Becker person doesn't really seem to like animals very much. Mammals *or* amphibians. Maybe even fish.'

There were fish in the tank in the library that I like a lot.

'And even if they did seem a little strange in the beginning, these new students are pretty nice. I'm making Plans for some of them. And wouldn't they be upset if one of us disappeared?' My mind was spinning like a hamster ball. 'And don't forget, Mrs Brisbane said she can't imagine teaching without us. She needs us, Og!'

'BOING!' Og said, taking an impressive (and splashy) dive into the water side of his tank.

'So, she's got to say no,' I ended. 'Doesn't she?'

'Richie called me and told me his goofy idea,' Aldo said as he dusted the tables that night.

'Imagine, moving one of you to Room 18. It's

a bad idea! I told him that!' The tables bounced up and down as he gave them a brisk dusting.

'I think you're right, Aldo,' I squeaked. 'But it would be nice to see Richie every day.'

'If Miss Becker wants a classroom pet, she should get her own,' he said. 'There are other hamsters and frogs looking for homes.'

I suddenly thought back to my early days at Pet-O-Rama . . . and of the hamsters, guinea pigs, mice, rats and chinchillas all hoping to find nice homes. (I never saw any frogs there. I guess the amphibians were in another section.)

'You're so right, Aldo!' I shouted, climbing to the top of my cage. 'Tell Richie that!'

Surprisingly, Aldo stopped and chuckled. 'Still, those kids just love you and Og,' he said. 'I guess I can't blame them for trying.'

I couldn't blame them for trying either.

Once Aldo had left for the night, I could hear Og gently floating in his tank – making the slightest possible splashing sounds.

My mind was still racing. I worried about the new kids in Room 26 and all their problems. Didn't they need both Og and me to help them?

I worried about Mrs Brisbane, who was *not* selfish. She was just telling the truth: she needed us to help her.

I worried about something else, too. Even though we were different species, even though I was warm-blooded and he was cold-blooded, even though I had fur and he didn't . . . I would miss Og if we got separated.

I crossed my toes, hoping that he'd miss me, too.

I felt restless and uneasy, so I decided to take a little stroll down to Room 18 to find out what my old friends were doing in class. Last time, I'd left in a hurry when there was the thunderstorm.

Og was unusually quiet. Just in case he was sleeping (which I'm never sure about), I opened the lock-that-doesn't-lock very gently and managed to slide down the table leg without making a sound. Then I darted across the floor, slid under the door, and made a right turn. When I got to Room 20, I made a left turn and there it was: Room 18.

Once I was inside, I got a funny feeling in my tummy. There were nice decorations on the walls and it was tidy and neat. It just didn't feel like home. I suppose if all my old friends, like Kirk and A.J., were sitting in the chairs, it would have felt more familiar.

The problem was, it was unsqueakably quiet. No splashing. No twanging. No one to talk to at night.

I wasn't even sure there was room for a cage or a tank on the table by the window.

I slid under the door and back into the hall-way, making a right turn at Room 20.

As I scurried past the other classrooms, I realized that if Og and I were separated, I could still come and visit him at night. I'd be able to tell him all about the problems in Miss Becker's classroom. But all I'd find out about what was going on in Room 26 would be the usual 'BOING!'

As I approached Room 26, I heard a VERY-VERY-VERY loud noise.

'Screee-screee!' It was Og's alarm call. Something must be terribly wrong!

I slid under the door so hard, I zoomed halfway across the classroom!

'Screee-screee!'

'I'm here, Og! What's wrong?' I asked.

Og was suddenly silent and I knew what was wrong. I'd been so quiet when I left Room 26, that when Og realized I was gone, he didn't know what had happened to me.

'Sorry, Oggie, I just went down to Room 18 to check it out,' I explained.

I reached the table and looked up at the blind cord hanging down. Even though I am always a little nervous about getting back up to the table, I grabbed hold of the cord and started swinging, higher and higher until I reached the top of the table and let go. I slid again, right up to Og's tank.

'Sorry you were worried,' I told him.

'BOING!' he replied. He sounded much calmer now.

Once I was back in my cage, I wasn't really that sorry. At least now I knew that if Og and I were separated, he'd miss me as much as I'd miss him.

I carefully slid my notebook out from behind the mirror and wrote what I felt in my heart:

Autumn, oh, autumn,
Bringing changes every day.
Autumn, oh, autumn,
I don't want to move away!

For the rest of the week, I didn't have time to write poetry. I was too busy trying to keep up with all the comings and goings in Room 26. Believe me, there were a lot of them!

After several days of remembering her homework, Phoebe forgot again.

'What about that reminder in your backpack?' Mrs Brisbane asked her.

'I forgot to look in my backpack,' the girl admitted. I thought she was going to burst into tears again.

Mrs Brisbane sighed. 'I think I'm going to have to call your grandmother.'

That upset Phoebe a lot. 'Oh, please, don't! I don't want to worry her. I promise I'll do better!'

'See that you do.' Mrs Brisbane let her go but that was a close call!

Then, during break one day, Mrs Brisbane had a talk with Helpful Holly about letting Rosie decide when she wanted help. Holly listened and agreed to try. Still, I saw Rolling Rosie get irritated several times when Holly wanted to push her wheelchair or tell other people to get out of the way.

Mrs Brisbane was annoyed when Thomas raced out of the cloakroom one afternoon and announced that there was a bug as big as his hand in there.

'Eek!' I squeaked.

But the bug turned out to be a harmless little fly.

That same day after school, Ms Mac stopped by to chat. She had problems, too.

'Humphrey, teaching first grade would be a lot easier with you around, but I can't ask Mrs Brisbane to give you up,' she told me.

I didn't think it would be polite to argue with her.

Just then A.J. and Richie came in to try to convince Mrs Brisbane to let either Og or me move to Room 18.

'You miss us, don't you?' Richie asked me as he generously slipped a few raisins into my cage.

'I do!' I squeaked back.

'You'd rather live in Room 18, wouldn't you?' A.J. said in his loud voice.

'Maybe not,' I mumbled.

I wasn't sure how I felt about moving to Room 18. And I couldn't tell what Mrs Brisbane was thinking because she was spending every spare moment playing with cards.

She'd line up the cards in pairs on her desk and mutter over them at break.

She stayed after school and moved them around, muttering some more. I could only hear bits and pieces of what she was saying – things like, 'Maybe that will help her,' and 'Those two will work well together.'

I am a very curious hamster, especially when it comes to what's going on in the classroom. One night, Mrs Brisbane left the cards out on her desk and I just couldn't stop thinking about them. I wanted to check them out, but I didn't dare risk leaving my cage until after Aldo was finished for the night.

'Hi, rodent and frog. Greetings from a primate!' Aldo announced when he came in to clean.

'What's a primate?' I asked.

Aldo pulled out a cloth and starting dusting the student tables. 'Primates are the group of mammals that humans belong to. Rodents are the group of mammals hamsters belong to. I guess you already know Og is a frog,' he explained. 'There are so many kinds of frogs, they have a whole group all to themselves!'

I was shocked to find out there were more frogs than hamsters in the world. Imagine that!

Aldo began to dust the teacher's desk.

'NO-NO-NO!' I squeaked. Mrs Brisbane had worked so hard arranging those cards!

'Whoops,' Aldo said. 'Mrs Brisbane's in the middle of something here.'

He looked at the cards more closely. 'Looks like she's got something planned here. Brisbane's Buddies!'

Brisbane's Buddies? I'd never heard of that before.

Aldo left the cards alone and mopped the floors. When he was finished, he stopped to eat his supper and talk to us.

'I told Maria that I'm lucky I get to clean Mrs Brisbane's room,' he said as he munched on a sandwich. Maria was Aldo's wife, and a special friend of mine. 'I get a lot of good ideas about teaching just from seeing what she's doing,' he added.

Aldo gave me a small piece of carrot and dropped a few Froggy Food Sticks into Og's tank before he left. He was a thoughtful friend.

Once Og and I were alone again, I couldn't stop thinking about those cards.

'Brisbane's Buddies,' I said. 'Og, do you have any idea what that's about?'

Og splashed lazily in the water. He obviously didn't have an idea.

'Now I can finally find out for myself,' I said.

I flung open the door to my cage and scurried to the edge of the table and slid down the cord hanging from the blinds.

Getting to Mrs Brisbane's desk was easy.

Getting on Mrs Brisbane's desk was VERY-VERY-VERY difficult. In fact, it would have been completely impossible, except for those little bars between the chair legs. I think they're called 'rungs', but don't ask me why.

However, climbing the chair that way meant reaching up as high as I could, grabbing hold and then pulling myself up, rung by rung, with all my might. (I'm strong because I get so much exercise.)

Then balancing on the top rung, I had to reach up high again, pull myself up and slide on to the seat of the chair.

After stopping to catch my breath, I reached up one more time, pulled myself up to the arm of the chair and rested again.

Luckily, Mrs Brisbane always pushes her chair under the desk, so from the arm of the chair, it wasn't too difficult to pull myself up on to the desktop.

Although I was eager to get to the cards, I couldn't help noticing Rockin' Aki's hamster ball.

I took a closer look. I've really only seen Aki up close when he was moving. Now, he was completely still. He actually didn't look much like a hamster at all. His fur wasn't shiny and golden like mine and his eyes were lifeless pieces of plastic. I felt a little sorry for him.

I decided to concentrate on the cards. One big card said 'Brisbane's Buddies' and the rest were laid out in pairs. Each card had one student's name on it. Above each pair was a label that said something different.

'It looks like some kind of game, Og!' I squeaked to my friend. 'I'll try to figure it out.'

I strolled up and down the rows of cards, reading the labels: Teacher's Assistants, Door and Line Monitors, Homework Collectors.

'They're classroom jobs, Og!' I squeaked. 'Mrs Brisbane is pairing up two people for each job, so they'll have to work together. Isn't that a good idea?'

'BOING-BOING!' Og twanged.

'Noticeboard Designers . . . oh, and listen to this job: Animal Handlers,' I told him.

'BOING-BOING-BOING!' Og replied, splashing loudly in his tank.

Now that I understood what Brisbane's Buddies were, I started reading the names she had paired together.

'Paul G. and Kelsey, Thomas and Phoebe, Holly and Rosie . . .' I suddenly stopped. Mrs Brisbane had worked hard and done a good job. But I had a few ideas of my own. Since part of my job as a classroom hamster is to help the teacher, I decided it would be okay for me to lend her a paw. She needed all the help she could get.

'I'm just going to make a few teeny-weeny changes, Og,' I explained to my friend as I carefully started moving the cards around.

What may seem like a little card to a human is actually a HUGE card to a small hamster so it took a lot of time and effort to move them and line them up.

I was thinking so hard about what I was doing, I forgot about Aki until I accidentally backed into his hamster ball. I guess I hit the switch, because lights began to flash and the ball started to loop and twirl across the desk.

'Rockin' Aki! Rock 'n' roll rules!' The ball spun wildly.

'Stop it, Aki!' I squeaked. Then I remembered he wasn't real.

The ball twirled across the cards, which slowed it down.

BUMPITY-BUMP-BUMP!

Aki had seemed like a lot of fun when it was daytime and all my friends were there. But now, his hamster ball was rocking and rolling out of control! Twice, it spun dangerously near the edge of the table. If it fell off, it would be broken for ever and Mrs Brisbane would be VERY-VERY-VERY upset.

There *had* to be some way to shut it off. I could see the little ON/OFF button as it spun across the desk, but every time I was close to it, the ball rolled away from me.

Then I spotted some pencils lying nearby. I quickly slid one pencil on either side of the ball to keep it from rolling. It worked! The ball stayed in place, but the lights still flashed and the music blasted out, 'Rockin' Aki!'

There was still a problem: I would have to switch the large button from ON to OFF.

'Don't worry, Og! I'll turn it off!' I squeaked. Not that Og could hear me over all that noise.

I wasn't sure how to approach the ball. But if I could explore the school, spin on my wheel and swing on a blinds cord, I could surely get to that button!

I took a running leap and jumped right on top of it. I'd once seen a TV show where cowboys rode on bucking broncos, trying their best not to get thrown off. While the ball wasn't moving, it was still shaking like mad.

'Yahoo!' I shouted, just like those cowboys.

The plastic was slippery but I stretched my paw WAY-WAY-WAY closer to the button.

'Ride 'em cowboy!' I yelled as the ball rocked and rolled.

'Rockin' Aki!' the music played.

I pushed the button with all my might and it slid forward. The music and lights stopped immediately. I hadn't thought about the stopping part and I slid off on to the desk.

'Ouch! I'm okay, Og! Nothing broken,' I said. 'At least I don't think so.'

As I lay there, catching my breath, I looked over at the little hamster in the ball, staring straight ahead with glassy eyes.

'Sorry, pal,' I said. 'I was only trying to help.'

Of course, I had to spend more time straightening out the cards which Aki had messed up.

By the time I finally got back to my cage, the room was getting lighter. Before long, Mrs Brisbane and the strange students would be back.

Of course, they'd never know about my exciting adventure. They probably thought that being a classroom hamster was easy.

But even if they didn't know what I'd accomplished, *I* was pleased that I'd done an unsqueakably good job!

I think Og was, too.

Humphrey's Rules of School

Whatever job you're given in the classroom, always do your best. Even if it makes you unsqueakably tired!

Hickory Dickory Dock

Friday morning I was tired and a little jumpy because I thought Mrs Brisbane might be upset that I mixed up her cards. I was also worried about Harry.

All week long, I'd held my breath after every bell, wondering if Hurry-Up-Harry would be tardy or not. After all, he'd made a deal with Mrs Brisbane.

He did unsqueakably well at keeping his end of the bargain. But on Thursday, he had been late to school because his mum couldn't find her car keys. (They were under the kitchen table.)

I wasn't sure whether he'd broken his end of the deal or not, so I still didn't know where I'd be spending the weekend.

But I forgot about everything else when Mrs Brisbane said, 'Boys and girls, I'm now going to announce your new classroom jobs.'

She explained Brisbane's Buddies and how the students would work in pairs. Then she described each job. Finally, she began to read off the names of the students who would share each job.

'For Homework Collectors, Rosie and Phoebe.' Mrs Brisbane looked surprised and I knew why. The night before, I'd moved Phoebe to the homework job.

Helpful Holly raised her hand. 'Don't you think *I* should do the job with Rosie?'

'No,' Mrs Brisbane said. 'I have another job for you, Holly. Just keep listening.'

Holly looked disappointed but Mrs Brisbane continued. 'Animal Handlers will be Joey and Kelsey.'

Again, Mrs Brisbane looked surprised. I just hoped that Be-Careful-Kelsey would be better at taking care of animals than she was at taking care of herself.

Joey and Kelsey both looked thrilled.

'It really is the best job,' I squeaked to Og.

'BOING-BOING!' he agreed.

'Door and Line Monitors will be . . .' Mrs Brisbane paused. She obviously knew these weren't the names she'd chosen, but she read them anyway. 'Harry and Simon.'

I thought that pairing Hurry-Up-Harry with Slow-Down-Simon was a brilliant idea. At least I hoped so.

Mrs Brisbane kept going. I thought maybe she'd ignore my next idea, but when she read the names, she actually looked pleased. 'Noticeboard Designers: Paul G. and Paul F.'

The two Pauls did *not* look thrilled, but I crossed my toes and hoped my idea would work.

When she got to the very end of the list, there were just two people left.

'These jobs just have one person,' she said. 'Thomas, you will be Class Reporter. That means you have to record what we do every day in a Class Log,' she explained. 'What we study, who participates and even what the temperature is. No exaggeration, okay?'

'Okay!' Thomas said as he gave her a 'thumbs-up'.

'Holly, you will be the Teacher's Assistant. That means when I need anything done, from taking a note to the office, answering the phone or cleaning the board, I will ask you. Do you think you can handle that?'

Helpful Holly did.

Near the end of the day, Mrs Brisbane made another announcement: Hurry-Up-Harry would be taking me home for the weekend.

'Yes!' Harry shouted. 'This is my lucky day.'

I hoped it was my lucky day, too.

I was tired from all that late-night work rearranging the cards, but a classroom hamster sometimes works around the clock. And I was anxious to get to Hurry-Up-Harry's house and meet his family.

I had to wait a while, though, because Harry's mum was unsqueakably late in picking us up from school.

Yep, I had my work cut out for me . . . again.

⚬

Harry's mum was NICE-NICE-NICE. So was his little sister, Suzy. I wasn't surprised. After all, Harry was NICE-NICE-NICE. He was also often LATE-LATE-LATE. And I wanted to find out why.

I got all settled on the coffee table in the Ito family living room.

'Nice mouthie,' Suzy said as she leaned in close to my cage.

'Nice *hamster*,' I politely corrected her.

'Mouth!' she said, twirling in circles around my cage until I felt slightly dizzy.

'He's a hamster,' Harry corrected her, thank goodness.

Suzy twirled around again but this time she said, 'Hamthter!!'

At least that was a little closer than 'mouth'.

Usually when I go home with a student, I am placed on a desk or table, admired and played with, and then the family has dinner.

At Harry's house, I was placed on a table, admired and played with. But dinner was a long way off.

I can't say the Ito family didn't have a clock. They had a large gold one in the living room, on the mantel above the fireplace, directly opposite from my spot on the table. I saw the time change from 6.00 to 6.30 and from 6.30 to

7.00. Each time the clock reached the half-hour point, it chimed a lovely, loud sound. Ding-ding! Ding-ding!

'Mummy, I'm hungry!' Suzy said. She stopped twirling and plopped down on the sofa.

'Sorry, honey,' Harry's mum said. 'I was hoping we'd all eat together, but I'll go ahead and give you some pasta.'

'Pathta-pathta-pathta,' Suzy said, jumping up and twirling around my cage again.

Harry decided to wait to eat until his dad came home, which was around 8.30.

'Sorry,' Mr Ito said, giving Harry's mum a kiss. (Which was unsqueakably nice.) 'I was clearing up some paperwork and I lost track of time,' he said.

The Itos lost track of time a lot. Harry's mum said it was no problem and it was 9.00 when she finally said the food was ready. Suzy had fallen asleep on the sofa, but the rest of the family ate together.

After dinner, Harry's mum took Suzy up to bed and Harry and his dad came into the living room.

'Wow, I didn't know it was so late,' Mr Ito

said, looking up at the large, shiny gold clock over the fireplace. 'It's bedtime for you, too, Harry.'

'Oh, Dad, it's Friday night. Can't I stay up a little while longer?' Harry asked.

Harry's dad said it was okay, especially since he'd got home late and hadn't had much time with his son. They started playing a game together. I decided to entertain them with some hamster acrobatics. I leaped around on my tree branch, then hopped on my wheel and started spinning faster and faster.

'Go, Humphrey, go!' Harry said and pretty soon he and his father forgot about their game and watched me.

'Tomorrow, we'll put him in his hamster ball,' Harry told his dad.

When Harry's mum came back downstairs, I started my act all over again. I was already tired from the night before, but a hamster's job is never done.

Mrs Ito glanced up at the clock. 'Harry has a football game in the morning,' she said with a yawn. 'We'd better get to bed.'

Mr Ito looked up at the clock, too. 'My

watch is a little slow,' he said, resetting it.

'Are you sure that clock is right?' his wife asked.

'Very sure. It may be an antique, but it keeps perfect time,' Mr Ito answered.

Mrs Ito nodded, then adjusted her watch, too.

After Harry and his parents had gone to bed, I was happy to settle in for a nice snooze myself. Like the Itos, I checked the clock.

It was 11.00.

The next morning, I sat in my cage in the living room and watched the Itos in action. There was the usual morning commotion of people getting up, eating breakfast, listening to the news.

Harry came into the living room to see me.

'Hi, Humphrey. Did you have a good sleep? Do you like my house?' he asked.

I was about to say yes, when Mrs Ito rushed into the living room, looking frantic.

'Harry, you've got to get dressed. The game is at 9.00!' she said. It was only fifteen minutes to nine and Mrs Ito was still in her dressing gown.

'What time's the game?' Mr Ito asked, wandering into the living room, still in his dressing gown, too.

'Nine!' Mrs Ito told him as she headed for the stairs. Mr Ito was right behind her.

Harry came back down in his football uniform at five minutes to nine. I crossed my toes and hoped that the football pitch was close to the house.

Finally, Mr and Mrs Ito came back into the living room, both dressed.

'Where's Suzy?' Mr Ito asked.

Mrs Ito ran back up the stairs. 'I'll get her dressed. Meet you in the car!'

Mr Ito looked at the clock and shook his head. It was one minute to nine.

'Okay,' he said. 'But we're going to be late!'

The last Ito finally left the house at three minutes past nine. They were definitely late . . . as usual.

I was exhausted from watching the family run around like that. But I realized that this was probably what went on in the Ito house every day that Harry was late to school.

Mr and Mrs Ito were grown-up human beings and seemed quite smart. How could a small hamster help them change their ways? I thought about that problem all day, between naps in my cage.

Then an idea began to take shape in my brain. The Itos weren't very good at keeping track of the time, but when they did, they seemed to check that clock on the mantel. I couldn't change the Itos, but maybe I could change the clock they trusted so much.

As I stared at the clock a long time, a little rhyme rolled around in my brain.

Hickory dickory dock
The mouse ran up the clock . . .

Suzy had called me a mouse (at least I think that's what she meant by 'mouth') and hamsters are a lot like mice. (According to Aldo, we're both rodents.) So if a mouse could go up the clock, I guess a clever hamster like me could, too, as long as I had a Plan.

I rested some more while the Itos were gone, knowing I had a busy night ahead of me.

Once the family was back from the game
(Harry's team won – hurray!), I learned that
the Itos were really fun as long as they didn't
have to worry about time. Harry showed Suzy
some of his football moves in the back yard.
Then they all went out for a while and came
back with lots of yummy food. Later, Mr and
Mrs Ito cooked a big dinner and Harry and
Suzy helped. And they gave *me* carrots.

After dinner, they all went downstairs to the
basement and Harry brought me along.

I was glad he did, because I got to sit in my
cage and watch the family play table tennis.
They didn't play tennis *with* a table. They
played it *on* a table, using a small bouncy ball
and paddles.

Suzy was too young to play, but they gave
her a paddle and let her try. Harry and his parents
were very good at hitting the ball back and
forth across a table with a little net going down
the centre. The game was quite exciting and
my neck got tired from turning my head back
and forth to follow the ball in its travels.

'Hey, maybe Humphrey would like to play,' Harry said.

I shivered and quivered a little bit, worried that the Itos were going to bat me back and forth with paddles. But Harry had a better idea. First, he put blankets all around the edges of the table so I wouldn't roll off. Then he placed me inside my hamster ball and set it on the table.

'Go for it, Humphrey,' he said.

The Itos all leaned in and watched as I rolled my ball across the table towards the net. I was able to pick up quite a bit of speed. As I hit the net, I bounced off, just like the little white ball.

'Score one for Humphrey!' said Harry. 'Let's give him a point every time he bounces off the net.'

I don't mean to brag, but I scored *ten points* before Harry's mum said she was tired and needed to go to bed.

She was tired – what about me? But I still had lots of work to do.

Once I was alone in the living room and the house was completely quiet, I opened the lock-that-doesn't-lock and slid down the leg of the coffee table. The moon shone through the big double doors and I could see that there was a set of metal shelves next to the fireplace. The shelves were spaced close together, which was a lucky break for me, because I could easily climb up and hop on to the mantel.

I haven't had any experience with clocks but I hoped that I could figure out how this one worked. It was an old-fashioned clock with numbers and hands – not the kind with lighted numbers. The time was exactly 11.25.

There was no way to set the time on the front of the clock, so I moved around to the back. There was a knob there, which I figured must be for setting the time.

I reached up and tried to turn the knob to the right. The thing didn't budge. My Plan wasn't going to work! I sat back down on the mantel and rested.

'Wait a minute, Humphrey,' I squeaked softly to myself. 'You turned off Rockin' Aki. Surely you can turn this little knob!'

I felt very determined as I leaped up and grabbed on to the top of the knob with all my might. I don't weigh much, but I hoped that if I could hang on long enough, I'd be heavy enough to move the knob.

I shimmied my body over to the right and tried to yank the knob down.

'Oof!' The knob budged a little bit.

Ding-ding! Ding-ding! Suddenly the chimes rang out.

I dropped back to the mantel.

Ding-ding! Ding-ding! The chimes were so loud, it felt as if they were ringing in my brain. It was enough to give me a huge hamster head-ache.

Still, I had a Plan and nothing was going to stop me. The ringing stopped, so I leaped up again, hung on for dear life and the knob moved a little more. I let go, then scurried around to the front, checked the time, and then returned to the back to move the knob again and again.

My paws were aching. When I went around to check the front of the clock again, I saw that I had set the clock ahead five minutes.

I was afraid to set it too far ahead – then the Itos might catch on. But maybe five minutes would make a difference.

Feeling unsqueakably pleased with myself, I looked for a way back to my cage. The thought of climbing down the wire shelves made my stomach a little queasy. But on the other side, there was a window with curtains and a long cord hanging down. Perfect! I grabbed on to the cord and began to slide.

'Eeek!' I hadn't realized that this cord would be so slippery. I slid WAY-WAY-WAY faster than when I slide down the cord to the blinds in Room 26! The room was a blur as I zoomed down to the floor, which I hit a little harder than I would have liked.

Once I recovered, I looked up at the clock. It was 11.45 by then. Of course, I knew that it was really only 11.40. I'm so glad I know how to tell the time!

I had another lucky break when I got back to the coffee table. There was a footstool next to it and I climbed up easily and hopped back on the table and into my cage.

I was never so happy to crawl into my sleeping hut as I was that night.

And to think, at that moment, Og was alone in Room 26, just swimming around in his tank!

The next morning I was a little sore, but anxious to see if all my hard work would pay off. It was a little later in the morning when again, there was a lot of running back and forth through the living room around 9.45.

'We'll be late to church!' Mrs Ito said, walking into the room in her robe.

'I'm all set,' Mr Ito answered. He strolled in, completely dressed for the day.

'You make sure the kids are ready,' his wife said. 'I'll get dressed.'

Mr Ito disappeared and I could hear footsteps upstairs as the whole family hurried around.

They finally reappeared in the living room again, dressed for church.

'Oh, no. We're going to be late again,' Mrs Ito said, looking at the clock.

'Only five minutes late,' her husband said. 'Let's go.'

When they left, I looked up at the clock. It said it was five minutes to ten. But I knew it was really ten minutes to ten. The Itos would probably make it to church on time. Barely.

The rest of the day was QUIET-QUIET-QUIET. I was dozing when Harry came and picked up my cage.

'Come on, Humphrey,' he said. 'You can help me with my homework.'

'Eeek!' I squeaked. I wasn't upset about the homework. I was upset because I didn't want to end up in Harry's room for the night. I already had a Plan to give the Itos a little more help.

Thank goodness, when Harry was finished, he carried my cage back downstairs to the table in the living room. My Plan was safe!

When the house was quiet that night after the clock chimed 11.00, I opened the door to my cage, took a deep breath and once again headed up the wire shelves to the mantel. With great effort, I turned the clock forward another five minutes. That would give the Itos an extra ten minutes in the morning.

Hopefully, the next morning I wouldn't be tardy. And neither would Harry.

Humphrey's Rules
of School

Homework can be extremely tiring,
especially if you're a classroom pet!

Brisbane versus Becker

Good news! The Itos never suspected what I'd done. In fact, Mrs Ito noticed that the clock was ten minutes ahead of her watch, so she changed her watch! Mr Ito did the same thing.

Believe it or not, we got to school five minutes ahead of the bell.

Harry was surprised, his mother was surprised, and Mrs Brisbane was surprised.

I was not.

'Harry, it's great to see you here on time,' Mrs Brisbane said.

Mrs Ito looked a little embarrassed.

'Mrs Brisbane, I know we got off to a bad start this year,' Mrs Ito told the teacher. 'But I'm really going to do my best to get Harry here on time every single day.'

That made Mrs Brisbane happy. I was happy, too. I just hope nobody *ever* changes the clock again – except for me!

I couldn't wait until break to tell Og about my adventures. But first, something even more important was going on. The students started their new jobs as Brisbane's Buddies.

'Here's hoping my Plan works,' I told Og.

Rolling Rosie and Forgetful Phoebe went to work right away collecting the homework assignments. The two girls put their homework in first. Yes, Phoebe had actually remembered this time! As I was hoping, she'd probably figured it would look BAD-BAD-BAD for a Homework Collector to forget her own assignments.

Thomas never went anywhere without his Class Log, which he wrote in a *lot*.

Mrs Brisbane kept Helpful Holly hopping. Holly took attendance and carried the report to the office. Later, Mrs Brisbane asked Holly to tidy up the little library in the back of the room and water her plants.

I think Holly finally got to be as helpful as she wanted.

Hurry-Up-Harry and Slow-Down-Simon made excellent Door and Line Monitors. When it was time for break, Simon opened the door and Harry led the students down the hall (he couldn't dawdle if he was first in line!). Then Simon closed the door and made sure there were no stragglers at the end of the line (so there was no way for him to race ahead!).

After lunch, there was free time for Tall Paul and Small Paul to work on the noticeboard. This was the pair I was most interested in, since they'd never actually talked to each other before.

It was a little hard for me to see what they were doing. I was in my hamster ball while Mrs Brisbane watched Just Joey clean up my cage. Once she got him started, she moved over to Og's tank to teach Be-Careful-Kelsey how to take care of *him*.

'I hope she's careful with you, Og!' I squeaked, knowing that Joey wouldn't be able to understand me.

'BOING-BOING!' Og twanged cheerfully.

While Joey was working, he talked to me.

'I can't believe it, Humphrey. I got the best job of all! Good things hardly ever happen to me,' he said.

I'd never seen Joey so happy. As he put me back in my cage, he said, 'It's just like having Giggles back. I can hardly wait until you come home with me.'

'Neither can I,' I squeaked, before I remembered Joey had that Frisbee-catching dog.

Then I climbed up to the top of my cage to get a better look at the two Pauls. They were taking down papers and old drawing pins that were still on the noticeboard. Tall Paul handled the top part of the board while Small Paul handled the bottom part. They weren't talking to each other but at least they were working together.

Near the end of the day, Mrs Brisbane called Holly up to her desk and told her that she was doing a wonderful job.

'I was thinking, Holly. Being my assistant takes up a lot of time. Maybe it would make sense for Phoebe to be Rosie's assistant,' she suggested. 'After all, they are Homework Collectors together.'

Helpful Holly looked relieved. 'I think that's a good idea,' she said. 'If it's okay with Rosie.'

'I'll ask her,' Mrs Brisbane said.

Of course, when she asked Rosie, it was no problem. And when she asked Phoebe to be Rosie's new assistant, Phoebe's face lit up.

Yes, my evening rearranging the Brisbane Buddies cards was definitely paying off. And the worst class ever was looking a lot better. I was pretty pleased with myself for a while.

But after school, something happened that shook me down to the very tips of my paws.

Miss Becker paid a visit to Room 26!

I'd never actually seen Miss Becker before. She was a short woman with great big glasses that made her eyes look huge. That might have been a little weird, but Miss Becker also had a great big smile that made me like her.

'I hope you don't mind, Sue,' she said as she came in the room. 'My students are very anxious for us to get a classroom pet, but I've never had one before.'

Mrs Brisbane smiled. 'My class was very

fond of Humphrey and Og last year.'

'Oh, I know! That's all I hear. Humphrey this and Og that. That's just about all they talk about,' Miss Becker explained. 'But I don't know. I never even had a pet as a child.'

'Why don't you come over and meet them?' Mrs Brisbane suggested.

My heart sank down to the bottom of my toes. Was Mrs Brisbane really going to give one – or both – of us away?

'I wasn't interested in having a hamster last year either,' Mrs Brisbane said. I remembered that well.

'Then Ms Mac brought Humphrey in while I was gone,' she continued. 'He added a lot to the classroom. So when Angie Loomis needed to get Og out of her classroom, I was happy to take him. It's funny, because sometimes I think they've actually become friends.'

Sometimes? Og and I are friends *all* the time.

'But do you have to, you know, *touch* them?' Miss Becker said. Her big smile had disappeared.

'Sure I do, but I don't mind,' she said.

Miss Becker leaned in close to my cage, so

close her eyes seemed gigantic.

'They say Humphrey does many cute things,' she said, her voice quivering a little.

Mrs Brisbane chuckled. 'I should say so! Show her, Humphrey.'

I've never been shy about showing off my great gymnastic abilities. After all, it seems to please humans to watch me leaping, spinning, rolling, climbing and to hear me say SQUEAK-SQUEAK-SQUEAK! But I was a little nervous about showing off so much that Miss Becker would want to move me to Room 18. Especially since she didn't even want to touch me.

But, I always try to do what Mrs Brisbane asks, so with a heavy heart, I hopped on my wheel and began to spin.

'Oh my word!' Miss Becker's big eyes grew even wider. 'He's certainly active.'

She didn't sound too pleased about that, so I decided to be a little more active. I jumped off the wheel and climbed up my tree branch as fast as my little legs could carry me. When I got to the top, I leaped on to the side of the cage.

Miss Becker gasped. 'How does he do that?'

'He's a very clever guy,' Mrs Brisbane said

proudly. 'But Og is no slouch either,' she said.

I had a chance to catch my breath while the two teachers turned their attention to Og's tank.

'He's a very handsome frog, isn't he?' Mrs Brisbane asked.

Now I consider Og a very fine fellow, but handsome? With that green skin, no fur at all, the huge mouth and those big googly eyes . . . which suddenly reminded me a lot of Miss Becker's eyes.

'BOING!' Og twanged. It was a pleasant sort of reply but Miss Becker jumped back from the tank.

'What was that?' she asked.

'That's the kind of sound he makes.' Mrs Brisbane was being very patient.

'And what does he do?' Miss Becker asked.

'He spends part of his time on the dry part of his tank and part of his time in the water,' Mrs Brisbane explained.

Og must have been listening (with those ears I can't see), because he suddenly leaped into the water and began splashing wildly.

'Oh, my word,' Miss Becker exclaimed.

'He's awfully noisy, isn't he?'

I'd had it then. We'd been very polite to Miss Becker but she certainly wasn't polite to us.

'Not as noisy as *you* are!' I squeaked.

Miss Becker looked back and forth between Og and me.

'How do you manage it all?' she asked.

'Oh, the children do most of the work,' Mrs Brisbane said. 'Though I do enjoy bringing them home when I can. I think the point is something Ms Mac told me when she brought Humphrey to Room 26. You can learn a lot about yourself by taking care of another species. That's proved to be very true.'

Miss Becker stared at Og and me for a while before she spoke again. 'I don't know what to say. The students love them so much.'

Just then, Ms Mac came in. 'Am I interrupting something?' she asked.

'No! You're the perfect person to talk to,' Mrs Brisbane said.

She was right. Ms Mac was a perfect person . . . at least to me.

'Some of my old students are begging for a classroom pet and Arlene's trying to decide whether to get one,' Mrs Brisbane explained. 'So she came to look at Humphrey and Og.'

Ms Mac smiled her wonderful, warm smile. 'Any class would do better with those two.'

For once, I was sorry Ms Mac had come to visit. I didn't want her to talk Miss Becker into taking me away.

'Thanks for your time, Sue,' Miss Becker said. 'I still have a lot to think about.'

After Miss Becker left, Ms Mac wanted to talk to Mrs Brisbane.

'It's great to see my students learning to read,' she said. 'But some of them are having a hard time and I want them to see how much fun books can be.'

Mrs Brisbane nodded. 'That gives me an idea. We could work together.'

She glanced at the clock. 'I've got to go now. I'll give you a call tonight and we'll talk.'

Just before Ms Mac left, she bent down so she was eye level with my cage and Og's tank.

'Maybe my students need a classroom pet, too,' she said.

Suddenly, I had a sinking feeling that *both* Og and I would be leaving Room 26!

When Aldo came in to clean that night, it was clear right away that he was still upset.

'Richie called and said he thinks one of you is coming to Miss Becker's class,' he said. 'I don't think that's a good idea!'

'Neither do I!' I squeaked loudly.

'BOING-BOING-BOING!' Og agreed.

'Of course, those kids love you,' he said, calming down as he swept the floor. 'But the new kids need you, too.'

It was true. Just about everybody seemed to need a helpful hamster.

Later that night, after Aldo left and Og was quiet, I slipped my little notebook out from its hiding place and started a couple of lists.

Reasons to stay in Room 26:

- Mrs Brisbane relies on me
- The new students have a lot of problems and need help

- To stay with Og (I hope)

Reasons for me to move to Room 18:

- To be with my old friends: Richie, Heidi, Gail, Kirk, Tabitha, A.J.
- To teach Miss Becker about pets

Reasons for Og to move to Room 18:

- To be with his old friends: Richie, Heidi, Gail, Kirk, Tabitha, A.J.
- To teach Miss Becker about pets

I stared at those lists for hours and hours and hours but I couldn't decide which would be the best choice for me.

In the end, I wouldn't make the decision, anyway. But just before I tucked my notebook away for the night, I worked on my poem.

> Autumn, oh, autumn,
> The golden leaves are blowing.
> Autumn, oh, autumn,
> I don't know where I'm going!

Humphrey's Rules
of School

Make sure you do your part to
make your classroom a better place.

Working Together

The next day, I was pleased to see that Phoebe remembered her homework again! I was certainly glad I'd changed the cards to make her a Homework Collector.

Holly seemed really happy being helpful all day long, especially because Mrs Brisbane kept her BUSY-BUSY-BUSY.

Slow-Down-Simon had slowed down quite a bit because as Door and Line Monitor, he had to wait for the rest of the students to line up. Hurry-Up-Harry was never tardy after break or lunch because he *had* to leave when the other students did. (And he was never late in the morning, either. I guess the Itos still hadn't figured out the living-room clock was fast.)

Be-Careful-Kelsey was extremely careful when she handled Og out of his tank.

'Don't be scared, Og,' she said. 'I'd never let anything happen to a special frog like you.'

Just Joey tidied up my cage again, even though it didn't really need it. When Mrs Brisbane came to check on him, she told him he'd done such a good job, she'd let him train all future Animal Handlers.

Joey was overjoyed. 'Did you hear that, Humphrey?' he asked me later. 'I'm a Trainer now, not just a Handler. Mrs Brisbane really trusts me.'

I could see Joey's job was doing him a lot of good. In fact, all of Brisbane's Buddies seemed happy with their jobs . . . except two of them.

Tall Paul and Small Paul had worked together to clear the noticeboard but they still hadn't put anything up there. Mrs Brisbane had taken out boxes full of art supplies and paper, maps and posters, but they just couldn't seem to agree on what to put up. Small Paul wanted to make the theme about autumn. Tall Paul wanted to make the theme about animals. Then Small Paul wanted the noticeboard to be about aeroplanes and Tall Paul wanted it to be about cars.

'How about aeroplanes *and* cars? Transportation,' Mrs Brisbane suggested.

The Pauls didn't think those went together.

I thought that the two *Pauls* didn't go together. I had obviously made an unsqueakably bad mistake when I decided to pair them up.

'Mrs Brisbane, I don't think Paul G. and I make very good Brisbane's Buddies,' Small Paul told Mrs Brisbane after lunch on Tuesday. 'Maybe you should switch us with somebody else.'

'You have to learn to work with people who aren't like you,' the teacher explained. 'You'll have to do it many times in your life.'

Small Paul looked miserable. 'He won't even try.'

'And what about you? Are you trying?' Mrs Brisbane asked.

Small Paul didn't answer.

'You can do it, Paul!' I squeaked from my cage.

Og tried to be encouraging, too. 'BOING-BOING!' he twanged.

Mrs Brisbane looked over at us. 'Look at

those two. Can you think of two animals who are less alike than Og and Humphrey?'

'That's right! He's an amphibian and I'm a mammal!' I agreed.

'And yet, they share that table and actually seem to enjoy each other's company,' Mrs Brisbane continued.

'He's cold-blooded and I'm warm-blooded!' I added.

'So I think two boys who are the same age and in the same class and both like things like planes and cars can learn to work together, don't you?' Mrs Brisbane certainly made sense to me.

'I guess,' Paul said. He didn't sound convinced, though.

'So give it another try,' Mrs Brisbane told him. 'For Humphrey and Og, okay?'

I crossed my toes and hoped they'd try.

The did have a chance to work together later in the day but they didn't talk at all. They just stared down at the boxes of art supplies.

Something I hadn't planned for happened next. Mrs Brisbane asked Holly to return some playground equipment to Mrs Wright. There were several bats and a box of balls.

Helpful Holly had a little trouble carrying them all at one time. The bats crashed to the ground, the box tipped over and the balls bounced all over the floor. She picked them up, then admitted she needed some help.

'Would you like to ask someone else to help?' Mrs Brisbane asked.

Holly looked around the room and I almost fell off my tree branch when she picked Rolling Rosie. The smile on Rosie's face told me she was pleasantly surprised.

'I can carry the box on my lap,' Rosie suggested. 'You can take the bats.'

'Good idea,' said Holly.

After they had left, Mrs Brisbane told the rest of the class, 'That's what I like to see in my classroom. Working together. That's why I came up with Brisbane's Buddies.'

Small Paul glanced at Tall Paul when he heard those words.

I couldn't hear him, but he said something to Tall Paul, who nodded. Soon, they were actually talking as they pulled things out of the box.

A little later, Small Paul asked, 'Mrs Brisbane, could we borrow your pictures of the kids in the class and go to the library? We need to scan them into the computer.'

She was surprised but of course she said yes and wrote a note to Mr Fitch, the librarian.

The Pauls were both smiling when they came back.

After school, Mrs Brisbane seemed unsqueakably pleased with herself. Just before she left, she came over to our table to say goodbye.

'Brisbane's Buddies seems to be working out,' she said. 'Even though I'm still not sure how those cards got switched around. Did Aldo do it?' She laughed. 'You wouldn't tell on him if he did.'

Which was true.

The next morning, Small Paul and Tall Paul – together – asked Mrs Brisbane if they could put up their noticeboard during break.

'Yes,' she said. 'I just hope Mrs Wright doesn't find out. She wants all students to get fresh air.'

Tall Paul laughed, ran over to the window, opened it and took a deep breath. 'There. I've got my fresh air.'

Small Paul raced over and did the same thing. 'Me too,' he said.

Then they returned to the noticeboard.

'I made a plan,' Small Paul said, showing Tall Paul a piece of paper. I was glad to hear someone else in Room 26 made plans besides just me.

Tall Paul studied it carefully. 'That should work,' he said. 'I guess I'll take the top part.'

'Okay,' Small Paul replied. 'I'll take the bottom.'

I climbed up to the tippy-top of my cage to watch as the noticeboard magically came to life.

Tall Paul put up letters across the top reading:

BRISBANE'S BUDDIES –
WE WORK TOGETHER

Meanwhile, on the lower half of the board, Small Paul put up pictures of students Mrs Brisbane had taken on the first day of school. The boys had enlarged them on the computer and printed them out. He put them in pairs according to their jobs.

Next, Tall Paul put pictures on the upper half of the board.

When they got to the middle, they worked together and didn't seem to mind one bit.

They worked quickly in order to finish before break ended.

'Now add the drawings we did last night,' Tall Paul said.

Soon, the job titles were accompanied by drawings the boys had made depicting each job. For Animal Handlers, there were excellent drawings of Og and me.

Suddenly, I had an awful thought. 'They won't need two Animal Handlers if they move one of us to Room 18,' I told Og.

Og splashed loudly in his tank. They were angry kinds of splashes.

By the time the other students in the room returned, the noticeboard was finished and it looked GREAT-GREAT-GREAT.

All the kids seemed to enjoy having their pictures on the board. I enjoyed having mine up there, too. But what I really enjoyed was seeing that my Plan worked after all!

Small Paul and Tall Paul walked out of the

classroom together at the end of the day, talking about getting together with their planes and cars. I don't think either of them noticed that they weren't the same size.

·ö·

'Whew!' I said when Og and I were alone again. 'We did it, but it was a lot of work.'

'BOING-BOING-BOING!' Og agreed.

Aldo came in later to clean the room. 'I'm glad to see you two are still together,' he said. 'Richie told me that Miss Becker said she'd decided on which classroom pet she wanted.'

My tummy did a flip-flop. 'Which one of us is it?' I squeaked.

'She said it would be a surprise,' Aldo added as he swept under our table. 'She'll tell them tomorrow. Oh, and she said Ms Mac helped her make up her mind.'

My tummy did a somersault. Ms Mac LOVED-LOVED-LOVED me, so of course, she told Miss Becker to pick me. I still miss my old friends from last year. So why did I feel sad about leaving Room 26?

Aldo spent a long time in our classroom that

night, because he brought in stacks of extra chairs and left them in the corner.

'Mrs Brisbane said she's going to need these tomorrow,' he explained.

Why did Mrs Brisbane need more chairs? Was she going to get more students? If so, wouldn't she need a helpful classroom pet more than ever?

ᐧöᐧ

Later, I made a few more notes in my notebook.

Reasons I'm sad about leaving Room 26:

- Leaving Mrs Brisbane
- Leaving Og
- Leaving my new classmates just when I'm starting to like them.

I opened the lock-that-doesn't-lock and strolled over to Og's tank.

'Og, old friend, I think I'm going to be leaving Room 26,' I said. 'Even though I don't want to.'

Og bounced up and down so hard, I thought he'd pop the top off his tank. 'BOING-BOING-

197

BOING-BOING!'

'I'm sure you'll still help the students with their problems,' I said. 'And I'll come and visit you every night.'

Og calmed down a little then.

'Maybe Mrs Brisbane will bring another pet in to keep you company. A cold-blooded animal, like you.' I thought that would make him feel better, but I don't think it did.

He dived into the water side of his tank, splashing furiously.

I understood.

I went back to my cage but I didn't sleep much that night.

My last night in Room 26.

Humphrey's Rules of School

Work together. Please!

The Best Class in the World

Everything in class was running smoothly now and suddenly, the new students of Room 26 didn't seem so strange any more. Too bad I'd be leaving so soon.

I tried to shake and wiggle my worries away but this time, it didn't work.

I waited and waited and waited to get the bad news but nothing happened until after lunch, when Miss Becker came in, accompanied by Richie and Gail. They were smiling, naturally, because they were happy they were getting me back.

'Mrs Brisbane, your students from last year wanted to share some news with you. Do you have a minute?' Miss Becker asked.

Mrs Brisbane looked surprised but she said, 'Sure, if you can share the news with my whole class.'

Miss Becker smiled. 'Yes, of course. ' She turned towards the class. 'Mrs Brisbane's students from last year wanted to get a classroom pet,' she told the class. 'Of course, they missed Humphrey and Og. So, I've finally made a decision. Richie and Gail, would you like to announce it?'

'Hermit,' Richie said, stepping forward.

That didn't sound like my name at all.

'Crabs,' Gail said, giggling.

That didn't sound like Og's name, either.

'What?' Mrs Brisbane looked amazed.

'We decided on something completely different. Six hermit crabs,' Miss Becker said. 'It was Ms Mac's suggestion.'

'Wonderful!' Mrs Brisbane said. 'How did you choose them?'

'We decided there would never be a frog as great as Og,' Richie said.

'Or a hamster as perfect as Humphrey,' Gail added.

I wasn't sure if that was true, but it was nice to hear.

'And,' Miss Becker added, 'Hermit crabs are very quiet. But they do better if they live in groups.'

'I hope you enjoy them as much as we enjoy Humphrey and Og,' Mrs Brisbane said. 'Perhaps we'll come and visit them some day.'

But at the end of the day, before she left, Mrs Brisbane said, 'You notice it takes six hermit crabs to replace the two of you.'

That made me feel VERY-VERY-VERY good.

'Whew! That was a close call, Og,' I told my neighbour when we were alone again.

I was unsqueakably delighted that I'd be staying in Room 26. After all, someone needed to keep a close eye on Kelsey, to make sure she didn't have any accidents. Joey wouldn't get to hear me giggle if I weren't around. Harry's family's clock could be set back at any time. I still wanted to find out why Phoebe was so forgetful, and I wasn't sure yet whether all of Thomas's stories were real or just tall tales.

I had a second surprise later that afternoon when Ms Mac appeared at the door.

'Are you ready?' she asked.

'Come on in,' Mrs Brisbane said.

I guess I'd been dozing when Mrs Brisbane had announced what was going to happen. Suddenly, my classmates were arranging the spare chairs stacked in the corner and setting them next to their own chairs. Then, I was SURPRISED-SURPRISED-SURPRISED when Ms Mac and her entire Reception class entered the room.

Ms Mac directed each of the Reception kids to sit next to an older student.

'The idea behind Brisbane's Reading Buddies is that the older children will share their favourite books with the younger children,' Mrs Brisbane told them. 'Any questions?'

A small boy who was missing both of his top front teeth raised his hand. 'What's over there?' he asked, pointing towards the table Og and I shared.

'Why that's our hamster, Humphrey, and

our frog, Og,' Mrs Brisbane explained.

'HI-HI-HI!' I squeaked, which made most of them giggle.

'Maybe you'll be in this class one day and they'll be *your* classroom pets,' Mrs Brisbane said.

That seemed to please the Reception kids. It pleased me, too.

What pleased me even more was watching the students in my class patiently sharing books with the Reception kids and helping them learn to read.

How on earth could I have ever thought they were the worst class in the world?

'ö'

The third surprise of the day came just before school was over for the day. Mr Morales stopped by for a visit. He was wearing a tie with colourful autumn leaves on it.

'Class, I just want to say that Mrs Brisbane has told me that in the last few weeks, your class has improved more than any class she's ever had. Mrs Brisbane has been teaching for a long time, so that's quite a compliment.' Mr

Morales paused and smiled at the class.

'She said you've made special progress in learning to work together,' he continued. 'So I would like to congratulate you and encourage you to keep up the good work!'

Every face in Room 26 had a smile on it. Even mine.

After school, Mrs Brisbane hummed to herself as she gathered up her papers and her purse.

'Fellows, this has been quite a week, hasn't it? It's the kind of week that makes me glad I'm still teaching,' she said.

That was nice to hear, because I didn't want Mrs Brisbane to stop teaching – ever!

'I still have to decide who takes you home this weekend, Humphrey,' she said. 'It will have to be a surprise.'

I didn't mind being surprised. The new students in Room 26 were my friends now.

That was a very nice feeling.

∙ö∙

When Aldo came into the room that night, the first thing he said was, 'Hermit crabs!'

He laughed so hard, his moustache shook. 'I never would have guessed she'd pick hermit crabs. They're crustaceans, you know.'

'No, I didn't know,' I told Aldo. 'But it doesn't matter whether they're crustaceans or primates or amphibians – they're classroom pets. And I'll bet they'll do a very good job.'

⚬

Of course I couldn't resist the temptation to pay a visit to Room 18 after Aldo's car had pulled out of the car park that night.

But as I slid under the door of Miss Becker's classroom, I was a little nervous. What if hermit crabs were as unfriendly as George?

I looked at the table by the windows but there were only stacks of folders there. An eerie glow from another wall caught my attention and there, on a table, was a large aquarium with a small light on it.

I inched closer and looked up at the unsqueakably odd sight of the hermit crabs. They weren't golden and furry, like me. And they weren't green and googly-eyed like Og. They were pinkish and shiny and had pincers that I wouldn't like to come in contact with. But I have to admit, they were interesting.

'Welcome to Longfellow School,' I said, even though they probably couldn't understand me. 'I hope you know that you're in one of the best classes in the world.'

They just kept wiggling, so I continued. 'And I'm in one of the other best classes in the world.'

Since they didn't have anything to say, I turned away, but before I left the room, I turned back.

'By the way,' I squeaked. 'My name is Humphrey. I'm the hamster in Room 26.'

I'm not completely sure, but I think one of the hermit crabs waved to me. I waved back.

⋅𝖔⋅

Once I was back to my classroom, I told Og about the hermit crabs.

'I guess it's nice that they're all crustaceans,' I told him. 'But personally, I'd rather have an amphibian as a neighbour. It makes life more interesting.'

'BOING-BOING-BOING!' he said, which

made me think he was happy to share the table with a mammal.

I took out my little notebook and I finished my poem, writing in the moonlight.

> Autumn, oh, autumn,
> You had my poor head spinning,
> But now I am happy
> To have a new beginning!

Humphrey's Rules of School

Love the class you're in. I do!

Humphrey's Top 10 Rules for Classroom Pets (hamsters, frogs and even hermit crabs)

1 Listen to your teacher. If it wasn't for your teacher, you wouldn't have a job and you might still be stuck in a boring old pet store!

2 When a student needs help, always lend a paw. (If you have pincers instead of paws, be VERY-VERY-VERY careful.)

3 If you have a lock-that-doesn't-lock, keep it a secret!

4 Remember: all doors are not the

same height, and being stuck under one is unsqueakably scary.

5 In case of emergency (and classroom pets have many of those), try and stay CALM.

6 Learn to tell the time. It's a skill that can come in very handy.

7 Be a friend to other classroom pets, even if they're a different species.

8 Even if they seem strange, new students can be every bit as nice as old, familiar students.

9 You can learn a lot about yourself by taking care of another species. (That's what Ms Mac said and she's unsqueakably smart.)

10 Humans need you. Please be kind to them!

Mysteries According to Humphrey

In memory of Humphrey's number one fan,
Sarah Williams
'Sweet-Sarah'

Contents

The Case of the Mysterious Detective

Outside the sun was shining, but inside Room 26 of Longfellow School, it was a dark and stormy night.

Mrs Brisbane, our teacher, was reading us a fur-raising mystery story from a big red book.

A mystery is like a puzzle. It can be something unsqueakably scary like a thing that goes THUMP in the night.

Or a mystery can be something ordinary, like what happened to Mrs Brisbane's glasses. Sometimes our teacher can't find her glasses when they're right on her head.

Even though my classmates and I can read by

ourselves, we love having Mrs Brisbane read to us. (It *is* surprising that I can read, because I am the classroom hamster, but I am also SMART-SMART-SMART, if I do say so myself.)

As I listened, I climbed up to the tippy top of my cage and looked out at my classmates. When school started in September, they were *all* mysteries to me. I didn't realize that at the beginning of the school year, a new class comes in. A class of *total strangers*.

It's taken me a while to work out why Hurry-Up-Harry is late so often and why Slow-Down-Simon moves so fast. I learned that Rolling-Rosie's wheelchair doesn't slow her down a bit. And I learned that Helpful-Holly is sometimes *Too*-Helpful-Holly.

Now it's October. I'm still getting to know some of the students who sit on the opposite side of the room from my cage. I haven't worked out why Do-It-Now-Daniel Dee always puts things off and why Stop-Talking-Sophie Kaminski has so much trouble being quiet.

In time, I hope I'll solve those mysteries, too. I guess being a classroom hamster is a lot like being a detective.

A detective is someone who solves mysteries. The story Mrs Brisbane was reading was about a detective named Sherlock Holmes, who was one smart human. In his picture on the cover of the red book, he wore a strange-looking hat. Mrs Brisbane said it was called a deerstalker hat. She also said he sometimes played the violin to help him think. (Which made me wish I had a violin of my own.)

There were a lot of stories in the book. This puzzling mystery had to do with a man with flaming-red hair, named Mr Jabez Wilson. He came to Sherlock Holmes and explained something strange that happened to him. It started when he saw an ad in the newspaper for a job that was *only* for a person with flaming-red hair. I guess that's why the name of the story was 'The Red-Headed League'.

Mrs Brisbane asked us, 'Why would they only want someone with red hair?'

Kelsey Kirkpatrick's hand shot up so fast, she almost hit Just-Joey, who sat next to her.

'Please Be-Careful-Kelsey,' Mrs Brisbane said. 'So what do you think?'

Kelsey said, 'They must be looking for

somebody smart! Everybody knows that red-heads are the cleverest people!'

My classmates all laughed, because Kelsey has red hair. Naturally, she would think red-haired people are the cleverest.

Mrs Brisbane laughed, too. 'Yes, Kelsey. Some red-haired people are very smart. But I don't think that was the reason.'

She asked if we had any other ideas.

I thought and thought. If the job needed someone smart, I think they might look for a clever hamster, like me.

Paul Fletcher, whom I think of as Small-Paul, had another idea. 'Maybe they needed someone who looked like someone else . . . a different person with red hair?' he suggested.

'That's an interesting idea, Paul. You'd make a good detective,' Mrs Brisbane said.

Paul Green, whom I think of as Tall-Paul, raised his hand. 'Maybe the person has to wear a costume,' he suggested. 'And they need red hair to go with the costume.'

'Excellent idea,' Mrs Brisbane said.

Thomas T. True looked puzzled and he raised his hand. 'Is this a true story?' he asked.

'I mean, is Sherlock Holmes a real person?'

Mrs Brisbane smiled. 'No, it's a made-up story. But Sherlock Holmes almost seems like a real person, and he's been popular for many years. When he solves a mystery, he looks for clues.'

She explained that a clue is information that helps you solve a mystery. And Sherlock Holmes was always looking for clues, because a good detective always has to be sharp-eyed.

Mrs Brisbane read some more. The red-haired man got hired, but it turned out that the job was nothing more than copying out the encyclopedia every evening.

What a strange job! Why would anyone need someone to copy the encyclopedia? And why would the person have to have red hair?

This was a mystery, indeed!

Suddenly, Mrs Brisbane stopped reading and closed the book.

'Eeek!' I squeaked. My classmates all groaned and begged her to read more, but it was almost time for afternoon break.

'When you come back, I'll have a different kind of mystery for you,' she said, which got us all excited again.

Soon, the classroom was empty, except for Og the frog and me. (Classroom pets like us don't get to go outside at break.)

Once we were alone, I squeaked to my neighbour, who lives in a tank next to my cage. 'Og, why do you think that ad asked for someone with red hair?' I asked.

Og splashed around a little in the water side of his tank and then leaped up and said, 'BOING-BOING!'

He sounds like a broken guitar string, but he can't help it. It's just the sound he makes.

I guess he doesn't know much about red hair. He doesn't have any hair or fur at all. And he's VERY-VERY-VERY green.

'I don't have any ideas, either,' I said. 'But I'm sure going to think about it.'

When my friends came back, they were anxious to hear about the *other* mystery.

'You know, class, when we read, we're all detectives,' the teacher said.

We all looked puzzled.

'Sometimes we come across a word we don't know, right?' she asked.

Everyone nodded, including me.

'So to work out what the word means, we look for a clue,' Mrs Brisbane continued. 'Just like Sherlock Holmes. Try this sentence.'

Then Mrs Brisbane wrote something very mysterious on the board.

The twins looked so much alike, I was piewhacked when I tried to tell them apart.

Piewhacked? That word had never been on our vocabulary list.

Lots of my friends giggled when they saw the word.

'Who knows what *piewhacked* means?' Mrs Brisbane asked.

Thomas raised his hand. 'I think it means "hit someone in the face with a pie".'

Everybody laughed, including me. But that didn't make much sense in the sentence about the twins.

'Let's try again,' Mrs Brisbane said. She wrote another sentence.

The rules of football can be very piewhacking if you've never seen a match before.

This time, more students giggled.

Piewhacked? Piewhacking? What was she trying to say? Were the pies flying at the football match?

'Look at how the word is used in the sentences to get some clues,' she told us.

Mrs Brisbane wrote one more sentence on the board.

When the teacher put the wrong
answers on the board, there was a lot of
piewhacksion in the classroom.

Piewhacksion? Was there a pie fight in the classroom? Or had my teacher lost her mind?

'I'm confused!' I blurted out, even though all that my human friends heard was 'SQUEAK!'

'Confusion!' Slow-Down-Simon shouted.

I'm sorry to say he forgot to raise his hand before speaking.

'Confused!' Too-Helpful-Holly said. She raised her hand, but she didn't wait for the teacher to call on her before speaking.

'Let's see if that word works,' Mrs Brisbane said with a smile. '"The twins looked so much alike, I was *confused* when I tried to tell them apart.'"

That worked for me.

'How about "The rules of football can be very *confusing* if you've never seen a match before",' she continued. 'And finally, "When the teacher put the wrong answers on the board, there was a lot of *confusion* in the class-room."'

Now I was pawsitive that *piewhack* meant *confuse*.

'For your homework tonight, here are five more mystery words to work out,' she said as she handed Rolling-Rosie homework sheets to pass out.

Unfortunately, Rosie didn't give me one, so I couldn't see what the mystery words were.

I tried making up my own mystery words, like *flapple* and *scarrot*, but they just made me hungry!

˙ö˙

At the end of the day, just before the bell rang, the door to Room 26 swung open and in walked Mrs Wright, the physical education teacher.

She was clutching a pink jacket and, as usual, wore a shiny silver whistle on a cord around her neck.

Mrs Wright likes to blow that whistle and when she does, it makes my ears wiggle and the fur on my neck stand up. It's LOUD-LOUD-LOUD. Way too loud for the small, sensitive ears of a hamster.

Mrs Wright also likes rules. Okay, she *loves* rules.

I can understand why someone who teaches children to play games would love rules, because rules are very important to games. But to squeak the truth, I think she loves rules just a tiny bit too much, and I think Mrs Brisbane agrees with me.

'Yes, Mrs Wright?' our teacher asked.

Mrs Wright raised the pink jacket up high. 'I believe this belongs to one of your students,' she said. 'Normally, I would put it in the lost property. But her name was inside and I thought she might need it. It's quite chilly out there. Phoebe Pratt?'

Poor Forgetful-Phoebe looked embarrassed as she walked over to get the jacket. 'Sorry, Mrs

Wright,' she said.

'Students must be responsible for their belongings,' Mrs Wright said. 'You'd be amazed at what treasures I have in the lost property.'

'Thank you, Mrs Wright,' Mrs Brisbane replied.

Mrs Wright paused at the door and fingered her whistle. I steeled myself for a loud blast, but luckily, she walked out the door silently.

Thomas T. True waved his hand and Mrs Brisbane called on him.

'Don't go to that lost property,' he said. 'I went there last year and it was a scary place.'

'Now, what was scary about it?' Mrs Brisbane asked.

Thomas's eyes grew wide. 'There were creepy things like spiders' webs and . . . claws!'

I felt a shiver. Some of my classmates giggled.

'Oh, and a dead snake.' Thomas stopped and thought. 'Maybe it was alive. And I'm pretty sure I saw a severed hand.'

I felt a quiver. There were gasps and more giggles and some of my friends went, 'Ewwww.'

Mrs Brisbane walked between the tables towards Thomas. 'Are you sure that's true?'

'Yes, Mrs Brisbane,' he said. 'At least that's what I remember.'

'Well, I don't think Mrs Wright would keep any of those things in the lost property,' Mrs Brisbane said. 'Maybe you just imagined it.'

Thomas thought for a second. 'Maybe, but I don't think so.'

Suddenly, the bell rang and my friends jumped up from their chairs.

Slow-Down-Simon was the first one out the door, and my other friends were close behind him.

After all of my classmates had left Room 26, Mrs Wright came back in.

'That Phoebe is quite forgetful,' she said. 'Have you noticed?'

'Yes, I have. We're working on it,' Mrs Brisbane said.

I'd certainly noticed that Phoebe had a problem remembering things like homework and lunches. But I hadn't worked out why. All I really knew about Phoebe was that she lived with her grandmother, who seemed like an unsqueakably nice human.

Mrs Wright nodded politely and headed for

the door. But before she left, she turned and said, 'Please try to encourage your students to visit the lost property. It's right in my office, inside the gym.'

'I'll do that,' Mrs Brisbane said.

Mrs Brisbane tidied up her desk for a few minutes. Then she wandered over to the table where Og and I live, next to the window. 'Have a good night, fellows,' she said. 'I hope today wasn't too *piewhacking* for you. See you in the morning.'

She laughed and then she left, just like on any other day.

'See you in the morning . . .' That's what she said.

I remember it so well.

·ö·

Later that night, Aldo came in to clean the classroom, as he does every night.

'Never fear, Aldo's here!' his big voice boomed. Then he laughed, which made his big, furry moustache shake.

He went right to work, moving the tables and sweeping the floors, humming a happy-sounding song. When he got close to Mrs Brisbane's desk, he stopped and picked up the red book.

'Hey, Sherlock Holmes! I love these stories,' he said, thumbing through the pages. 'I remember that one about the red-headed guy.'

'Tell me what happens!' I shouted.

Even Og splashed around in his tank. 'BOING-BOING!' he twanged.

'Sorry, I don't have time to read it to you,' he told us. 'Too bad you can't read it yourself.'

Aldo probably knows me better than any of my human friends, but even he doesn't know that I can read. It's not easy for a small hamster to read a BIG-BIG-BIG book. That's why I like it when Mrs Brisbane reads to us. I decided I could wait until the next day to hear more of 'The Red-Headed League'. But it was nice to know that Aldo liked Sherlock Holmes as much as I do.

After Aldo left, the room was silent. Og didn't splash. He didn't even say 'BOING!'

What was he thinking about? We're good friends, but Og will always be a mystery to me.

Humans are also very mysterious. Although I've learned a lot about them, there are still so many things I don't understand. I took out the little notebook I keep hidden behind my mirror and started scribbling in it with my tiny pencil.

Mysteries about humans:

Why do they keep odd and unpleasant pets like dogs and cats when they could have a very nice hamster . . . like me?

Why do they throw bits of leftover food away when they could store it like I do – in my bedding or in my cheek pouch?

Where are humans' cheek pouches?

Why do humans laugh when they talk about poo? Especially my poo?

Mysteries about frogs:

Why don't frogs have fur? Or even hair?

Why can't frogs act just a little bit more like hamsters?

I wasn't sure those mysteries would ever be solved.

Humphrey's Detectionary

Even smart detectives like Sherlock Holmes can't solve a mystery without a clue.

The Case of the Missing Mrs

I'm always excited for the start of a new day in Room 26. But the next morning, I could hardly wait to hear Mrs Brisbane read more about Sherlock Holmes.

I waited for the key to turn in the door and for Mrs Brisbane to bustle into the classroom.

I waited for the bell to ring and for my friends to arrive.

I waited and waited and waited some more. In fact, I waited so long, the bell rang, but *nobody* came in.

I knew it wasn't Saturday. I never spend Saturdays at school because I go home with one of my classmates at the weekends. Sometimes I go home with Mrs Brisbane.

Either way, I have a hamster-iffic good time. (Og usually stays in Room 26 at the weekends, which must be lonely for him, poor frog.)

'Og, something's wrong!' I squeaked loudly to my neighbour.

'BOING-BOING-BOING-BOING-BOING!' he replied. He sounded as worried as I was.

I could see some of my friends' faces looking through the window in the door.

'Humphrey, let us in,' I heard Simon's muffled voice calling.

It was the only time in my life I wished I wasn't a hamster so I could be big enough to open that door.

Long after the bell rang, I finally heard some jiggling and joggling and the door swung open at last!

But Mrs Brisbane wasn't the human opening the door. It was our head teacher, Mr Morales. Behind him were my fellow students.

'Come on in, boys and girls,' he said.

Mr Morales is the Most Important Person at Longfellow School because he's in charge of everything. He was wearing a tie with tiny little question marks all over it. He has *lots* of interesting ties.

'Take your seats,' he said.

My fellow students were worried, too. I could tell, because they were quieter than usual. (I guess that was a clue.)

'It looks as if Mrs Brisbane is going to be late,' he said. 'We're trying to get in touch with her now.'

Mrs Brisbane is NEVER-NEVER-NEVER late. This was a very *piewhacking* morning.

'I'll take the register,' Mr Morales said.

Holly jumped up and offered to help.

'Thank you,' he said to her. 'But I think I can handle it.'

Then he called out names and each student answered 'Present' in return.

Everyone was present *except* Mrs Brisbane.

Mr Morales looked uneasy. 'So, what do you usually do first in the morning?'

Helpful-Holly raised her hand. 'We had homework last night,' she said. 'I can collect it.'

'Thank you,' Mr Morales said.

Holly went up and down the aisles collecting the homework. How I wished I could get a look

234

at those five mystery words!

Everybody turned in a homework sheet except for one person: Forgetful-Phoebe. When Holly passed by her table, Phoebe blushed and said, 'Oh, no! I forgot it! I'll bring it in tomorrow.'

As helpful as Holly is, she sometimes gets carried away. That's when I call her Too-Helpful-Holly. She frowned and said, 'You were supposed to bring it *today*.'

Mr Morales stepped forward. 'It's okay, Holly. We'll sort things out when Mrs Brisbane gets here,' he said.

Whew! I was GLAD-GLAD-GLAD to hear him say that Mrs Brisbane was on her way.

Just then, the phone in the classroom rang. Mr Morales said, 'Oh,' and then, 'I see,' and finally, 'Very well,' while my classmates were completely quiet.

Mr Morales hung up the phone. 'Boys and girls, Mrs Brisbane won't be here today,' he said. 'A supply teacher is coming to take care of the class.'

The last time I'd had a supply teacher was when Ms Mac was here. But I didn't know she was a substitute, because I didn't know much about school when I first arrived. I've certainly learned a lot since then!

Mr Morales seemed a little confused about what to do next and he kept looking at his watch.

'Read to us – from "The Red-Headed League"!' I squeaked loudly.

My classmates all giggled when they heard me.

Mr Morales walked over to my cage. 'Oh, so you want to take the class, do you, Humphrey?' he said.

I jumped on my wheel and spun it fast.

'Maybe Humphrey thinks we should do some exercise,' Mr Morales said.

That made my classmates giggle even more.

Rosie made her wheelchair spin in a circle. 'I love to spin, too,' she said, and everybody laughed.

Just then, the door to the classroom opened and a young man rushed into the room.

˙ȯ˙

The first thing I noticed about him was his red hair. (I think Sherlock Holmes would have noticed that, too.)

I also saw that he was wearing round glasses, and on his shirt was a big badge with writing on it that said *Give Peas a Chance*.

I love any veggies, including peas, so this human and I definitely had something in common.

He had a big cloth bag slung over his shoulder, sort of like Santa Claus. It was lumpy and bumpy and way too big for a lunch bag!

Mr Morales stepped forward and shook his hand. 'Welcome. I'm the head teacher,' he said. 'Mr Morales.'

'Hi,' the young man said. 'Ed Edonopolous.'

The head turned to the class and said, 'Here's your supply teacher for today. I expect you to give him your full attention.'

Mr Morales left and Mr Edonopolous gave us a friendly smile. 'Hi, kids,' he said. 'I know Edonopolous is a mouthful, so you can call me Mr E.'

There were a few giggles and Slow-Down-Simon repeated the name out loud the way I'd heard it: 'Mystery!'

Mr E smiled and nodded. 'Mystery! That's a good one. Hey, you know my name, but I don't know yours. I'm going to come up and down the aisles and you tell me who you are.'

He walked around the students' tables, one by one, asking, 'What's your name?'

He high-fived each student and said something like, 'Cool shirt,' or, 'Glad to know you,' or, 'Awesome.'

'My name is Holly and I collected the homework this morning,' Too-Helpful-Holly said when Mr E got to her. 'It was our Mystery Words sheet. I put it on the teacher's desk. Only one didn't get turned in.'

'Uh, thanks,' Mr E said.

'I'm Sophie and I really like your badge. I like to wear badges with sayings, too,' Stop-Talking-Sophie said. 'Do you remember where you got it?'

Mr E didn't remember where he got it. Sophie kept on talking until he said, 'I think I'd better give the rest of the class a chance.'

He moved on to the next table.

'I'm Thomas T. True,' Thomas said. 'My dad's a detective. Like Sherlock Holmes!'

'Not,' I heard Just-Joey mutter.

Mr E turned towards the class. 'What's the

problem?' he asked.

'He told me that his dad's an aeroplane pilot,' Just-Joey said.

'So?' Thomas said. 'He can be both.'

'He told *me* that his dad's a ship's captain,' Small-Paul grumbled.

Mr E just laughed. 'Sounds like a talented father.' Then he moved on again.

When he got to my side of the room, he finally noticed Og and me.

'Whoa,' he said. 'These are some funny-looking students.'

I heard some giggles, but I wasn't laughing. I can see how you might call Og funny-looking, but not a handsome golden hamster like me!

Mr E leaned in and looked right at me. 'What's its name?'

'Humphrey!' I squeaked loudly. 'And I am not an *it*!'

'Whoa,' he said again. 'I think he's talking. What is he – a rat?'

It was clear that this teacher didn't do his homework when it came to animals. Imagine, mistaking me for a rat!

Luckily, my friends all shouted out, 'Hamster!'

'His name is Humphrey,' Holly added.

Mr E said, 'Cool.' Then he turned to Og. 'I know this is a frog – right? What's its name?' he asked.

'BOING-BOING-BOING!' Og twanged loudly. He probably doesn't like being called an 'it' either.

'His name is Og,' Rolling-Rosie explained.

'Og the frog,' Mr E said. 'I like it.'

He was quiet for a few seconds as he looked around the room. 'You know, I was still sleeping when I got the call to come over here, so I don't know what your teacher's plans were today,' he said. 'Why don't you tell me what *you* would like to do?'

My friends looked surprised. I'm sure I looked surprised, too.

Hurry-Up-Harry waved his hand and Mr E called on him.

'I'd like to go home!' he said.

Everybody laughed. It was a funny thing to say. But I don't think Mrs Brisbane would have laughed.

'I understand,' Mr E said. 'But I don't think that's going to happen. Hey, I know . . . why don't we play a game to help me remember your names?'

Everybody seemed to like the idea of a game.

I was amazed at what happened next. Mr E pointed at a student. The student stood up and said his name and then the teacher made a little rhyming song with the name. He took parts of each name and added things to it, like 'banana fana' and 'fee fi fo'. After a few names, the whole class joined in.

The rhyme made my friends giggle, but I found it very confusing. After he'd finished the whole class, Rosie raised her hand and asked if they could do *my* name.

I can't remember it all but it ended:

> *Fee fi mo Mumphrey,*
> *Humphrey!*

Bumphrey-Mumphrey-Fumphrey-whhoaa! How was this going to help him remember our real names? Og's name sounded even stranger: Bog-Fog-Mog.

I don't know what Og thought, but I was in a bit of a fog myself! I was still thinking about

Mumphrey and Mog when the bell rang for break.

As soon as my classmates were gone, Mr E picked up his big sack and looked inside. 'Let's see,' he mumbled. 'What next? Maybe this.'

Then he glanced over at Og and me and chuckled. 'I don't know why I'm talking out loud when I know you can't understand me.'

Og piped up first. 'BOING-BOING.'

'You are WRONG-WRONG-WRONG!' I squeaked, wishing with all my might that Mr E could understand me.

He didn't notice. He was too busy rummaging around in that big cloth sack.

Suddenly, he stopped and smiled. 'Okay. I've got it!'

That's all he said.

I thought I'd pretty much worked out humans in my time as a classroom hamster so far. But Mr E was a real mystery to me.

When my friends were back in their seats, Mr E announced that it was time for maths.

Some of the students groaned, until the teacher reached into his bag and pulled out a basketball.

'We're going to play another game,' he said. 'It's called Mathketball!'

My friends looked puzzled. I didn't blame them.

'Of course, we could just have a maths quiz,' Mr E said. 'If you'd like.'

'No!' the students all yelled. 'Mathketball!'

Mumphrey. Mog. Mathketball – all mystery words. I was learning a whole new language today.

First, Mr E threw the ball to Slow-Down-Simon. 'Quick! Four plus four.'

Simon caught the ball and said, 'Eight!'

'Great,' Mr E said. 'But in Mathketball, instead of saying the answer, you bounce it.'

Simon looked confused for a second and then he understood. He bounced the basketball one-two-three-four-five-six-seven-eight times.

'That's it,' Mr E told him. 'Now throw it back.'

The teacher caught the ball and threw it to Be-Careful-Kelsey. 'Ten minus five,' he said.

Kelsey bounced the ball one-two-three-four-five times.

'Great,' Mr E said. 'Now throw it back.'

Kelsey dropped the ball and it bounced across the floor.

'Careful,' Mr E said as he scooped it up.

Just-Joey caught the ball next and when Mr E said, 'Twelve plus three,' Joey bounced it one-two-three-four-five-six-seven-eight-nine-ten-eleven-twelve-thirteen-fourteen-fifteen times. I know because I counted!

Then the ball went to Paul G. 'Six plus five,' Mr E said.

Tall-Paul bounced it one-two-three-four-five-six-seven-eight-nine-ten times. Then he stopped.

'One more time!' I squeaked. I guess he didn't hear me.

Mr E gave him another chance, which was nice, and Tall-Paul got the problem right.

As the game went on, the pace went faster and faster. As it got more exciting, it also got louder and louder.

And then . . . the door to Room 26 swung open. Standing in the doorway was Mrs Wright.

Mr E looked pretty surprised when he saw her. Maybe he noticed her whistle. I certainly did.

'Hello?' he said. It was more a question than a greeting.

'You're the stand-in for Mrs Brisbane?' she asked.

'Yep. I'm Mr E,' the substitute said.

Mrs Wright looked puzzled. 'Mr E?' she asked. 'That's your name?'

Mr E laughed. 'My name is Edonopolous, but Mr E is fine with me.'

Mrs Wright frowned. I guess Mr E wasn't fine with her.

'And you are . . .' Mr E asked.

'Mrs Wright,' the PE teacher answered.

To my GREAT-GREAT-GREAT surprise, Mr E laughed. 'Mrs Wright? I guess you're never wrong!'

Some of my classmates giggled, but Mrs Wright wasn't the giggling type. She stepped into the classroom and looked around.

'Is that basketball the property of Longfellow School?' she asked.

The substitute shook his head. 'Nope. I brought it from home.'

That didn't seem to please Mrs Wright at all. 'You're probably not aware that basketballs are only allowed outside on the playground. No ball-playing in the classroom,' she said. 'And only official Longfellow School equipment is allowed.'

'Really?' Mr E seemed surprised.

'Really,' Mrs Wright said. 'I'm the chairperson of the Committee for School Property. There are safety issues with having a ball in the classroom. And by the way, the noise level in this classroom is unacceptable. I could hear you all the way down the hall.'

'We were doing maths,' Mr E said. 'Right, class?'

My friends all nodded.

Mrs Wright fingered the whistle and I braced myself for an unsqueakably loud noise. Luckily, none came.

'That's funny,' she said. 'I thought you were playing basketball.'

Mr E smiled and looked at my classmates. 'What were we playing?'

'Mathketball!' my friends all answered.

Mrs Wright frowned even more, if that's possible. 'Perhaps you can do maths more quietly in the future,' she said. 'Of course, I'm sure Mrs Brisbane will be back tomorrow.'

I crossed my paws and hoped that she was right.

Oh, how I hoped that she was right.

Because school with Mr E was making me VERY-VERY-VERY *piewhacked*!

(That means 'confused'.)

⋅⋅ Humphrey's Detectionary ⋅⋅

It's not easy to solve the mystery of a missing person. Especially if you miss that missing person a lot!

The Case of the Mystifying Mr E

After Mrs Wright left, Mr E said, 'We've had enough Mathketball for today. But if I'm here again tomorrow, we're going to have a Word War!'

My friends seemed excited about that, but I was worried. Wasn't Mrs Brisbane coming back tomorrow? Where was she? What was wrong?

I had no clue.

I was ready for a nap, but right away, Mr E started another game called 'Who's Missing?'

First, he picked Daniel to sit with his back to the classroom. Then, all the other students had to run around and switch places at their tables, except for one. He silently led Forgetful-Phoebe to the cloakroom to hide.

Next, Daniel had to turn back and guess who was missing. It was a lot harder than it sounds, but he guessed Phoebe on the third try. (Which was a good thing, since Mr E only gave him three tries!)

The class played the game again and again because everybody wanted a chance to be the guesser. I got drowsy after a while and went into my sleeping hut for a nap. And you know what? No one even noticed that *I* was missing! I know, because I ALWAYS-ALWAYS-ALWAYS wake up when I hear my name.

When I came out again, my classmates were begging Mr E to read to them. He smiled and said, 'Okay.'

He reached into his big bag and pulled out a book.

'No!' Stop-Talking-Sophie said. 'We want Sherlock Holmes!'

'It's the red book on the desk,' Hurry-Up-Harry said. 'Mrs Brisbane's reading us the story "The Red-Headed League."'

Mr E made a face. 'That's too serious. My

book is a lot more fun.'

'Sherlock Holmes – please!' Tall-Paul and Small-Paul both said.

Soon, all my friends were saying, 'Sherlock Holmes! Sherlock Holmes!'

But Mr E sat down and opened his book.

'Can you hear us? We REALLY-REALLY-REALLY want Sherlock Holmes!' I squeaked so hard my whiskers wiggled and my ears jiggled.

Even Og agreed. 'BOING-BOING!'

But Mr E went right ahead and read us jokes from his big joke book.

I like jokes a lot, really I do, especially ones like this one: *Why are frogs so happy? Because they eat whatever bugs them!*

I thought Og would like that!

Mr E's jokes were funny. At least in the beginning they were funny.

Like: *Where do you put a sick insect? In an ant-bulance!*

My friends laughed hysterically.

I chuckled, too, but after a while, I started worrying about Mrs Brisbane again. Then I couldn't laugh at all.

Finally, the laughter got quieter and quieter.

Too-Helpful-Holly yawned and raised her hand. 'Now could you read from the Sherlock Holmes book?' she asked. 'It's a mystery.'

Mr E chuckled. 'Why do you need Sherlock Holmes? *I'm* a Mister E!'

The mystery about Mister E was this: When was he going to teach us anything?

Lunch time came at last and the classroom was quiet again, which was a relief.

Then the door opened and something wonderful happened. Ms Mac walked in.

Ms Mac was the supply teacher who brought me from Pet-O-Rama, my first home (if you can call it that), to Room 26 of Longfellow School. But later, Mrs Brisbane came back and Ms Mac left and my heart was broken.

Now Ms Mac was a full-time teacher at Longfellow School, but in another classroom.

Of course, I love Mrs Brisbane, too. If I could have one wish come true, it would be that Ms Mac and Mrs Brisbane could both be my teachers at the same time!

'Hi.' Ms Mac was smiling. 'I'm Morgan McNamara from first grade.'

Our substitute teacher shook her hand. 'I'm Eddie Edonopolous, but the children call me Mr E.'

Ms Mac smiled her big, beautiful smile. 'I'm sure they like that. I stood in for Mrs Brisbane last year so if you need anything, just ask. Have you found her lesson plans?'

'Uh, no. Not yet,' he said.

Ms Mac opened one of Mrs Brisbane's desk drawers. 'She keeps them in here in this file. Mrs Brisbane always has very thorough lesson plans.'

'Great,' Mr E said. 'I've been getting to know the kids, you know, having a little fun.'

'I just heard she might be away for a while,' Ms Mac told him. 'She really worries about her students when she's not here.'

That was nice to hear because, to squeak the truth, I was really worried about Mrs Brisbane.

'If you have any questions, I'm right down the hall,' Ms Mac said.

'Thanks,' Mr E said.

Of course, Ms Mac wouldn't leave Room 26

without saying hello to Og and me.

She came over to our table by the window. 'How's it going, Humphrey, you handsome hamster?' she asked.

No wonder I love Ms Mac! I scurried over to the side of my cage so I could get a closer look at her.

'It's been such a STRANGE-STRANGE-STRANGE day,' I replied. 'Where is Mrs Brisbane?'

'I know you miss Mrs Brisbane,' she said. Then she turned to Og. 'And how's my favourite frog today?'

Og leaped into the water side of his tank and splashed loudly, which made Ms Mac laugh. I love to hear her laugh.

'I've got to eat,' she said, turning back to Mr E. 'Can I show you where the cafeteria is?'

'Sure, thanks,' he said, following her out the door.

I rarely leave my cage during the day because it's just too risky. However, this was an emergency. So while we were alone, I jiggled the lock on my cage and scurried over to Og's tank. I'm so lucky to have a lock-that-doesn't-lock.

Humans always think it's fastened tight, but I know how to wiggle it open.

'Og,' I squeaked. 'Something's wrong!'

'BOING-BOING!' he said. Then he dived from the land side of his tank to the water side.

I had to scramble to stay dry. (Hamsters should never get wet.)

Once he stopped splashing, I went back to the tank and said, 'Mrs Brisbane wouldn't miss school unless something is terribly wrong! And Ms Mac said she might be away for a while. Ms Mac always tells the truth – right?'

Og splashed frantically again, and again I scrambled for a dry spot.

'Og, if you could splash a little less, I'd appreciate it,' I told him. 'Although I know you are a frog and frogs do splash.'

He must have understood because he stopped.

'Sherlock Holmes always looks for clues,' I said. 'So keep your ears open, okay?'

I felt terrible as soon as I said it because Og doesn't have any ears (that I can see, anyway).

I glanced up at the clock. I didn't have much time before the class returned from lunch.

'Oh, and by the way, I don't think you're an

"it",' I said as I headed back to my cage. 'And I know you don't think I'm a rat.'

'BOING-BOING-BOING!' Og twanged.

I managed to pull the cage door shut behind me just as my friends returned to their desks.

The afternoon went pretty much like the morning. There was no Mathketball, but Mr E pulled out three smaller balls from his big sack and juggled them.

Yes, he juggled! It was quite amazing to see him toss the balls into the air and keep them going. Mrs Brisbane had certainly never done that. It made my brain whirl when I tried to keep my eyes on the balls.

Then Mr E let my friends try juggling.

Harry couldn't keep even one ball in the air, but he didn't seem too upset about it.

Next, it was Thomas's turn. 'You should see my dad juggle. He can juggle fifteen balls at a time,' he said.

Mr E looked amazed.

'And knives, too. He can juggle knives,' Thomas added. 'And . . . baseball bats!'

Juggling large, sharp objects sounded down-right dangerous.

I heard Rolling-Rosie say, 'Give me a break!'
Just-Joey rolled his eyes.

Thomas managed to juggle the balls a few seconds, but then he dropped them and they rolled across the classroom.

'Perhaps your dad can give you some pointers,' Mr E said.

Phoebe caught the balls on her first try but then dropped them. When Daniel tried, he managed to keep two of the balls going for a few seconds.

It looked like fun, but I couldn't help thinking about Mrs Brisbane.

She'd be teaching us something interesting about the clouds or the ancient Egyptians or reading something wonderful like Sherlock Holmes.

And here we were, going through an entire afternoon without learning anything except how to juggle!

Near the end of the day, when Mr E finally stopped juggling, Helpful-Holly raised her hand.

'It's time to take care of Humphrey and Og,' she said. 'They need to be fed, and Humphrey needs fresh water. Tomorrow he gets his cage cleaned.'

'I don't know how to do those things,' Mr E said.

Holly explained that the students took turns at the job. This week it was Phoebe's turn to look after me and Harry's turn to look after Og.

When Harry threw some Froggy Food Sticks into the tank, Og made a huge, splashy leap to get to them.

I could tell my friends were impressed.

Mr E was impressed, too. 'He's quite a jumper.'

'That's nothing,' Thomas said. 'Once I saw Og leap up out of his tank and land all the way on Mrs Brisbane's desk!'

Some of my friends laughed.

'That didn't happen,' Simon said.

'You're exaggerating,' Holly said.

Thomas just shook his head. 'I know what I saw,' he told them.

I'd seen Og pop the top of his tank a few times, but I'd never seen him leap to Mrs Brisbane's desk!

Phoebe gave me fresh water, which tasted

much better than the old water in my bottle.

'Oh, no!' Phoebe suddenly said. 'Mrs Brisbane always brings fresh veggies for Humphrey.'

Yes, she does, and I look forward to them. I always have Nutri-Nibbles and Mighty Mealworms, but there's nothing as crunchy and munchy as fresh veggies. In fact, I hide them in my cheek pouch and in my bedding. But the cage cleaner always finds them and takes them away.

'You don't have any?' Mr E asked.

Phoebe looked WORRIED-WORRIED-WORRIED as she shook her head.

'I do!' a voice called out.

Thomas rummaged through his backpack. 'I didn't eat my carrot sticks,' he said. 'Humphrey can have them. I don't like them.'

I was extremely grateful to Thomas, though why anyone wouldn't like carrot sticks is a mystery to me.

My friends take very good care of me.

At the end of the day, Helpful-Holly raised her hand again. 'We need to be given homework,' she said.

A lot of the other students tried to shush her,

but Holly was determined. 'Mrs Brisbane always gives us homework.'

Mr E replied that he had a big surprise for the class: our only homework was to bring in a riddle or joke for the next day.

'You don't even have to write it down,' he said. Then he tapped his finger on the side of his head. 'Just remember it up here.'

It was pretty strange homework. But then, it had been a pretty strange day.

When the bell rang, my friends all looked happy as they left the class.

'Bye, Mr E!' Thomas said on his way out of class. 'See you tomorrow.'

'Bye, Mo-Momas,' Mr E said. I thought he was mixed up until I remembered the name game.

I heard Hurry-Up-Harry tell Slow-Down-Simon, 'Pretty sweet – no homework.'

'Mr E is a great teacher!' Simon said.

'He's so funny!' Kelsey told Rosie.

After the students had left, Mr E sighed a big sigh and said, 'That went well.' He strolled over to the table by the window where Og and I live. 'I think they liked me.'

'YES-YES-YES,' I shouted. 'And they like Mrs Brisbane, too.'

Of course, all he heard was 'SQUEAK-SQUEAK-SQUEAK.'

Mr Morales came into the room. 'I'm glad I caught you, Ed,' he said. 'Are you available to teach tomorrow?'

Mr E said yes, and then the head teacher said, 'I wasn't able to talk to Mrs Brisbane, but her husband said her lesson plans are in the desk.'

'Yes, I know,' Mr E said.

'Good!' Mr Morales said. 'I'll see you tomorrow.'

The two men shook hands and Mr Morales left.

When the door closed, Mr E chuckled. 'That's good news for me.'

Then he opened Mrs Brisbane's desk drawer and took out the file with the lesson plans in it.

Whew! He was finally thinking about teaching his students. I watched him as he turned the pages.

'Maths problems, vocabulary, art project, science – wow, she really packs a lot in,' he said aloud.

'YES-YES-YES!' I agreed.

'I don't know about all this,' he said. He turned another page. 'And that's not going to work.'

Og started splashing around in his tank. I was worried, too. After all, these were Mrs Brisbane's lesson plans. And Mr E didn't seem to like them.

Mr E closed the file. 'I'm going to have to make these subjects a lot more fun to make this work,' he said. 'A *lot* more fun.'

He was still muttering under his breath when he picked up his big bag and left Room 26.

I had no idea what he was muttering about.

And I still had no idea what had happened to Mrs Brisbane.

But I had a BAD-BAD-BAD feeling that it wasn't something good.

Humphrey's Detectionary

A detective without any clues is like a classroom without a real teacher!

The Case of the Curious Clues

Once the room was quiet, I hopped on my wheel and spun as fast as my legs would go. Spinning helps me think, and I had a lot of thinking to do.

I waited and waited for Aldo to come in and clean. Maybe he would tell me what had happened.

Suddenly, I was blinded and Aldo's voice boomed, 'Hey, guys, how's it going?'

'Things are unsqueakably bad!' I told him as my eyes adjusted to the lights.

Aldo wheeled his cleaning trolley into Room 26 and towards our table. 'I guess you heard about Mrs Brisbane,' he said, leaning down to look in my cage.

'WHAT-WHAT-WHAT happened?' I screeched.

Aldo shook his head. 'Who'd have thought it? I don't have to tell you what I think of Mrs Brisbane. She inspired me to want to be a teacher.'

Aldo goes to school in the daytime so he can teach in school some day. He's an excellent cleaner, but I think he'll be a great teacher, too.

'Like I said to Maria, boy, you never know what's going to happen next.'

Maria was Aldo's wife and a special human to me.

'I don't even know what happened today,' I tried to tell him.

'I know, I know,' he said. 'You miss her.'

Then Aldo went to work. Usually, I love to watch him clean. He sweeps and swoops. He dusts and polishes. He hums and sings and sometimes does a dance.

But he was quieter that night. Oh, he did get the room very clean, but there was no humming, singing or dancing. Every once in a while he'd stop, shake and mumble, 'What a thing to happen,' or, 'You just never know.'

I certainly didn't know what was going on and I wished someone would tell me.

When he was finished, Aldo took out a sandwich and his thermos of coffee and sat in front of Og and me. He usually had his dinner break with us, and he always remembered to bring me veggies.

'Here you go, Humphrey, old pal,' he said as he pushed a sweet, crunchy celery stick into my cage.

'THANKS-THANKS-THANKS,' I squeaked.

Then he dropped a fishy frog stick into Og's tank. My neighbour splashed happily.

'Hey, I was thinking about that Sherlock Holmes book,' Aldo said. 'I think I'm going to read that story about the redhead again.'

'Read it now!' I begged him. 'Please!'

But Aldo just ate and packed up his cleaning supplies and wheeled his trolley out of Room 26.

'You two have a good night,' he said as he switched off the lights.

I was disappointed to see him go. It might be a long time before I had the chance to hear the end of that story.

But after I thought about it some more, I decided to take things into my own paws.

When I saw the lights of Aldo's car leave the car park near my window, I jiggled the lock-that-doesn't-lock and opened my cage.

First, I needed to talk to Og. 'I was thinking, if we knew how Sherlock Holmes solved a mystery, maybe we could solve our mystery,' I squeaked.

'BOING-BOING?' Og twanged.

'I mean, the mystery of what happened to Mrs Brisbane,' I explained patiently.

I try hard to be patient with Og because frogs don't always think like hamsters. I guess they wouldn't, since we're different species.

'Don't worry, Og,' I said. 'I have a Plan.'

Aldo had very kindly left the blinds open so the streetlight outside lit up the room inside.

I moved to the edge of the table and grabbed onto the leg. Taking a deep breath, I glided down. I've done it many times before. It's thrilling and slightly scary and definitely dangerous. Once I hit the floor, I scurried over to Mrs Brisbane's desk.

That desk is extremely tall from a hamster's-eye view.

I had another lucky break. Mrs Brisbane's chair was pushed close to the drawers of her desk, so getting to the big red book on top wouldn't be too difficult. I stood on my tippy-toes and reached up to grab the bar between the chair legs. I used every ounce of strength I could gather to pull myself up. Then I grabbed the next highest bar and – *OOOF* – pulled myself up again.

All the exercise I get spinning my wheel and rolling in my hamster ball has made me a super-strong hamster! (Those veggies help, too.)

Next I grabbed onto the arm of the chair and inched my way up to the seat.

Whew! I was so tired my whiskers were wilting, but I was only halfway to my goal!

Og sent me some encouraging BOING-BOINGs.

I rested for a few seconds, then reached up

again, grabbed the edge of the desk, pulled myself UP-UP-UP and threw myself onto the desktop. Whew!

Og splashed excitedly.

After I caught my breath, I hurried over to the big book with the thick red cover.

Along the side, in big black letters it read: *The Adventures of Sherlock Holmes.*

I felt a little shiver as I looked at the picture of the great man with his deerstalker hat.

'BOING-BOING-BOING!' Og called impatiently.

'Okay, okay, I'm going to open the book,' I squeaked back. 'We'll find out how to be detectives soon!'

I reached up to touch the edge of the top cover.

'Umph!' I pushed hard with both paws.

Nothing happened.

I pushed again – harder.

Nothing happened. *Again!*

'It's very heavy, Og!' I squeaked, but I was so out of breath I'm not sure he could hear me. 'I wish there weren't quite so many stories about Sherlock Holmes!'

When I failed to budge the cover the third time, I decided to try something else. I looked around the desktop and saw a pencil. Maybe I could use that to push the cover open.

I rolled it over to the book, propped it up under the cover and gave it a mighty push.

It pushed right back, I guess, and I fell backwards. The pencil rolled off the edge of the desk. (I hate to think what would have happened if *I'd* rolled off the edge.)

As I tried to catch my breath, I heard Og splashing wildly.

'BOING-BOING-BOING-BOING-BOING!'

'I'm all right, Og,' I called to him. 'But I can't get the book open.'

I'm not one to give up easily, but I was exhausted and I knew it wouldn't be long before school began. It hadn't been a successful night, but it would be even worse if I got caught outside my cage.

So I slid down the side of the desk (much faster than when I'd climbed up). I raced across the floor and grabbed onto the long cord that hangs down from the blinds.

Then came that hard part, where I had to swing back and forth, higher and higher, until I was level with the top of the table. I let go and slid across the table, past Og's tank, right up to the door of my cage.

'I made it, Og!' I told my friend.

'BOING!' He sounded relieved.

I was planning on a nice doze when I got back in my cage. But when I closed my eyes and was about to drift off, I remembered Mrs Brisbane saying, 'A clue is information that helps you solve a mystery. Sherlock Holmes is very good at finding clues.'

I didn't just remember her words, I could hear them in my tiny ears.

I jumped up and raced to the side of my cage. 'Og! Mrs Brisbane said to look for clues. Let's see if we have any clues to what happened to her.'

I grabbed the tiny notebook Ms Mac gave me long ago and the teeny pencil that goes with it. I keep it well hidden behind the mirror in my cage.

I opened it and began to write.

Clue 1: Mrs Brisbane didn't plan to be absent. The day before, she said, 'See you in the morning.'

Clue 2: Mr Morales didn't know Mrs Brisbane would be absent. He said they were trying to get in touch with her. That's why he took over the class until they could find a supply teacher. Whatever happened was unexpected.

Clue 3: Mrs Wright said she was sure Mrs Brisbane would be back tomorrow. But later in the day, Ms Mac and Mr Morales both said she might be away for a while. So the story changed as the day went on.

Clue 4: Aldo seems worried that something happened to Mrs Brisbane. And that makes me unsqueakably worried, too.

My paw started shaking, so I stopped writing.

I wondered if Sherlock Holmes had ever been as worried as I was that morning.

'ö'

Miss Swift unlocked the door to let Mr E in. He had on a badge with a big smiley face, and his big cloth bag looked even fuller than it had the day before.

Once my fellow classmates arrived, Mr Morales came in. His tie for the day had little red birds on it.

'Class, your families were all notified last night about Mrs Brisbane,' he said. 'As you know, Mr E will be taking over.'

My friends all looked perfectly happy, but I was not!

Mr Morales might have told all the families about Mrs Brisbane, but nobody had told me! Would Mr E be taking over just for now . . . or would it be forever?

I was so worried I could hardly concentrate on our classwork that morning. Not that there was much. Mr E started off the day by having all the students share their jokes. That was their homework, after all.

My friends' jokes were pretty funny.

Hurry-Up-Harry had a good one. 'Why does a stork stand on one leg?' he asked. His answer: 'Because if it raised both legs, it would fall down.'

And Rolling-Rosie made everyone groan when she asked, 'What's brown and sticky? A stick!'

Phoebe forgot to bring a joke. 'But I know one,' she said. 'What do you say to a crying whale? Stop blubbering!'

Everyone seemed so happy, I began to think maybe nothing bad had happened to Mrs Brisbane after all. Maybe she'd just gone on holiday.

But then I remembered her saying, 'See you in the morning.'

I've learned enough about humans to know that they don't go on holiday without planning ahead.

Especially a human like Mrs Brisbane.

᛫ᵒ᛫ ᵒ᛫ *Humphrey's Detectionary* ᵒ᛫ ᵒ᛫

Clues can make you WORRY-WORRY-WORRY.

The Case of the Afternoon Accident

The rest of the morning was a blur.

First, Mr E reached in his sack and pulled out a big rolled-up map. He tacked it on the notice board and taught my friends a game called Map Attack. I couldn't really see what was going on because they stood in front of the map and blocked my view. It got very noisy, and the rest of the class seemed to have fun.

Next came Animal Addition. This time, Mr E pulled out finger puppets in different animal shapes and the class played some kind of adding and subtracting game. I don't know why they needed *fake* animals when there were two perfectly good *real* animals in the room. But nobody seemed to notice Og and me.

My classmates enjoyed the game, but I thought the problems were a little easy for them. Especially for Small-Paul, who is a maths whizz.

Then right after lunch, something odd happened.

The door opened and my friends all streamed in, talking and giggling as usual.

But when they were all in their seats, I noticed that one chair was empty. Were they playing the game they'd played yesterday?

'Who's missing?' I squeaked loudly.

I guess I didn't squeak loudly enough.

Luckily, Helpful-Holly also noticed that someone was missing.

'Excuse me, Mr E?' she said.

'Yes, Holly?' he asked.

She pointed at the empty chair. 'Harry hasn't come back from lunch.'

Mr E looked at the empty chair and scratched his head. 'Oh,' he said. 'Does anyone know where he is?'

I didn't have any idea, and neither did any of my friends.

Holly's hand shot up. 'I'll go and look for him,' she said.

'I'm sure he'll turn up in a minute,' Mr E said.

I don't think Mrs Brisbane would ever say that. She'd worked hard since the beginning of school to help Hurry-Up-Harry learn to be on time.

Mrs Brisbane spends a lot of time thinking up ways to help her students. Or at least she *did*.

I spent a lot of time thinking up ways to help Mrs Brisbane. But how could I help her if she wasn't here?

Mr E was trying to tell my friends how to play Word War when the door opened and Harry strolled in.

'Welcome back,' Mr E said. 'Glad you could join us.'

'Thanks,' Harry said.

That was it! Did Mr E think it was fine for Harry to come to class whenever he felt like it?

The game began when Mr E wrote a word on the board. Then two students ran up and made a list of new words by adding letters to the beginning or end. They started with *ate* and wrote *mate* and *hate*, then *hated, late, later,* and *slate*.

Whoever came up with the most words won that round. I could tell my friends enjoyed being able to run in the classroom.

They got louder and louder as they cheered each other on as the game got more and more exciting.

Then Mr E wrote another word on the board: *Eat*.

'I've got it!' Slow-Down-Simon shouted as he raced to the board.

'I know!' Be-Careful-Kelsey said as she ran up to the board.

Simon didn't slow down.

Kelsey forgot to be careful.

The two of them rammed right into each other.

'Ow!' Simon yelled, holding the side of his head.

'Ow!' Kelsey shouted, clapping her hand over her eye.

Kelsey cried a little and Simon kept saying, 'Ow! Owww!'

How many times had Mrs Brisbane tried to think of ways to slow down Simon?

How many times had Mrs Brisbane encouraged Kelsey to think before doing things? And now that Mrs Brisbane was gone, look what had happened!

Mr E decided to send them to the nurse's office.

'I could go with them,' Holly volunteered.

'I think they can manage on their own,' Mr E told her.

That was the end of Word War, thank goodness.

'What next?' Mr E said.

Helpful-Holly raised her hand. 'It's time to look after Humphrey and Og,' she said.

'Oh, right,' Mr E said.

Then Holly said, 'Humphrey needs his veggies.'

'Did anybody bring veggies for the hamster?' Mr E asked the class.

The hamster. As if I didn't even have a name.

'Oh, no!' Phoebe exclaimed. 'I forgot. Sorry, Humphrey.'

I might have felt discouraged, except for the

fact that six hands went up in the air. A lot of my friends had remembered to bring me a treat.

Just-Joey offered a piece of lettuce. Tall-Paul brought me a blueberry. Small-Paul brought sunflower seeds – my favourite. Rolling-Rosie had some yummy celery, and Holly offered a tiny bit of broccoli. Thomas gave me his carrot sticks again (which isn't really a good thing because he should eat his veggies every day).

There were so many hamster-licious things to eat, I hid some of them in my cheek pouch and the rest in my bedding.

It's always nice to save a little something for later.

I was still busily nibbling when Simon and Kelsey came back.

Simon was holding an ice pack on the side of his head. Kelsey held an ice pack on her eye.

'Everything all right now?' Mr E asked.

They both nodded and took their seats.

'I think it's story time,' Mr E said.

My ears twitched when he said that. Was he

finally going to read the rest of that Sherlock Holmes story from the big red book?

My friends were on the edges of their chairs as well.

Mr E reached in his sack and pulled out a piece of paper, which didn't look anything like a book.

'Let's write our own silly stories,' he said.

I sighed. Was I ever going to hear the rest of 'The Red-Headed League' and learn how a real detective works?

Mr E then asked the class to give him different words: nouns, verbs, words that describe things – oh, I didn't know there were so many different kinds of words. He wrote each of them on the piece of paper. Then he made up a silly story using all those words.

The story made no sense at all, but my friends liked it.

The door suddenly burst open and standing there was Mrs Wright. Her fingers were on her whistle, which made me nervous.

Luckily, she didn't blow it.

In one hand, Mrs Wright held a clipboard.

'It's Mrs Wright!' Mr E said. 'Right?'

'Mr Ednopop . . . Ednolopopolopolis,' Mrs Wright said. 'I'm co-chairperson of the School Safety Committee. I understand there've been injuries in the classroom.'

'A little accident,' he said. 'Kids will be kids.'

Mrs Wright shoved the clipboard towards him. 'You will have to fill out an accident report. Their parents will be notified.'

'It was just an accident,' Mr E said.

'There were injuries on school property,' she said. 'A report must be filed.'

Mrs Wright took a few more steps into the classroom and looked around. 'I also had a report of a student wandering the halls after the lunch bell rang. Was that one of yours?' she asked.

'I don't know,' Mr E said. 'Was it?'

'The corridors should be empty after the bell rings,' Mrs Wright said. 'I've put a copy of the *rules* under the accident report.'

She fingered that silver whistle around her neck. 'The report is due in the morning.'

I was REALLY-REALLY-REALLY worried that she was about to blow the whistle.

Instead, she turned and walked out the door.

I was glad to see her go. But I was also glad to see that someone was concerned about my classmates besides Og and me!

In the afternoon, I dozed through some other kind of game, but I woke up when I heard Mr Morales's voice.

It's always important to listen to what the head teacher has to say. I darted out of my sleeping hut and saw him in front of the class, holding a piece of paper.

'Class, I just received a note from Mrs Brisbane that she wanted me to share with you all,' he said.

'Did you hear that, Og?' I squeaked at the top of my lungs. 'A note from Mrs Brisbane!'

Og splashed wildly, so I guess he heard.

'The note says, "Dear class, I miss you all and I miss Longfellow School. I miss being home, too. But the good news is that they say I'll be up on my feet and dancing before long! It's funny to think that this all came about because of Humphrey. Please listen to Mr E and make me proud of you. Your teacher, Mrs Brisbane."'

This all came about because of Humphrey.

Was it really my fault that Mrs Brisbane was gone?

If she's going to be up on her feet, she must be sitting. But where *is* she?

Why would she leave her class to go dancing? I'd never seen her dance before.

I wasn't just *piewhacked*. I was super-duper *piewhacked*.

After Mr Morales left, Holly's hand shot up. 'Mr E, where is Humphrey going this weekend?'

'I give up,' Mr E answered. 'Where is he going?'

Holly explained how I go home with a different student each weekend.

'Okay,' Mr E said. 'So who wants to take Humphrey home?'

Every single student raised a hand. Every one!

'Mr E!' Holly said. 'You have to get written permission from the parents.'

Sometimes, I think Holly will grow up to be just like Mrs Wright. That's not a bad thing, unless she also gets a whistle.

Just then the bell rang, ending the school day.

Some of the students rushed out to catch the school bus. Others crowded around Mr E, begging to take me home.

'Whoa!' he said. 'Calm down. I'm sure Humphrey will be fine on his own this weekend.'

Sorry, but I would *not* be fine without tasty treats and clean water and a poo clean-up!

A red-haired woman hurried into the classroom looking worried. She saw Kelsey with the ice pack on her eye and gave her a hug.

It didn't take Sherlock Holmes to work out that she was Kelsey's mum.

'Are you okay?' she asked, moving the ice pack. 'The nurse called.'

'Yes,' Kelsey said. 'Sort of.'

'Wow, you're going to have a black eye,' her mum said.

'Mum, could we take Humphrey home for the weekend?' Kelsey asked.

I rushed to the front of my cage to hear what Mrs Kirkpatrick had to say.

'Humphrey? Oh, little Humphrey! Well, sure. Why not? He'll help take your mind off your eye,' she replied.

Mr E came over and introduced himself and said he'd be very grateful if she'd take me home. 'I think we need some kind of written permission,' he said.

'In the middle drawer!' I shrieked. 'That's where she keeps the forms.'

Mr E didn't understand of course, but Mrs Kirkpatrick just wrote on a plain piece of paper and before I knew it, Kelsey was carrying my cage out of Room 26.

'Sorry, Og! I mean, bye! I mean, have a nice weekend!' I shouted.

'BOING-BOING!' he said. It was a slightly sad sound.

I always feel guilty when I go off for the weekend and leave Og behind.

But that Friday, I felt absolutely rotten. After a few days without Mrs Brisbane, he would probably be extra lonely this weekend.

˚ ˚ Humphrey's Detectionary ˚ ˚

A mystery: why are some people, even teachers, pawsitively clueless about how to care for a hamster?

6

The Case of the Baffling Ballerina

In the car, Mrs Kirkpatrick wanted to hear about how Simon and Kelsey bumped heads.

But Kelsey just wanted to talk about me!

'I can't believe it,' she said. 'I've wanted to bring Humphrey home since the first day of school.'

That made me feel very nice. But thinking about what Mrs Brisbane said still made me feel not-so-nice.

This all came about because of Humphrey.

What on earth had I done to send Mrs Brisbane away?

And how could I undo it?

Kelsey's house was white, with bright orange shutters around the windows that reminded me of Kelsey's hair – and her mum's.

Her big brother, Kevin, was already home from school. He was very tall, and his hair was darker than Kelsey's.

'What's that?' he said, pointing at me.

'Humphrey!' Kelsey answered. 'Our classroom hamster.'

'Oh,' Kevin answered. 'Mum, what's there to eat? I'm so hungry, I could eat anything in sight.'

I was glad I'd hidden all those yummy treats in my cheek pouch and bedding. I like to share, but I'm never quite sure when I'll be fed again.

Kevin and his mum went to the kitchen while Kelsey took my cage to her room.

'Humphrey, you're the cutest hamster I ever saw,' she told me.

'Thanks,' I squeaked. 'And you're one of the nicest girls . . .'

Before I could finish my sentence, I looked at Kelsey. She was nice, but the skin around one of her eyes had turned a bright shade of purple with streaks of green and black.

'Eeek!' I squeaked.

Luckily, Kelsey just giggled. That was one time I was happy a human couldn't understand my squeak. I would never want to hurt a friend's feelings.

Kelsey made sure that everything in my cage was in order. Then her mum came in to check on us.

'Oh, Kelsey! Look at your eye!' her mum said. 'I'm afraid it will look a lot worse before it goes away.'

Kelsey raced to the mirror and looked at herself.

Oddly enough, she smiled. 'I'll probably be the only girl at Longfellow School with a black eye,' she said. 'Probably the only person!'

Kelsey's mum bit her lip and looked at the eye more closely. 'I guess I don't need to take you to the doctor,' she said. 'The nurse said it was fine.'

Kelsey assured her mum that she could see all right.

'I hope you can go to your ballet lesson to-morrow,' Kelsey's mum said. 'I'd hate you to miss the very first one.'

287

At the mention of the word *ballet*, Kelsey suddenly looked unsqueakably unhappy. She reached up and touched her purple eye. 'It does hurt a little,' she said.

Mrs Kirkpatrick shook her head. 'Poor Kelsey. Tell me again how it happened. That boy, Simon, ran into you?'

Kelsey nodded, but there was more to the story than that, and I knew it.

'You ran into each other!' I squeaked.

'And you were just standing there?' Kelsey's mum asked.

Kelsey squinched up her face and thought for a bit. 'No. I was running up to the board to answer a question. We both were running up to the board.'

'Ah,' Mrs Kirkpatrick said. 'So you bumped into each other.'

'YES-YES-YES!' I squeaked.

'I think I'll call Simon's mother to see how he is,' Kelsey's mum said.

'He's fine, Mum,' Kelsey said, rolling her eyes. 'It's no big deal.'

But Kelsey's mum had already left the room. A little while later, Kevin wandered into

Kelsey's room. He was eating a large (and yummy-looking) sandwich. 'What's up with your eye?' he asked.

'A boy ran into me,' Kelsey said.

Kevin stared at her eye. 'Wow, that's going to be an amazing shiner, Clumsy. I mean Kelsey.'

'How rude!' I squeaked loudly.

Clumsy! Kelsey wasn't always careful, but I didn't think she was clumsy!

And what on earth was a 'shiner'? Another mystery word!

'Birdbrain,' Kelsey muttered.

Kevin just chuckled and wandered out again. I was glad he was gone.

Once we were alone, Kelsey flopped down on the bed. 'That's what I am, Humphrey. Clumsy Kelsey, like Kevin said.'

I climbed up the side of my cage and looked right at Kelsey. 'That's the silliest thing I ever heard,' I told her.

'I am,' Kelsey said. 'I'm always running into things and getting bumped and bruised.'

'Because you aren't careful,' I explained. 'That's what Mrs Brisbane says. You need to take your time.'

'Mum thinks ballet will make me graceful,' she said. 'But I think it will just make me more clumsy.'

I knew ballet was some kind of dancing. In her note, Mrs Brisbane said she was going to be dancing soon.

Maybe she was learning ballet. Did she think it would make her more graceful?

'What's so great about twirling around on your toes?' she asked.

I thought about it. Twirling was kind of like spinning on my wheel, which is something I LIKE-LIKE-LIKE to do. And I use my toes for all kinds of things, from climbing on my cage to grooming myself.

'Sounds pawsitively great!' I said.

Kelsey got up off the bed, looked in the mirror and smiled. 'It's a great shiner,' she said. 'But whoever heard of a ballerina with a black eye?'

'I don't know,' I squeaked. 'I've never actually seen a ballerina.'

Kelsey walked over to her dresser and picked up a pink box. 'Here, Humphrey. I'll show you,' she said.

Sometimes I wonder if humans really *can* understand me.

After setting the box next to my cage, Kelsey opened the lid and I saw an amazing thing. There was a tiny dancer – smaller than me – in front of a small mirror. Tinkly music began to play as the ballerina twirled around.

The ballerina was all in pink, with a short pink skirt, and she danced right up on her tippy-toes. I was spellbound as I watched her go ROUND-ROUND-ROUND again and again.

'See, that's a ballerina,' Kelsey said. 'She never trips and falls. She never gets a black eye.'

I was disappointed when she suddenly slammed down the lid of the box. The ballerina disappeared from view and the music stopped playing.

'I could never be graceful like her,' Kelsey said. 'Watch.'

Kelsey started spinning around the room. I have to admit, she didn't exactly look like the twirling ballerina. While the tiny dancer twirled in one place, Kelsey lurched around wildly until I was afraid she was going to stumble right into my cage.

She didn't. Instead, she wobbled and fell backwards, landing on her tail. (Well, the place where humans would have a tail, if humans had tails.)

'Ouch!' she said.

'Eeek!' I squeaked.

Just then, Simon raced into the room. His mum and Kelsey's mum were right behind him.

'Hi, Kelsey,' he said. 'My mum wanted to check you were okay.'

'Kelsey, what are you doing on the floor?' Mrs Kirkpatrick asked.

Kelsey got up and rubbed her rear end. 'Practising ballet,' she said.

Simon walked up to Kelsey and looked closely at her eye. 'Wow, that's amazing,' he said.

'Does it hurt?' Mrs Morgenstern asked.

'Not really,' Kelsey answered. She pointed at the side of Simon's head. 'Hey, you've got a bump.'

Simon rubbed his head. 'I'd rather have a shiner.'

So . . . a shiner must be a bruised eye!

He turned and saw me. 'Hi, Humphrey! Look at my bump.'

'Eeek!' I squeaked again. But Simon didn't seem to mind.

'We thought if we all went out for ice cream, you two might forget your injuries for a while,' Mrs Kirkpatrick said.

Kelsey and Simon seemed happy and didn't even remember to say goodbye to me when they all left the room.

When I was alone, I thought about the twirling ballerina.

I can spin on my hamster wheel or in my hamster ball, but twirling looked like fun.

I stood up and tried to twirl, but I tumbled head over toes instead. Somersaults are fun . . . unless you aren't planning on doing one.

I got up and tried again. This time I managed to twirl around once.

But something was missing: the music!

I knew that it would take my friends a while to get ice cream, so I jiggled my lock-that-doesn't-lock and pushed on it. Once I was out of my cage, I hurried over to the pink box.

I could barely reach the lid, and the first time

I pushed, the lid popped up and crashed right back down. But even standing on my tippy-toes, I wasn't tall enough to open it.

However, I don't give up easily. So I scurried over to the side of the box near the hinge. I pushed with all my might and finally the lid swung open. Phew, it was heavy!

The music began to play, and I raced to the front of the box to watch the pretty little ballerina go round and round.

Kelsey was right. The ballerina was a graceful dancer. I watched her whirl and twirl until I felt a little dizzy.

Then, I raised myself up and tried twirling again. I stood UP-UP-UP on my toes and spun myself around in a circle. Then I made another circle. And another. I was twirling and not falling over!

I wished Kelsey could see me. If a furry little hamster could learn to twirl around gracefully, I knew she could, too!

Although I was unhappy about Mrs Brisbane leaving Room 26, I hoped she would enjoy dancing as much as I was.

My twirling was interrupted by a loud bang

and footsteps. Kelsey and Simon were back!

I raced back to my cage and pulled the door behind me. The ballerina was still dancing and the music was playing.

.ö.

'Humphrey! We brought you a strawberry,' Kelsey shouted as she raced into the room.

Simon was right behind her. 'Where's the music coming from?' he asked.

'My music box,' Kelsey said. 'That's funny. It was closed when I left.'

Simon laughed. 'Maybe Humphrey opened it.'

That made Kelsey laugh. 'Sure, it was Humphrey.'

With the music still going, it was my chance to show Kelsey that anybody could learn to twirl . . . even a hamster!

I got up on my toes and spun around again and again.

'Look! Humphrey's dancing!' Simon pointed at me.

Kelsey leaned down to watch. 'He makes it look easy,' she said.

They giggled, of course. The music was

getting slower and slower. So was I.

'Can you make it go again?' Simon asked.

Kelsey closed the lid and opened it again. The music was back to speed and the ballerina was spinning.

'Let's do a Humphrey dance,' Simon said. He started twirling around the room and laughing.

Kelsey chuckled and started twirling again, too.

'The trick is to pick one place to look,' Simon said. 'Each time you spin around, look at that spot.'

He was a pretty good twirler.

'Hey, it works,' Kelsey admitted.

She wasn't staggering. She wasn't stumbling. She was just spinning.

The music slowed down again and we all stopped dancing.

'I have to start ballet lessons tomorrow,' Kelsey said. 'I don't know how I'll ever dance on my toes.'

'My sister takes ballet. You don't start by dancing on your toes. You start with simple stuff,' he said.

Slow-Down-Simon's sister was Stop-Giggling-

Gail. She'd been in Mrs Brisbane's class last year. I knew she was a great laugher, but I didn't know she took ballet lessons, too!

'Really?' Kelsey said.

'Really,' Simon said.

'Let's watch Humphrey dance again,' he said.

So I DANCED-DANCED-DANCED some more until, finally, it was time for Simon to go home.

Before she went to bed that night, Kelsey watched the music-box ballerina again for a while.

'It would be nice to have a pretty pink tutu like that,' she said. 'Maybe I'll like ballet after all.'

Tutu? I was *piewhacked* until I realized she was talking about the dress.

Well, I liked ballet, but there was no way *I* was going to wear a pink tutu – ever!

I guess Kelsey read my mind because she said, 'Of course, boy ballet dancers don't dress like that. They wear tights. And they don't dance up on their toes – they lift the girl dancers way up in the air.'

Whew! I was relieved to learn that.

Kelsey slept well that night. And even though I'm usually awake for some of the night, I slept unsqueakably well, too.

I guess it was all that twirling.

On Saturday afternoon, Kelsey left for her ballet class. I crossed my toes and hoped that she would enjoy her first lesson.

While she was gone, I couldn't resist leaving my cage to watch the tiny ballerina dance again, and I made sure I was back in my cage long before she got back.

'Humphrey, Humphrey!' Kelsey shouted as she raced into the room. 'Wait until I show you!'

She stood in front of my cage and noticed that the music box was open.

'I closed that before I left,' she said. 'Maybe there's something wrong with the lid.'

I didn't squeak one word.

'Anyway, I want to show you what I learned in my ballet class,' she said.

'GOOD-GOOD-GOOD,' I replied.

She pointed at her shiny pink shoes. 'These are my ballet slippers,' she said.

Next she showed me five positions for the feet. And then she did some very graceful dipping moves.

'It was so much fun, Humphrey! And I can be graceful. I just have to pay attention to what I'm doing. That's what our teacher said,' Kelsey explained. 'At the end of the class, we got to dance around the room with scarves. It was beautiful.'

The next day, Kelsey's eye was a rainbow of colours. But it didn't seem to bother her. She spent a long time practising the five positions.

I practised, too, but I guess a hamster's feet work a little differently from human feet. The first three positions weren't too bad, but the fourth and fifth were . . . well, let's just say, I'm going to have to practise a whole lot more.

And pay attention to what I'm doing.

Humphrey's Detectionary

I don't know if Sherlock Holmes ever tried ballet dancing, but he should have because it's FUN-FUN-FUN.

7

The Case of the Colourful Cards

When Kelsey brought me back on Monday morning, everybody rushed over.

'Whew! That's some black eye!' Rosie exclaimed.

Actually, it was purple and grey with pink and green stripes, but I didn't correct her.

'How's it feel?' Mr E asked her.

'Fine,' Kelsey said.

She set my cage on the table in front of the window and walked very carefully – and gracefully – back to her desk.

'BOING-BOING!' Og greeted me cheerily.

Then Simon came in and everybody wanted

to touch the bump on his head.

'Okay,' he told Small-Paul. 'But not too hard.'

'That's nothing,' Thomas said, holding the back of his head. 'I hit my head and had to get ninety-five stitches here.'

'That explains a lot,' Just-Joey muttered as he walked by.

Tall-Paul bent down and looked at Thomas's head. 'Funny, there's no scar.'

'Ninety-five?' Simon asked. I'm pretty sure he didn't believe Thomas. 'Are you sure?'

'If you got ninety-five stitches in your head, you'd be sure,' Thomas said.

My friends all went to their seats, and as soon as the bell rang, Helpful-Holly raised her hand.

'Mr E, we always have a vocabulary test on Monday,' she said.

There were lots of groans from the other students and some of them went 'Sssh! Sssh!'

'Well, we won't have one this Monday,' Mr E replied. 'Because today we'll have – '

He didn't finish his sentence because just then Mr Morales walked into the classroom. He was wearing a tie with little horses all over it. (I wonder if they make a tie with little hamsters all over it?)

'Class, I have another note from Mrs Brisbane. She says, "I'm getting stronger every day. Today, I was actually able to put on my slippers. I think of you all every day."'

Slippers? Kelsey said that's what ballerinas wear. And Mrs Brisbane had said she'd be dancing soon.

So, just as I thought, Mrs Brisbane really was learning ballet!

'I have an address for her now,' Mr Morales said. 'So I think it would be nice if you all made cards and we'll send them off to her.'

'Great idea,' Mr E said. 'We'll start on it right away.'

After Mr Morales left, Mr E passed out colourful paper. He told my classmates to start writing their messages to Mrs Brisbane while he gathered up art supplies.

Holly's hand shot up in the air. 'They're over there on the shelves. I can show you!'

'No thanks, Holly. You start writing,' Mr E replied. 'Now be sure to make your card reflect your personality.'

'Can I take this home and work on it tonight?' Daniel asked.

'Try to Do-It-Now-Daniel,' Mr E told him. 'If you don't finish, you can take it home.'

Soon, all of my classmates were all bent over their tables, working.

All except for Joey. He stared at his paper, but he didn't write one word.

I scrambled up to the top of my cage to see if I could read what my other friends were writing, but I couldn't make out the letters from so far away.

I wanted to write to Mrs Brisbane, too, but I didn't dare take out my notebook in case someone saw it. And as much as I like my friends, my notebook is private. (No one should *ever* read something that's private.)

While my friends wrote, things were clinking and clanging and rattling and rolling about as Mr E poked around in the art supply bins. Soon, there was a big mound of felt-tips and boxes of coloured pencils and crayons on the desk. I saw more construction paper, brightly coloured wool, scissors, glue, and jars of buttons, beads and glitter.

When Mr E told my friends to take what art supplies they needed for their cards, everyone raced forward at once.

'I wanted those felt-tips!' Simon said.

'I got here first,' Thomas replied, clutching the pens to his chest.

'Oooh, feathers!' Phoebe said.

Rolling-Rosie rolled towards the desk. 'Hey, I need those,' she said.

'Ow! Rosie ran over my foot!' Sophie complained.

'Did not!' Rosie said.

My friends never acted like that when Mrs Brisbane was in the classroom.

I could hardly tell what anyone was saying because there was so much commotion.

Suddenly, my whole body was shaken by the shrill and painful blast of a whistle!

Everyone went quiet then.

I didn't even have to look to know that Mrs Wright was standing in the doorway.

'What's going on here?' she asked.

'We're making cards for Mrs Brisbane,' Mr E answered.

'What you're making is an uproar,' she said.

'I could hear you all the way down the corridor. And according to the school policy, you should *not* be able to hear what's going on in a classroom from the corridor.'

Mrs Wright walked into the classroom, and I saw that she wasn't alone. Hurry-Up-Harry was with her.

'I don't suppose you noticed that one of your students was missing,' she said.

Harry hung his head and looked extremely unhappy.

'I guess I'm still getting used to everyone,' Mr E said. 'Come on in, Harry. Come and make a card for Mrs Brisbane.'

Mrs Wright fingered the whistle hanging down from her neck. I braced myself, just in case she blew it again.

'Mr Edopoppy, at Longfellow School we don't permit our students to roam the halls whenever they want,' Mrs Wright said. 'I found Harry staring into the window of Room 14!' She sounded shocked.

'They're building an amazing tower,' Harry explained.

'What's amazing is that you weren't in your

classroom, like all the other students at school,' Mrs Wright said. 'I will have to report Harry to the head teacher.'

'I'll handle this,' Mr E said.

Mrs Wright looked surprised. 'Really? You'll put in a report?'

Mr E nodded. 'That's right, Mrs Wright.'

I was surprised – and relieved – when Mrs Wright and her whistle left the room. But I was sorry that Hurry-Up-Harry was going to get in trouble. He'd got into trouble a lot at the beginning of the year for being late. But he'd been so much better . . . until Mr E arrived.

'Do I have to go to the office?' Harry asked.

'No, Harry. But this class is just as much fun as Room 14,' Mr E said. 'Come on. Let's make cards! Make them funny and bright with lots of pizzazz!'

Pizzazz? What on earth was *pizzazz*? I'd never heard that word before. I'd never seen it on a vocabulary list, either.

Was it like glitter and beads and glue? Or was it like pizza?

Whatever it was, it was definitely a mystery word that I found very *piewhacking*!

My friends spent the rest of the morning on the cards, working furiously. Feathers flew, scissors snipped and there was glitter everywhere.

Joey still seemed to be struggling as he stared at his card. Maybe Joey needed help, but Mr E didn't seem to notice.

I think Mrs Brisbane would have noticed.

When the bell for lunch rang, my friends raced out the door while Mr E restacked the art supplies.

'Everything okay?' Ms Mac said as she poked her head in the door.

'Fabulous,' Mr E said. 'Better than I ever expected. Wait . . . I'll walk to the cafeteria with you.'

At last, Og and I were alone!

'Og!' I squeaked excitely.

'BOING!' he twanged.

'The class is a mess without Mrs Brisbane!' I shouted. 'The students are falling back into their bad habits! Harry's late again, and there's too much noise and no vocabulary quiz or Sherlock Holmes!'

Og splashed wildly in the water side of his

tank. 'BOING-BOING-BOING-BOING!'

I could tell he was almost as upset as I was.

'*And* I want to make Mrs Brisbane a card!' I said.

'BOING-BOING!'

'*And* I want to find out where she is!' I added.

'BOING-BOING-BOING!'

There was so much to think about.

I wondered if Harry would get back to class on time.

I wondered if Mr E would teach us something in the afternoon.

I wondered if Mrs Brisbane would EVER-EVER-EVER be back!

My fellow students came back after lunch – all except one.

Hurry-Up-Harry wasn't missing, but Forgetful-Phoebe was!

However, she showed up just after the bell rang.

'Sorry, Mr E,' she said.

'Not a problem,' he answered. 'Take a seat, because now we're going to play . . . Maths Monsters!'

He took his fingers and pulled out the corners of his mouth and the corners of his eyes. He looked pretty creepy, especially when he made a scary laugh, like a witch.

'After all . . . you know what's coming soon!' he continued.

There was a pause and then Thomas shouted, 'Halloween!'

Then everyone else chimed in, shouting, 'Halloween!'

My classmates seemed happy about it. But I remembered last year's Halloween, with creepy smiling pumpkins and ghosts and goblins and monsters. Now it was coming back? Eeek!

·ö·

After school, Og and I had some visitors.

'Hello,' Mr E greeted them. 'What can I do for you?'

'We were in this class last year,' a soft voice said. It was Speak-Up-Sayeh! She was one of my best friends in Room 26 last year. 'We came to see Humphrey and Og.'

'Be my guest,' Mr E said, and soon Og and I were surrounded by familiar, friendly faces.

'Hi, Humphrey Dumpty! Boy, bad news

309

about Mrs Brisbane!' That was good old A.J.'s loud voice.

'YES-YES-YES!' I agreed.

'Poor Humphrey! Poor Og! You must miss Mrs Brisbane a lot,' said Golden-Miranda. She was such a wonderful friend . . . with a terrible dog. 'But I'm sure she misses you, too.'

'Hi, Humphrey! Winky says hi!' said Mandy, whose hamster, Winky, was a friend of mine.

It was great to see my old friends. But it was sad, too, because they reminded me of happy days in Room 26 with Mrs Brisbane.

My teacher.

Or was she?

·ö· ·ö· Humphrey's Detectionary ·ö· ·ö·

It's a mystery to me why humans enjoy a very frightening holiday like Halloween!

The Case of the Mysterious Messages

'*Mamma mia!* What happened here?' Aldo said as he pulled his cleaning trolley into the room and looked around.

I looked around, too, and what I saw was almost as scary as Halloween.

The room was a pawsitive mess. On the floor were scraps of paper, wool, buttons, beads, felt-tips and crayons. On top of the tables were scissors and overturned glue bottles. And there was glitter glistening on the floor like snow.

'EEEK-EEEK-EEEK!' I squeaked.

'BOING-BOING-BOING!' Og twanged.

Aldo leaned on his broom and shook his

head. 'I can tell Mrs Brisbane wasn't here today. She never leaves her room messy at the end of the day.'

'That's for sure!' I agreed.

Aldo didn't have much time to talk. He was too busy sweeping and spraying and scrubbing and mopping up the room.

He stopped when he saw the stack of cards. 'Oh, they're making cards for Mrs Brisbane. Good idea!' he said. 'I'd like to send her a card myself.'

'Me too!' I squeaked.

'BOING-BOING!' Og agreed.

After the room was tidy and the art supplies neatly stacked on Mrs Brisbane's desk, Aldo took out his lunch and pulled up a chair close to Og's tank and my cage.

When he finished eating, he went over to Mrs Brisbane's desk, took a piece of paper and wrote something on it. He folded it in half. Then he wrote on a smaller piece of paper and stuck it on top of the folded paper.

'Now the supply teacher will include my card with the others,' Aldo said.

'Can you write one for me?' I squeaked. Aldo

usually seems to understand me. But that night, he didn't.

'Well, I've got to run,' he said. 'I'll be late getting home tonight and I have to study for a test.' He looked around the room, 'But at least the place is clean.'

'Yes, Aldo! You did a GREAT job,' I told him. I meant it, too. Aldo is VERY-VERY-VERY good at his job.

'Thanks, Humphrey,' Aldo said. He wheeled his trolley out of the room and turned off the light.

Luckily, a big full moon was making the room nice and bright. It had been a difficult day, but I was feeling brighter myself.

'Og, I think I'll check out those cards,' I said after Aldo's car left the car park. 'And maybe I'll find more clues about what happened to Mrs Brisbane.'

'BOING-BOING!' Og said. I'm not sure if he thought my idea was good or if he was just excited about his Froggy Food Sticks.

I took my usual path to get to Mrs Brisbane's desk and had no trouble.

'I made it, Og!' I told my friend, who was

splashing around in his tank.

I looked UP-UP-UP. The stack of cards was about six hamsters high. There was a bright yellow card with sparkles near the bottom. It was sticking out a bit from the rest of the pile, so I decided to grab it and pull.

That was a big mistake, because as the card came out of the stack, the whole pile tumbled down around me and *on* me. Luckily, paper doesn't weigh too much. I wasn't hurt – just surprised.

Still, I now had the chance to look at all the cards and possibly gather more clues about Mrs Brisbane's 'disappearance'.

The yellow card with sparkles was from Rosie. The front had red hearts and bright buttons. Inside, it said:

Mrs Brisbane, I miss you the most! Come back and I'll pop a wheelie for you!

Love, Rosie

The last part was in a big red heart. I'm not

sure Mrs Brisbane would be happy to see Rosie 'pop a wheelie' for her. That's a trick she can do with her wheelchair, but Mrs Brisbane made her promise not to do it at school any more. I guess Rosie just meant she'd be happy to see our teacher back in the classroom.

Then I looked at a blue card. It was from Small-Paul. On the front was a drawing of a rocket. Inside, it said:

I hope you'll be launched back into Room 26 soon. I miss you!

Paul F.

'Eeek!' I squeaked. Had Mrs Brisbane been launched into outer space?

Next, I looked at one that was bright pink. It had lots of fancy writing on the outside and the inside said:

Dear Mrs B,

When you come back to Room 26, I promise to help you all the time. You don't have to worry about anything, because I'll be here for you now and forever! If you ever need something, please call on me.

Your TRUE friend for all time,

Holly

Thomas's card was covered with red, white and blue wool. It read:

You are the best teacher in the universe!

Thomas

Sometimes Thomas exaggerates, but this time, I thought he was right. But I was shocked when I read what he wrote at the bottom:

PS I am the best juggler in the class. I can juggle for hours without dropping a ball, just like my dad!

That just wasn't true. Why did a nice boy like Thomas make up things like that?

The next card was white with fancy purple letters. It said:

Sometimes I forget things, but I never forget all the nice things you do for us.

Come back soon!

Love, Phoebe

I felt a little pang for Phoebe. She was forgetful, but she was also extremely nice.

Kelsey's card had a drawing of a ballet dancer on it. Inside, it said:

Hope you'll be up on your toes soon!

From Kelsey

There was a very plain orange card with blue letters. No glitter, no beads, no buttons. It said:

I'm not good at fancy words, but I miss you.

Just Joey

Joey's card was nice and simple. I knew Mrs Brisbane would like it, because it sounded like him.

'Og, these cards are so nice!' I shouted to my friend. 'Our friends did a great job!'

He splashed around in a happy-sounding way.

I read all the cards. The more I read, the more I wished I could make a card for Mrs Brisbane, too.

I looked at the art supplies. Felt-tips, crayons, glue and glitter make a very nice-looking card. But I also knew they were dangerous . . . at least to hamsters.

Hamsters like me don't wash our paws in soap and water. In fact, soap and water aren't good for us at all. NO-NO-NO! We groom ourselves using our tongues and paws. So if I got glue or felt-tips on my paws and licked it off, I might get very sick.

Maybe I could add some *pizzazz*. Mr E had suggested that. But I looked and looked and couldn't find any jar or bottle or box marked *pizzazz*.

I'd have to make a plain card like Just-Joey's.

I went slowly back to my cage. All the cards were great, but one stuck in my mind.

Kelsey had said she hoped Mrs Brisbane would be up on her toes soon.

Up on her toes? That sounded like a clue. Was Mrs Brisbane actually going to be a ballet dancer?

I tried to imagine our teacher, with her short grey hair and her sensible shoes, twirling around like a ballerina. She didn't look like the dancer in Kelsey's music box. But if Mrs Brisbane wanted to be a ballerina, then that's what she should be. (Even though I think she makes a better teacher.)

I pulled out my little notebook and pencil from behind my mirror.

First, I added a clue to my list:

Clue 5: Mrs Brisbane may be learning to be a ballet dancer.

I wasn't sure about that, so I added a few question marks.

????

Next, I turned the page and thought about what to write to my teacher.

I wanted to say just the right thing. I thought and thought and thought some more. Sometimes it's easier to say something you feel in your heart with a poem. And so I wrote:

> Roses are red,
> Violets are blue,
> Oh, Mrs Brisbane –
>
> How much I miss you!

I looked it over and liked it, so I signed it:

> Humphrey

I read it to Og.
'BOING-BOING!' my friend twanged loudly.
'Oops! Sorry, Og,' I replied.
Then I added:

> Og, too

'I signed your name, too, Og,' I assured my neighbour. (He can't write. At least I don't think he can write. And he doesn't have a notebook. If he did, it would have to be waterproof!)

I tore the page from the notebook, but when I looked at it, it seemed a little too plain.

I didn't know how to make it fancier.

I looked around my cage and dug around in my bedding. All I came up with was a tiny piece of carrot I'd saved and a strawberry Aldo had brought.

It was the juiciest strawberry I'd ever seen.

'Og, I have a great idea!' I squeaked.

I rubbed my paws all over the strawberry to get them nice and juicy. Then I made little red paw prints around the edge. It looked very nice, if I do say so myself.

And when I was finished, I licked the red juice off my paws. Yummy!

Of course, then I had to take the card over to the desk. I picked up the paper with my teeth, jiggled the lock-that-doesn't-lock and opened the door to my cage.

Og splashed gently in his tank as I passed by.

'Oh!' I said. Of course, as soon as I opened

my mouth, the paper dropped to the table.

'Sorry, Og,' I said. 'I wish you could add your mark, too.'

'BOING!' Og answered, splashing.

'Or maybe you can! I'm leaving the card here,' I explained. 'Then I'll go behind my cage. Splash some water, and then I'll come back for the card.'

I left the paper near his tank, scurried away and squeaked, 'Now!'

Og splashed and splashed some more.

'Not too much,' I said. 'You can stop now.'

I waited until Og stopped splashing and raced back to the paper.

There were several little water marks on the paper now. I HOPED-HOPED-HOPED Mrs Brisbane would know that Og had made them.

I picked up the paper with my teeth again and made my second trip of the night down the table leg and back to the desk.

The stack of cards was now a mound of cards. There was no way a small hamster could stack them all up again, so I just pushed my card into the pile. Then I made the long trek back to my cage and closed the door behind me.

Morning light streamed in through the window and I was worn out.

'Goodnight, Og,' I said as I crawled into my sleeping hut. 'I mean, good morning.'

I guess he was tired, too, because he didn't answer. Not even one 'BOING.'

Or if he did answer, I couldn't hear him because I was sound asleep.

Humphrey's Detectionary

Finding clues can make you unsqueakably tired!

The Case of the Problem Pupils

'I've lost my watch,' I heard Phoebe whisper to Kelsey before class began the next morning. They were standing right next to my cage and Phoebe looked worried. In fact, I'm pretty sure she had tears in her eyes.

I REALLY-REALLY-REALLY hate to see a human cry.

'Oh, no! Your daisy watch? Where did you lose it?' Kelsey asked.

'If I knew where I lost it, I could find it!' Phoebe answered.

That made sense to me.

'Maybe it's in the lost property,' Kelsey suggested. 'You should have a look.'

Phoebe rolled her eyes. 'No way. You heard what Thomas said about the lost property!'

'It sounds like a creepy place,' Kelsey agreed.

Phoebe nodded. 'Besides, I don't want to go to Mrs Wright's office. She doesn't like me. Anyway, the last place I saw it was in the toilets, but when I went back there, it was gone. I just feel terrible,' she said. 'My parents gave me that watch, and Grandma would be disappointed if I lost it.'

'I'm sorry,' Kelsey said.

'Okay, class. Take out your homework from last night,' Mr E announced.

I was spinning on my wheel at the time and I was so amazed to hear him say 'homework' that I almost fell off!

Mr E gave homework? When did that happen?

I guess I must have dozed off during class yesterday.

'Who got the answer?' he asked.

I was surprised again when none of my friends raised a hand.

'Let me write that paragraph on the board so

we can all look at it together,' Mr E said.

I raced to the front of my cage so I could watch as he wrote and wrote and wrote some more. This is what he wrote:

This is an unusual paragraph. I'm curious how quickly you can find out what is so unusual about it. It looks so plain you would think nothing was wrong with it! In fact, nothing is wrong with it! It is not normal, though. Study it, and think about it, but you still may not find anything odd. But if you work at it a bit, you might find out! Try to do so without any coaching!

The paragraph didn't look unusual to me. Just sentences strung together with no mystery words like *piewhack* or *pizzazz*.

'Did anyone work it out?' Mr E asked.

A few hands went up. Mr E called on Rosie.

'I think it's unusual because it has so many exclamation marks,' she said.

'Good answer,' the supply teacher said. 'But there's something even more unusual.'

Next, he called on Thomas.

'I think it's unusual because it's so long,' he said.

Mr E nodded. 'It's long. But I've seen paragraphs that are a lot longer.'

While all of this was going on, I read that paragraph over and over again.

'I'll give you a hint,' Mr E said. 'Something is missing.'

'Eeek!' I squeaked as my friends all stared up at the board.

Finally, Small-Paul raised his hand. 'There's no letter *e* in it,' he said.

'*e!*' I squeaked. He was right!

'That's correct. Did you know that *e* is the letter that shows up more than any other letter in the English language?'

Mr E would know that. I'm sure he liked the letter *e* a lot. But I didn't know it. I think it was the first time I'd actually learned something since he arrived in Room 26!

'So now, why don't you try to write a paragraph without using the letter *e*?' Mr E said.

'While you do that, I'll get these cards ready to send to Mrs Brisbane.'

My friends all went to work, but I didn't. I was too busy watching Mr E stack up the cards. I wanted to make sure that my tiny card was still with the others. Whew! It was!

Then Mr E looked at some of the cards. 'Joey? Would you like to work on this card a little more?' he asked. 'It doesn't have much pizzazz.'

'That's okay,' Joey answered. 'I don't have much pizzazz either. I like things simple.'

'Some buttons? Some wool? A little glitter and glitz?' Mr E asked.

Joey shrugged. 'No, I like it the way it is.'

This time Mr E didn't argue.

But I was excited because now I had some clues to work out what *pizzazz* really meant!

'Og, *pizzazz* isn't like pizza at all!' I squeaked to my friend. 'It's glitter and glitz. It's zing and bling! It's that little something extra,' I explained.

'BOING?' Og sounded a little *piewhacked*.

'It's fancy instead of plain,' I said. 'If you had a very fancy pizza, then I think you'd have a pizza with pizzazz!'

Og leaped into the water side of his tank for a swim. I'm not sure he understood what I said, but at least *I'd* worked out that mystery word.

Now if I could only work out what had happened to Mrs Brisbane.

And why Mr E was a teacher who didn't really teach.

And where-oh-where Phoebe's watch had gone?

°ö°

After lunch, Mr E gave the class free time. He gave them a *lot* of free time!

Some students read. Some drew pictures. Some of them wrote. Some of them walked around the classroom. Some of them even talked. (Something Mrs Brisbane would not have allowed. For her, free time meant quiet time.)

Only one of them talked to me: that was Phoebe.

'Humphrey, I brought you a piece of apple,' she said. 'This time I remembered.'

'That's unsqueakably nice of you,' I replied. I was very honoured that Forgetful-Phoebe

329

had remembered me.

Phoebe leaned down close to my cage so I was almost nose to nose with her.

'But I can't remember what I did with my daisy watch,' she said. She looked around to see if anyone was listening. No one was . . . not even Og, who was swimming in the water side of his tank.

'My parents gave it to me before they deployed,' she said. 'They're both in the military, and I miss them a lot. They weren't supposed to be gone at the same time, but then they had to be.'

So that's why Phoebe was living with her grandmother.

'I just have to find it. I wouldn't want my mum and dad to know I lost it,' she said.

'YES-YES-YES!' I told her. 'You have to try very hard!'

I hoped that somehow Phoebe understood me.

Phoebe sighed. 'I think about Mum and Dad all the time. I guess that's why I don't remember things very well. Mrs Brisbane was sending reminders home with me every night and calling my grandma when something important was coming up,' she explained. 'Mr E doesn't do that.'

Then she grinned. 'Of course, he doesn't give us real homework and tests!'

'I noticed,' I told her.

'Would it be okay if I looked in your cage?' Phoebe asked. 'I was thinking maybe it fell off while I was cleaning it.'

'Of course! Please look,' I replied. To squeak the truth, I was sure it wasn't in my cage because I know every hiding place there is. But I thought it was a good idea to look, and it was awfully nice of her to ask first. After all, my cage is my home, and as much as I like humans, I don't want them sticking their hands inside all the time.

Phoebe opened the cage door and poked all around. She was doing such a good job of looking, I was afraid she'd find my notebook hidden behind my mirror.

Luckily, she didn't!

'I guess it's not there,' she said at last. 'I was wishing that you had found it and saved it for me, Humphrey.'

I wished her wish had come true!

After free time, Mr E said something that curled my toes and wiggled my whiskers. 'Folks, it's almost Halloween. While we have the art supplies out, why don't we decorate the room?'

'Eeek!' I squeaked. All I could think of was the leering orange pumpkin someone put close to my cage last year.

'BOING-BOING! BOING-BOING!' Og sounded as alarmed as I was.

But my friends were happy and excited about Halloween.

'Let's give our decorations some pizzazz! We want the ghastliest ghosts! The goriest goblins! The creepiest creeps! And the weirdest witches!' Mr E's red hair seemed to shine a little brighter.

I felt a shiver . . . and a quiver.

'Let's make it the most haunted Halloween ever,' he added.

I just couldn't look. I dashed into my sleeping house. But I didn't sleep a wink.

I couldn't stop thinking about Phoebe. Finally, I understood why she was so forgetful. But I didn't have a clue about how to help her.

Also, there were some eerie sounds going on in the classroom.

I heard a ghostly 'Oooooo'. Then a ghastly laugh . . . like a witch. And a fur-raising howl. Halloween was turning into Howl-a-ween!

I finally had to take a peek outside. Luckily, I didn't see any ghosts or goblins – just my friends drawing, colouring and cutting paper.

So I went back into my sleeping house again. And this time, I took a nap.

Later in the afternoon, Mr E announced that he had a letter from Mrs Brisbane! I dashed out of my sleeping hut and climbed up high in my cage so I could see and hear everything.

'Pay attention now, Og,' I told my froggy friend. 'There may be clues.'

Og hopped up on a rock and was very quiet.

'Dear class, I hope you are all doing well,' Mr E read. 'I miss you all, but everyone here is very nice and they've got me on my feet. My days are a whirl and they say I'm performing very well. Please be kind to your supply teacher and to one another. Fondly, Mrs Brisbane.'

My friends all applauded when Mr E was finished.

'Did you hear that?' I asked Og. 'She *must* be learning to dance. She said she's performing and she's up on her feet.'

Og didn't know anything about ballet, and it was hard to explain to him.

After school, when the classroom was empty except for Og and me, I took out my notebook and looked at my list of clues. I took my little pencil and added two more:

Clue 6: Mrs Brisbane is on her feet and in a whirl.

Clue 7: She is performing very well. Mrs Brisbane definitely must be at ballet school!

I had plenty of clues, but they didn't help me understand why Mrs Brisbane would leave the class to learn ballet, especially with all the problems my friends were having.

And I didn't know how one small hamster – me – could solve their problems all by myself.

I *had* helped Kelsey. She hadn't bumped into anyone all week, and I'd heard her telling her friends about ballet class.

On the other paw, Hurry-Up-Harry seemed to have forgotten everything Mrs Brisbane had taught him about getting back to class on time. Tell-the-Truth-Thomas was stretching the truth further and further every day and losing friends. And even though I knew why Forgetful-Phoebe was so forgetful, I couldn't think what to do about it.

It was still a mystery to me why Mr E didn't do a little more teaching. After all, he was a teacher. He needed help, too.

It was quiet in the room now – so quiet I could hear the big clock on the wall tick away the seconds.

TICK-TICK-TICK. TICK-TICK-TICK. I wished that clock would STOP-STOP-STOP because it reminded me of Phoebe's watch.

'Og, I wish I could find Phoebe's watch,' I squeaked to my friend.

Suddenly, Og wasn't quiet any more.

'BOING-BOING-BOING!' he twanged.

'You're right,' I said. 'I *should* find it.'

'BOING!'

'I *must* find it.'

'BOING-BOING!'

'I *will* find it!' I stomped my paw.

'BOING-BOING-TWANG!' Og splashed around in his water.

Now I just had to work out *how* to do it.

⠶ ⠶ Humphrey's Detectionary ⠶ ⠶

One mystery, like what happened to your teacher, can lead to another mystery, like why the supply teacher isn't really teaching.

The Case of the Wandering Watch

When Aldo looked around the room that night, he shook his head – again.

'What a wreck,' he said. 'Room 26 was always the neatest classroom in the whole school. Now it's the messiest.'

Once again, Mr E had not bothered to ask the students to clean up. In fact, when Helpful-Holly started to collect all the art supplies, he'd stopped her. 'We have to use them tomorrow,' he'd said. 'Just leave them out.'

Of course, they didn't have to leave the scraps of paper and glops of glue and piles of shiny glitter everywhere too.

But Aldo went to work and soon the floor was clean, the art supplies were stacked and the student tables were straightened.

When Aldo sat down to eat dinner with us, he said, 'Guys, I sure hope Mrs Brisbane is back soon. I'll bet you do, too.'

'Do you think she'll be back, Aldo?' I squeaked. 'Or will she become a famous ballet dancer?'

'I know you think she's not coming back, Humphrey, but she is,' Aldo assured me.

I was happy to hear that!

'But this messy room, that's nothing,' Aldo said. 'You should see all the stuff kids leave lying around. I take it all to the lost property. Coats, socks, even shoes. Wouldn't you notice you were missing one shoe? Jewellery and toys. Lots of notebooks and pencils. Why, once I even found a tuba! That's a huge musical instrument. 'Aldo chuckled. 'I can't imagine losing a tuba, but there it was. No name on it, either. I took it to the lost property. I take everything to the lost property.'

'Really? That gives me a GREAT-GREAT-GREAT idea!' I squeaked.

Personally, I keep a close eye on my possessions: my wheel, my sleeping hut, my hamster ball, water bottle, food dish, climbing tree and ladder. I know where everything in my cage belongs, including my poo – which is only in my special poo corner – and the food I hide in my bedding. And of course, I always make sure my notebook and pencil are in their place.

Aldo pushed a lovely bit of cauliflower through the bars of my cage. 'Time to move on,' he said.

I looked out of the window after he left, waiting for his car to leave the car park.

There was a big orange moon that looked a lot like a Halloween pumpkin. And the man in the moon looked like a jack-o'-lantern.

In the moonlight, I could see that the trees had lost most of their leaves. It was almost time for Halloween, all right.

Once Aldo was gone, I raced out of my cage.

'Og, Phoebe's watch must be in the lost property,' I squeaked. 'I'd like to go and get it, but Thomas said there were claws and hands and snakes in there.'

'BOING-BOING!' Og replied.

'I know. Thomas does exaggerate sometimes. And Aldo didn't mention any of those things,' I said.

'BOING-BOING-BOING-BOING!'

I don't really understand frog language, but I could tell what Og was trying to say.

'You're right,' I admitted. 'I think I have to go.'

'BOING!'

'But first, I have to find Mrs Wright's office, because that's where the lost property is,' I explained.

Og dived down into his water with an impressive splash.

I scurried down the leg of the table and headed towards the door. 'Wish me luck!' I squeaked.

'BOING-BOING,' Og said.

I slid through the narrow space under the door and there I was, out in the corridor of Longfellow School.

It's dark in the corridor at night, of course, but there are little lights along the way, so I could see where I was going.

I remembered that Mrs Wright had said that the lost property was in her office, inside the gym.

I've been to the library, the playground, the head teacher's office. But I've never ever seen the gym.

I hurried past the other classrooms, turned down another corridor, past the head teacher's office, and past the cafeteria. That was as far as I'd ever gone in my nighttime adventures at Longfellow School. But that night, I saw there was another corridor past the cafeteria.

I was in uncharted territory when I saw two gigantic doors. I stopped and looked up.

The sign on one door read GYMNÁSIUM.

Gym was in the word, so this must be it.

The doors were tall and looked heavy, but there was a narrow space below them. It was a little tight, but I squeezed through.

Even in the dim light, I could see that the gym was enormous! Of course, everything looks large to a small hamster, but this was the biggest room I'd ever seen. Ever!

It was TALL-TALL-TALL and WIDE-WIDE-WIDE. I'm not sure what they did in the gym, but there were hoops with nets on poles at either end and a shiny wooden floor. There was a big clock. And a huge sign with numbers on it.

As large as the gym was – and as little as I am – I was determined to find Phoebe's watch. There was a smaller door to the right of the main doors. I looked up and saw a sign that said MRS WRIGHT.

The space under the door was unsqueakably narrow. I took a deep breath, exhaled and then pushed. Ooof! At first I didn't go through at all. But I gave another big push and suddenly, there I was in Mrs Wright's office.

Now all I had to do was find the lost property!

One wall had a cabinet with a big lock on it. I hoped that wasn't the lost property, since I didn't know how to open a lock without a key. Luckily, the sign on it read EQUIPMENT.

I looked around and saw a desk against the opposite wall. On the shelf next to the desk there was another sign: LOST PROPERTY.

'That's it!' I squeaked, even though there was no one around to hear me. At least I hoped there was no one around to hear me!

There was a stack of boxes next to Mrs Wright's desk. I was able to climb them like steps and make my way to the top of her desk.

I paused to catch my breath, and I suddenly realized that Mrs Wright wouldn't be happy to see me on her desk.

Mrs Wright liked to see everything in its place. And she thought my place was in my cage.

Then I saw something terrible: MRS WRIGHT'S WHISTLE! It was lying right there on her desk.

Funny, I'd always imagined that she wore that whistle everywhere. But I guess she went home without it. (Luckily for her family.)

It was silver and shiny and hard. I walked right up to it – so close I could see my reflection in it.

'You're not so scary!' I squeaked.

The whistle didn't say anything. I hadn't expected an answer, but still, I was relieved.

'You're not so big!' I yelled at the whistle.

Again, the whistle was silent.

'You're not so loud!' I yelled again.

The room stayed QUIET-QUIET-QUIET.

I could have stayed there a lot longer just yelling at that loud, rude whistle, but I had work to do.

Mrs Wright's desk was tidy, and so was the lost-property shelf.

As neat as it was, I thought about the creepy things Thomas said he'd seen, so I decided to check it out from the desk first. I didn't see anything like a snake or a severed hand. Or even anything large, like the tuba Aldo mentioned.

What I did see were big plastic bins labelled CLOTHING, NOTEBOOKS, PENS AND PENCILS, BOOKS, LUNCH BOXES, JEWELLERY, OTHER.

Jewellery? Phoebe's watch could be in that bin.

I was able to hop directly from the desk to the lost-property shelf. As I hurried towards the jewellery bin, I could see through the little holes in the other boxes I passed.

In the clothing bin, I saw a sweater with blue polka dots, one striped sock, a green mitten, a pink backpack, a single red sneaker.

The next bin held dozens of pens, pencils,

notebooks, a dictionary, and a book of music.

Then there was the bin filled with plastic lunch boxes and a thermos.

I finally reached the bin marked JEWELLERY and stopped to peer inside.

OH-OH-OH! There were chains of gold and silver, sparkly rings and those things girls wear in their hair and big, bright shiny things.

But I was only looking for one thing: Phoebe's watch. I needed to take a closer look.

I scrambled up the side of the bin, clinging to the edges of the holes. When I got to the top, I crossed my paws, held my breath . . . and dived right in!

I landed with a CLATTER-CLATTER-CLATTER and began to make my way through a sea of jewellery. It wasn't easy, because the items kept shifting beneath my toes.

I poked around with my paws and carefully began to dig through the tangle of rings, bracelets and necklaces. If only their owners had thought to check the lost property!

Then I spied something round that had numbers on it in a circle. Yep, that was a watch all right. I liked the red band and the stars in between the numbers. I flipped it over. There was no name on it except Timewell, which I think was the name of the company that made the watch. At least I didn't know of any students at Longfellow School named Timewell.

It was a very nice watch, but it didn't fit Phoebe's description.

After some more poking, I found another round clock face. I tugged it out of the pile. It had a gold band, and in the centre of the clock face was a smiling yellow flower. There was no name at all on the back of that watch.

I heard Phoebe's voice in my head. 'My daisy watch,' she'd called it.

Even Kelsey had called it 'your daisy watch'.

Well, a daisy is a yellow flower. This had to be Phoebe's watch!

To humans, I'm sure a child's watch doesn't seem too big, but it looked HUGE-HUGE-HUGE to me! I tried using my teeth to drag it an inch or two, but I soon realized that if I dragged it all the way back to the classroom, it would probably get scratched and dented.

I might get a little scratched and dented, too.

So I stopped and looked at the watch. The

band was a stretchy circle, and it wasn't very big.

I put my front paws into the centre of the circle and lifted one side over the back of my head. The band just fitted around my middle. I took a few steps and was relieved that the watch didn't fall off.

Getting out of the bin took all my strength, because the watch made my body heavier.

Once I was out, I scurried across the shelf and leaped onto the desk. The weight of the watch made me slide and I just missed running into Mrs Wright's whistle. Scary!

I came to a stop next to a pad of paper that had this word on it: Military.

Normally, I wouldn't have paid attention, but I'd just heard Phoebe talking about her parents being away in the military and how much she missed them.

So I took a closer look. The paper read:

MKC: MILITARY KIDS' CLUB

A brand-new club!

If you are a student with a parent in the military, join us for weekly fun outings, tasty treats, thoughtful discussion groups and a chance to make friends with kids who are just like you!

There was a telephone number to call at the bottom.

The Military Kids' Club sounded perfect for Phoebe. She needed fun outings, and if she had friends to talk to who were going through the same things she was, maybe she would be able to relax. Maybe she wouldn't be so forgetful.

And everyone – even me – loves tasty treats!

But how could I get the information to Phoebe? I certainly couldn't carry a whole pad of paper back to Room 26.

Gently, I took the bottom edge of the top paper and tugged. It tore off the pad and I could see that there were identical notes beneath it.

So with the note for Phoebe in my teeth and her watch around my body, I started down the stair-step boxes but – whoa! The heavy watch made me feel all wobbly and I had to slow way down. I landed hard on the floor and made my way to the door.

I'd forgotten how small the space was under the door. With the watch around my middle, I couldn't fit. So I wiggled my way out of the watch and pushed it under the door.

I squeezed through the gap next. Once I was on the other side, I put the watch around my waist again.

The trip back *from* the lost property took twice as long as the trip *to* the lost property, and the watch felt heavier and heavier with every step.

When I got back to Room 26, I had to push the watch under the door again.

By the time I finally slid under the door to Room 26, it was already getting light outside.

'I found it, Og!' I squeaked.

Of course, as soon as I opened my mouth, the paper fell out, but I managed to grab it with my teeth again.

'BOING-BOING-BOING-BOING!' Og replied. He must have been awfully worried about me while I was gone.

There was no time to waste, and I was exhausted. But I still had to make sure Phoebe got the watch.

'BOING-BOING!' Og warned.

I looked up at the clock. School would start soon, and I didn't want to be caught outside my cage!

It would take a long time to climb all the way to Phoebe's table, leave the watch and get back down again.

I made a quick decision and headed to our table by the window.

There was the blind cord. Swinging myself back up to the table is always tricky, but with Phoebe's watch (which now seemed to weigh a ton) and the paper in my mouth, I knew it would be harder than ever.

What I didn't expect was that the weight of the watch would make me swing faster than usual. It was a wild ride and my tummy felt queasy and uneasy.

Whew! I leaped onto the tabletop and slid FAST-FAST-FAST past Og's tank and right up to my door.

I wiggled my way out of the watch and left it on top of the MKC paper right in front of my cage.

'I got the watch, Og!' I said. 'I'll tell you more later.'

Then I darted inside, pulled the door behind me and ran into my sleeping hut.

In seconds, I was fast asleep.

Humphrey's Detectionary

Surprisingly, while you're solving one mystery, like where to find a watch, you might find a solution to another mystery, like how to help a friend.

11

The Case of the Creepy Classroom

As soon as the morning bell rang, I leaped out of my sleeping hut because I wanted to make sure Phoebe found the watch and the MKC notice.

While I was waiting for her to arrive, Thomas came in and tapped Just-Joey on the shoulder. He had a big friendly smile and said, 'Hey, Joey . . . want to play football after school?'

Joey looked surprised. He didn't smile at all. 'I'm busy,' he said.

'Maybe tomorrow?' Thomas asked.

Joey shook his head. 'I don't think so.' And then he walked away.

Thomas wasn't smiling any more.

I think Thomas is a nice boy. I know for a fact that Joey is a nice boy. But I didn't think Joey was being very nice to Thomas.

'What's going on, Og?' I asked my froggy friend.

'BOING-BOING!' he replied.

'I'm not sure I want any more mysteries to solve,' I squeaked.

Og dived into the water and splashed around.

Just then, Phoebe came into the classroom and went straight to her table.

'Over here, Phoebe!' I squeaked at the top of my lungs.

She didn't pay any attention, so I jumped up and down.

'PHOEBE!' I screamed. 'OVER HERE!'

She still didn't respond, so I climbed up to the top of my cage.

'WILL SOMEBODY PLEASE TELL PHOEBE TO COME OVER HERE?' I shrieked.

I heard Rosie giggle. 'Look at Humphrey. He's acting silly!'

She rolled her wheelchair over to the table

for a closer look. Simon, Joey and Kelsey rushed over.

'Phoebe, come and see Humphrey,' Kelsey said.

Thank goodness!

Finally, Phoebe came over, too.

Since an audience had gathered around me, I decided to give them a show.

Clinging to the top bars of my cage, I made my way, paw over paw, across to the other side.

'Go, Humphrey, go!' Simon cheered me on.

'Where's he going, anyway?' Rosie asked.

I knew exactly where I was going – to the side of my cage near Phoebe's watch and the MKC paper. I took a deep breath and I dropped down into the soft bedding.

I did a double flip-flop. I hadn't planned on it, but my friends all said, 'Oooh!'

I looked over at the watch and the paper, crossed my paws and hoped.

'Hey, Phoebe, isn't this your watch?' Kelsey asked.

Phoebe stared at the watch. 'It is!' She picked it up. 'But I looked here yesterday. How did I miss it?'

'Maybe the caretaker found it,' Rosie suggested.

Phoebe put on her watch and smiled.

I crossed my paws tighter.

Kelsey picked up the MKC notice. 'It was sitting on this,' she said.

She handed the paper to Phoebe, who stared at it and stared some more.

The bell rang and the students all headed for their chairs.

Phoebe slipped the paper into her pocket.

It worked! I could finally uncross my paws. Phoebe had her watch back, and maybe she'd call that number for MKC.

I was proud of myself, but my joy didn't last long, because when I looked over at Thomas, he was staring at his desk and looking about as unhappy as a human could look.

'Class, get ready for a ton of fun!' Mr E announced.

I wasn't in the mood for fun, so I crawled into my sleeping hut and had a nice dream about Phoebe's daisy watch.

When I awoke, I thought I was having a bad dream. In fact, I thought I was having a nightmare!

There were ghosts hanging from the ceiling! There were witches and broomsticks and black cats flying above the notice board! And there were leering pumpkins of every shape and size pinned onto it.

'Eeek!' I squeaked.

I don't think anybody heard me.

'I'll bet this is the best-decorated room in all of Longfellow School,' Mr E told my friends.

To squeak the truth, he was probably right. But I didn't think looking at those hideous grinning pumpkin faces and ghastly ghosts all night long would be best for me.

'And don't forget, there'll be a costume party on Halloween next week,' Mr E reminded the class.

'Eeek!' I squeaked again.

As if my paws weren't already full (of problems), now I had to come up with a costume.

Humans just don't realize how much a classroom hamster has to do.

After school, Mr Morales came into the

classroom. 'Nice decorations, Ed,' he said.

Mr E looked very proud. Mr Morales took a piece of paper out of his pocket. 'Have you got a moment?'

'Sure,' Mr E said.

The two men sat in some student chairs. Grown-up humans always look funny sitting in those small chairs.

'How have things been going with the class?' the head teacher asked.

'Great,' Mr E said. 'The kids are the best.'

Mr Morales nodded. 'Yes, and I can tell they like you a lot.'

Mr E smiled and I think his red hair glowed a little brighter.

'But there have been a few problems,' Mr Morales continued.

'Yes, there have!' I squeaked. 'Problems like Phoebe-Harry-Kelsey-Simon-Rosie-Holly-Thomas!'

I know all that the head heard was 'SQUEAK-SQUEAK-SQUEAK,' and it made him laugh.

'Yes, Humphrey, I know you're listening,' he said.

Mr E cleared his throat. 'What, um, problems?'

The head looked down at the paper. 'Well, Mrs Wright has complained about some safety issues, some injuries, a problem with noise. And a problem with students roaming the halls during class.'

'Oh,' Mr E said. 'I guess Mrs Wright and I don't see eye to eye.'

Mr Morales smiled. 'Mrs Wright does like to follow the rules. But rules are there for a reason, after all.'

Mr E nodded nervously. 'Yes, I understand.'

If he understood, why didn't he follow them? That was part of the mystery of Mr E.

'And a few parents have called to say that they're concerned about a lack of homework,' Mr Morales continued.

Mr E chuckled. 'I'll bet the students haven't complained about that.'

'No,' the head teacher replied. 'But we're here to teach the children. I believe that learning is fun, but there should be work involved, too.'

Mr E nodded. And nodded some more. He looked so nervous, even his red hair looked pale.

'And then there's Mrs Brisbane.' Mr Morales wasn't smiling any more. 'She's wondering if you're keeping up with her lesson plans. She said you haven't called her with any questions.'

'Oh,' Mr E said. 'Well, I've been following the lesson plans but adding my own touches. Maybe I haven't been following them closely enough.'

At least Mr E was honest. I liked that about him.

'The district-wide maths test is coming up. Are the students prepared for that?' Mr Morales asked.

'Not completely,' Mr E said. 'Not yet.'

'Ed, I want to give you a chance. You're a new teacher, and I know you really want to continue,' Mr Morales said. 'But the learning comes first.'

'It certainly does!' I squeaked.

'BOING-BOING-BOING!' Og agreed.

'Are you letting me go?' Mr E asked.

'No, Ed,' Mr Morales said. 'I think you can be a good teacher. But I need to see a change, starting tomorrow.'

'Yes, yes, I'll change,' Mr E said. 'Thank you

for giving me another chance. I won't let you down.'

The two men shook hands and Mr Morales left.

Once he was alone again, Mr E began to mutter something I couldn't understand. I did hear the word 'failed'.

I know that my fellow classmates don't want to fail. Maybe teachers don't want to fail, either.

After a while, he got up and paced around the room.

'Don't give up,' I squeaked. I was trying to be helpful.

I guess Mr E heard my squeaks, because he looked my way.

'I'll tell you one thing, I'm not giving up yet,' he said.

He sounded very determined, which gave me hope.

'Take out the lesson plans,' I squeaked. 'In the file. In the drawer!'

I didn't think he was likely to listen to me, since he thought of me as an 'it'. But surprisingly, he marched over to the desk, opened the drawer and took out the file.

He stuffed it into his large sack. Then he came over to the table where Og and I live.

'You have it easy,' he said. 'You're just classroom pets. Everybody loves you and you don't have to worry about tests.'

Then he stared out the window, his shoulders slumped. He sighed once or twice.

After a while I couldn't stand it. 'You can do a better job!' I squeaked. 'TRY-TRY-TRY!'

Mr E looked down at me and *almost* smiled.

'Would you like to change jobs with me, Humphrey?' he asked.

I think it was the first time he used my name.

'I could sit in your cage and take naps and you could teach the class,' he said.

I was sorry to hear that he thought all that I did was sit in my cage and take naps. But then, he didn't know about the lock-that-doesn't-lock.

'I really like my job,' I squeaked. I was too polite to say that I didn't think Mr E would be a very good classroom pet.

'I really like my job,' Mr E said. 'And I want to make this work.'

'I want this to work, too!' I replied.

Just then Ms Mac walked in. Why do good things always happen when Ms Mac walks in?

'Hi, Ed,' she said. 'How's it going?'

Mr E sighed. 'Not very well, I'm afraid.'

'What happened?' Ms Mac asked.

'Mr Morales just told me there have been a lot of complaints about my teaching. Too much noise, not enough homework . . . and Mrs Brisbane doesn't think I'm following her lesson plans,' he explained.

'Are you?' Ms Mac asked in the friendliest way possible.

Mr E shook his head. 'Yes, and, uh, no.'

Ms Mac said, 'Oh.' She came a little closer to my cage and leaned down. 'Hi, Humphrey,' she said with a wink.

'I really want to be a teacher,' Mr E said. 'There were no job openings, so I signed up to be a supply teacher.'

'That's how I got started,' Ms Mac said.

Yes, and if she hadn't, I wouldn't have my wonderful job!

'I've never told anybody what happened,' Mr E said.

Ms Mac smiled. 'I'm a good listener.'

Mr E nodded. 'Okay.'

'Listen up, Og,' I squeaked to my neighbour. 'Maybe we'll solve the mystery of Mr E.'

'BOING-BOING!' Og agreed.

'My first day as a supply teacher was a nightmare,' he said. 'I tried to teach the kids, but they wouldn't be quiet, wouldn't sit down, wouldn't listen to a word I said. When I tried to give them homework, they threw paper wads at me.'

'What?' I squeaked. 'That was RUDE-RUDE-RUDE!'

'BOING-BOING-BOING!' Og was just as shocked as I was.

Ms Mac was surprised, too. 'Was that at Longfellow School?' she asked.

'No,' Mr E said. 'I tell you, I was ready to give up teaching forever. And I decided that the next time I got a placement I'd make everything fun. If the kids liked me, maybe they'd behave better.'

'I understand,' Ms Mac said. 'But you can have fun and learn things at the same time. Students can have respect for you and like you at the same time. Look at Mrs Brisbane!'

'Yes, look!' I squeaked.

'I wish I knew her,' Mr E said. 'This is such a great class, and I don't think I've lived up to her standards. But it was so awful to know that the students in that first class didn't like me.'

You'd think I'd have learned it by now, but sometimes I forget: teachers are humans!

'I have an idea,' Ms Mac said. 'I'm going to visit a friend tonight, and I'd like you to come along. Are you free?'

'Yes,' Mr E said. 'But I have to prepare for tomorrow.'

Ms Mac smiled mysteriously. 'I think you can do both.'

Before long, they were gone.

'Og, I'm sorry to say I thought Mr E just didn't care,' I told my friend when we were alone. 'I'm glad I was wrong. But I wonder if Mrs Brisbane still cares.'

'BOING?' Og sounded confused.

'She's abandoned her students to go off and become a ballerina,' I explained. 'That doesn't seem right!'

There. I'd said it. I love Mrs Brisbane with all the heart a small hamster has to offer. But I had to admit, I was *piewhacked* by her behaviour. And a little disappointed, too.

I guess Og was disappointed, too, because he dived into the water and splashed wildly.

I'm not one for splashing, so I hopped on my wheel for a good, long spin.

Humphrey's Detectionary

When you solve a mystery, you might learn some very shocking information (involving very badly behaved students).

12

The Case of the New Mr E

As the light in the room grew darker that evening, the pumpkins on the wall grew brighter. For some reason, those jack-o'-lanterns really bothered me.

Aldo liked them, though. When he came in to clean that night, he said, 'Whoa! I almost thought I was in the wrong room.' He stopped and admired all the decorations. 'They did a really good job. Speaking of Halloween, I have a present for you, Humphrey.'

I LOVE-LOVE-LOVE presents!

He wheeled his trolley to the middle of the room. Then he reached into his lunch sack and pulled something out. 'Maria helped me with this,' Aldo explained as he walked towards my cage.

He opened the door and put something orange in my cage. 'A little Halloween treat,' he said.

In front of me was a tiny little jack-o'-lantern. It was actually a piece of pumpkin, with carrots and seeds that made a little face.

It looked perfectly hamsterlicious!

'Thank you, thank you – a million times,' I squeaked excitedly.

'It's my pleasure,' Aldo replied.

I started to nibble on the pumpkin right away while Aldo gave Og his nightly Froggy Food Sticks.

Poor Og. I guess he'll never know how tasty pumpkin is, especially the seeds.

When Aldo was ready to leave, he said, 'I've got a joke for you two. What do ghosts eat on their cereal?'

'I have no idea,' I said.

Og didn't say a thing. Not even BOING.

'Booberries!' Then Aldo burst out laughing and kept on chuckling as he rolled his trolley out of the door.

After he'd gone, when I looked up at the row

of pumpkins on the wall, they didn't look scary.

They just looked yummy!

'Class, it's time to begin,' Mr E announced the next morning. 'We have a lot to do today.'

'Can we play Mathketball?' Simon asked.

'Not right now,' Mr E answered.

'Word Wars?' Rosie asked.

'Not today,' Mr E said. 'We've got a lot of work to do.'

There were a few groans, but not many.

'We're going to start with Mrs Brisbane's mystery words,' he said. 'Take out a sheet of paper.'

Mr E still had small round glasses and red hair. But this was a different Mr E from the one I'd seen before. This was a real teacher.

Besides, I was HAPPY-HAPPY-HAPPY that we were going back to mystery words.

I knew what *piewhack* meant. And *pizzazz*.

But today, Mr E gave us a new word to work out: *pursizzle*.

I wondered if it meant a hot handbag.

He wrote this sentence on the board:

When you go to the store, please
get some *pursizzle* for tomorrow's
lunches.

Gosh, *pursizzle* had to be some kind of food.
But it could be anything: carrots, apples, celery
or other crunchy things.

Then he wrote another sentence:

My grandmother spent the
afternoon teaching me how to
bake *pursizzle*.

I don't think a grandmother would spend a
whole afternoon teaching somebody how to
bake a carrot or an apple. (I like them raw.)

The third sentence was:

My favourite breakfast is
pursizzle with jam.

Jam. It's a sweet, fruity spread. I know that.
And as far as I knew, humans usually ate jam
on: bread!

Pursizzle was *bread*!

369

I got 100 per cent on my assignment. My friends were all shouting out 'bread', so they got 100 per cent, too.

I was most excited because Mr E was following Mrs Brisbane's lesson plan, and as far as I could tell, everybody still liked him.

Personally, I liked him a little more than I had the day before.

I didn't have much time to think about *pursizzle* with jam because Mr E then went into a maths lesson that didn't involved basketballs or running or shouting. My friends worked hard and didn't talk unless they were called on.

Just before break, Mr E talked about Egypt. He had me on the edge of my seat – er, cage – talking about pyramids, mummies and the River Nile. I tell you, I was shivering and quivering during that lesson.

And when my friends went out to play, Mr E sat at Mrs Brisbane's desk and studied the lesson plans in her file.

We got so much done that day, I'm not sure Mrs Brisbane could have kept up . . . but my classmates and I did.

Mr E even gave out homework. *Real* homework. No one complained because he explained why it was important.

Late in the afternoon, Helpful-Holly reminded Mr E that he needed to choose who would take me home for the weekend.

Mr E asked my friends to raise their hands if they hadn't taken me home yet and thought their parents would give permission.

A lot of hands went up. How was Mr E going to choose?

He looked at the clock. 'I think we have time for a quick spelling bee to decide.'

He asked Rosie, Joey, Tall-Paul, Thomas and Sophie to spell different words.

They all got through the first round. On the second round, Rosie missed on the word *symbol*. (I was surprised there was a *y* in it, too.)

On the third round, Tall-Paul missed on the word *misery*. I completely understood, because the *s* does sound like a *z*.

Sophie went down on the word *mystify*. I would have too!

It was down to Joey and Thomas. And for the next two rounds, neither of them missed a word. They were difficult words, too: *disease*, *fierce, schedule*!

The spelling bee was suddenly very exciting, and it was almost time for the bell to ring.

'I'll tell you what,' Mr E said. 'You've done such a great job, would you agree to share Humphrey?'

The boys both looked puzzled. I was a little concerned, too. I hoped they weren't planning to split me in half!

'Thomas could have him Friday night. Then Joey could pick him up at Thomas's house on Saturday and have Humphrey Saturday night,' Mr E explained. 'Would your families agree to that?'

Neither boy looked happy. But they both nodded.

'Bring back notes from your parents tomorrow,' Mr E told them just as the bell rang.

'How did it go?' Ms Mac asked after school.

'Not bad.' Mr E smiled. 'We got a lot done and nobody threw anything at me. Thanks for taking me along last night. I think I'm on the right track now.'

'Great,' Ms Mac said. 'And the Halloween surprise is really going to be something. We just need to make sure no one finds out our secret.'

'Finds out what?' I squeaked.

'BOING-BOING!' Og twanged.

Ms Mac must have heard us because she laughed.

'No one must find out . . . even Humphrey and Og!' she said.

When Mr E and Ms Mac left for the day, I was annoyed.

'It's not nice to keep secrets,' I told Og. 'And it's especially not nice to keep secrets from classroom pets!'

'BOING-BOING-BOING,' Og agreed.

But I had something else on my mind besides the Halloween surprise. I could tell that Joey didn't want to be around Thomas. I wasn't sure why, but I think it had to do with the way Thomas exaggerated.

They should have been friends, but they weren't. And I was *piewhacked* about how to help them.

I had another problem to think about: my costume. I'd felt so proud when I won the prize for Best Costume last Halloween. And I hoped

I'd win it again.

Friday was a busy day . . . and a day that made me HAPPY-HAPPY-HAPPY.

We learned more about Egypt and a new kind of maths problem and we got a new vocabulary list. The day went by in a hurry because we were so busy.

At the very end of the day, Mr E made a special announcement. If the class all did well in our maths test on Monday, he'd finish reading us 'The Red-Headed League'.

Everybody cheered at that news! No one cheered louder than me.

⚬

I was really looking forward to meeting Thomas's dad. After all, according to his son, Mr True was a juggler-aeroplane-pilot-ship's-captain-detective!

When he came to pick us up from school, he just looked like a normal nice dad.

'Do you mind sharing Humphrey this weekend?' he asked as he drove us home from school.

'Not really,' Thomas said. 'Maybe when Joey

comes over tomorrow, we can play football.'

'Sure,' Mr True said. 'I'll take you to the park.'

I wasn't sure if Joey would like that, but I crossed my paws and hoped that he'd say yes.

When we got to the house, I was suddenly a little nervous. So far this school year, Thomas had told a lot of stories about his shark teeth collection, the gigantic fish he'd caught and huge spiders and colossal snakes. *And* all those tall tales about his dad.

Luckily, I didn't see any spiders, snakes, or fish – with or without teeth – at his house.

Thomas's dad helped get me set up. His little sister, Theresa, came in to watch me. I spun on my wheel for her, which made her laugh.

Then Thomas's mum brought me a celery treat.

Later that night, they all watched me roll around in my hamster ball. While I rolled, I wished I could help the boys become friends. All that rolling helped me think and before long, I had a Plan that would force them to spend time together, at least for a little while.

I crossed my paws and hoped it would work.

If they got to know each other better, maybe

Joey would find out what I knew: Thomas was a nice, normal boy. And Thomas would find out that if he wanted friends, he needed to stop exaggerating and tell the truth. Otherwise, how could anyone trust what he said?

Humphrey's Detectionary:

If you don't have a violin like Sherlock Holmes, rolling in a hamster ball can also help you think.

The Case of the Battling Boys

On Saturday afternoon, I was rolling around the living room in my hamster ball when the doorbell rang.

Thomas ran to open the door and said, 'Hi, Joey.'

It was time for my Plan. I started running like crazy in my ball so it rolled and rolled and rolled way, way under the couch, where it was dark and a little dusty. Perfect!

Thomas and Joey were talking, but their voices were hard to hear because there was a piece of cloth around the bottom of the couch that reached to the floor.

'Hey, Joey. My dad said he'd drive us to the park. We could play football,' Thomas said.

'No,' Joey said. 'My mum's waiting in the car.'

'My dad would take you back later,' Thomas said. 'He could talk to your mum.'

I thought I heard Joey say 'no' again. Then he asked, 'Where's Humphrey?'

Thomas said something I couldn't understand and then Joey said, 'Well, he must be around here somewhere.'

They said something about searching for me. Then all I heard were footsteps clomping all over the room.

'I used to have a hamster named Giggles,' Joey said. 'He loved his hamster ball. Humphrey reminds me of him.'

Then Thomas said, '*I* used to have a pet ostrich! He giggled, too.'

'No way,' Joey said.

'I did!' Thomas insisted. 'His name was Ozzie.'

Joey sighed. 'Let's just find Humphrey.'

The boys were quiet again except for their footsteps.

'He must be under something,' Joey said.

More footsteps. Then Thomas said, 'Not under the chair.'

Even more footsteps. Then Joey said, 'What about the couch?'

Before I knew it, a hand lifted up the cloth. Thomas and Joey were staring right at me.

'Humphrey!' Thomas said. 'What are you doing there?'

I didn't dare squeak the truth, so I stayed silent.

Joey reached way, way back and grabbed the hamster ball. 'Where's his cage?'

'In my room,' Thomas said.

Joey carried me to Thomas's room and put me back in my cage. 'Okay, Humphrey. We're ready to go,' he told me.

'Wait,' Thomas said. 'Don't you want to come play football with my dad and me? He used to play professionally.'

'Professionally? Look, I just don't want to, okay?' Joey said.

I was surprised to hear Joey talk like that. Just-Joey usually got along with everyone.

'Why are you so unfriendly?' Thomas asked.

'Why are you always telling lies?' Joey asked.

'Your dad did not play football professionally and he's not a detective or an aeroplane pilot or any of that stuff, right?'

Thomas hesitated. 'No,' he admitted. 'But he is in the transportation business. He sells cars!'

'You don't have to make up all that stuff. You're lucky to have a dad around. Not everybody does,' Joey said. 'My dad lives far away and I don't get to see him much. But I don't lie about him.'

'Sorry,' Thomas said. He sounded sorry.

I was sorry that Joey didn't get to see his dad much, too.

But Joey wasn't finished with Thomas. 'What about the lost property?'

Thomas rolled his eyes. 'It *was* creepy in there. But maybe the severed hand was just a glove.'

'And the ostrich?' Joey asked.

Thomas laughed. 'I did have an ostrich named Ozzie! But it was a toy I had when I was little.'

Joey grinned. 'I believe that. And the shark teeth?'

'That's true,' Thomas said. 'I'll show you.'

He opened a drawer and handed a box to

Joey. 'Here they are.'

Joey's eyes got really big when he looked inside the box. 'Wow. These really *are* shark teeth.'

'My uncle gave them to me,' Thomas said. 'He's in the Navy. And that's true.'

I scrambled to get a peek at the shark teeth. Eeek! They looked unsqueakably sharp!

Joey stared at the teeth. 'Do you know what kind they are?'

Thomas shook his head.

'The library has a book on sharks. We could look them up,' Joey said.

'Together?' Thomas asked.

Just-Joey grinned. 'Yeah, if you don't make stuff up.'

Thomas nodded and said, 'I just like to make things sound more interesting.'

'You don't need to,' Joey answered.

Thomas seemed surprised. 'I don't?'

'Just be you. Just-Thomas,' Joey said.

Thomas thought for a second. 'Okay. So, do you want to play football before we go to the library?' he asked.

Joey did, which made me feel GREAT-GREAT-GREAT. He went out and talked to his mum. Then Mr True took Joey and Thomas away for a long time.

When they came back, they had a new idea. Joey would spend the night at Thomas's and they would look after me together.

That meant I wasn't going to Joey's house after all. I wasn't all that disappointed, since he had a dog called Skipper who caught Frisbees in his teeth. I'd seen the tooth marks, so I'm pretty sure he wasn't exaggerating.

I'd rather be around shark's teeth with no shark attached than a dog with teeth still in its mouth.

And on Sunday, I was thrilled when Thomas and Joey studied for the big maths test – together!

⠐ö⠐

Before class started on Monday, Joey told his friends about Thomas's amazing shark tooth collection.

'You mean that was true?' Simon asked.

'Yes,' Joey said. 'It really was.'

Then Thomas said. 'I guess I exaggerated about some other things. Sorry about that. I just like a good story.'

'Me too,' Do-It-Now-Daniel said. 'Especially Sherlock Holmes.'

'Sherlock Holmes? We've got to do well on our test so we can hear the end of that story,' Tall-Paul said.

'I studied,' Harry said.

'Me too,' Simon said.

'Yep, I did, too,' Small-Paul said.

That was good news!

After the register, Mr E got right to work and the maths test began.

I watched my friends thinking, writing, rubbing out, writing some more.

After the test was over, my friends begged Mr E to mark them right away. So while they were at break, he sat at Mrs Brisbane's desk and marked each one. When he was finished, he smiled.

'Good,' he said. 'Very good.'

'Did you hear that, Og?' I squeaked. I looked over just as my friend did a magnificent dive into his water. I guess he had heard.

When my classmates came back after break, all eyes were on Mr E.

'Well, class, I'm sorry to tell you . . .' Mr E paused. My friends looked VERY-VERY-VERY nervous.

'. . . that I'm going to have to read you the rest of "The Red-Headed League"!'

Everybody cheered, including me.

'You all did very well on the test,' he said.

Naturally, with all that cheering, the door opened and there was Mrs Wright.

'I could hear your class all the way down the hall,' she said.

Still smiling, Mr E walked towards her. 'I'm sorry, Mrs Wright. We were celebrating the great job my students did in their maths test.'

Mrs Wright looked surprised. 'Oh. Well, that *is* good news.'

'We'll cheer a little more quietly next time,' Mr E said.

'Thank you, Mr Edonopolous,' Mrs Wright replied. She actually smiled.

Humans can be very *piewhacking*.

After she left, Mr E said, 'Mrs Brisbane would be pleased with you.'

Mrs Brisbane would be pleased with us. That was nice to hear.

But I wasn't very pleased with Mrs Brisbane. How could she start reading an exciting story and then run off and go to ballet school without even finishing it? Really, it was a mystery to me.

And then I remembered what she'd said in her letter: *It's funny to think that this all came about because of Humphrey.*

What had I done? What had I said?

Maybe Sherlock Holmes, the great detective, would help me understand.

Mr E pulled a tall stool from the corner and moved it to the front of the classroom. He took off his sweater and everyone laughed. He had on a black T-shirt that had *Mr E* in red wavy letters and a cartoon of a man with bright-red hair that looked a lot like him.

He sat on the stool and in a mysterious voice said, 'A mystery read by Mr E!'

He opened the big red book and said, 'And now, the exciting conclusion of "The Red-Headed League".' He began to read. He was an excellent story reader . . . every bit as good as Mrs Brisbane!

It turns out that Mr Jabez Wilson went to his

385

strange job each evening and was paid well. Then one day when he came to work, the office was locked and a sign read THE RED-HEADED LEAGUE IS DISSOLVED.

That's when he visited Sherlock Holmes (which was an unsqueakably good idea).

I don't want to give away the whole story, but Sherlock Holmes solved the puzzle and caught the bad guys in the act! And – what a surprise – the Red-Headed League turned out to be a trick!

Sherlock Holmes showed me that a detective can't always assume things are what they seem to be. Could I have been wrong about what happened to Mrs Brisbane? I hoped that one day, I'd find out.

'What did you think?' Mr E asked. 'Did any of you work it out?'

Thomas T. True's hand shot up in the air. 'I did!'

'Really?' Mr E asked. 'When?'

I saw Just-Joey turn to watch Thomas. I think he was pretty sure Thomas was going to exaggerate. Maybe Thomas noticed Joey's look, too.

Thomas grinned. 'When you read us the

ending!'

Everybody laughed, and Joey high-fived Thomas.

After he was finished with the story, Mr E gave us a lesson on Egypt, a lesson on writing sentences, and a new maths problem. He even showed us different kinds of clouds with cool pictures on a projector.

We were BUSY-BUSY-BUSY.

Near the end of the day, Mr Morales stopped by Room 26. He was wearing a tie with little gold stars all over it.

'I don't want to interrupt your studies,' he said. 'I just want to say that I heard this class did a tremendous job in the maths test today.'

Mr E nodded. 'They really did. Are you proud of yourselves?'

My classmates cheered and clapped. I hopped up and down and squeaked, 'YES-YES-YES!'

'Congratulations, Mr E and class. Keep up the good work,' the head teacher said.

I was unsqueakably proud of Mr E. It looked as if he was turning into a good teacher. And my friends still liked him.

I guess I liked him, too.

☙ ☙ *Humphrey's Detectionary* ☙ ☙

Sometimes a detective learns
something surprising about himself.
(He might even learn that someone
he didn't like is really a good human
after all.)

The Case of the Weird, Weird Witch

Mr E worked so hard the next few days that my class caught up with Mrs Brisbane's lesson plans. But it wasn't all hard work. He also read us a fur-raising story about a secret code. And it turned out that the secret code was also a maths problem!

During the day, I was busy trying to keep up with the lessons. At night, I'd make notes in my notebook so I'd remember what we'd learned in class.

But there was more than just schoolwork going on. Mr E talked to Hurry-Up-Harry about getting back to class on time and suddenly, Harry wasn't late any more.

One day, Phoebe came up to my cage smiling. She held up her wrist with the daisy watch on it.

'See, Humphrey, I still have it,' she said. 'And guess what? Yesterday after school, I went to a meeting of this new club. It's only for kids whose parents are in the military. We talked about our parents and we played a game and we're having a Halloween party, too!'

'That's pawsitively great!' I squeaked. I could tell Phoebe was feeling better already. And she remembered her homework all week, too.

Joey and Thomas were together all the time. I even heard them whispering about their Halloween costumes. They said something about 'hats', or maybe it was 'bats'. And they also mentioned 'grasses'. Maybe they meant 'glasses'. Were they going to dress up as bats with glasses? Or wear hats made of grasses? You can never guess *what* humans will wear for Halloween.

There was so much talk about Halloween, I couldn't help thinking about last year's party. I didn't know much about Halloween then.

All I knew is that humans wore costumes and that the class would have a party.

But last year we had a different class. We had a different teacher. And I was a different hamster.

Oh, I was still Humphrey. But I was just starting to learn about school.

Now, I knew a LOT-LOT-LOT more.

I just didn't know what my costume would be.

The night before Halloween, Aldo came in Room 26 and stopped. He looked around and said, 'Will you look at that? It's almost as clean as when Mrs Brisbane was here.'

'And where is she now?' I squeaked loudly.

I guess Aldo didn't understand me.

'How do you like my costume?' Aldo twirled around.

He looked the same as usual. He had on a blue shirt and black trousers and he was pushing his cleaning trolley.

'This *is* my costume! Get it?' Aldo roared with laughter, and I realized that he was joking.

I like jokes. I think most hamsters do.

'I need a costume, too,' I squeaked.

'BOING-BOING!' Og agreed.

'I know you're excited,' Aldo said. 'I talked to Richie today. He's excited, too.'

Richie was his nephew, and he'd been in Room 26 last year.

'He's going to be a monster,' Aldo explained.

It was hard to imagine Richie as a monster. He was a very nice human. Maybe there are nice monsters, too. I'll bet there are.

When Aldo sat down to have his dinner, I was hoping for a pumpkin treat, and I wasn't disappointed.

'Trick or treat, buddy,' he said.

'Thanks, Aldo. Trick or squeak!' I called after him.

Later, when Aldo was gone, I told Og, 'Tomorrow is Halloween.'

'BOING-BOING!' he replied.

'I need a costume,' I said, walking towards the edge of our table. 'Don't you?'

'BOING-BOING-BOING!' He didn't seem to like the idea of wearing a costume.

'You don't have to wear a costume, Og. But I want one,' I said. 'I had an idea today when I was thinking about the Sherlock Holmes story. And I have a Plan.'

Og dived into his water with a giant splash. I dashed away to keep from getting wet.

I slid down the table leg and scurried across the room to the shelves where the art supplies were stored.

Luckily, they were low to the ground, so I could easily scramble up the side of a bin and slip over the edge. Once I was inside, I found what I wanted. I gnawed and gnawed until I had exactly what I needed for my costume.

Holding my treasure in my mouth, I climbed up a stack of glue sticks, hopped on a tall jar of glitter and slid back over the edge.

I swung back up to the table and went straight to my cage. I hid my costume in my bedding and closed the cage door behind me.

'BOING-BOING!' Og twanged.

'My costume is a surprise, Og. You'll find out what it is tomorrow,' I squeaked back at him. '*Everybody* will find out tomorrow.'

There were no costumes on Halloween morning. There were just the usual lessons. But after lunch, Mr E sent everyone out of the room to change into their costumes. Simon's mum and Small-Paul's dad were there to help.

When the room was empty, Mr E turned towards Og and me and said, 'You're about to have a *big* surprise.'

'So are you!' I squeaked.

Then he left the room, too.

While the room was empty, I made sure my costume was still under my bedding.

·ö·

It seemed like a LONG-LONG-LONG time before the door finally opened again.

In walked a tall pirate and a short ninja. I guessed they were Tall-Paul and Small-Paul.

Then a princess with a sparkling crown on her head came in. That was Holly.

More kids came into the classroom in amazing costumes. Phoebe wore a camouflage military uniform. Kelsey was a ballerina in a pink tutu. Her eye was back to normal, and she looked very graceful.

Then a very surprising pair came in. They were dressed alike in long coats and those deerstalker hats like Sherlock Holmes wore, and they carried huge magnifying glasses.

Thomas and Joey were both dressed like

Sherlock Holmes. So they had been talking about hats and glasses, not bats and grasses!

Right behind them was Simon in a super-hero costume with a blue cape, along with Harry, who was all wrapped in white like a mummy.

Then something amazing happened. A table rolled through the door. There was a plate on the table with a knife and fork next to it. And on the plate was Rosie's head!

'Eeek!' I squeaked.

Rosie smiled and everybody laughed. Someone had put a box over her shoulders with a hole for her head. She had painted a tablecloth, and the plate, knife and fork were glued on.

It was the best costume I'd seen so far!

My friends sat at their tables and waited. Or in their tables, in Rosie's case.

We all waited quite a while before the door opened again.

I thought I'd see Mr E, but that's not what I saw at all.

In came a grinning pumpkin head on a skinny skeleton body and a truly horrible old witch. She was all hunched over and leaned on a crooked wooden cane. Her face was hideous, with huge warts and a pointed nose and green skin.

The room was silent as they walked to the front of the room and faced us.

'How do witches tell the time?' the pumpkin skeleton asked in a strange, high-pitched voice.

'With a witch-watch!' the witch answered. And then she cackled wildly. The sound made my fur stand on end.

'What do you call a nervous witch?' the pumpkin skeleton asked.

'A twitch!' the weird witch answered, and cackled loudly again.

I was about to go and hide in my sleeping hut when the pumpkin skeleton asked another question.

'And which witch are you?' the pumpkin skeleton asked.

This time, the witch didn't answer.

'Class, who knows which witch this is?' the skeleton asked us.

For a few seconds, no one spoke. Or squeaked.

And then Small-Paul shouted, 'Mrs Brisbane!'

Mrs Brisbane was a *witch*? And all this time, I thought she was a ballerina!

The witch reached up and took off her witchy face, which was just a mask.

And there was Mrs Brisbane, smiling happily at us.

Everyone in the class cheered and clapped.

Og splashed loudly. 'BOING-BOING-BOING-BOING!'

I climbed up to the top of my cage and shouted, 'Welcome back!'

Mr E took off his pumpkin head and grinned.

'I'm so happy to see all of you,' Mrs Brisbane said in her normal voice. 'Mr E came to visit me, and we planned this surprise for you. I'm so proud of how well you did in your maths test.'

The door opened and a mad scientist with wild white hair and a white coat came in, along with a clown with a round red nose and a pink-, blue- and green-striped wig.

'Happy Halloween!' The clown sounded just like Mrs Wright. In fact, I was sure it was Mrs

Wright when I saw that the clown had a whistle around her neck.

'Welcome back!' The mad scientist sounded just like Mr Morales.

'It's good to be back,' Mrs Brisbane said.

Still leaning on her stick, Mrs Brisbane hobbled over to see Og and me.

'Of course, I missed my friends Humphrey and Og,' she said.

'I'm so glad to see you!' I squeaked.

Og jumped for joy. 'BOING!'

'Hi, Og. Hello, Humphrey,' Mrs Brisbane said. 'You know, Humphrey, you're the cause of this.'

My heart sank to my toes. 'What did I do!?' I squeaked.

Our teacher turned to the class. 'You see, I was running a little late for school that morning. I was already in my car when I realized I'd forgotten Humphrey's fresh vegetable treat. As I ran back to the house, my heel caught on the front step and I tumbled down and broke my ankle.'

She lifted a corner of her long witch's skirt and showed us her cast.

'I'm unsqueakably sorry!' I said.

'I couldn't reach my phone and Mr Brisbane wasn't home, so I couldn't call the school to tell them I wouldn't be in,' she explained.

So that's why Mr Morales had been so confused that morning!

'My neighbour finally found me and took me to hospital. I had to have an operation on my ankle before I could start walking again,' she continued. 'But of course, it was all *my* fault and not Humphrey's. What did I forget to do, Kelsey?'

'You forgot to pay attention to what you were doing,' Kelsey answered.

At least I wasn't *piewhacked* about what had happened any more! The mystery was solved at last.

I was happy to have our teacher back, but I wished she'd learned to be a ballet dancer instead of breaking her ankle. Ouch!

Mr E brought a chair for Mrs Brisbane, and it was time for Mr Morales and Mrs Wright to judge the costumes.

I dived down into my bedding, found my wool and put on my costume.

Mr Morales and Mrs Wright smiled and

whispered as they watched my friends parade around the room.

No one was watching me, so to get their attention, I began squeaking loudly.

'SQUEAK-SQUEAK! Look at me!' I repeated over and over.

Finally, Mrs Brisbane turned to see what was wrong, and she burst out laughing. 'What on earth is Humphrey wearing?'

Everyone rushed over to my cage, so I stood up on my rear paws and squeaked some more.

'He's got red wool on his head,' Rosie said.

Thomas leaned in and held up his magnifying glass. 'It's red wool, all right.'

Joey leaned in and held up his magnifying glass. 'It looks like hair. Red hair.'

Kelsey giggled. 'He looks like a redhead. From "The Red-Headed League" story.'

I guess it took a redhead to recognize another redhead.

Everyone was laughing and pointing except Mr Morales and Mrs Wright. They were whispering and pointing.

'Who gave Humphrey that wool?' Mrs Brisbane asked.

No one answered.

'Whoever you are, you're a very clever person,' she said.

For once, Mrs Brisbane was wrong. I am a very clever *hamster*.

Mr Morales announced that he and Mrs Wright had made a decision. He reached in his pocket and pulled out a blue rosette that had Best Costume written on it. 'It's a tie between Rosie Rodriguez and . . . Humphrey!'

'BOING-BOING-BOING-BOING!' Og cheered. He knew I'd wanted to win.

Everyone else cheered, too, and Mr Morales put the rosette on my cage. He had another Best Costume rosette, which he gave to Rosie. I was proud to share the honour with her.

'Of course, you're all winners in Room 26,' he said. 'Mrs Brisbane is coming back to teach next week. So I think we should all thank Mr E for doing a great job.'

He reached in his pocket and pulled out a gold rosette that had Best Supply Teacher written on it. Mr E looked very happy to accept it.

'Now, boys and girls, Mrs Murch is going on a sick leave next week, so Room 29 needs a supply teacher. Do you think I should recommend Mr E?'

Everyone cheered wildly – even Mrs Wright!

Then they passed out treats for everyone – including some sunflower seeds for me.

All I can say is: it was a SUPER-SUPER-SUPER-GREAT-GREAT party!

That night, when Og and I were alone in Room 26, I guess I was the happiest hamster on earth.

I'd made my friends laugh, and I had a shiny blue ribbon on my cage.

My favourite teacher, Mrs Brisbane, was coming back.

My next-favourite teacher, Ms Mac, was just down the hall.

My other favourite teacher, Mr E, would still be at Longfellow School for a while.

And even though I'd just solved a lot of mysteries in Room 26, I knew that as long as I was a hamster living in a classroom full of humans, I'd always have plenty mysteries to solve . . . just like Sherlock Holmes!

·ö· ·ö· Humphrey's Detectionary ·ö· ·ö·

Sometimes even excellent clues can lead you in the wrong direction, but it doesn't really matter if everything ends well and your teacher comes back!

Humphrey's Top 10 Tips For Beginning Detectives

1   To be a detective, you need to find a mystery to solve. They are everywhere, especially when humans are around. (Humans need a lot of help!)

2   To find the clues you need to solve a mystery, it's important to watch and listen to EVERYTHING. (A cage is a good watching place.)

3   It's also unsqueakably important to write your observations in your notebook. You will also need a pencil or pen. (It's a good idea to hide your notebook behind a mirror or some other secret place.)

4   If you don't understand something – like a mystery word – studying things

around it will help you work it out.

5   If you're going to watch and listen, you have to be VERY-VERY-VERY quiet and not make a peep — or a squeak!

6   Some detectives, like Sherlock Holmes, wear funny hats. I'm not sure why. Maybe it makes them think better. But you don't HAVE to wear a hat to be a detective.

7   It's important to know when it's safe to go searching for clues, especially when you're going in and out of a cage.

8   One mystery often leads to another. And one solution often leads to another.

9   Never, ever give up! This is a good rule for detectives and everyone else!

10   Read a lot of good mystery stories. They're fun . . . and they make you think!

Christmas According to Humphrey

To my niece, Jennifer Powell Radman, and
my nephew, Todd Vincent Powell –
'Jenny' and 'Todd' all grown up!

Contents

What a Lark

'Humphrey! Where are you?' a voice called out.

I wasn't quite sure where I was, because I'd been sound asleep in my cage until I heard the voice.

My cage is a wonderful world all to itself. I have everything a hamster needs: a wheel to spin on, a sleeping hut, a climbing ladder, food, water, a mirror, tree branches and a corner just for my poo. (And that, of course, isn't near my food or water or sleeping hut.) And my bedding is like a lovely quilt that keeps me warm when it's cold.

I poked my head out of the bedding.

So that's where I was. Room 26 of Longfellow School!

'Oh, so that's where you're hiding.' Mrs Brisbane, my teacher, leaned down to look into my cage. I do like to play hide-and-squeak at times, but all I could think of that morning was keeping warm. During the winter at Longfellow School, they turn the heat down at night and turn it up again in the morning.

'Brrr, it's chilly,' Mrs Brisbane said. She was still wearing her heavy coat and a woolly cap. 'I hope the heat goes on soon.'

'YES-YES-YES!' I agreed.

But since I am a hamster and she is a human, all she heard was 'SQUEAK-SQUEAK-SQUEAK.'

'BOING-BOING!' my neighbour Og said. He's the other classroom pet in Room 26 and he makes a very strange twanging sound. He can't help it. He's a frog.

'Morning, Og,' Mrs Brisbane said, taking off her cap. 'Winter is definitely here.'

Soon my classmates began to arrive. They were all wearing heavy coats and hats, scarves and gloves.

'Hi, Humphrey-Mumphrey!' Slow-Down-Simon shouted as he raced into the room.

He'd been calling me that ever since we played a funny name game. I liked my nick-name.

'Hi, Oggy-Moggy,' Be-Careful-Kelsey called out as she passed by Og's tank.

'BOING!' Og replied.

Rosie rolled into the classroom in her wheel-chair. She had a bright red cap and a bright red nose. 'It's cold out there,' she announced.

'It's freezing out there! It's twenty below zero!' Thomas T. True said as he entered. Just the thought of twenty below zero made me shiver and quiver.

I was about to dive under my bedding again when Mrs Brisbane corrected him. 'Thomas, it's actually two degrees *above* zero, which is cold, but not quite freezing. Now go and hang up your jacket.'

The students who had already hung up their coats stood around, talking.

'Wait until you see the present I'm making you,' I heard Helpful-Holly tell Kelsey. 'You'll love it.'

'What is it?' Kelsey asked.

'It's a special surprise,' Holly said.

Kelsey smiled. 'Great!'

Holly turned to Tall-Paul, who was standing behind her. 'I'm making you a special present, too,' she told him.

Tall-Paul looked puzzled. 'Why?' he asked.

'Because you're my friend,' Holly said.

'You too,' she told Small-Paul, who was standing next to Tall-Paul.

The two Pauls exchanged puzzled looks.

Then Holly came over to my cage. 'Don't worry, Humphrey,' she said. 'I'll make a present for you, too.'

'That's unsqueakably nice of you,' I replied.

My squeaks made her giggle.

She turned to Og's tank. 'I have a great idea for your present, Og.'

'BOING-BOING!' Og twanged happily.

'I've got a big list of things to make,' Holly said. 'It's a lot of work. I even sneaked out of bed last night and worked at my desk with a torch. It's the only way I'll get them all done.'

I wanted to get a present from Holly, but I didn't want her to go without sleep to make it!

The bell rang and Holly rushed to her table.

Hurry-Up-Harry arrived just as the bell

stopped ringing, but at least he made it on time.

'Class, as you can tell by the weather, winter is here,' Mrs Brisbane announced after she took the register. 'And that means we've got to get busy practising.'

'We do?' I asked. I know I'm supposed to raise my paw before squeaking, but it slipped out.

'This year, Longfellow School is putting on a show to celebrate the Christmas holidays. It's called *Winter Wonderland*. Each class will do a special performance that has to do with winter,' she explained. 'It takes place the evening before the holidays start, and your friends and families are all invited.'

Some of my friends went 'Oooh.'

Some of my friends went 'Ahhh.'

Thomas T. True said, 'All right!'

I said, 'SQUEAK', because when you celebrate something, it's fun.

'Ms Lark will be in later this morning to tell you about your part in the show,' Mrs Brisbane said.

I'd heard of Ms Lark, the music teacher. Sometimes the rest of the class goes to her room, but Og and I stay behind. My friends always come back humming.

Mrs Brisbane changed the subject and passed out sheets of maths questions.

I, on the other paw, kept thinking about the winter show. I know winter can be COLD-COLD-COLD. But it can be pretty when it snows.

But what on earth was a wonderland? I wondered what it would be like all through maths class.

While Mrs Brisbane was cleaning the board, the door opened and in came a woman who almost looked like a student. She was slim with curly brown hair, and she was shorter than my tallest classmate, Paul Green. (I call him Tall-Paul.) She had a big smile on her face and she carried a stack of papers.

'Hello, Ms Lark,' Mrs Brisbane greeted her. 'We've finished maths class and are ready to hear about the show.'

I scrambled up my tree branch and shouted, 'Yes! Tell us now!'

Suddenly, Ms Lark froze. 'What was that noise?' she asked.

'Oh, that's our classroom hamster, Humphrey,' Mrs Brisbane said. 'I think he wants to say hello to you. Would you like to come and meet him?'

Some of my friends laughed, but Ms Lark didn't.

She stared in the direction of my cage . . . and I think she shivered.

Mrs Brisbane walked towards my cage, but Ms Lark didn't follow. In fact, she took a step back.

Just then, Og said, 'BOING!'

Ms Lark backed up again. 'What was that?'

'That's Og the frog,' Helpful-Holly said.

The music teacher's eyes grew wide and her voice sounded strange as she said, 'You have a lot of animals in this class.'

Mrs Brisbane chuckled. 'Yes, and they're not all in cages and tanks.'

The rest of the class laughed, but Ms Lark didn't even smile.

She kept staring in the direction of my cage until Mrs Brisbane said, 'We're all excited to hear about the winter show. Why don't you tell us about it?'

At last, Ms Lark smiled and moved to the

front of the classroom. 'It's going to be an exciting celebration of everything the season has to offer. And I think Room 26 has the best part of the show.'

It's hard for a small, excitable creature like me not to squeak up when I hear something wonderful, but I managed to stay silent.

Og splashed around in his tank. I guess it was hard for him to stay silent, too.

'Your class is performing two songs. There'll be swirling snowflakes and prancing horses and jingle bells!' Ms Lark's eyes sparkled.

'Oh, I love horses and bells!' I heard Sophie say. Then she turned to Kelsey, who was next to her, and started to tell her a story.

'Stop-Talking-Sophie,' Mrs Brisbane said.

Sophie said she was sorry and I think she meant it.

Rosie raised her hand. 'Will there be real horses?' she asked.

'No,' Ms Lark said. 'But there will be prancing and dancing and singing and ringing!'

All my classmates were excited at her answer.

'Yippee!' I squeaked. I didn't mean to, but it slipped out.

Suddenly, the sparkle went out of Ms Lark's eyes.

'Does that hamster ever get out?' she asked.

'Sometimes,' Mrs Brisbane replied. 'When he rolls around in his hamster ball.'

This time Ms Lark definitely shivered. And it wasn't even cold any more.

'Could you explain how we're going to prepare for our musical numbers?' Mrs Brisbane asked.

'We'll be rehearsing in here,' Ms Lark said. 'The music room is being used to store the scenery for the show.' Then she started talking about schedules and rehearsals and costumes.

My friends were especially excited about the costumes.

'Some of you will be floating snowflakes,' Ms Lark explained. 'And some of you will be jingle-bell horses.'

There was a lot of murmuring in the classroom.

Og splashed a little louder.

'I'll be sending a letter home to your parents,' Mrs Brisbane said. 'Now, let me say that this will be a lot of work and I want to make sure that you're all prepared to do your best.'

'I WILL-WILL-WILL!' I squeaked, but luckily, I don't think Ms Lark heard me because all of my friends were talking, too.

'Quiet, please,' Ms Lark said. Once everyone quietened down, she added, 'It will be work, but it will also be fun and I know it will be wonderful! Now, I'm sure you all know the song "Jingle Bells", but there will be a brand-new snowflake song, too. I wrote it myself and I brought copies for you.'

Helpful-Holly jumped up. 'I'll pass them out.'

Ms Lark gave her the papers and Holly made sure all her friends had one.

All her friends except Og and me!

'I'll be working with you on the melody,' Ms Lark explained. 'And one more thing: does anyone in this class play the piano?'

Do-It-Now-Daniel's hand went up. 'I do,' he said. 'I take lessons.'

'Great,' Ms Lark said. 'Would you like to play for the performance?'

'Sure,' he said.

'I'll play the new song and I'd like to have you play "Jingle Bells". I'll get you the music so you can practise,' she said.

Be-Careful-Kelsey's hand went up. 'I take ballet lessons!'

I already knew that and, I must say, Kelsey is a little more careful since she started ballet.

'That will be a big help,' Ms Lark said.

Thomas's hand went up next. 'I play a musical instrument.'

Mrs Brisbane didn't look convinced. 'Tell-the-Truth-Thomas,' she said.

Thomas sometimes stretches the truth a little.

'I do,' he insisted. Then he puckered his lips and began to whistle.

There are several things humans can do that I wish hamsters could do. Whistling is one of them.

Ms Lark and Mrs Brisbane both laughed.

'That's not a musical instrument,' Mrs Brisbane said.

'Sure it is,' Thomas said. 'My mouth!'

'I think we need that mouth for singing,' Ms Lark said.

Soon, the bell rang for playtime and my friends ran to get their coats.

'Stay buttoned up,' Mrs Brisbane told them. 'It's cold out there.'

Mrs Brisbane walked towards the door with Ms Lark. 'It will be hard work, but I know the children will love the programme,' Mrs Brisbane said.

'I can see it now.' Ms Lark had her sparkle back. 'A real winter wonderland.'

After she left, Mrs Brisbane came over to see Og and me. 'You know, I don't think Ms Lark likes animals very much,' she said. 'I feel sorry for her.'

Poor Ms Lark. I felt sorry for her, too. She doesn't know what she is missing.

Humphrey's Merry Christmas Musings:

I wonder how an intelligent human being could not like a handsome hamster with long whiskers and beautiful golden fur.

Singing Snowflakes

After playtime, my friends wanted to talk about the winter show.

Mrs Brisbane, on the other paw, wanted to talk about science.

'I tell you what,' she said. 'Since you'll be singing about snowflakes, let's talk about them.'

It turns out that snowflakes are SO-SO-SO interesting! I discovered that:

- Snowflakes are made of little crystals of ice.
- Each snowflake has six sides.
- Snow forms in clouds where the temperature is below freezing.
- No two snowflakes are ever the same.

- Ice crystals form around tiny bits of dirt! Can you believe a beautiful snowflake starts with a piece of dirt?
- As they get heavier, the snowflakes fall towards the ground.

'If we're lucky, we'll get to do a science experiment with real snow,' Mrs Brisbane said. 'What else can we do with snow?'

'Oooh, I love to go tobogganing,' Sophie said. 'We live on a hill and last year it snowed and the kids in the neighbourhood tobogganed all day. The hill was bumpy so we bounced all the way down. And then my cousins came over and some friends and my mum made chilli. And then the next day . . .' Sophie paused for a breath.

'Thank you, Sophie,' Mrs Brisbane said quickly. 'Who else has an idea?'

I don't think Stop-Talking-Sophie was finished talking. To squeak the truth, she never is.

She can talk more than any human I know!

'I like building snowmen,' Holly said. Then she yawned a HUGE-HUGE-HUGE yawn.

My other friends came up with so many interesting things to do, like skiing, building snow castles, making snow ice cream and throwing snowballs.

I've never done any of those things because hamsters don't like the cold, despite our fur coats! Still, I enjoy watching the snow from the warmth of my cage.

Then Mrs Brisbane said, 'And, of course, one of your songs is about the idea that no two snowflakes are exactly alike. I like the words to the song Ms Lark gave us today. I think it's true for this class.'

The words? What words? I wanted to get my paws on that song and find out what it said. After all, if I was going to be in the show with my friends, I needed to know my part!

Soon, all of my friends hurried off to lunch – except for one.

Holly was still at her desk, yawning.

Mrs Brisbane noticed, too. 'Holly, are you feeling all right?'

'I'm fine,' Holly answered in a weak voice.

Mrs Brisbane walked over to her table. 'You seem tired today. Maybe you should go and see the school nurse. Or I could call your mother to pick you up, if you're sick.'

Holly yawned. 'No, I'm fine,' she said again.

Then Mrs Brisbane did a strange thing. She put her hand on Holly's forehead. I tell you, humans never stop surprising me with their odd behaviour!

'Did you bring your lunch?' Mrs Brisbane asked.

Holly nodded.

'You can eat in here, if you'd like. It's nice and quiet. We could eat together,' Mrs Brisbane said.

Mrs Brisbane brought her lunch bag over to Holly's table and they took out all kinds of yummy-looking food, like sandwiches and hamsteriffic carrot sticks. They didn't talk for a while as they ate. Then Mrs Brisbane asked, 'Are you all ready for the holidays?'

'Not really,' Holly said. 'I still have a lot of presents to make.'

'It's nice to make presents,' Mrs Brisbane said. 'But it's a lot of work.'

'You can squeak that again,' I said. 'Holly's working so hard, she's not even sleeping. It might make her ill!'

I know that all Mrs Brisbane could hear was

SQUEAK-SQUEAK-SQUEAK, but I wished she could understand me.

'Who are you making presents for?' Mrs Brisbane asked.

'Everyone in the class,' Holly said. 'Oh, and I forgot! I have to make something for Ms Lark!'

Mrs Brisbane looked puzzled. 'We don't exchange gifts in this class.'

'I know,' Holly said. 'But I figured it out. I'm going to deliver them outside of class.'

Mrs Brisbane chewed a bite of her sandwich and then said, 'That's nice of you, but why do you want to do this?'

'I love to make things! And I love to give gifts to show how much I like everybody,' Holly said. 'Then they'll like me back.'

Then Mrs Brisbane did something I don't see her do very often. She frowned.

'Holly, your classmates do like you,' she said. 'You know that, don't you?'

Holly thought for a moment. 'I guess they do.'

'You don't need to give people presents to make them like you. People like you for

429

who you are,' Mrs Brisbane explained.

I was so glad to hear my teacher squeak up.

'That's right!' I agreed.

'It's important to get enough sleep, Holly,' Mrs Brisbane said. 'You don't want to be ill for the holidays.'

It's amazing! Even if she didn't understand what I said, Mrs Brisbane seemed to know what I was thinking. I guess that's what makes her such a great teacher.

Holly yawned again.

Mrs Brisbane and Holly chatted a little more while they finished lunch. Then my teacher said, 'Why don't you put your head on your table and rest until the others come back?'

'Couldn't I work on making my presents instead?' Holly asked. 'I brought some of my projects with me.'

Mrs Brisbane shook her head. 'No, Holly. Please drop the idea of making presents for everyone. Put your head down and rest.'

Holly agreed, and soon she was fast asleep.

Of course, Holly woke up when our friends came back into the class. (Maybe she didn't wake up all the way, though.)

Later in the day, Mrs Brisbane read to us from a wonderful book about a girl named Alice falling down a rabbit hole (which sounds terrifying to a small creature like me). And just like our show, it took place in a wonderland, but not the kind where it snows.

It was hard to follow the story, though, because while Mrs Brisbane was reading, Holly kept yawning and the yawns kept getting longer and longer.

'Yawn. Yawn. Yawwwwn. Yawwwwwwwn.'

Then I noticed something funny. Once Holly started yawning, all the other humans in the room began to yawn.

Even *I* started to yawn, and I'm not a human.

I finally crawled into my sleeping hut for a nap. I was only sorry that Holly couldn't fit in there too!

'Og, do you remember the time you and I got snowed in?' I asked my neighbour that night when the school was empty.

'BOING-BOING!' Og replied.

'It doesn't seem that long ago,' I said. 'In

fact, it was earlier this year. But so much has happened since then. And now winter is back!'

'BOING?' Og sounded surprised.

'I wonder if it will snow again. I wonder what a wonderland looks like. And I wonder what that snowflake song is like,' I squeaked.

Og splashed around in his water a little, but he didn't answer my questions.

It was beginning to get dark in Room 26, but my hamster eyes see well in the dark. And as I looked across the room, I noticed a sheet of white paper under Be-Careful-Kelsey's table.

'I wonder . . .' I squeaked. 'Og, do you think that's a copy of the snowflake song?'

Og splashed a little louder.

I was thinking about opening the lock-that-doesn't-lock on my cage and trying to read the paper when I heard a familiar RATTLE-RATTLE-RATTLE coming down the hall outside the classroom.

The first time I'd heard that rattling, I'd thought a ghost was coming. But now I knew that it was only Aldo coming in to clean. He isn't anything like a ghost, thank goodness.

Suddenly, the door swung open and bright light filled the room as Aldo appeared, pushing his cleaning cart.

'Never fear . . . 'cause Aldo's here,' his voice boomed out.

'Greetings, Aldo!' I squeaked at the top of my tiny lungs.

'Hello, Humphrey! Hello, Og! How are my favourite classroom pets?' he said.

I was glad we were his favourites. George, the frog with the deep voice in Miss Loomis's class, isn't one bit friendly. Sometimes it's difficult to understand Og, but I don't understand the hermit crabs in Miss Becker's room at all.

I've liked Aldo since my first night in Room 26. It was fun to watch him, especially when he showed me his trick of balancing a broom on his fingertip.

Aldo came over to our table and bent down so his face was level with my cage and Og's tank. I love to see Aldo up close because he has a big furry black moustache that wiggles when he talks. Sometimes I wonder if he stores extra food in there, the way I do in my cheek pouch.

'Say, have you heard about this *Winter*

Wonderland show?' he asked. 'It's going to snow in the gym . . . and that's no joke! Get it? That's *snow joke*.'

When he laughed, his moustache shook.

It made me cold to think of snow outside. But the thought of snow inside the school made my teeth chatter.

'Here's a snow joke for you,' Aldo said. 'How do snowmen travel around?'

I had no idea, so I was happy when Aldo said, 'By icicle! Get it? An icicle, like a bicycle.'

'That's funny,' I squeaked.

'Here's another one,' Aldo continued. 'What do you call a snowman in the summer? A puddle!'

Aldo's moustache shook even harder as he laughed at this joke – along with me.

Then Aldo went to work cleaning the classroom. He dusted the tables and was careful not to disturb anything on Mrs Brisbane's desk. Aldo admires Mrs Brisbane (so do I). He's even going to school to learn to be a teacher like her someday.

Next, Aldo got out his big broom and started sweeping.

I climbed up to the top of my tree branch so I could have a better look.

He had collected quite a pile of dust and paper trimmings by the time he reached the piece of paper near Kelsey's table.

He bent down and picked it up. 'What's this?' He studied the paper. 'Oh, it's a song. Hey, I'll bet this is the song for the winter show.'

'What's it say?' I squeaked loudly.

'BOING-BOING-BOING!' Og twanged excitedly.

Aldo started to whistle. I'm not quite sure how he did that, because I couldn't see his mouth under that big floppy moustache.

'I like it,' he said. 'That's a nice idea.'

'PLEASE-PLEASE-PLEASE bring it over here!' I squeaked.

I guess Aldo didn't understand, because he put the paper back on Kelsey's table.

After he finished his work and the tables were in neat rows again, he pulled a chair up next to my cage and took out his dinner. He always eats his dinner with Og and me.

'Richie said his class is going to build a snowman in the gym,' Aldo told us.

Richie is Aldo's nephew. He was in Room 26 with me last year.

Aldo chuckled. 'Now that's something, isn't it?'

'It certainly is!' I squeaked. It would have to be COLD-COLD-COLD in that gym if they didn't want the snowman to melt. I shivered a little.

'I like that snowflake song, though.' Aldo pushed a crunchy piece of lettuce between the bars of my cage.

'Sing it to us, Aldo,' I said.

He didn't sing but he hummed a little. Then he sang, 'Each one is special, just like me and you.'

Aldo chuckled again. 'I guess you two snowflakes aren't alike at all,' he said. 'And you're both special, all right.'

After he finished his meal, Aldo threw a few Froggy Food Sticks into Og's tank. My friend took a deep dive in the water to catch them.

Before I knew it, Aldo had rolled his cart out into the hallway and turned off the lights.

'Night-night,' he said before closing the door.

The room was dark and quiet. I waited until

I saw Aldo's car leave the car park a little later. Then I jiggled the lock-that-doesn't-lock on my cage and scrambled over to Og's tank.

'Did you hear that, Og?' I asked. 'He called us snowflakes!'

'BOING-BOING!' he said.

'And he said we're special. I guess that's what the song says,' I explained.

I glanced at Kelsey's table and saw the paper lying there. 'I wish I could go over there and read it,' I said.

Since I've been the classroom pet in Room 26, I've learned to read. I can even write in the little notebook hidden behind my mirror.

And I've learned to open my lock-that-doesn't-lock, get out of my cage and explore Room 26 at night.

But there was no way that I could get from my cage to Kelsey's tabletop, because I can't shimmy up such a tall, smooth leg. And I couldn't leap from her chair to the table because her chair was pushed all the way in.

'I guess we'll have to wait until tomorrow,' I squeaked to my neighbour. It was suddenly getting chilly in Room 26. I looked forward to burrowing down in my nice warm bedding.

'BOING-BOING,' Og answered. If the students in Room 26 were snowflakes, certainly no two were alike. Slow-Down-Simon was always in a rush, while Hurry-Up-Harry was often late. Do-It-Now-Daniel put things off, while Helpful-Holly did everything right away. One Paul was tall and the other Paul was short. Oh, and Stop-Talking-Sophie was the complete opposite of quiet Speak-Up-Sayeh from last year's class.

It sounded as if he agreed with me, so I said goodnight and went back to the comfort of my cage.

Hamsters are often wide awake at night, so I had plenty of time to think.

Even the classroom pets, Og and I, were as different as night and day.

I have beautiful golden fur. He is green and has no fur at all.

He likes water and I should NEVER-NEVER-NEVER get wet.

I say 'SQUEAK' and he says 'BOING!'

And those are only a few of our differences.

I guess I wasn't wide awake after all because

I drifted off to sleep and dreamed about snow-flakes and jingle bells and prancing horses.

Humphrey's Merry Christmas Musings:

Could there possibly be any two snowflakes as different as Og and me?

Jingle-Jangle

I had to wait two days to see Ms Lark again. The morning before she was due in class seemed unsqueakably long.

First, we had to do maths questions. One was about a train going east and a train going west and as far as I could figure out, those two trains were going in circles!

Then, there was the vocabulary test. I hid in my sleeping hut with my notebook and took the test with the rest of the class. I'm sorry to say I missed three words. The first was 'drizzle'. I thought it only had one *z*. I should have known it had two. After all, Mrs Brisbane once gave us a made-up word, 'furzizzle,' and that had two *z*s.

Next was 'frozen'. I thought it had two *z*s. I

also missed 'icicle'. I got carried away and wrote 'icicicicle' (I guess Mrs Brisbane was using our spelling to get us in the mood for the *Winter Wonderland* show.)

'Og, do you think Ms Lark is really coming back today?' I squeaked to my neighbour when we were alone in the room at breaktime.

Og splashed a little but he didn't answer. I guess he didn't know, either.

But once my classmates were back and in their chairs, the door swung open and Ms Lark came in. She gave a nervous glance in the direction of my cage, then moved to the front of the classroom. She was carrying a piano keyboard with her. It was just the keyboard part – not the whole piano.

'Did you have a chance to look at the snowflake song?' she asked, placing the keyboard on the desk.

My friends all nodded, even Forgetful-Phoebe, who sometimes doesn't remember her homework.

'Great,' Ms Lark continued. 'Let's warm up by singing a chorus of "Jingle Bells". Then I'll teach you the new song.'

She flipped a switch and started playing the keyboard. It may have been small, but it was LOUD-LOUD-LOUD.

My classmates began to sing and I squeaked along.

Jingle bells, jingle bells, jingle all the way,
Oh, what fun it is to ride in a one-horse open
    sleigh-ay!
Jingle bells, jingle bells, jingle all the way,
Oh, what fun it is to ride in a one-horse open
    sleigh!

It's a happy song and I loved it so much, I kept on going.

'Squeak squeak squeak, squeak squeak squeak. Squeak . . .'

Just then, I noticed that the rest of the class had stopped singing. My friends sitting near my cage giggled.

I stopped singing.

Ms Lark looked in my direction and frowned.

But then she forced a smile (it looked forced to me) and told my friends what a good job they'd done.

Next, we sang the first verse of the song. I didn't know that part, so I listened.

Dashing through the snow, in a one-horse
  open sleigh,
O'er the fields we go, laughing all the way.
Bells on bobtail ring, making spirits bright,
What fun it is to ride and sing a sleighing song
  tonight! Oh . . .

When they went back to singing the 'jingle bells' part, I joined in again. But this time, I remembered to stop when my friends did.

Ms Lark explained what some of the words meant, which was quite surprising.

I'd thought that the horse's name was Bob and that he had bells on his tail. That's why the song said 'Bells on Bob's tail ring'. But I was WRONG-WRONG-WRONG! The horse's tail was cut short so it wouldn't get caught in the reins, and that was called a bobtail. OUCH!

(I have a small tail myself, but I'm not sure how I feel about putting bells on it.)

'I want you to practise the song on your piano when you get home so we can rehearse with you playing soon,' she told Daniel.

'Okay,' he said.

'You will remember, won't you?' Mrs Brisbane asked. 'Remember. Do-It-Now-Daniel.'

Mrs Brisbane often had to remind Daniel not to put things off.

Then Ms Lark moved on to the new song about the snowflakes.

I could tell my friends were as excited as I was to hear a brand-new song. They leaned forward in their chairs to listen.

I scrambled up to the tippy-top of my cage so I could watch Ms Lark sing and play. She had a lovely voice. The melody sounded like 'Twinkle, Twinkle, Little Star'. And I liked the words Ms Lark had written.

> No two snowflakes are the same,
> Though they're lacy white.
> No two snowflakes are alike,
> Almost . . . but not quite.
>
> Each one is special,
> That is true.

Each one is special,
Just like me and you.

Snowflakes floating through the air
Make a lovely sight.
No two snowflakes are alike,
Almost . . . but not quite.

Each one is special,
That is true.
Each one is special,
Just like me and you.

Snowflakes covering the ground
Make the whole world bright.
No two snowflakes are alike,
Almost . . . but not quite.

Each one is special,
That is true.
Each one is special,
Just like me and you.

By the time she got to the end, the whole class joined in on the chorus. I wanted to, but I managed not to squeak because I was afraid I'd upset Ms Lark.

When she stopped, Mrs Brisbane applauded and everybody cheered.

'That's a beautiful song,' our teacher said.

'Thank you,' Ms Lark replied. 'But now I'll tell you the best part. Half of the class will be prancing horses for "Jingle Bells". Those children will wear tails, horse manes and bells.'

'I want to be a jingle horse!' Stop-Talking-Sophie blurted out.

By the nods and whispering, I could see that the rest of the class wanted the same thing.

'The other half of the class will be glittering snowflakes whirling around the stage for the second song,' Ms Lark said.

'Oh, I want to be a snowflake!' Sophie exclaimed.

'Sorry, but you can't be a horse *and* a snowflake,' Ms Lark told her.

Sophie looked disappointed, but she was quiet for once.

'I don't want to be a snowflake,' Simon said. 'I'd rather be a horse.'

All the boys nodded and said they wanted to be horses.

Ms Lark turned to Mrs Brisbane. 'What do you think?'

Mrs Brisbane thought for a second and then said she thought it would be a good idea if the girls were snowflakes and the boys were horses.

'Did you hear that, Og?' I said. 'Since we're boys, I guess we get to be horses.'

Being a horse wouldn't be that hard for a hamster. After all, unlike humans, I already have a tail.

'BOING!' Og twanged loudly.

The class practised the new song several times and then it was lunchtime.

When the classroom was empty again, I burrowed under my bedding to warm up and to think.

I was thinking that Og wouldn't make a very good horse.

I'd never seen a picture of a green horse before.

And horses don't hop.

Still, I was HAPPY-HAPPY-HAPPY that we boys were going to be horses and I'm sure Og was, too.

For the rest of the day, it was hard to concentrate on our studies, because I kept hearing 'Jingle Bells' and the snowflake song going round and round in my brain.

Late in the afternoon, Mrs Brisbane began talking about real snowflakes again. That got my attention.

Our teacher had started to explain how the ice crystals formed when Small-Paul Fletcher raised his hand.

'Mrs Brisbane,' he said when she called on him. 'I did some reading about snowflakes last night and I found out that something we talked about yesterday is wrong. And Ms Lark's song is wrong.'

'Wrong?' Mrs Brisbane looked puzzled.

Paul pushed up his glasses. 'Yes, Mrs Brisbane. The song says no two snowflakes are alike, but that's not true.'

Not true? What was Paul saying?

'Oh, my! Has anyone seen two that are alike?' Mrs Brisbane asked.

'I'm not sure about that,' Paul said. 'But it's scientifically possible that there could be two identical snowflakes.'

'I see,' Mrs Brisbane said. 'If you'd like to do a little more research on that, I'd appreciate it, Paul. Can you report back to the class tomorrow?'

As soon as Paul said he would, more hands were raised.

'Maybe we should change the song,' Helpful-Holly suggested.

Mrs Brisbane smiled. 'I'm not sure that singing "Sometimes two snowflakes might be alike" would sound as good, are you?'

'You'd have to change all the words,' Thomas said.

'Does this mean we can't have glittery snowflake costumes?' Rosie asked. She looked VERY-VERY-VERY disappointed.

'You can still have glittery snowflake costumes,' Mrs Brisbane said. 'And I think we can keep the song as it is. We'll talk to Ms Lark about it tomorrow.'

All of my friends seemed pleased with her answer.

'Speaking of tomorrow, whose turn is it to take Humphrey home for the weekend?' Mrs Brisbane asked.

I looked around the room. Which house would I be visiting for the weekend? Each week it's a different place, which makes my life interesting.

Holly waved her hand wildly. 'It's me!' she said.

'Don't forget to bring in the permission slip tomorrow,' Mrs Brisbane told her.

I was pretty sure that Helpful-Holly wouldn't forget!

Later that night, when Og and I were alone, I opened the lock-that-doesn't-lock and scampered over to his tank.

'Og, since we're boys and we'll be jingle horses, do you think we should practise singing "Jingle Bells"?' I asked.

My friend didn't answer, so I decided to practise by myself. 'Jingle bells, jingle bells, jingle all the way . . .' I began.

I was happy when Og chimed in. 'BOING-BOING-BOING, BOING-BOING-BOING, BOING-BOING-BOING-BOING-BOING!'

It didn't sound like 'Jingle Bells', but at least Og was trying his best.

Later, I snuggled under the bedding in my cage with the notebook and pencil I keep hidden. I tried to draw two snowflakes that were exactly alike, but you know what? I couldn't do it!

I liked the idea that no two snowflakes – and no two people or hamsters or frogs – are exactly alike. I knew that Small-Paul was smart and knew a lot about science, but was he right about this?

Still, I didn't want to change the song.

Humphrey's Merry Christmas Musings:

Are any two hamsters ever alike?
It's STRANGE-STRANGE-STRANGE
to think that somewhere there
might be a classroom hamster named
Humphrey who's just like me!

*S*our *N*otes

I was on tenterhooks until Friday, waiting for Ms Lark to come back.

Would she be upset when she found out that the words to her song were wrong?

Would the girls be upset if she said they couldn't be snowflakes after all?

Would everyone be upset with Small-Paul for ruining the whole song? Would I?

_{·ö·}

'Ms Lark, Paul Fletcher did some research and found that there's a problem with one of the lines in your song,' Mrs Brisbane explained when the music teacher arrived. 'It is possible for two snowflakes to be identical.'

Ms Lark looked surprised. 'Really? That's not what I learned at school.'

Mrs Brisbane called on Small-Paul to explain.

'What I read said that while there probably have never been two snowflakes that are alike, there is a possibility,' he said. 'And of course, who would know for sure? Because you'd have to look at every snowflake that ever fell.'

'Wow, that's a whole lot of snowflakes,' Thomas said.

Ms Lark blinked a few times as she thought. 'Let's take a vote,' she said at last. 'Raise your hand if you think we should change the song.'

Not one hand – or paw – went up. I saw Small-Paul start to raise his hand, but then he lowered it again. I guess he liked the song, too.

'Good,' Mrs Brisbane said. 'And I think I have an idea that will make everything clear. I'll tell you later. For now, I'll let you sing.'

And SING-SING-SING we did as Ms Lark played on her keyboard.

First the boys sang all of 'Jingle Bells'. I squeaked right along with them, but I think they drowned me out.

Then the girls sang 'No Two Snowflakes Are Alike'. I didn't squeak along with them, since I'm not a girl. Instead, I hopped on my wheel and spun to the music.

I forgot one thing, though. My wheel makes a noise. It's not a little SQUEAK-SQUEAK-SQUEAK like mine, but a loud SCREECH. The more I spin, the more it screeches.

Suddenly, Ms Lark looked up and stopped playing the music.

Some of the girls kept on singing, until they noticed she had stopped.

Ms Lark stared in the direction of my cage, so I stopped spinning my wheel as well.

'Is that the—?' she asked.

'Oh, that's Humphrey's wheel. He enjoys spinning to music,' Mrs Brisbane said.

'So do I,' Rosie said as she spun her wheelchair in a circle.

'Can we cover the cage with a cloth or something?' Ms Lark asked. 'So we don't have to hear him?'

Cover my cage with a cloth? Could my tiny hamster ears actually have heard those words?

'Oh, no!' Sophie gasped. 'He'd feel terrible if you did that!'

I was so happy that someone was thinking about me!

'I don't think we need to cover his cage,' Mrs Brisbane said. 'Let's just sing a little louder.'

I was so worried that Ms Lark would cover my cage, I didn't squeak – or screech – at all as the boys practised 'Jingle Bells' again.

They sounded fine to my small ears.

But Ms Lark stopped again and said, 'Who's that?'

The singing ended again.

'It wasn't me,' I squeaked.

After all, I can't be blamed for everything!

'Sing again, boys,' she said. 'This time I won't play.'

The boys cheerfully repeated 'Jingle Bells'. But this time, Ms Lark walked away from the keyboard and stood in front of the boys, looking hard at each one.

When she was standing in front of Just-Joey, she frowned.

'I'm afraid it's you, Joey,' she said.

The boys stopped singing.

'What did I do?' Joey asked.

'I'm afraid your singing is a little bit off-key. In fact, I'm afraid your singing was way off-key,' she said.

'Off-key?' he said.

'Yes,' Ms Lark said. 'You're not singing the right notes. Could you sing a little more softly?'

Joey nodded.

When the boys started singing again, Joey didn't just sing more softly. He didn't sing at all. His mouth was closed and he stared down at his feet.

It was the saddest 'Jingle Bells' I ever heard.

'Poor Joey. I think he felt terrible about singing off-key,' Mrs Brisbane told Ms Lark when my friends left for break.

'I hated to say anything,' Ms Lark answered. 'But Joey's singing was awful. He almost sounds like that frog over there. He's so off-key, he'll throw everyone else off, too.'

'I'm sure he'll try to do better,' Mrs Brisbane said.

'He certainly will!' I squeaked.

Ms Lark sighed. 'I know, but will he be better by the time of the show? It's very important to me.'

'BOING-BOING-BOING!' Og twanged.

I don't blame him for sticking up for frogs (although I have to admit, the sounds Og makes don't sound much like singing).

Ms Lark shuddered as she glanced over at Og and me. 'Don't those animals bother you while you're teaching?' she asked.

'Not a bit,' Mrs Brisbane said. 'The children learn a lot from them.'

'And you could learn a lot from Mrs Brisbane,' I squeaked. If only humans could understand me – at least once in a while!

I'm not quite sure Ms Lark believed Mrs Brisbane . . . or me.

'They won't . . . bite?' she asked in a shaky voice.

'Og certainly doesn't. And Humphrey doesn't, either, though some hamsters may give you a nibble if they're scared. It's not their fault,' she said.

I'm not sure, but I think Ms Lark squeaked.

She might not like hamsters, but she sounded like one!

'They won't hurt you,' Mrs Brisbane said. 'Now, why are you so worried about the show?'

'It took a lot of hard work to persuade Mr Morales to let us have a winter show,' Ms Lark said. 'Finally, he said we could try it this once and see how successful it is. So I want everything to be perfect.'

Mr Morales is the head teacher and the Most-Important Person at Longfellow School. So naturally, Ms Lark would want him to be pleased.

Mrs Brisbane put her arm around Ms Lark's shoulder. 'I do understand, Mary. But try to relax. I know the children won't let you down. And the parents will love the show.'

'They will!' I squeaked.

'BOING-BOING!' Og agreed.

Ms Lark left, thank goodness. After the way she treated Joey, I didn't care if she never came back at all! For the rest of the day, I thought about Joey. I didn't think he, or his family, would enjoy the show if he didn't get to sing.

And once we were alone at the end of the day, I opened the lock-that-doesn't-lock on my cage and hurried over to Og's tank.

'I'm sorry about what Ms Lark said about your croaking,' I said. 'I thought you and Joey sounded GREAT-GREAT-GREAT.'

It wasn't actually true, but for once, I thought it was all right to bend the truth a little.

After all, I wouldn't want to hurt anyone's feelings.

I wouldn't want to be like Ms Lark.

·ᵒ·

Right before school finished for the day, Mrs Brisbane gave the class an assignment.

When she said the word 'homework', everybody groaned as usual. But my classmates cheered up quite a bit when she told us what it was.

'On Monday, I want you to talk about what you like best about the Christmas holidays,' she said. 'We're all going to share our traditions and memories. And if you'd like to bring something in that has a special meaning for you, please do.'

There were nods and smiles. Sophie leaned over and whispered something to Phoebe, until Mrs Brisbane told her to stop talking.

Being a young hamster, I didn't have any traditions. I'd spent last Hanukkah at Stop-Giggling-Gail's house – she's Simon's sister. They lit candles and sang and they opened presents. Oooh, it was wonderful. Then I spent Christmas at Mrs Brisbane's house and had a hamsteriffic time! They opened presents under a sparkling tree.

But Og didn't come into Room 26 until after the holidays.

'Og, do you know about all the celebrations that happen during the winter break?' I asked him.

He splashed around in the water but he didn't have anything to say.

Poor Og didn't even know about holiday fun.

Suddenly, all I wanted was for my goofy, googly-eyed neighbour to receive a present for the holidays.

And I wanted it to be from me!

Humphrey's Merry
Christmas Musings:

I wonder what kind of a gift a
frog would like? I do know what
a frog's favourite drink is. Croaka-
cola!

PRESENTS-PRESENTS-PRESENTS

'I wanted to take you home for Christmas, but we're going to my grandparents' farm,' Helpful-Holly explained in the car.

It was Friday afternoon and I was on my way to her house for the weekend.

I couldn't see where we were going because her mum put a blanket over my cage so I didn't get cold. I tried burrowing under my bedding, but every time the car turned a corner, I slid from one side of the cage to the other.

My tummy felt a little wobbly from all that sliding and, at one point, I got dangerously close to my poo corner – something I try to avoid!

'Why couldn't Humphrey come with us to Grandma and Grandpa's farm?' Holly asked her mum, who was driving.

'I told you, Holly. It's too long a drive for a hamster, especially in the cold,' Mrs Hanson answered. 'And Grandma and Grandpa have enough animals on the farm already.'

I'd never been on a farm, but I'd heard about them. And I wasn't interested in meeting some of those farm animals, such as large horses and cows and chickens with sharp beaks.

'But they don't have a hamster! And I'd make sure nothing happened to him,' Holly said.

The car slowed down and then stopped.

My wobbly tummy felt better right away.

'How can I give Humphrey his present when he's somewhere else?' Holly asked. 'I was even going to make a little stocking for him.'

I thought about that while she carried me to the house. Why would Holly make me one stocking when I have four paws?

My cage thumped and bumped as Holly carried it into the house. At last, the blanket came off and I realized that my cage was sitting on Holly's desk.

I turned to look around and saw four eyes staring at me!

'Eeek!' I squeaked.

'Billy and Lilly, this is Humphrey,' Holly said.

I looked again and saw that the four eyes belonged to two bright orange fish, swimming in a tank on the desk. In the middle of the tank was a bright orange castle.

'Humphrey, these are my goldfish. Do you like them?' Holly asked.

'Yes,' I squeaked, and Holly giggled.

I wasn't sure how much I liked Billy and Lilly, but I tried to be polite.

'I'm going to do my homework right away,' Holly explained. 'Then I can spend the rest of the weekend making presents.'

'Remember what Mrs Brisbane said,' I squeaked. If only she could understand me!

'She didn't want me to give gifts, but I'm already started and I don't want to stop now,' she said.

I've gone home with many students before and Holly was the first one who ever did her homework on Friday afternoon. And she did it unsqueakably fast!

'Of course, I can't let you see your present, Humphrey,' she told me. 'I want it to be a surprise.'

I like surprises, as long as they're the good kind. And I LOVE-LOVE-LOVE presents! My mind started racing as I tried to imagine what Holly would make for me.

I already knew that Holly was not lazy. She was always the first to raise her hand when Mrs Brisbane asked for a helper.

I'd also noticed that Holly could be a little too helpful at times. Mrs Brisbane's favourite plant died when Holly gave it way too much water, because she thought it would grow more that way. (The poor plant drowned!)

Rolling-Rosie Rodriguez got annoyed because Holly wanted to push her wheelchair when she didn't need help. And Forgetful-Phoebe didn't like it one bit when Holly reminded her of things that she hadn't even forgotten.

I knew Holly meant well. But I didn't know if it was a good idea for her to try to make so many gifts. Especially since Mrs Brisbane had told her to stop.

'See, I have this giant book of holiday crafts.' Holly picked up a thick book and opened it. As she thumbed through it, I saw page after page of things to make, with instructions on how to make them.

As she showed me the pictures, she told me about some of the gifts she was planning.

She was making a bookmark for the librarian, and a lanyard for Mrs Wright's LOUD-LOUD-LOUD whistle. Mrs Wright is the PE teacher at Longfellow School and as far as I'm concerned, I'd like her better if she didn't have a whistle at all!

'I'm making a calendar to help Phoebe remember dates and this cloth bag for Rosie to hang on the side of her wheelchair to keep things in,' she told me. 'Oh, and I'm making a miniature garden for Mrs Brisbane, to replace the plant that died.'

Holly's list was so long, I couldn't remember everything she was making. She did say she was making something special for Og's tank, but she didn't say a thing about my present.

Then she started snipping and clipping and gluing.

She had music playing in the background, which was nice, until I heard 'Jingle Bells' and thought about Joey. I hoped he felt better.

'Holly, don't you want to watch a movie with us?' Mr Hanson asked when he came in after dinner.

'I need to work on my presents,' Holly said. 'It's only two weeks until the Christmas holidays and I have twenty-five presents to make.'

'So many?' Mr Hanson's eyebrows went up. 'Who are they for?'

'Everyone in my class,' Holly said. 'And the teachers and the head teacher and everyone I know.'

Mr Hanson shook his head. 'I don't think everyone in your class will be making a present for you.'

'That's fine,' Holly said. 'I like giving presents. I don't need to get them in return.'

'Well, don't stay up too late,' her dad said.

After he was gone, I watched Holly cut and paste, colour and tape, fold and glue.

She used yarn, cloth, paper and cardboard.

She worked so long, I finally crawled in my sleeping hut and closed my eyes, even though

I'm usually wide awake at night.

I must have dozed off, but I woke up when Holly's mum came in and told her she had to go to bed right away.

'It's an hour past your bedtime.' Mrs Hanson turned off the music.

'But all I've made is a bookmark and two snowman finger puppets,' Holly complained.

'Holly, you're trying to do too much,' her mum said.

'YES-YES-YES,' I squeaked. I was getting tired of watching Holly work.

Holly didn't agree. 'Mum, it's Christmas and Hanukkah and that's when you give presents to people you like, right?'

'Yes, but you could give them each a card,' Mrs Hanson said. 'Now put on your pyjamas. You don't want to keep Humphrey awake, do you?'

Mrs Hanson was a very thoughtful human!

I don't know about Holly, but I was so tired, I fell asleep as soon as she went to bed, until a bright light woke me up.

I crawled out of my sleeping hut and saw that she was busy again, weaving the lanyard for Mrs Wright's whistle. A torch was propped up on the desk.

'Hi, Humphrey,' Holly whispered. 'I'm going to make a few more presents.'

'Okay,' I squeaked, although to squeak the truth, I didn't think it was okay for her to do it so late at night.

After all, both humans and hamsters need plenty of sleep!

I'm not sure about fish, though, because Billy and Lilly always have their eyes (and their mouths) open!

Holly picked up her scissors and cut some paper.

Then she yawned.

Holly picked up a marker and coloured the paper.

Then she yawned.

I yawned, too.

She was gluing some yarn on the paper when the door opened and Holly's dad came in.

'Holly, get into bed – now!' he said.

He sounded upset, so Holly didn't argue. She went right back to bed.

'Humphrey, I'm counting on you to make sure she stays in bed,' Mr Hanson told me.

'Me?' I squeaked. 'I'll try!'

He chuckled and turned off the light.

When he was gone, I kept an eye on Holly. I wasn't sure what I'd do if she tried to get up again, but luckily, she slept soundly the rest of the night.

I guess I did, too, because the next thing I knew, bright sunlight streamed through the window.

Humphrey's Merry Christmas Musings:

How many presents could Billy and Lilly make? They never seem to sleep at all!

A Sweet Idea

Usually when I go home with a classmate for the weekend, we do fun things. But all Holly wanted to do was to work on her presents.

Luckily, on Saturday afternoon, her mum insisted that Holly go shopping with her.

Once they were gone and I was sure they weren't coming back for a while, I decided to take a break from my cage.

I was curious about Holly's list of presents.

I was especially curious about one name on the list. A name that starts with a *hum* and ends with a *phrey*.

It didn't take me long to jiggle the lock on my door open. As I strolled across Holly's desktop, I was careful not to knock over any of the jars of glitter or paint or to step on something sharp, like a paperclip or a pair of scissors!

I could feel four eyes following me as I passed by Billy and Lilly. 'Don't mind me,' I told them. 'I'm just looking for the list.'

The fishes' mouths opened and closed. It looked as if they were talking, but there was no sound except the bubbling water. Were they trying to tell me something?

I paused to look at them and they stared back at me and never, ever blinked.

When I have adventures outside my cage, I try to make sure no one will see me. It felt odd to have Billy and Lilly staring at me. But I was almost pawsitive that they couldn't tell Holly that I'd been out of my cage.

I hurried past the tank and found the list sitting between a box of watercolours and the giant book of crafts.

It was a long list, so I started at the bottom and worked my way up to the top.

Of course, it's not easy for a small hamster to read the great big letters humans write, but Holly's writing was neat and I could make out the names.

Just as she had said, there was Mr Fitch's name with 'Bookmark' written after it.

And 'Lanyard' with Mrs Wright's name next to it.

I saw Phoebe's calendar and Rosie's carry-all and a few things I didn't know about, such as tissue-paper wreaths for some of my friends.

I moved up the list a little more and saw Og's name. Next to it, Holly had written 'Mermaid'.

Og was getting a mermaid for his tank? Now that was a surprise – especially because I didn't think mermaids were real!

I wanted to give Og his first gift, but I didn't think I could come up with anything close to a mermaid.

I was almost to the top of the list and, right above Mrs Brisbane's name, I saw a great big 'HUMPHREY'.

But I was unsqueakably disappointed to see this after my name:

'????'

What kind of a gift is that?

I heard a door slam, so I scurried back to my cage.

When Holly came in, she went straight to

work on her presents some more while I watched.

I watched her glue candy canes to a picture frame which was a useful and yummy gift.

Then she made a bookmark with the words 'Reading rocks' on it.

By the time her parents told her it was time for bed, she'd checked off quite a few gifts on her list.

But she hadn't crossed off 'Mermaid'.

And I was pretty sure my name still had those question marks after it.

Holly went to sleep right away. She must have been exhausted from working so hard.

Even in the dark, I could feel Billy and Lilly staring at me and opening and closing their mouths. What were they trying to tell me? I finally crawled into my sleeping hut and after a while, I dozed off.

I had a strange dream about a tiny package sitting in my cage. It had a tiny card that said, 'To Humphrey from Holly'.

I gnawed off the ribbon and opened the box and in it was a little carrot. I LOVE-LOVE-LOVE carrots, so I nibbled off a piece. It was yummy. But to my amazement, the carrot suddenly grew bigger!

Since I'm a curious hamster, I took another bite. This time, the carrot grew bigger and bigger until it was bigger than I am!

And it kept on growing and growing. I had to jiggle open the lock-that-doesn't-lock and escape before the giant carrot took over my cage . . . the room . . . and the entire world!

Luckily, I woke up before that happened.

My heart was pounding, but it quietened down when I realized that it was only a dream.

I'd been thinking a lot about Holly's gift to me. But now, I wasn't quite sure I wanted anything more than the peace and quiet of my comfy cage for the holidays.

I guess Holly had finally worn herself out, because the next morning, she slept and slept and slept some more. Finally, her mum and dad came in to see if she was all right.

As soon as Holly woke, she sat straight up in bed and said, 'I've got to get to work!'

'Wait, Holly.' Her mum sat on one side of the

bed and her dad sat on the other.

'I have to keep going or I won't finish them all!' Holly cried.

'We've got to talk about this,' Mrs Hanson said. 'I called Mrs Brisbane last night to ask about gifts and she said she'd already told you there was no gift-giving in your class.'

Holly moaned. 'But I want everybody to like me!'

'Holly, you don't give presents to get friends,' Mr Hanson said.

'But I want them to know how much I like them!'

Then it was really nice, because Holly's mum and dad both hugged her.

I like to see humans hug. (But if a human hugged me, it might hurt a lot! A little stroke of a finger on my back is fine with me.)

'You're trying to do too much and I'm afraid your friends will feel bad because they didn't make a present for you,' Mrs Hanson said. 'Did you ever think of that?'

I was truly SORRY-SORRY-SORRY to see Holly's eyes filling with tears.

'She had a suggestion,' Mrs Hanson said.

'She said if you wanted to make one gift for the whole class, that would be very nice. And we could donate the presents you've made to children in care. Think how happy they'd be to receive them.'

'But what could I make?' Holly said. 'Everybody is so different. I can't give the whole class one bookmark or picture frame.'

'We'll figure something out,' Mr Hanson said. 'Now let's have breakfast.'

'Pancakes?' Holly asked.

Her mum and dad looked at each other and smiled.

'Pancakes,' they both said.

Holly smiled and left the room with her parents.

Which left me alone to think and think and think some more.

What could Holly make for the whole class? She was right when she said everybody was different. My classmates were like snowflakes – one present wouldn't fit them all. Or would it?

I decided to check out Holly's great big book while the Hansons were making and eating pancakes. Maybe I could come up with a Plan.

I jiggled my lock-that-doesn't-lock and hurried across the desktop.

Then I saw them: Billy and Lilly, swimming around with their wide-open eyes staring at me.

As their mouths opened and closed, opened and closed, I thought maybe they wanted to tell me something. I stopped in front of their tank.

'Hi, Billy. Hi, Lilly,' I said. 'My name is Humphrey.'

They swam. They stared. Their mouths opened and closed. But they still didn't say anything.

'Well, nice chatting with you,' I said. Then I hurried over to the huge book.

Luckily, it was open. (I'm strong for a hamster, but I might not be strong enough to open such a BIG-BIG-BIG book.)

I glanced at the pages I could see. There were instructions for making a reindeer out of a paper bag, a menorah made of sticks, and a clothespeg angel. They were nice ideas, but not quite right for the whole class.

It wasn't easy to turn the page on such a

large book, but I found that I could wiggle my nose between the pages, push my head in first and then the rest of me. Next, I walked towards the middle of the book and the pages flipped over my head.

I looked at more interesting gifts: a paper-cup bell, a stocking made of felt, a thumbprint Santa.

I was about to give up when I turned a page and saw it: the most beautiful house in the world!

It was made of gingerbread, with cake frosting on the roof, a candy-cane chimney and yummy sweets glued along the sides. The garden was covered with white and fluffy flakes, like snow. (I think they call it coconut.)

I stared and stared at that little house, wishing I had one just like it. All my friends would love a little gingerbread house like that, too.

Then I heard footsteps. I dashed across the desk, past Billy and Lilly, and back to my cage, slamming the door behind me.

I crossed my paws and waited.

Sure enough, Holly went straight to her desk and sat down.

'Humphrey, we didn't think of a single thing that would be nice for the whole class,' she said. 'What am I going to do?'

'You could look at the picture in the book,' I squeaked.

I knew she couldn't understand me, but I wanted to help.

Holly reached her hand towards the book. Yes!

'I've looked through this book a hundred times,' Holly said. 'There's nothing there.' Then she moved her hand and was about to close the book entirely.

'Oh, no!' I squeaked. 'PLEASE-PLEASE-PLEASE see that little house!'

I closed my eyes. I couldn't stand to see her miss out on this wonderful idea.

'Wait,' she said.

I opened my eyes.

Holly hadn't closed the book. Instead, she was staring at the page with the house.

'Look at this gingerbread house!' she said. 'Everybody would like it, don't you think?'

'I sure do!' I told her.

She stared at the page some more. 'I love to

bake with Mum and Grandma. Mum could help me bake it and I could decorate it.'

Holly looked happy for the first time all weekend as she scooped up the book and headed out of the room. 'Mum! I've just had a great idea!' she shouted.

It was nice to see Helpful-Holly smiling.

Even if the great idea was actually mine.

Humphrey's Merry Christmas Musings:

I wonder what it would be like to live in a house made of sweets. Or better yet — a house made of carrots. Yum!

481

7

In a Spin

'Holly is making a special present for the whole class! And she has two strange goldfish named Billy and Lilly and they live in a tank with a castle!' I told my friend when I was back in Room 26 on Monday.

'BOING-BOING!' Og twanged.

Then the bell rang and class began, so I didn't have time to tell him more.

As usual, Mrs Brisbane started the day with maths.

Then we had a spelling test. I would have got 100 per cent, except for the word 'flurry'. I think I had a piece of bedding stuck in my ear because I thought Mrs Brisbane said 'furry.' Still, it was my best spelling test of the year!

When it was playtime, Mrs Brisbane said it was terribly cold outside, so my friends got to stay inside and decorate the room. They made paper snowmen and -women, yummy-looking candy canes, and all kinds of funny gingerbread people.

Then everyone gathered in a circle to answer our homework question: 'What do you like best about the Christmas holidays?'

Thomas was first to shout out, 'No school!'

All the rest of my friends shouted 'Yes!'

I didn't join in, because school is my home. It's my favourite place.

Unlike my classmates, I also didn't have any idea of where Og and I would be spending the holidays.

Next, Mrs Brisbane called on Tall-Paul Green.

'Presents!' he answered. 'I get a present every night during Hanukkah!'

A lot of my classmates said, 'Oooh!'

'We light the menorah and add another candle every night for eight nights,' he added.

'I like presents, too,' Daniel said. 'Santa leaves them under our tree.'

'I like making presents for other people,' Helpful-Holly said.

I certainly knew that was true.

'And I help my grandma make biscuits when we go to the farm,' Holly continued. 'I love to help my grandma. I'm making a special present for her.'

Mrs Brisbane smiled. 'I guess we all like presents.'

Rolling-Rosie raised her hand next. 'I love the Christmas pudding,' she said. 'My mum and I make it together, and I get to mix in the coin!'

'That's the best job of all,' Mrs Brisbane said.

Christmas pudding sounded yummy, but I'm not sure I'd like to sink my hamster teeth into a coin! I hope no one hides any metal objects in my Nutri-Nibbles.

Sophie's hand was waving wildly, so Mrs Brisbane called on her next. 'I get to set up the little nativity scene that goes under our tree. The people and the carved animals are tiny, so I have to be careful not to break anything, especially the baby in the manger. See? Here's one of the wise men.' Sophie pulled out a small carved figure of a man in robes riding a camel.

484

'Ooh, and I love the presents and mince pies and stockings,' she said. 'And if it snows, I like snowball fights and sledging. And oh, did I mention the tree?'

It all sounded GREAT-GREAT-GREAT. I would love to see that nativity scene sometime.

Stop-Talking-Sophie probably could have gone on for quite a while, but Mrs Brisbane said it was Kelsey's turn to talk.

'My mum and dad took me to see *The Nutcracker* last week,' she said. 'That's a ballet and I love ballet!'

She held up the programme with a picture of a little girl dancing on her toes in front of a beautiful Christmas tree.

Mrs Brisbane asked her to share part of the story with us.

'There's a little girl named Clara. And the dancer was actually a little girl,' Kelsey explained. 'At midnight on Christmas Eve, all the toys come alive and then mice come in and they get in a big fight. And then there's dancing sweets from around the world and – oh, it's hard to explain! But someday, I hope I can dance in *The Nutcracker*.'

She explained it well enough for me to wish I could see *The Nutcracker*, too.

'I like the Christmas crackers. I love to hear them snap. When I was little, I had a hard time pulling them, but I'm good at it now,' Forgetful-Phoebe said. 'I always laugh when Mum and Dad put on the paper hats.'

I don't like loud noises, but I do like paper hats and presents.

'This year, my parents won't be home for Christmas, but I'm looking forward to talking to them on the phone,' she added. 'That's the only present I want.'

Phoebe lives with her grandmother while her parents are far away in the military.

I REALLY-REALLY-REALLY hope she gets that call.

'Of course, Phoebe. After all, the holidays are about family,' Mrs Brisbane said.

'That's what I like,' Hurry-Up-Harry Ito said. 'Everyone comes to our house. I have six cousins. First we play board games. Then we play ping-pong and end up chasing each other all over the house!'

I've seen Harry play ping-pong, but I'd like

to see him with his cousins – all six of them.

Slow-Down-Simon raised his hand. 'I like Hanukkah, the way Paul G. does. I like the eight days of presents. I like lighting the menorah. But my favourite part is spinning the dreidel!'

It sounded as if he said 'dray-dull'. Who would like something dull?

Simon reached in his pocket and pulled out a small, wooden top. So that was a dreidel! I'd heard about it last year when Simon's big sister Gail took me to their house for Hanukkah, but I'd been too far away to see what it looked like. He put it on the table in front of him and made it spin.

I dashed up to the tippy-top of my cage to get a better look.

The dreidel had markings on each of the four sides. 'Those are letters from the Hebrew alphabet,' Simon said.

He explained that you spin the dreidel and depending on what side it lands on when it stops, you either get money or give up money.

'But it's not real money,' he told us. 'It's made of chocolate!'

I think chocolate money would taste a lot better than real human money.

Simon let his friends try spinning the dreidel and he even taught them a little song.

'Dreidel, dreidel, dreidel . . .' everybody sang. I squeaked along.

I was hoping that maybe I'd get to go home with Simon for Hanukkah!

'I like to go carolling,' Tell-the-Truth-Thomas said next. 'We go door-to-door around the neighbourhood, singing songs. Then everybody comes to our house and we drink hot chocolate. My mum makes the best hot chocolate.'

This time, I didn't think Thomas was exaggerating at all.

Small-Paul finally spoke up. He said he liked adding things to his elaborate train set to make it look like the holidays.

'I put a Christmas tree in the middle and decorate it,' he said. 'And I put candy canes in all the carriages. I even put Santa's sleigh with his reindeer on the roof of one of the houses. If you want to see it, come on over,' he said. 'Just call first.'

It sounded wonderful. But I'd had an unsqueakably scary experience on that train, so I didn't mind skipping that one.

Mrs Brisbane looked at the clock. It was almost lunchtime.

Then she noticed Just-Joey. He was looking down at his feet again.

'How about you, Joey?' she asked. 'There must be something you like about the holidays.'

Joey looked up. 'One year, my dad and I made a regular snowman. Then we made a second snowman, but that one was standing on his head. That was hard to do but it was fun.'

'I guess you're hoping it snows this Christmas,' Mrs Brisbane said.

'Not really,' Joey answered. 'Even if it snows, Dad might not get here this year.'

'Oh, dear,' Mrs Brisbane said.

My tail twitched and my whiskers wiggled. I was SORRY-SORRY-SORRY to hear that.

'I'm sorry, Joey. My mum and dad won't be able to come to the *Winter Wonderland* show, either,' Phoebe said. 'But my grandmother will be here.'

'Well, my mum will be here,' Joey said.

I was glad to hear some good news.

I crossed all my toes, wishing that Joey's dad would get home for the holidays.

I hoped Phoebe would be back with her family soon.

And I wished with all my heart that it would snow.

(For Joey. As I said, I don't particularly like snow.)

Mrs Brisbane stood up. But then Holly said, 'What do you like about the holidays, Mrs Brisbane?'

I think our teacher was surprised at first. She hadn't expected to be included.

'Thank you for asking, Holly,' she said. 'I was a little sad because our son, Jason, and his new wife live too far away to get home this Christmas. But I've just found out that my sister is coming to visit. And she's bringing my niece and her husband and their two young children. So I'll also have my great-niece, Jenny, and great-nephew, Todd, for the holidays. I'm looking forward to having a big family celebration.'

Early that evening, when Og and I were alone, I looked out of my cage and noticed something sitting nearby.

It was dark outside, but the street light lit up our table.

'Look, Og! It's Simon's dreidel,' I squeaked. 'He must have left it here.'

Og splashed noisily in his tank.

I thought about how Simon had spun the dreidel.

Spinning is something I like a lot. I spin on my wheel to pass the time, and it makes me STRONG-STRONG-STRONG. And when I'm rolling across the floor in my hamster ball, it sometimes goes into a spin that makes my tummy do a funny flip-flop.

'I don't think he'd mind if I gave it a spin . . . do you?' I asked my neighbour.

'BOING!' Og agreed.

So I opened the lock-that-doesn't-lock and hurried over to the top. It was about the same size as I was and I saw that the sides were flat.

I got up on my tippy-toes and stood the dreidel up on its spinner.

'Here goes!' I said, and I gave the top a spin.

But – oops – I hung on a little too long. When I finally let go, I was feeling a little dizzy and I tipped over. The dreidel tipped over, too, and landed right on me!

'BOING-BOING-BOING!' Og twanged.

'Don't worry, I'm fine,' I said.

I'm not the kind of hamster who gives up easily, so I stood the dreidel up again and gave it a spin. This time, I quickly let go and scrambled out of the way.

It whirled and twirled all around me. In order for me to keep my eyes on it, I had to spin around, too.

'Dreidel, dreidel, dreidel,' I squeaked, the way Simon had taught us.

The dreidel slowed, wobbled, then toppled over.

I was about to see what side it landed on when I heard RATTLE-RATTLE-RATTLE coming down the hall.

'Eeek – it's Aldo!' I scrambled back to my cage and pulled the door behind me.

I like Aldo, but I don't want him to find me outside my cage. A hamster has to have some secrets.

'Greetings, my friends,' he said as he turned on the lights.

He pulled his cart into the room and then came over to our table. 'How are my favourite hamster and favourite frog tonight?'

'FINE-FINE-FINE,' I answered.

Og hopped up and down. 'BOING-BOING!'

'What's this?' Aldo asked as he picked up the dreidel. 'Oh, I know. Dreidel, dreidel, dreidel,' he sang with a smile. 'I'd better put this in a safe spot.'

He took the dreidel to Mrs Brisbane's desk, which is a very safe spot.

But before he went to work, he gave the dreidel a good spin. It was such a good spin, it spun right off the desk and landed on the floor.

I was glad that it hadn't spun onto the floor when I was hanging onto it!

Aldo chuckled and put the dreidel back on the desk.

Later, after Aldo was gone, I looked over at the dreidel.

I love spinning, but I decided to leave it alone for the rest of the night.

On quiet nights in Room 26, I have a lot of time to think. That night, I thought about what all my friends had shared earlier in the day. I thought Mrs Brisbane was right when she said the holidays were all about family.

But then I had a truly terrible thought.

I jiggled the lock-that-doesn't-lock on my cage and hurried over to Og's tank.

'Og!' I squeaked. 'Remember all those things they said in class about families?'

'BOING-BOING!' he replied.

'But what about us?' I asked. 'I don't have a family. I mean, I used to, but I hardly remember them.'

I must admit, I do remember the wonderful smell of my mum. And I remember quite a few tiny brothers and sisters. But that's about it.

'BOING-BOING-BOING!' Og twanged in his weird way.

'Oh, no!' I said. It just slipped out. But I suddenly remembered a lesson on frogs we had long ago, when Og first came to Room 26.

As it turns out, frogs are amphibians. They come out of eggs! So Og probably didn't remember his mum at all. I wondered if he remembered his egg.

Not only that – frogs come out as little tadpoles. They aren't even frogs yet.

I wondered if he remembered being a tadpole.

I stared through the glass at my neighbour, with his green skin, his huge mouth and his googly eyes.

'BOING!' he repeated.

'I know, Og,' I said. 'It's okay. I'm sure we'll spend the holiday . . . well, I don't know where, but with some family.'

He began to splash around in his water.

'Besides,' I squeaked softly, 'I kind of think that maybe, well, you and I are like a family. Because we live together and we share what goes on here. What do you think?'

Og splashed and splashed and splashed some more.

His splashing made me feel a lot better. It turns out that having a frog in the family is a GREAT-GREAT-GREAT idea!

Humphrey's Merry Christmas Musings:

I wonder if my family ever wonders what happened to me, because sometimes I wonder what happened to them.

Sad Lad, Glad Dad

The next day, after our morning maths and vocabulary, Ms Lark came back to help our class rehearse for the *Winter Wonderland* show.

First, the girls practised their snowflake song. They were getting better and better.

Then the boys sang 'Jingle Bells'. They sounded good! Maybe it was because Joey wasn't singing along. He kept his mouth firmly closed.

'You know, Joey, I miss hearing your voice,' Ms Lark said when the song had finished. 'Please join in with the others.'

'That's okay,' Just-Joey said.

'Well, I want you to,' Ms Lark told him.

'So do I,' Mrs Brisbane said, smiling brightly

at Joey. I was smiling, too. At least I was smiling inside.

The boys sang 'Jingle Bells' again. Joey sang along – in a softer voice – but I have to admit, he did sound a little bit like a frog.

Next, Ms Lark talked about costumes for the number.

And what costumes they would be!

The girls would wear white clothes. Then they were going to make big snowflakes to wear on their backs and smaller ones to wear on their wrists. They'd be shiny and glittery and the girls would spin around like falling snowflakes.

The thought of all that spinning made me head straight for my wheel. After all, spinning is something I'm VERY-VERY-VERY good at.

The boys were going to make tails to wear and they'd have bells that would jingle and jangle as they pranced around like horses.

I hopped off my wheel and tried prancing. I'm not sure I looked like a horse, though.

My classmates were as excited as I was about the costumes and after Ms Lark left, Mrs Brisbane had a little trouble getting them to settle down.

But Mrs Brisbane is such a good teacher, she knew exactly what to do.

She started talking about snowflakes again, and this time, she told us there are seven different types of snowflake. She showed pictures of interesting shapes and patterns and then my friends got to draw their own snowflakes.

'Og, don't you think snowflakes are beautiful?' I squeaked to my neighbour as the class was busily drawing.

'BOING!' he replied. He dived into the water side of his tank and splashed like crazy.

The bell for lunch break rang and most of my friends hurried out of the classroom.

All except Hurry-Up-Harry. He came over to my cage and said, 'Hey, Humphrey, I've got a song for you!' Then he sang, 'Jingle bells, your feet smell . . .'

'Hurry-Up-Harry! We've got to get to lunch,' Slow-Down-Simon shouted.

'See you later, Humphrey,' Harry said.

After he left, I sniffed my paws. Harry was right. My paws smelled like strawberries and carrots and my favourite Nutri-Nibbles. I think they smelled hamsterlicious.

When I woke up a little later, I heard a voice say, 'Are you in there, Humphrey? I can't see you.'

I poked my head out of the sleeping hut, but all I could see was a gigantic eyeball!

I didn't dare leave my little house with a thing like that outside.

But then the eye blinked and then a face moved and I could see that the eyeball belonged to Just-Joey and not a giant at all!

I scurried out to show him I was really there.

'Hi, Joey!' I squeaked.

'Oh, hello, Humphrey,' Joey said. 'Mrs Brisbane said I could give you some fresh water.'

A giant hand reached in the cage and removed my water bottle. 'I'll be right back.'

It's a little disturbing when someone removes my water bottle, but so far, no one has ever forgotten to bring it back, not even Forgetful-Phoebe.

Sure enough, Joey quickly returned and put it back in place.

'Here you go, Humphrey,' he said. 'It's raining, so we couldn't go out for playtime.'

I looked out of my cage and saw that the rest of the class was busy drawing and cutting things out and talking to each other.

'Mrs Brisbane said we could work on our costumes for the *Winter Wonderland* show.' Joey sighed. 'I wish there wasn't going to be a *Winter Wonderland* show.'

I wiggled my nose. Did he mean that?

'What's the point? I can't even sing because my voice is so bad,' he said.

'It's not that bad,' I squeaked, but Joey didn't understand.

'Just as well,' he said. 'My dad doesn't think he's going to be able to come. He lives far away, and he doesn't know if he can get off work on time. And the roads will be bad if it snows.'

'Eeek!' I squeaked. I knew that Joey wished he could see his father more.

'Come on, Joey. We've got to work on our tails,' Thomas said.

When playtime was over, Mrs Brisbane made my classmates put away their costume pieces and talk about science again.

'It's too bad it's raining and not snowing,' she said. 'Then we could go out and gather snowflakes and study them.'

'Wouldn't they melt right away?' Sophie asked.

'Yes, but I have an idea about that. We would have to look at them quickly,' Mrs Brisbane said.

She went on to explain how snow actually helps crops grow by protecting them from the cold.

It was interesting, but for some reason, I couldn't stop thinking about how the *Winter Wonderland* show was making everybody feel GOOD-GOOD-GOOD except for Joey.

It was making him feel BAD-BAD-BAD.

When Og and I were alone after school, I was still thinking about the problem. 'I think Joey sings fine, don't you?' I said.

'BOING!' Og replied.

'Not like a frog at all,' I said. Then I quickly added, 'Not that there's anything wrong with the way a frog sings.'

Og dived into the water and splashed around.

A little later, Aldo came into the room to clean. He greeted us as usual, then went about his work, dusting and sweeping Room 26.

And, since Aldo is generally a happy human, he even sang a little song about a reindeer with a red nose. That would be something to see!

But he didn't talk until it was time for his dinner break.

Then he pulled a chair close to the table by the window where Og and I live and took out his paper bag.

'Well, fellows, the holidays are almost here,' he said.

'YES-YES-YES!' I squeaked.

Aldo took a tiny carrot out of his bag and pushed it through the bars of my cage. 'Season's greetings,' he said.

I didn't say anything, because I was busy chewing my crunchy treat.

'I always love Christmas,' Aldo said. 'But this

year is a special one.' Aldo looked at us and smiled a big smile that made his furry moustache look like a half-moon on its side.

'You see, boys, I got some exciting news from Maria,' he said. 'She's going to have a baby in the coming year. That means we're going to be a real family! I'm going to be a dad!'

Aldo's smile just grew and grew!

'That's wonderful!' I shouted, wishing with all my heart that he could understand me. 'Isn't it, Og?'

My neighbour was strangely silent.

'Og, didn't you hear that? Aldo and Maria are having a baby!' I repeated.

I guess Og heard me that time because he suddenly leaped up and said, 'BOING-BOING-BOING-BOING-BOING!'

That made Aldo's smile even bigger and he let out a loud laugh. 'Thank you, fellows,' he said. 'Your congratulations are appreciated.'

Then Aldo took out a huge sandwich and began to eat.

I stopped eating and hid some of the carrot in my cheek pouch.

I wasn't in the mood to eat right then. I was

too busy thinking about Aldo and Maria and their baby.

'Yep, this time next year, we'll be celebrating with our own baby,' Aldo said. 'Isn't that amazing?'

I absolutely, pawsitively thought that it was!

I only wished that Joey could celebrate with his dad this year.

Humphrey's Merry Christmas Musings:

I wonder if Aldo's baby will have a moustache like his. If so, I hope it's not a girl!

9

More Sour Notes

Over the next few days, the most amazing things began to happen.

First of all, large white sheets of cardboard turned into great big snowflakes that the girls could fasten onto their bodies by putting their arms through elastic loops. Smaller snowflakes went onto their wrists like bracelets.

Second, long pieces of colourful yarn were woven together into handsome tails for the boys. They also wore caps with paper ears on them.

By Thursday, the girls learned to swirl around like snowflakes as they sang:

Snowflakes floating through the air
Make a lovely sight.

No two snowflakes are alike,
Almost . . . but not quite.

They looked wonderful, especially Rolling-Rosie, who could spin her wheelchair in perfect circles.

Meanwhile, the boys learned to prance while they sang:

Dashing through the snow,
In a one-horse open sleigh . . .

But there were problems, too. One day, things got WILD-WILD-WILD and Tall-Paul pranced right into Be-Careful-Kelsey, and Forgetful-Phoebe almost knocked Small-Paul over when she swirled out of control.

Just-Joey pranced over to my cage.

'Look, Humphrey – I'm a horse,' he said. Then he made a weird noise that sounded a lot like a horse.

'*Wheeehngeeeeh!*' he said. Or something like that. I think it's called a whinny.

I've never actually seen a horse in real life, but I once saw an amazing movie at Mrs

Brisbane's house that had lots of people riding around on the backs of enormous horses. At least they looked enormous to me.

'Do it again, Joey!' I squeaked.

Guess what? He did! '*Wheeehngeeeeh!*'

Hurry-Up-Harry and Slow-Down-Simon heard him and rushed right over.

'That was amazing!' Harry said.

'How did you do that?' Simon wanted to know.

Joey did it again.

Harry and Simon tried to whinny, too, but they didn't sound like horses at all.

'Settle down, class. Back to your seats,' Ms Lark said. 'Now, girls, you will be decorating your snowflakes with paint first and then glitter. Boys, you need to finish up your ears and tails. I'll bring in jingle bells for you to practise with as well.'

All of my friends seemed so excited and pleased. I was, too!

'Daniel, why don't we try the song one time with you playing the "Jingle Bells" music,' Ms Lark said.

'Now?' Daniel asked.

'Yes, now,' Ms Lark replied.

Daniel shuffled his way to the front of the room where Ms Lark had her keyboard.

'I'm not used to playing on that,' he said.

'I know,' Ms Lark said. 'But it's just like a piano. And we'll have a real piano for the show.'

She placed the music near the keyboard and Daniel took his place.

'I'll count to four,' Ms Lark said. 'On the count of four, you start playing. And remember to follow my direction.'

Daniel nodded.

'One, two, three,' Ms Lark counted. 'Four!'

I was relieved when Daniel started to play and the boys started to sing, following Ms Lark's hands as she waved them.

Before long, I realized that something was WRONG-WRONG-WRONG!

The boys sang, 'Dashing through the snow, in a one-horse open sleigh . . .'

But by the time they were singing 'sleigh', Daniel was still playing the note for 'snow'.

Not only that, it was the wrong note. It sounded so terrible, my ears twitched and my whiskers wiggled.

'Eeek!' I squeaked. No one could hear me, of course, because there was so much noise.

Ms Lark kept waving her arms.

'O'er the fields we go,' the boys sang.

But Daniel played, 'In a one-horse open sleigh.'

He hit a couple more clunkers, too. I never knew how bad music sounded if someone hit the wrong notes.

And there was another sound: the girls were giggling.

I couldn't blame them.

Daniel wasn't laughing, though. He turned red and there was a look of panic on his face.

'Stop!' Ms Lark said.

Daniel froze and everyone stopped singing.

'Sorry, Daniel, but you need to keep up with the boys,' Ms Lark said. 'It sounded as if you were performing two different songs.'

'They were going too fast,' Daniel complained.

'I know it's difficult to play while people sing if you're not used to it,' the teacher said. 'Have you practised at home?'

Daniel rubbed his nose. 'Sort of,' he mumbled.

'I hope you will spend some time practising this weekend,' Ms Lark said. 'We'll try again on Monday.'

Daniel shuffled his way back to his chair.

He looked so miserable, the girls stopped giggling.

Ms Lark left and Mrs Brisbane took over the class, but Daniel didn't look any happier.

And when they left class for playtime, I heard Simon say to Harry, 'I hear piano players run in his family.'

'Run far away, I hope!' Harry replied with a laugh.

Which was kind of funny, except that it was true.

Later in the day, Mrs Brisbane let my friends work on their costumes. The girls seemed especially excited to make their snowflakes glitter. But before they got started, suddenly Mrs Wright walked into Room 26.

Mrs Wright is the PE teacher, who always wears a shiny (and loud) whistle around her neck.

She also likes to make sure that everyone at Longfellow School follows the rules.

'Mrs Brisbane, I want to alert you that there is to be *no glitter* at the *Winter Wonderland* show,' she said.

Some of the girls gasped.

'Oh, no!' Sophie said out loud.

I held my breath as Mrs Wright put her hand on the whistle. I crossed my paws and hoped she wouldn't blow it because hamsters have very sensitive ears!

'Oh, but we need it to make our snowflakes sparkle,' my teacher said. 'We were just about to start.'

Mrs Wright shook her head. 'I'm sorry, but at our planning meeting, we decided there would be *no glitter*. It's too much extra work for Aldo. And I don't want to find glitter in my gymnasium for the rest of the year!'

'You do have a point,' Mrs Brisbane said. 'I certainly don't want to make Aldo's job harder.'

Aldo works hard. I know – I watch him every night of the week as he sweeps, dusts and mops our room. I didn't want him to have extra work, either.

But I hated to see the girls looking so un-happy.

'Thank you for your cooperation,' Mrs Wright said. 'I'm sure we can have a perfectly nice glitter-free performance.'

After Mrs Wright left, the girls all started talking.

'It's not fair!' Be-Careful-Kelsey complained.

'We need glitter to make our snowflakes shiny,' Rolling-Rosie said.

'I'll sweep up the gym,' Helpful-Holly said. 'I'll make sure there's not one single piece of glitter left behind.'

Mrs Brisbane smiled. 'Mrs Wright has a point. There are other ways to make your snow-flakes shiny. We could try tinfoil. Now . . . back to learning.'

The girls didn't seem convinced, but soon, Mrs Brisbane was talking about something coming up called the winter solstice, which is the shortest day of the year! Since I'm usually wide awake at night, I thought an extra-long night would be FUN-FUN-FUN!

On Friday, the girls were a lot happier as they glued shiny shapes made of tinfoil on their snowflakes. And they were as sparkly as could be.

That afternoon, Do-It-Now-Daniel said, 'Humphrey, it's my turn to take you home for the weekend!'

People like Fridays. I guess it's because they have a whole weekend ahead of them. I love Fridays, too, because I get to go home with a classmate and learn something new about humans.

What I don't like about Fridays is having to leave Og behind. He stays alone in Room 26 because he doesn't have to be fed. And transporting his tank is more difficult than carrying my cage.

While Daniel waited for his grandfather to pick him up, I told Og I'd see him soon. 'Have a good weekend!' I said.

'BOING-BOING,' he answered. It sounded as if he was going to miss me.

Mrs Brisbane stood looking out the window at the grey sky.

'You know what?' she said.

I wasn't sure who she was talking to, but I squeaked anyway. 'What?'

'I'm taking you home for the weekend, Og,' she continued. 'It feels like snow and I don't want you to get stuck here in case school is closed on Monday.'

I guess she remembered the time Og and I got snowed in. It was SCARY-SCARY-SCARY to be alone at school with no one to feed us or give us water.

I was HAPPY-HAPPY-HAPPY for Og. Now I could enjoy the weekend knowing he'd have fun, too.

After the rest of the class had gone home, Daniel's grandfather arrived.

'Grandpa, meet Humphrey,' Daniel said as the old man came in.

Mrs Brisbane introduced herself to Mr Popwell, which was Grandpa's real name.

Grandpa Popwell wore a heavy tartan jacket and a funny hat with flaps that came down over his ears.

Maybe those flaps kept him from hearing too well, because he said, 'Nice to meet you, Mrs Bizzbane.'

Mrs Bizzbane – I mean Mrs Brisbane – helped Grandpa Popwell cover my cage with a blanket and carry it out.

'Bye, Og! Have a great weekend,' I squeaked to my friend. I already knew he would, since he was going home with Mrs Brisbane.

'BOING-BOING!' he answered happily.

'It looks as if we'll have the house to ourselves for a few days,' the old man said as we drove away from school. 'Your mum has a conference.'

'I know,' Daniel said. 'And Dad's out of town.'

'Just you and me,' Grandpa said. 'The boys.'

'Just you and me and Humphrey,' Daniel reminded him. 'He's a boy, too. But not Lulu. She's a girl.'

I heard Grandpa chuckle.

I wasn't sure who Lulu was. Maybe Daniel had a sister.

Once we were at Daniel's house, the blanket came off my cage. Right away, I knew who Lulu was, because she started barking.

That's right – Lulu was a dog and she was barking at me!

She was a small dog with curly black fur. But even if she was small for a dog, she was still a lot bigger than I am, and when she barked, I could see some very white, very sharp teeth.

'Settle down, Lulu,' Grandpa Popwell told her.

She didn't settle down.

'Lulu, be nice!' Daniel said.

But Lulu wasn't nice.

'I'll put her in the den,' Daniel said, and he carried her out of sight, thank goodness.

My heart was still pounding, but once Lulu was gone, I looked around and saw that I was sitting on a table in the living room.

And right across the room was a piano! I certainly hoped that Daniel was planning on practising all weekend.

Grandpa and Daniel went into the kitchen for a snack, so I scratched around my bedding and found a small piece of broccoli I'd stored there. I like to save bits of food in case some human forgets to feed me – but that hasn't happened yet.

When they came back to the living room, Grandpa said, 'Do you have homework to do, Daniel?'

Daniel made a face. 'It's Friday! I've been working all week. I'll do it later this weekend. Can we watch TV?'

'Your mother said she didn't want us watching TV all weekend,' he said. 'Oh, and she said you need to practise piano for the show at school.'

'I'll practise,' Daniel said.

I was glad to hear that, because from the way he played at rehearsal, he needed LOTS of practice.

'Later,' Daniel said.

He said 'later' a lot.

'Is it okay if I read for a while?' Daniel asked.

'Sure,' his grandfather answered. 'And I'll finish that crossword puzzle I started this morning.'

I crossed my paws and hoped that when Daniel practised 'later' it wouldn't be too late!

Humphrey's Merry
Christmas Musings:

If you say 'later' every time you need to do something, do you ever actually get that thing done?

Practice Makes Perfect

When we got to his room, Daniel set my cage on the dresser, pulled a book out of his backpack, then flopped down on his bed to read.

He was quiet for a long time. There wasn't much else to do, so I hopped on my wheel for a spin. That always gets my whiskers wiggling and my tail waggling.

I was concentrating so hard on wiggling and waggling that I almost fell off my wheel when Daniel suddenly said, 'Yes!' I thought he was trying to encourage me, so I spun a little faster.

Daniel said, 'Way to go!'

'Thanks,' I squeaked, though I have to admit I was out of breath.

'Whoa!' he said.

That surprised me so much I stopped spinning completely.

When I looked out, I saw that Daniel wasn't even looking at me. He was still reading his book.

'Humphrey, this book is the best,' he said.

Then he finally looked over at me.

'You should read it,' he continued.

'I'd like to!' I squeaked.

I meant it, too. I would LOVE-LOVE-LOVE to read more. Does anybody write hamster-sized books?

Daniel sat up and leaned closer to my cage. 'See, this boy has a magic backpack and anything he needs comes out of it whenever he needs help. So, there's this part where another boy is bullying him and he reaches into his backpack and pulls out a cream pie! So he throws the pie in the bad guy's face. And when the bully tells the teacher, the pie and the mess magically disappear. I wish I had a backpack like that!'

I guess anybody would like that.

'And it can take you places. You put it on and think of a place you want to go and – whoosh – you're there,' he said.

That got my brain spinning. I imagined being in my cage and putting on a magic backpack and – whoosh – I'd be on top of Mount Everest (although it would be a little cold there for a hamster). Or I'd be surfing on the Pacific Ocean (although it would be a little wet there for a hamster). I could be on the streets of a big, bustling city (although it would be a little dangerous there for a hamster).

Maybe a magic backpack wasn't such a great idea after all, at least for a small creature like me. But that cream pie sounded YUMMY-YUMMY-YUMMY!

I glanced over at Daniel and could see that his mind was miles away.

'Boy, if I had that magic backpack, when it was time to practise piano, I could put it on and fly to an amusement park,' he said.

'Don't you like playing piano?' I asked, wishing that he could understand.

'I like the piano,' Daniel said. 'But every time I practise, I make so many mistakes, it sounds awful. That's why I don't like to practise.'

I saw his point, but I also thought that if you don't practise something, you'll never, ever get better at it. There was no use trying to explain that to Daniel, though. I knew that all he'd hear would be squeaks.

Daniel stared at the cover of the book. 'This D. D. Denby is a genius,' he said. 'Imagine writing a book like this.'

Then he opened the book again and leaned back on his pillow. 'I've got to find out what happens next.'

Reading is great, but it's not too interesting to watch someone read. So I hopped back on my wheel and did some more spinning. I went faster and faster and faster until I suddenly screeched to a stop.

My brain was still spinning, though, because I had an idea. What if there was a story about a hamster who had a magic wheel? He could spin that wheel and go anywhere he wanted! Now *that* was a story I'd like to read in a book. I got so caught up thinking about that idea, I didn't notice that it had grown dark. Daniel had turned on the lamp by his bed.

He suddenly closed the book and sat up. 'That's it!' he said. 'Finished.'

He stared down at the cover. 'I wish I had a

magic backpack to help me get out of playing piano at school,' he sighed.

'But you don't!' I squeaked. 'So you need to practise.'

Daniel read the back of the book's cover. 'There are five more magic backpack books,' he said. 'I hope I get the next one for Christmas.'

Just then, Grandpa Popwell came into the room. 'It's awfully quiet,' he said. 'I thought maybe you'd fallen asleep.' Then he chuckled. 'I guess maybe I dozed off myself. So, how about showing me what a great piano player you are?'

'I'm hungry,' Daniel said. 'Can we do it later?'

'I'll tell you what,' Grandpa said. 'You play a song for me now and then we can eat.'

Daniel wrinkled his nose. 'Just one song?'

Grandpa agreed.

They started out the door, but Grandpa came back for my cage. 'I bet Humphrey would like to hear you play, too,' he said.

He was RIGHT-RIGHT-RIGHT. But I was prepared to dive under my bedding if Daniel's playing sounded as terrible as it had at school.

Back in the living room, Grandpa put my cage right on top of the piano so I had a hamster's-eye view of the keys. I was unsqueakably thankful!

Daniel sat down on the piano bench, opened a piece of music and began to play.

I was expecting to hear 'Jingle Bells', but instead he played another song. I knew that song, too. It's called 'Twinkle, Twinkle, Little Star'.

I was sorry that Daniel wasn't practising 'Jingle Bells', but at least he hit the right notes for 'Twinkle, Twinkle'.

Grandpa clapped when Daniel finished. 'Well done,' he said. 'But wasn't that a song you played when you first started lessons?'

Daniel nodded.

'I'd like to hear one of your new songs. I think your mum said something about you playing "Jingle Bells",' his grandfather said.

'But you said I just had to play one song,' Daniel told him. 'You didn't say which song to play. And I'm so hungry!'

'Play it one time through and we'll eat,' Grandpa said.

Daniel grumbled under his breath, but he

found the music and set it on the piano, right by my cage.

'It's pretty hard,' he complained.

'Practice makes perfect,' Grandpa said. 'Try it.'

Daniel tried, I guess.

He even hit some of the right notes.

But he hit a lot of wrong notes, too.

When Ms Lark played 'Jingle Bells', I could almost see the prancing horses and a sleigh gliding through the snow.

When Daniel played 'Jingle Bells', I could see horses tripping on the snow and a sleigh caught in a snowdrift!

'See? I told you I can't play it,' Daniel said when he was finished.

'Sure, you can play it,' his grandfather told him. 'All you need is practice.'

Daniel patted his tummy. 'But I'm starving!'

Grandpa chuckled. 'Okay. Let's eat.'

He and Daniel went into the kitchen, leaving me in my cage on the piano.

While good smells started coming out of the kitchen, I stared down at the keys. I wasn't sure how they worked. There was a piece of paper propped up above the keys. But the paper didn't have words on it – only lines and dots. Somehow, those showed people what keys to push. And when a person pushed the keys, sounds came out.

When Ms Lark pushed the keys, the music sounded good.

When Daniel pushed the keys, the music sounded bad. At least when he played 'Jingle Bells'.

I thought of how the song goes. 'Jingle bells, jingle bells, jingle all the way.'

SQUEAK-SQUEAK SQUEAK. SQUEAK-SQUEAK SQUEAK.

That part didn't seem too difficult, if you could find the right key and hit it three times, then three times again.

And what was the next part? 'Jingle all the way.'

Or, as I imagined it in my head: SQUEAK-SQUEAK SQUEAK SQUEAK SQUEAK.

That time, you played the same note as the first part once, then three other notes, then ended up on the note where you started!

SQUEAK-SQUEAK SQUEAK SQUEAK

SQUEAK. The first note, then a note that was higher, two notes that were lower, then back to the first note.

If only I had a way to get on that keyboard, I thought I could play those notes.

Then I might be the only piano-playing hamster in the world!

But I wouldn't want to get caught out of my cage. For one thing, there was always the possibility that Lulu would get out of the den and come straight for me.

And even if I survived Lulu, there was the possibility that Grandpa Popwell would change my lock-that-doesn't-lock and I'd be stuck in my cage forever!

So I stayed in my cage and thought and thought and thought some more, until I knew 'Jingle Bells' so well, it was almost a part of me.

After dinner, Daniel and his grandpa came back in the living room.

'Let's give Lulu a break and take her for a walk,' Grandpa said.

That was fine with me, as long as she didn't walk close to my cage!

'Now?' Daniel asked. 'It's cold out.'

'We'll bundle up,' Grandpa said. 'Lulu needs the exercise. Come to think of it, so do we, after all that chilli.'

Soon, Daniel and Grandpa Popwell were wearing coats and hats, gloves and scarves. Then they went into the den and came out with Lulu. Luckily she was on a lead. And she was actually wearing a sweater, which seemed strange to me.

She barked at me, of course, but Daniel took her outside while Grandpa locked the front door.

'We'll see you later, Humphrey,' he said as they left.

'Bye!' I squeaked in reply. 'Don't hurry back!'

And there I was. No Lulu, no humans, just me and the piano.

Humphrey's Merry Christmas Musings:

I wonder why a dog needs a sweater when she already has a fur coat?

The Keys to Success

I stared down at the keys. There were big shiny white keys. And in between some of them were thinner shiny black keys.

I wondered how long Daniel and his grandfather would be gone. On the one paw, it was cold outside and they might hurry back. On the other paw, it might be the only chance I'd ever have to be alone with a piano, without Lulu around. And I didn't have far to go.

So without hesitation, I jiggled the lock-that-doesn't-lock and slid down onto the keys.

CLANK-CLINK-CLUNK! CLUNKETY-CLINK-CLINK!

When I tumbled down on the keys, the notes sounded even worse than Daniel's playing.

I stopped to catch my breath before I looked down at the keys I was standing on.

I remembered that Daniel was playing the keys in the middle of the piano, so I carefully made my way there, note by note.

BING-BANG-BING!

I settled on the middle key and pushed it.

TINKLE!

That didn't sound quite right. I pushed the next key with my paw but that didn't sound right, either.

JANGLE!

I s-t-r-e-t-c-h-e-d my paw up one more key and pressed it.

JINGLE!

That was it! That was the note where Daniel had begun. (At least he got that part right.) I scurried up to that key to begin and I hit that key three times.

'Jingle bells.'

Then I pressed it three times again.

'Jingle bells . . .'

Next came the tricky part. I had to *stretch* my paws up, skip the next key and push the one next to that. Then, I quickly turned and *stretched* my paws the other way and pressed the note two keys down from the starting point.

So far, so good. I pressed the next key up and then pressed the key I started with.

'Jingle all the way!' I squeaked.

I'd hit the right notes, but it still sounded wrong. The music was too jerky.

Then I remembered that Grandpa Popwell had said, 'Practice makes perfect.'

So I played that part again. And again.

The more I practised, the more it sounded like the way Ms Lark played it. (Of course, she played with two hands, but I wasn't ready to tackle that yet! I do have four paws to work with, but I can only stretch so far.)

It was a GREAT-GREAT-GREAT feeling. In fact, I was having so much fun, I lost track of the time. So I was surprised to hear the door open and footsteps. Daniel, Grandpa and Lulu bounded through the door.

The dog started barking at me right away. I was so shocked, I fell back on the keys with a CLINK-PLINK-PLUNK!

Daniel shouted, 'Humphrey's out of his cage!' Grandpa Popwell dragged Lulu off to the den and slammed the door.

'How did he get out?' the old man asked.

Daniel had his hands cupped around me so I wouldn't fall. 'I don't know. I checked to make sure the cage was locked.'

'Well, put him back in,' Grandpa said. 'I hate to think what would happen if Lulu got near him.'

I hate to think about it even more than Grandpa. I imagine if she got near me, she'd use those sharp teeth in a highly unfriendly way!

Daniel relaxed his hands a bit. 'Maybe Humphrey wants to play the piano,' he said with a laugh.

'See what he does,' Grandpa said. 'But keep your hands there so he won't fall. It's a long way down.'

'I'll be careful!' I squeaked, which made Daniel and his grandfather chuckle.

I was SORRY-SORRY-SORRY to be caught out of my cage. But at least I had the chance to show Daniel what a little practice can do.

I made sure I started on the right key and played what I'd learned so far.

'Jingle bells, jingle bells, jingle all the way,' the notes played.

Daniel gasped. 'How did he do that? He played "Jingle Bells"!'

'It sounded like "Jingle Bells", but I'm sure it was a fluke,' his grandfather said.

'What's a fluke?' Daniel asked.

'Like an accident. Something that happened by chance,' Grandpa Popwell replied.

He thought it was an *accident* that a hamster could play the first part of 'Jingle Bells' perfectly? What about 'practice makes perfect'?

To prove that it was no fluke, I played the notes again, taking great care to make sure I hit the right keys.

'Wow, that really was "Jingle Bells",' Daniel said. 'Humphrey can play the piano!'

Grandpa looked down at me, shaking his head. 'I guess so, but nobody would believe it if we told them. In fact, maybe we should keep quiet about it, so folks don't think we're crazy. But he definitely played "Jingle Bells".'

'Play it again, Humphrey,' Daniel said.

So I played it again, without any mistakes.

'Grandpa, we should make a show with

Humphrey in it,' Daniel said. 'We could be rich if we had a piano-playing hamster. And Humphrey would be a star!'

Grandpa shook his head. 'I don't know,' he said. 'That would be a lot of work for a little hamster. Humphrey might not like working so hard.'

Daniel was disappointed, but I have to admit, my paws were feeling quite sore.

Thank goodness Grandpa told Daniel he'd better put me back in my cage for a rest.

My nice soft bedding felt especially good after scrambling around those hard piano keys.

As I settled in, Daniel said, 'If a hamster can play "Jingle Bells", then I can, too.'

Those words were music to my ears! It was exactly what I was hoping.

Daniel sat right down and practised playing 'Jingle Bells'.

The music sounded shaky at the beginning and he hit a lot of wrong notes. But the more he played, the better the music sounded.

Grandpa sat on the couch and listened. When Daniel's playing started to get better, he said, 'Good job!'

And then he said, 'That sounds great!'

Finally he said, 'Daniel, that was perfect!'

Practice makes perfect. I guess it works after all.

○

That night, I rested quietly in my cage in Daniel's room.

Lulu was in the den with the doors closed, according to Grandpa.

But I kept one eye open all night, just in case.

The next day, Daniel practised again, with my cage on the piano. He played so well, I could finally see the prancing horses and a sleigh gliding gracefully through the snow!

Late that afternoon, Daniel's mum came home.

'Mum, Humphrey played "Jingle Bells" on the piano!' he said.

His mum laughed. 'Humphrey? The little hamster? That's a good joke.'

'Well, he did,' Daniel said. 'Didn't he, Grandpa?'

Grandpa chuckled. 'Yes, he really did.'

Daniel opened my cage and took me out. 'I'll show you.'

He set me on the keys. I stopped and thought for a second.

On the one paw, I was proud to show off what I'd accomplished to help Daniel.

On the other paw, I knew Daniel would tell everyone at school what had happened. And he'd said I might become famous as the world's first piano-playing hamster. I might even end up on TV, which would be GREAT-GREAT-GREAT!

But wait. If I became a famous TV star, I wouldn't live in Room 26 any more. I'd miss my friends and my job as a classroom hamster.

So I made up my mind. I scurried up the keys and then back down.

BING-BANG-CLINK-CLUNK-BANG-BANG-BING!

Daniel's mum laughed. 'That doesn't sound like "Jingle Bells" to me!'

'Play it, Humphrey, please!' Daniel begged me.

I hated to disappoint Daniel, but I also wanted to stay in Room 26, so I scampered up and down the keys again.

CLINK-CLINK-BONG-BANG-CLUNK!

'I should have known better than to leave

you two together – making up stories like that,' Daniel's mum said. 'What I want to hear is *Daniel* playing "Jingle Bells".'

And he did.

The third time he played it, his grandpa and mum sang along.

I squeaked right with them.

Later that night, while Daniel was sleeping, I heard Lulu whining outside his bedroom door.

I almost felt sorry for her.

After all, she might have sharp little teeth, but I doubt that a dog could ever play the piano. Poor Lulu!

When I got back to Room 26 on Monday morning, I had good news for Og.

'Daniel practised "Jingle Bells", Og. And he's LOTS-LOTS-LOTS better now,' I said.

Of course, no one else would find out he was better until Ms Lark arrived.

As usual, when my friends came into Room 26, there was a lot of commotion as coats and hats were hung up and the children headed for their desks.

Stop-Talking-Sophie was telling Phoebe and Kelsey all about the tree her family put up over the weekend.

Small-Paul was showing Tall-Paul a drawing of his plans to expand his train layout.

And over in the corner, Thomas, Harry and Simon were gathered around Just-Joey.

I couldn't hear what they were saying, but suddenly Joey let out a loud horse whinny.

'*Wheeehngeeeeh!*'

'Let me try,' Thomas said. '*Weeheenwoooo . . .*' I'm sorry to say that while Joey's whinny sounded like a real horse, Thomas's sounded more like a sick cow.

'My turn!' Simon shouted. He tried to whinny, too. '*Waaaghaawaagh!*' It didn't sound like a horse. More like a large dog.

'My turn!' Harry said. Unfortunately his whinny sounded like a cat left out on the porch.

'*Wowwwoowowow!*'

'Goodness, what's going on over here with you boys?' Mrs Brisbane asked as she headed to the corner.

'We're whinnying like horses,' Simon said.

Mrs Brisbane laughed. 'Your horses sound as if they're in pain.'

'Not Joey's,' Thomas said. 'He sounds just like a horse. Show her.' He nudged Joey.

'*Wheeehngeeeeh!*' Joey whinnied.

He sounded just like a horse.

'That's terrific,' Mrs Brisbane said. 'Can you do it again?'

'*Wheeehngeeeeh!*' Joey repeated.

'You do sound like a horse,' Mrs Brisbane said.

'My dad taught me to do it,' Joey said.

Mrs Brisbane seemed excited. 'I have an idea! I'm going to tell Ms Lark about this.'

The bell rang and Mrs Brisbane took the register.

I was also unsqueakably excited about what I'd heard and seen.

'Og, did you hear it? Did you see what happened?' I asked my neighbour.

'BOING-BOING-BOING-BOING!' he answered.

Og didn't sound anything like a horse. But he did sound like a very excited frog!

Humphrey's Merry Christmas Musings:

If Og ever played the piano, would the music make everyone hoppy?

Keep Calm and Focus

'Class, as you know, today we're having a dress rehearsal for the *Winter Wonderland* show,' Mrs Brisbane said later in the morning.

Dress rehearsal? Not only did I not know we were having one, I didn't know what a dress rehearsal was.

'Ms Lark will take us into the gym so we can practise onstage. We'll take all our props with us,' Mrs Brisbane explained.

Rolling-Rosie raised her hand. 'How can it be a dress rehearsal? We girls aren't wearing white. And we haven't finished decorating our snowflakes.'

'I know,' Mrs Brisbane said. 'But at least we can try the song on the stage and you can wear your snowflakes as they are. We'll finish decorating them this afternoon. Daniel, are you ready to play the piano?'

Daniel looked pleased as he said, 'Yes, Mrs Brisbane. I practised this weekend.'

'Yes, he did!' I squeaked.

Everybody giggled.

Then Mrs Brisbane had my classmates line up. They took their snowflakes, bells, tails and ears with them.

Just as she reached out to open the door, Forgetful-Phoebe said, 'We forgot Humphrey and Og!'

For someone who can be forgetful, Phoebe was good at remembering important things – like us!

'Humphrey and Og are staying here,' Mrs Brisbane told her.

'But . . . then they won't get to see us onstage,' Phoebe protested.

Daniel looked truly upset. 'I don't know if I can play it without Humphrey,' he said. 'He helped me play the song!'

'Oh, dear,' Mrs Brisbane said.

'I want Humphrey and Og to see us,' Thomas

said. 'After all, they saw us learn the songs and make our costumes.'

'They should be there,' Holly added.

Suddenly the class was abuzz with my friends begging Mrs Brisbane to bring us along.

'But what will we do with them?' Mrs Brisbane asked.

Daniel had a suggestion. 'We can put them on top of the piano. That's where Humphrey was at my house.'

'Please! Please!' my friends begged.

Mrs Brisbane shook her head, which was bad. But then she smiled, which was good.

'Oh, I guess it won't hurt,' she said. 'But let's be careful with them.'

Then she carefully put my cage and Og's tank on a book cart she keeps in the room. 'Who's going to push?' she asked.

Of course, every single child wanted to push.

Mrs Brisbane chose Phoebe, because it was her idea.

Phoebe gave us a nice easy ride down the hallways of Longfellow School, right past Mr Morales's office.

He was standing in the doorway as we approached. 'Whoa, looks like a parade,' he said.

Mr Morales was wearing a tie with little stars on it.

'We're on our way to dress rehearsal,' Mrs Brisbane explained.

'And what are Humphrey and Og going to do?' he asked.

'They'll be the audience,' Sophie said.

Mr Morales leaned down to look in my cage. 'I hope you like the show.'

'I'm pawsitive that I will!' I squeaked back.

As we rolled along some more, I heard a familiar voice say, 'Hi, Humphrey-Dumpty!' That was A.J., one of my favourite friends from last year's class. He was the first human to give me a nickname.

And then we arrived. The gym is huge! I had only been there once before and I hadn't even noticed that there was a stage.

Ms Lark was waiting for us. When Phoebe rolled the cart past her, Ms Lark looked SHOCKED-SHOCKED-SHOCKED.

'What are *they* doing here?' she asked.

'The children wanted to bring them and I thought it couldn't hurt,' Mrs Brisbane replied.

'I don't think it's a good idea.' Ms Lark was looking pale.

'You won't even know they're here,' Mrs Brisbane said.

'Oooh, look at the stage!' Harry shouted.

What a sight! The back wall of the stage was all white with bright green pine trees made out of paper. In front of that was a low fence with snow on top. I guess it wasn't real snow, because it was warm in the gym and snow would melt. But it looked hamsteriffic.

The piano was at one side of the stage. Mrs Brisbane helped Phoebe put my cage and Og's tank on top.

Ms Lark's keyboard was on the opposite side of the stage, on a stand.

'All right, class. Let's get organized. Put on your costumes quickly.' Ms Lark looked around nervously.

There was a lot of talking, giggling and jingle-jangling as the girls put their snow-flakes, and the boys picked up their jingle bells and put on their tails and ears.

'Take your places!' Ms Lark said.

It took a while, but they managed to get lined up with the boys on the sides so they couldn't be seen by the audience (there wasn't an audience yet, except for Og and me). The girls lined up in the centre of the stage.

'Okay – so first the girls will begin the snowflake song. As soon as they finish, I'll signal you, Daniel. You start playing the introduction to "Jingle Bells". Then the boys prance onstage singing,' Ms Lark explained.

'And then the girls will sing a chorus of the snowflake song while the boys are still singing "Jingle Bells",' she said.

It sounded confusing to me, but I knew what Ms Lark wanted. I only hoped my classmates knew, too.

Ms Lark stood at the keyboard and raised her hand.

'One, two, three . . .' Ms Lark said, and the music began.

Then the most amazing thing happened. The girls twirled up the stage, spinning like snowflakes in a flurry. (That was one of my spelling words, remember?) The tinfoil on their costumes twinkled like stars. Mrs Brisbane was right – they didn't need glitter!

No two snowflakes are the same,
Though they're lacy white.
No two snowflakes are alike,
Almost . . . but not quite.

Each one is special,
That is true.
Each one is special,
Just like me and you.

Even though they weren't wearing white, I thought the girls looked wonderful whirling like snowflakes across the stage.

'And one, two, three . . .' Ms Lark said. 'Go, Daniel!'

She pointed at the piano. I saw a look of panic on Daniel's face, so I was relieved when he started to play 'Jingle Bells'.

With each note he hit, my heart went THUMP-THUMP-THUMP, but I didn't have anything to worry about. This time, Daniel hit all the right notes.

The boys came prancing in from both sides of the stage. Bells were jingling and the boys looked a lot like horses.

I loved it when they started to sing.

Jingle bells, jingle bells, jingle all the way,
Oh, what fun it is to ride in a one-horse open
    sleigh-ay!

I didn't love it when I noticed that Joey wasn't singing along.

Jingle bells, jingle bells, jingle all the way,
Oh, what fun it is to ride in a one-horse open
    sleigh!

I have to admit, I wasn't prepared for what happened next. Ms Lark pointed at Joey.

And Joey let out an earsplitting '*Wheeehn-geeeeh!*'

So *that* was Mrs Brisbane's idea!

It was a very fine whinny. And he repeated it at the end of the next verse.

The girls started twirling again and sang their song at the same time as the boys sang their song. Instead of sounding mixed-up and confusing, it sounded great!

There were a few *teeny-tiny* problems, though.

The swirling snowflakes got a little carried away. I think Be-Careful-Kelsey imagined that she was dancing in *The Nutcracker* and whirled right into Rolling-Rosie's wheelchair. Rosie spun into Phoebe and well, let's just say instead of twirling, the snowflakes were stumbling across the stage.

Meanwhile, the boys pranced like frisky horses . . . until Slow-Down-Simon took a wrong turn and the line of boys toppled like a row of falling dominoes!

'Stop!' Ms Lark shouted.

She stopped playing her keyboard, but Daniel was concentrating so hard on his playing, he didn't even notice. He kept on jingling all the way.

When the jingling-jangling-twirling-swirling-stumbling-tumbling stopped, Ms Lark asked, 'Is everyone okay?'

My classmates all nodded. That was a big relief!

'You were doing very well,' Ms Lark said. 'Just stay calm and focus on what you're doing.'

'You can do it!' I squeaked.

'BOING-BOING!' Og agreed.

'Ms Lark, we'll work really hard,' Sophie said. 'Won't we, everybody? We did well in rehearsal and our costumes look so good, I know we can do it! I think if we all pull together and—'

'Thank you, Sophie,' Ms Lark interrupted. Not that I blamed her. Sophie did tend to, well, talk a lot!

'Joey, you were great,' Ms Lark said. 'You made the song so much better.'

Joey's smile filled his whole face.

'We'll practise one more time before the show,' Ms Lark said. 'But I need you to *focus*. Oh, and Sophie, Mrs Brisbane will talk to you later.'

I was a little worried that Sophie was in trouble for talking . . . again.

Then, right before Phoebe wheeled us back to Room 26, Daniel leaned in close to my cage and said, 'Thank you, Humphrey.'

'You're welcome, Daniel,' I squeaked back.

'You're my lucky charm,' he said. 'You make me play better.'

I know he meant it as a compliment, but I wished I could tell him that he didn't need a lucky charm or a magic backpack to play better.

He played better because he practised!

Humphrey's Merry Christmas Musings:

If a horse lived next door to you, would he be your neigh-bour?

Helping Hands

When Holly arrived the next morning, her dad was with her. And he was carrying a HUGE-HUGE-HUGE box.

Slow-Down-Simon rushed up and asked, 'What's that?'

Soon, Holly and Mr Hanson were surrounded by curious classmates.

'Please, class . . . let Mr Hanson get through so he can put the box down,' Mrs Brisbane said.

They backed away and Mr Hanson set the box down on a table that Mrs Brisbane had cleared for him.

'But what *is* it?' Simon asked.

'It's a present for the whole class,' Holly said. 'And I made it.'

'And we're going to wait until everyone is here before we open it,' Mrs Brisbane said.

Simon and the others groaned. 'We'll have to wait forever for Harry!'

Harry and Simon were good friends, but Simon got annoyed when Harry was late, which was often.

All my classmates were eager to find out what was in the box. Even though I thought I knew what it was, I couldn't wait to see it, either.

Thankfully, by the time the bell rang, Harry was in his chair.

After Mrs Brisbane took the register, she said, 'Class, Holly has brought something special for everyone. I'll let her tell you about it.'

Holly stood next to the box on the table. 'I wanted to make each of you a gift to celebrate the season. But I ended up making one gift for the whole class.'

'Open it – please!' Simon said.

Holly carefully lifted the big lid and my classmates gasped. 'It's a gingerbread house and I made it myself. Well, with some help from my mum.'

'Wow! Can we eat it?' Thomas asked.

Holly looked horrified. 'No! Mum sprayed something on it that would keep it from spoiling. It's not good to eat.'

'There will be no nibbling, class. Besides, we wouldn't want anything to ruin this beautiful house,' Mrs Brisbane said. 'You did a wonderful job.'

'Can we see it closer?' Rolling-Rosie asked.

Mrs Brisbane said that the children could come closer. 'But you must be very careful not to touch the house or shake the table.'

When they moved up, my friends blocked my view.

'I'd like a better look, too,' I squeaked, but I'm sure no one heard me over all the talking.

'BOING!' Og splashed wildly in his tank.

'I want to live there,' Kelsey said, leaning in.

'Me too,' Tall-Paul agreed.

'It reminds me of the witch's house in *Hansel and Gretel*,' Phoebe said. 'But much nicer.'

'There's a card that goes with it,' Holly said. 'It says, "To all my friends in Room 26, from Holly".'

'Thanks, Holly,' Rosie said.

'Thanks!' all my friends chimed in.

'Could you tell us how you made it, Holly?' Mrs Brisbane asked.

'Og, I wish I could get a better look,' I squeaked.

'BOING-BOING-BOING!' Og agreed.

I climbed all the way up to the tippy-top of my cage and got a glimpse of the little house. It looked SWEET-SWEET-SWEET.

'My mum and I baked the gingerbread,' Holly explained. 'Then we cut it in different shapes. We followed a pattern my dad made. Then we put it all together, using icing as the glue.'

'Yum!' Rosie said.

'I needed my mum and dad to help with that. Then I put icing on the roof and put biscuits on it to look like – what do you call those?'

'Roof tiles,' Mrs Brisbane said.

'Then I put all kinds of sweets all over the house, with candy canes on the chimney and around the door,' Holly continued.

'Oh, and there are chocolate drops!' Harry said.

Kelsey pointed to something. 'And candy cane trees with gumdrops hanging from them!'

By this time, my friends were leaning over

the little house. Mrs Brisbane asked them to step back and not touch the table.

'After all, Holly worked hard on this,' she said.

Everybody moved back while they admired the house.

'I like the liquorice stick fence,' Small-Paul said.

'I like the candy-floss smoke coming out of the chimney,' Phoebe said.

They stood silently for a moment. Then Simon pointed and said, 'Oh, look in the window!' He leaned forward and pointed. 'A gingerbread man!'

'Where?' my friends shouted.

My whiskers wiggled with excitement.

But my excitement turned to shock when all at once, my friends leaned forward to get a closer look.

'Stop!' Mrs Brisbane shouted.

But it was too late. The table shook, the little house swayed from one side to the other and then—

CRASH! The gingerbread house collapsed into a heap.

'Og, it's fallen to pieces,' I squeaked to my neighbour.

'SCREE-SCREE!' he replied. That's a sound he only makes in case of emergency.

Og was right – this was definitely an emergency.

'Oh, no!' Holly moaned. 'No!'

Mrs Brisbane made everyone stand back. 'Stay calm, everyone.'

Holly was not calm. Her face was red and tears started running down her face.

'I'm so sorry this happened,' Mrs Brisbane said, giving Holly a hug. 'You worked so hard on it. I should only have let one student at a time come up to look.'

'I'm sorry, Holly,' Rosie said.

'Me too,' Thomas added. 'It was the most beautiful house on earth.'

Small-Paul stepped forward to look at the wreck of a house. 'It's broken, but it's not smashed,' he said.

'Waaah!' Holly wailed.

Mrs Brisbane asked Small-Paul what he meant.

'It might be possible to rebuild it,' he said.

Holly was sniffling so loudly, I'm not sure she heard him.

'Let's think about it,' Mrs Brisbane said, handing Holly a tissue. 'Right now, it's time for maths. Please go back to your seats.'

Then she began talking about multiplication.

'Doesn't she care?' I asked Og.

'BOING!' Og seemed as surprised as I was.

Tears were still flowing down Holly's cheeks and she began to hiccup. Sometimes it's funny to hear a human hiccup, but this time it wasn't funny at all.

'Holly, why don't you go to the nurse's office and lie down for a while?' Mrs Brisbane said. 'I'll call her and tell her you're on the way.'

Holly nodded and left the room, loudly blowing her nose.

Mrs Brisbane wrote some maths questions on the board, but I'm sure my friends weren't paying attention.

'Can't we help her?' Kelsey whispered to Small-Paul.

He nodded.

'There must be something we can do,' Sophie whispered.

Mrs Brisbane turned to face the class.

'What's going on?' she said. 'This isn't time for talking.'

Small-Paul raised his hand. 'We'd like to put that house back together,' he said.

Everybody agreed. 'Yes,' they said. 'We want to help Holly.'

'Me too! Me too!' I squeaked.

Mrs Brisbane glanced at the clock. 'All right, let's try. It's almost playtime,' she said. 'Those of you who would like to work on the gingerbread house may stay in. But just this once.'

Small-Paul started scribbling on a piece of paper.

The bell for playtime rang and guess what?

Everyone in the class decided to stay inside to rebuild the house.

Everyone wanted to help Holly.

Mrs Brisbane had them gather around the table.

Small-Paul examined the broken pieces. 'Luckily, when it collapsed, some of the bigger pieces didn't break,' he explained. 'So we should be able to glue them back together. Then we can put the sweets on again.'

'But we don't have that special icing,' Rosie said.

'Why don't we use real glue?' Tall-Paul suggested. 'We're not going to eat it anyway.'

Small-Paul nodded. 'And real glue might hold it together better.'

They went to work quickly.

The two Pauls and Mrs Brisbane got the walls back up again and glued them.

Kelsey and Phoebe put on the biscuit roof.

Thomas and Joey rebuilt the liquorice fence.

Rosie pieced the gingerbread man back together again.

Then the rest of my friends helped glue the sweets back on.

Everybody helped. I wished I could help, too. At least I could encourage my friends. 'Good job!' I shouted.

'BOING-BOING!' Og twanged.

They were almost finished when the door swung open and Mrs Wright walked in. She was bundled up in a thick jacket and had a scarf wrapped around her neck.

But I could still see her whistle hanging from her neck.

'Mrs Brisbane, what are your students doing inside? You know they're supposed to go out for playtime,' she said. 'The rules say—'

Mrs Brisbane is usually polite, but this time she interrupted Mrs Wright.

'I know about the rules,' she said. 'But we had an emergency in the class.'

She explained about the gingerbread house, the accident, and how upset Holly was.

'I think we can break the rules just this *once* so my students can help a friend who's in pain, don't you?' Mrs Brisbane smiled.

I could see that Mrs Wright was surprised, but then she shocked me.

'I think so,' she said. She looked at her watch. 'You'd better get back to work. Playtime will be over soon.'

And she left without blowing her whistle even once.

By the time the bell rang, the house was put back together again.

To squeak the truth, it didn't look quite the same. Even from my cage, I could see that it was a little crooked.

But it didn't matter. What mattered was that

561

the whole class had worked together to help Holly.

A few minutes after my classmates were back in their seats, the door opened and Holly came in. Her eyes were red, but she wasn't crying any more.

'Welcome back,' Mrs Brisbane said with a smile. 'We have a little surprise for you.' She pointed at the gingerbread house.

Holly's eyes were wide as she hurried to the table. 'But who? I mean what? I mean . . .'

I don't think Holly knew what she meant.

'All your classmates wanted to help you, Holly. So during playtime, they put the house back together,' Mrs Brisbane explained.

Holly stared down at the little house. I was afraid she was going to cry again.

But instead, she smiled!

'You did this . . . to help me?' she said, turning to the class.

'Sure, Holly,' Kelsey said. 'You're always helping us.'

All my friends were smiling and nodding, including me.

'You gave your friends a gift,' Mrs Brisbane

said. 'And they gave you a gift back.'

'Thank you,' Holly said.

I had a warm feeling from the ends of my whiskers to the tip of my tail.

Humphrey's Merry Christmas Musings:

I wonder if a gingerbread man puts a baking sheet on his bed.

The Perfect Present

On Thursday afternoon, things suddenly changed.

'Oh, my gosh – look!' Thomas shouted. 'It's snowing!'

I turned and looked out the window behind me. Big, thick snowflakes were tumbling down from the sky.

My friends ooh-ed and ahh-ed and Mrs Brisbane told them they could come to the window and look out.

'Do you think any two of them are the same?' Phoebe wondered aloud.

'Our experiment!' Small-Paul said. 'You said if it snowed we could study the snowflakes.'

'That's right!' Mrs Brisbane said.

Then, so many things happened. Mrs Brisbane sent Paul F. (that's Small-Paul) down to the office to ask someone in the head teacher's office to get something from the freezer. She and my classmates got their coats on and then Mrs Brisbane took a magnifying glass out of her desk drawer.

Small-Paul came back with a package of black paper that Mrs Brisbane had frozen. (Humans are strange, you know.)

Mrs Brisbane handed Paul his coat and then they all raced outside.

Suddenly, it was QUIET-QUIET-QUIET in Room 26.

'Og?' I asked. 'Do you know what happened?'

My froggy friend didn't answer. He only splashed around in the water.

Then I saw them out my window. They were catching snowflakes on pieces of black paper, then bending over them with the magnifying glass.

'They're looking at snowflakes,' I told Og. 'I hope they'll tell us about it,' I said.

'BOING-BOING,' Og replied.

And guess what? When they were back in the classroom, they did!

'The paper had to be frozen ahead of time so the snowflakes wouldn't melt right away,' Mrs Brisbane said. 'So what did you see?'

'There were about a million broken snow-flakes,' Thomas T. True answered.

Thomas does like to exaggerate.

'A lot of them were broken,' Mrs Brisbane said. 'But how many of you saw snowflakes with six sides?'

All my friends' hands were raised.

'And they were all different,' Sophie said. 'No two were alike. So maybe Paul F. was wrong about that.'

'You'd have to look at trillions of snowflakes to know,' Paul replied.

'They were beautiful,' Rolling-Rosie said.

Mrs Brisbane let my friends take time to draw the types of snowflakes they'd seen.

While they worked, she called Sophie up to her desk and talked to her so softly, I couldn't hear a word they said.

At first, I thought Sophie was in trouble for talking too much, again. She loves to talk!

But when I saw her smile, I knew she couldn't be in trouble.

So what was Mrs Brisbane telling her?

Sophie nodded and then nodded again.

Mrs Brisbane took a piece of paper out of her drawer and handed it to her.

I was only sorry Mrs Brisbane forgot to tell me what was going on. After all, I am the classroom pet!

It had been an exciting day in Room 26! I was staring out the window, trying to get a good look at the falling snowflakes, but I guess I dozed off. I woke with a start when I heard Mrs Brisbane say, 'So, class, tomorrow is the big day. We'll rehearse the songs in the classroom before the show. After *Winter Wonderland* is over, you'll go home with your families for the Christmas holidays.'

Tomorrow! I couldn't believe my tiny ears.

I wish I had a tiny calendar hidden behind my mirror, along with my notebook.

'Don't forget to practise tonight, Daniel,' Mrs Brisbane said as my friends left for the day. 'You too, Sophie.'

I knew Daniel would be playing 'Jingle Bells',

but I had no idea what Sophie would be practising.

And I still had no idea where I would be
spending the winter break.

Everybody in the class would be celebrating,
but what about Og and me? Would we have
anything to celebrate?

Og! I suddenly realized that I hadn't been
thinking enough about my next-door neighbour. I wanted to give him a gift . . . but so far,
I hadn't done anything about it.

It's not easy to think of a gift for Og.

For one thing, he's always splashing around
in water, so he'd ruin just about anything.

For another thing, he's always watching me.
He never closes his eyes (that I've seen). So if I
wanted to make him something, he'd see me
and it wouldn't be a surprise.

Besides, what do frogs like except flies and
crickets and other icky things to eat?

Thinking about what Og liked to eat gave me
an idea.

If I could only think of a way to distract him.

I pulled out my notebook and began to make
a Plan.

After school, while it was still light out, I decided to put my Plan to work.

I jiggled the lock-that-doesn't-lock on my cage and scurried over to Og's tank.

'Og, there's something I need to do, but I'm worried that Aldo will come in and find me,' I said. 'Could you watch the clock for me and warn me if it's time for him to clean?'

I don't know if Og can read or write. But in the past, he has often warned me about things, particularly when I've lost track of time. So he must know something about clocks.

'BOING!' Og hopped up onto the land part of his tank and faced the front of the room where the big clock is located.

Hooray – he understood!

I darted behind his tank and raced over to the corner where our food is stored.

While I looked longingly at my beloved Nutri-Nibbles, Mighty Mealworms, Veggie Dots and Hamster Chew-Chews, I passed right by. I glanced at the can of crickets – EWWW! – then headed for the jar of Froggy Food Sticks.

The small sticks were perfect for what I wanted to do. But how was a small hamster going to get them out of a plastic container with a lid?

Luckily, when I was making my Plan, I had thought about this.

I took a run at the container and managed to knock it on its side. (I almost got knocked on my side, too!)

I went up to the plastic cap and tapped it. Just as I feared, it was fastened tightly.

However, I'm VERY-VERY-VERY strong for a VERY-VERY-VERY small creature.

So I stood on my back legs and put both front paws against the lid and pulled.

The edge only bent back a little, so I tried again, pulling even harder. 'Ooof!'

But it still didn't come off.

I don't give up easily, so I looked around. Lying on our table, not too far from my cage, was a pencil. I hurried over and rolled the pencil up to the Froggy Food Sticks.

'Keep your eyes on that clock!' I told Og.

'BOING-BOING!' he replied.

I held the pencil with both of my front paws,

put the pointed tip under the edge of the lid and gave it one big push. All at once, the lid popped off and a pile of Froggy Food Sticks tumbled towards me.

Ewww! My whiskers wilted as the sticks gave off a smell like stinky fish. But this was a gift for Og, after all. He loves stinky stuff.

'Everything all right, Oggy?' I squeaked.

'BOING!' he said.

It would take too long to carry the sticks to the side of Og's tank. I had a better idea. I stood up on two feet and pushed the pile with my front paws, moving them in the direction of his tank.

Then I did it again and again, until I had a nice pile of Froggy Food Sticks in place. Luckily, Og was still looking towards the clock.

'I won't be long now,' I told him.

'BOING-BOING,' Og twanged.

Since I had it all planned out, it didn't take long for me to use my nose and paws to arrange the sticks in the shape of a Christmas tree.

I wasn't sure I'd ever get the smell of stinky

fish off my paws, but, after all, you shouldn't be selfish if you're giving a gift.

Then I scurried back to my cage and tore out a page of my notebook where I'd made a little card for Og earlier in the afternoon.

I had a little trouble with the card. I'd started out writing 'Happy Hanukkah', but I didn't know how to spell 'Hanukkah' so all I'd written was 'Happy'.

Then I'd tried to write 'Merry Christmas', but I didn't know how to spell 'Christmas' so all I'd written was 'Merry'.

I'd been in a BIG-BIG-BIG hurry at that point, so I'd written, 'Frog'.

That's all I had time to write. It wasn't much of a holiday greeting, but it would have to do.

'Og, could you come over to my side of the tank now? I have something for you,' I said.

Then I scampered back to my cage.

It took Og a while to move from one side of the tank to the other. I think he liked looking at the clock.

But when he finally saw the food stick tree and the note, he said, 'BOING!'

'It's a present from me, Og. It's a Christmas tree with a note that says, "Happy Merry Frog". Oops, I forgot to sign my name,' I explained. 'I hope you like it.'

Og stared and stared at the tree and the note with those bulging eyes of his.

I was afraid he had no idea what I was talking about.

Then all of a sudden, he started hopping up and down, up and down, crying, 'BOING-BOING-BOING-BOING!'

He liked it!

Og kept hopping and BOING-ing.

He was a very happy and merry frog.

I was feeling happy and merry myself.

·ͦ·

I was resting comfortably in my cage when I heard Aldo approaching.

RATTLE-RATTLE-RATTLE! I think the wheels of his cart needed oiling.

The door opened and there he was!

'Hello, my friends!' Aldo shouted as he came into Room 26. 'Season's greetings!'

'Hello, Aldo!' I squeaked.

Og splashed around in his tank.

'How do you like the snow?' Aldo said. 'Hey, what do snowmen wear on their heads?'

I thought and thought, but I had no answer.

'Snow caps!' Aldo replied. And he laughed and laughed and laughed.

I laughed, too.

Aldo went right to work, cleaning our class-room.

'Say, fellows, I was happy to find out that they decided there would be no glitter at the show tomorrow,' he said. 'You've got glitter once, you've got it forever. I've swept up pieces of glitter that have been hiding for years.'

'Then I'm glad too, Aldo!' I said. When Mrs Wright had first said our class couldn't use glitter, I was upset with her. But I decided that this time, Mrs Wright was right.

'After all, I want to get home after the show and be with Mama Maria,' he said. 'I've got to start thinking about being a dad.'

I was sure that Aldo would be a great dad.

He's already a great cleaner, a great student, and an unsqueakably great friend.

Aldo dusted and swept all the tables in the

room until he finally came to our table.

'What's this?' he asked as he looked down at the Froggy Food Sticks tree. 'It's a little Christmas tree!'

Then he laughed until his moustache wobbled. 'And a little card. "Happy Merry Frog",' he read. 'I guess somebody in this class likes you, Og. What am I saying? Everybody likes you and your friend Humphrey.'

'BOING-BOING!' Og agreed.

'But you haven't got to enjoy your present yet,' Aldo said. 'Here . . . open wide.' He scooped up a handful of the Froggy Food Sticks and threw them into Og's tank.

'BOING-BOING-BOING-BOING-BOING!' Og said as he opened his huge mouth wide to catch them all.

Aldo laughed some more as he watched my friend. 'I think somebody gave you the best present in the world,' he said. 'Right, Og?'

Og splashed and splashed until drops of water spilled over the top of the tank.

Aldo was still laughing as he sat down to eat his dinner. 'Tomorrow's the show,' he said. 'So if I don't see you after that, I wish you both the happiest holidays ever. Whatever you celebrate, may you celebrate it well.'

'I wish that for you, too, Aldo!' I squeaked with great excitement. 'And for Maria and the baby. And for everybody!'

Aldo chuckled. 'Humphrey, there's nobody like you.'

I certainly hope not! Maybe there are two snowflakes alike somewhere, but there are no two humans who are alike.

And I'm pretty sure no two hamsters are alike, either!

Nights are long in the winter, and if you're a wide-awake hamster, they seem to go on for-ever. On Thursday night after Aldo left, I spun on my wheel, climbed my tree branch, made a trip to my poo corner, rummaged around for food . . . and it was still early.

I sat in my cage, looking out at the classroom lit by the streetlamp outside the window.

'Og,' I squeaked. 'Isn't Holly's gingerbread house the most wonderful thing you've ever seen?'

Og splashed around, but he didn't seem too interested. I guess if the house had been made of crickets or something stinky, he would have liked it more.

'Have you noticed that it's just my size?' I asked.

Og was quiet, so I guess he hadn't noticed.

I continued. 'Holly will probably take it home for the holidays. I was just thinking that I might go over and have a peek at it while I have a chance.'

'BOING-BOING-BOING!' Og sounded worried.

'Oh, I'll be careful,' I told him as I jiggled the lock-that-doesn't-lock and scurried out of my cage.

I slid down our table leg and hurried over to the bigger table where the gingerbread house sat. The table is next to a reading area where Mrs Brisbane keeps a tall wire rack full of books. If my friends have free time, they can pick out a book to read or check it out and take it home.

The book rack reminded me of my climbing ladder, so I knew what to do. Very carefully, I pulled myself up from one wire to the next until I was on the same level as the gingerbread house.

As I climbed, I saw some unsqueakably interesting book covers. One showed a dinosaur with huge teeth. I hurried past that one. But there was another one with a mouse wearing knight's armour, standing in front of a castle. I hope Mrs Brisbane will read that one to the class someday.

I hopped onto the table and there it was: the gingerbread house, covered in the most yummy-looking sweets I'd ever seen!

'BOING-BOING!' Og warned.

I'm glad he did, because I was just thinking that no one would notice if I took a teeny bite of a candy cane or a nibble of a gumdrop.

'BOING-BOING-BOING-BOING!'

I almost thought Og could read my mind. But he was right. Holly had said that her mum had sprayed something on the house and no one should eat it.

'All right, Og! I won't take a bite,' I squeaked.

As I inched closer, I noticed that instead of smelling like delicious sweets and cake, the gingerbread house smelled like something Aldo used to mop the floor. And it was a lot shinier than biscuits usually looked.

The smell was strong, so I held my breath and gazed at the liquorice stick fence and the candy cane chimney with the candy-floss smoke. I took another breath and held it just long enough to peek in the windows of the house and see the gingerbread man inside. He gave me a jolly smile.

I felt a little dizzy, so I gave the gingerbread house one more look, then scampered back to the book rack and made my way to the floor.

When I returned to our table, I grabbed on to the blinds cord, as usual, swung my way back up, then let go and leaped onto the tabletop.

(I have to be VERY-VERY-VERY careful with the timing of that move.)

As I passed by Og's cage, I said, 'Thanks for reminding me that just because something looks tasty, it doesn't mean it's good to eat!'

'BOING-BOING-BOING!' he agreed.

Back in my cage, I wondered about what I'd said. If something doesn't look tasty – like an icky insect – is it possible that it still could be good to eat? Og certainly thought so. But I wasn't about to try a diet of flies and crickets and Froggy Food Sticks . . . ewww!

Humphrey's Merry
Christmas Musings:

If I got a present and Og did not, would he be green with envy?

15

On with the Snow

On the day of the show, my friends were full of energy, but Mrs Brisbane calmed them down and they finished up their schoolwork.

In the afternoon, Ms Lark came to the classroom to wish us luck.

'I know you'll do a great job this evening,' she said. 'Remember, keep calm and stay focused. Daniel, you'll practise again after school?'

He nodded.

'Sophie, you know what you're doing?' she asked.

Sophie nodded.

I was glad she knew what she was doing, because I certainly didn't.

581

Ms Lark continued, 'You'll meet here and get in your costumes. Then ten minutes before you go on, I'll stop by to help you line up and walk to the gymnasium.'

Mrs Brisbane thanked her and we went on with the rest of the day.

When class was almost over, Mrs Brisbane let my friends practise the songs while sitting in their seats.

It sounded so good, I was SURE-SURE-SURE it was going to be a great show!

Then Holly raised her hand and asked who would be taking Og and me for the holidays.

My ears pricked up, because it was something I'd wondered for a long time.

Mrs Brisbane smiled and said, 'I guess it's selfish of me, but I'm taking them both home. I want Todd and Jenny to get to know them. Besides, you'll all be busy building snowmen, because I heard on the radio that it's supposed to snow late tonight.'

My friends seemed pleased to hear about the snow, except for Joey.

He looked at the window and then he closed his eyes for a second.

I knew he was wishing that his dad could make it home before the snow arrived.

When the bell rang at the end of the day, everyone raced out of the room, except for Mrs Brisbane.

'I think I'll leave you two here for now,' she said. 'I'll pick you up after the show.'

'GOOD-GOOD-GOOD,' I said. 'Because I want to be here to see my friends.'

Mrs Brisbane chuckled. 'I guess you're as excited as the rest of the class.'

She was right!

·ö·

It was dark when everyone returned to Room 26.

'Aren't you excited, Og?' I squeaked.

'BOING-BOING!' He dived into his tank and splashed around.

Mrs Brisbane arrived first with her husband, Bert.

He rolled his wheelchair over to our table. 'So, I hear you guys are coming to visit,' he said. 'That's enough of a present for me!'

'Me too!' I agreed.

The girls were all dressed in white: white tights, white shirts and white trousers. Mrs Brisbane helped them get their snowflakes on their backs and wrists.

They were shiny and shimmering and no two were alike.

The boys wore dark shirts and trousers. Mr Brisbane helped them with their tails and ears. Once they had their bells, the room was jingling and jangling like mad!

In fact, everybody was talking and laughing.

Rosie showed Mr Brisbane how to twirl like a snowflake in his wheelchair.

I heard Phoebe tell Kelsey that she was so excited because her grandmother was making a film of the show so her parents could see it.

Sophie was talking and talking . . . to herself this time!

And Joey was practising his whinny. '*Wheeehngeeeeh!*'

'Children, why don't we start to line up now?' Mrs Brisbane said. 'Ms Lark will be here soon.'

While she helped them form a queue, Daniel came over to my cage. 'Okay, Humphrey. I need you to bring me good luck again.'

He picked up my cage and moved towards the queue.

'What about Og?' I squeaked. But just then, Daniel tilted the cage and I slid all the way across. 'Eeek!'

'Aren't we taking Og?' Phoebe asked Daniel.

He shrugged. 'I don't know.'

The door opened and Ms Lark came in. I couldn't get a good look at her from my cage, but I heard her tell everyone how great they looked.

The queue started to move into the hallway. Suddenly, Ms Lark said, 'What are you doing with that cage?'

Daniel said, 'I'm taking Humphrey. He's my good-luck charm.'

Then I could see her. Ms Lark wasn't tall, but as I looked up at her from my cage, I saw a giant face. A giant, no-nonsense face.

'There is no way you're taking that creature into the gym,' she said.

'But I need him for luck,' Daniel said. 'I can't play without him.'

'Put him back,' she demanded.

'But you let him come the other day . . .' he began.

'Against my better judgement,' Ms Lark told him. 'Put him back now.'

'Yes, Daniel. I know you'll be fine without him,' Mrs Brisbane said.

Daniel carried my cage back and set it on the table by the window. 'I can't play it without you,' he said.

'Yes, you can!' I squeaked, even though I was disappointed I'd miss the show.

Suddenly, Daniel opened the door to my cage and scooped me up. 'Come on, Humphrey. No one will know.'

And he put me in his pocket, which was down near his knee.

A pocket isn't a good place to put a hamster.

The bad news was that it was dark and hot in there. The good news was that I was going to the show after all!

'Bye, Og!' I yelled, though I'm sure he couldn't hear me.

BUMP-BUMP-BUMP, BUMP-BUMP-BUMP. The class headed down the hall.

Once the bumping stopped, I knew we were

somewhere near the gymnasium.

'Hey, we can see the stage from here,' I heard Daniel tell Thomas.

'Wow – it's all snowy,' Thomas replied.

I used my paws to climb up the inside of the pocket and poked my head out of the top.

We were standing in the hallway, but I could see the stage from an open door into the gym.

The children from Miss Loomis's class were onstage, wearing bright sweaters, scarves and earmuffs, and singing about a winter wonderland.

I recognized some of them from my class last year: Golden-Miranda, Speak-Up-Sayeh, Wait-for-the-Bell-Garth, and Sit-Still-Seth. And they were all gathered around a great big snowman!

'Eeek!' I squeaked. 'He'll melt!'

Daniel pushed me back down into the pocket and I couldn't see anything. I did sniff out two raisins stuck to the cloth. They were squashed but still tasty.

After a while, we started moving again. I could feel us moving up some steps and then up onto the stage.

THUMP! That was Daniel sitting down on the piano bench.

'Now Mrs Brisbane's class will perform for you. But first, an introduction from Sophie Kaminski.'

I peeked out of the pocket again. Sophie walked to the centre of the stage and faced the audience. She wasn't wearing her snowflake costume.

The audience! I turned and saw them: mothers and fathers, sisters and brothers, grandmothers and grandfathers and lots of friends. The gymnasium was packed with people.

Sophie stared out at the crowd. Everyone waited for her to say something, but for the first time ever, Stop-Talking-Sophie didn't seem to feel like talking.

I wished I could tell her to squeak up!

Luckily, Mrs Brisbane cleared her throat loudly.

Sophie suddenly opened her mouth and said, 'Most people think that no two snowflakes are identical. However, scientists aren't sure. Just for tonight, we'll say that no two snowflakes are the same, because in our class, no two students are the same. And we're happy about that!'

Then she walked to the side of the stage and Mrs Brisbane helped her put on her snow-flakes.

'One, two, three, four . . . ' Ms Lark said.

The music began to play and the girls came twirling and whirling and sparkling onstage, singing their song.

No two snowflakes are the same . . .

People were ooh-ing and ahh-ing at the lovely sight.

When they finished, Ms Lark pointed to Daniel, and he began to play as the boys came onstage, prancing and shaking bells and sing-ing with all their hearts.

Jingle bells, jingle bells, jingle all the way,
Oh, what fun it is to ride in a one-horse open
sleigh-ay!
Jingle bells, jingle bells, jingle all the way,
Oh, what fun it is to ride in a one-horse open
sleigh!

Just-Joey let out a fine '*Wheeehngeeeeh!*' and the audience roared with laughter.

Every single time Joey whinnied, the crowd reacted happily.

Then the girls whirled in again and sang their snowflake song while the boys sang 'Jingle Bells'.

It sounded so good, I had to have a better look, so I pulled myself UP-UP-UP –and then something terrible happened.

I started falling DOWN-DOWN-DOWN!

I had to stop myself, so I grabbed on to Daniel's trouser leg. He kept playing, but some of the notes he hit weren't quite right.

I was barely listening, though, because I started sliding DOWN-DOWN-DOWN.

Whew! I made it safely to the floor. I was going to try to get safely behind the piano, but as soon as I turned, Be-Careful-Kelsey twirled right towards me.

I darted away, just as Rolling-Rosie whirled dangerously close to me.

I took a sharp right turn and here came the horses, jingling and jangling so close, one of them almost pranced on my tail.

'Humphrey!' I heard Harry exclaim.

'Humphrey!' other friends shouted.

There was a stir in the audience, but I wasn't bothered by that.

I was bothered by the fact that my friends were all whirling and prancing to avoid stepping on me, which meant they were crashing into one another.

Then I heard a sound unlike anything I've ever heard before.

'Eeeeeeeek!' someone was screaming. 'Eee-eeek!'

I didn't know a human could make such a loud sound.

Everybody stopped to look in the direction of the 'Eeeeeek!'

It was Ms Lark. She was standing on a stool and screaming. 'Get it out! Get it out!'

And then the thing I always dread happened. Mrs Wright blew her whistle.

SCREEEECH!

I was jittery enough as it was, but that shrill blast almost made me jump out of my fur coat!

'Everyone stop where you are!' she shouted.

I stopped. The music stopped. The whirling and twirling and prancing stopped.

Even Ms Lark stopped screaming.

Mrs Brisbane ran onto the stage, gently picked me up and held me in the palm of her hand. I was trembling from all the excitement (and the whistle), but she stroked my back with her finger and that calmed me down.

She stepped to the front of the stage and spoke to the audience.

'Families and friends,' she said. 'Some of you may not have met Humphrey the Hamster. He's the classroom pet in Room 26 and we all love him. I don't know how he got in here . . .' She shot a knowing look in Daniel's direction. 'But everyone seems to be safe and sound. So do you think we should try the number again?'

The audience cheered and clapped.

Someone yelled, 'Encore,' which I think means 'some more'.

Mrs Brisbane carefully handed me to Joey. 'Don't take your eyes off him,' she said.

'I won't,' Joey promised. He also gave my back a soft and reassuring rub.

Mrs Brisbane helped Ms Lark off her chair.

She still looked a little shaky, but she went over to her keyboard.

Mrs Brisbane got everyone back in place, took me back from Joey and moved to the far side of the stage.

'One, two, three . . .' Ms Lark began again.

I carefully peeked over the edge of Mrs Brisbane's hand and I was amazed at what I saw and heard!

Every note was perfect. Every prance and whinny, every jingle and jangle, every whirl and twirl was wonderful.

Until all of a sudden:

'*Wheeeh*—!' Joey stopped in the middle of a whinny. He was staring at the door.

I twisted my head to look. A tall man with a bright red cap was standing in the doorway, smiling. He took off his cap and waved it.

I looked back at Joey. He was waving, too.

His great big smile let me know that the man was Joey's dad. He'd made it!

Then Joey opened his mouth wide and let out his biggest whinny yet. '*Wheeehngeeeeh!*'

When the number was finished, the audience stood up and applauded.

Ms Lark made my friends take a bow.

'Bravo!' the crowd shouted.

'Bravo!' I squeaked. I wasn't exactly sure what it meant, but I knew it was something good!

Our class left the stage and Mrs Brisbane rushed me back to Room 26 and my cosy cage.

'Humphrey, I don't know how that happened, but please don't ever do that again. I almost fainted!' she said.

'Me too! Me too!' I squeaked.

'BOING-BOING-BOING!' Og twanged.

'Don't worry, Og. I'll tell you all about it,' I said.

Mrs Brisbane went back to the gym and while we were alone, I described everything to Og. When I told him the part about Ms Lark, he hopped up and down, saying, 'BOING-BOING-BOING-BOING!'

And when I told him about Joey's dad and the cheering at the end, he dived in the water and splashed happily.

Then, I rested while I waited.

My friends all went home with their families, but Mr and Mrs Brisbane came back to Room 26 to pick up Og and me.

Mr Brisbane was chuckling as they entered the room. 'You certainly put on a show that no one will forget,' he said. 'Not as long as they live.'

'You know who to thank for that,' she said. 'Humphrey. It seems that Daniel put him in his pocket for good luck.'

'It turned out to be good luck after all,' her husband agreed.

Mrs Wright popped her head in the doorway. 'Is the hamster all right?'

Mrs Brisbane assured her that I was fine.

'Good thing I had this.' Mrs Wright fingered her whistle. 'Have a wonderful holiday!'

And she popped her head out of the doorway again.

I have to say, I could have done without that whistle, but it was nice to hear that Mrs Wright cared if I was all right.

The door opened again and Ms Lark entered. 'Sue, I'm so embarrassed about what happened,' she said. 'I apologize. I told the children to keep calm and focus. But I didn't follow my own advice.'

'It turned out all right in the end,' Mrs Brisbane said. 'But tell me, why are you so afraid of a little hamster?'

'I don't know,' Ms Lark said. 'I've always been terrified of animals. My mother said I must have been scared by something furry when I was a baby.'

'That's a shame,' Mr Brisbane said.

'I know,' Ms Lark agreed. 'I wish I could change.'

'Well, you can go on holiday now knowing you put on a great show,' Mrs Brisbane said.

'The children did all the work,' Ms Lark said.

'Oh, there you are!' Mr Morales said from the doorway. He was wearing a candy-striped tie with his suit, and a Santa hat on his head.

'Congratulations,' he told Ms Lark. 'You were right about the show. We'll have to do this every year.'

'What about the part with the . . . hamster?' she asked.

Mr Morales laughed so hard, his Santa hat shook. 'Believe me, Mary, that was the best part of all!'

Humphrey's Merry Christmas Musings:

I wonder how the show would have gone if Daniel hadn't put me in his pocket? It would have been entertaining . . . but not nearly as exciting.

Decking the Halls

Og and I have stayed at the Brisbanes' house many times.

But this time, it had changed completely. For one thing, there were tiny twinkling lights around the doors and windows. There was a wreath on the door and lights that looked like candles on the windowsills.

Inside, a gigantic tree took up a whole corner of the living room. It was covered with lights and little ornaments. I couldn't see them all from my cage on the table but I did see elves and reindeer and shiny round things.

There were also yummy-looking gingerbread trees and stars and angels!

I also saw long stockings hanging from the

mantelpiece. So that's the kind of stocking Holly was talking about!

There were decorations everywhere.

'Merry Christmas, Humphrey and Og,' Mrs Brisbane said as we got settled in. 'Tomorrow will be a big day!'

She certainly wasn't exaggerating. The next morning, Mrs Brisbane's sister arrived with her husband. There was a lot of hugging and talking and more hugging.

Then the doorbell rang and Mrs Brisbane's niece and her husband arrived.

And with them were two children, a little younger than the children in Room 26. Once their coats were off and the suitcases carried inside, Mrs Brisbane brought them over to meet us.

'Jenny and Todd, this is Humphrey. He's our classroom hamster!' she said.

'Pleased to meet you!' I squeaked.

Jenny and Todd giggled.

'And this is our classroom frog, Og,' she continued.

'BOING-BOING!' Og said.

Jenny and Todd laughed out loud.

It was fun meeting new children. Jenny and Todd helped their Aunt Sue (that's what they called our teacher) and Uncle Bert (that's what they called our teacher's husband) take care of us. They even helped clean out my poo – and they didn't even say 'Ewww!'

When Mrs Brisbane took me out of the cage and put me in my hamster ball, Jenny and Todd loved following me all around the living room.

They also loved throwing Froggy Food Sticks into Og's tank.

Late that night, when it was time for bed, Mrs Brisbane brought Jenny and Todd into the living room. They were both in their pyjamas, ready for bed.

'Tonight, Santa will come with presents,' she said. 'And he'll fill these stockings for you.'

'How will he know we're here and not at home?' Jenny asked.

'Because Santa knows everything,' Mrs Brisbane said. 'Don't worry, he'll be here. So we'd better leave out a mince pie for him, and a glass of milk.'

'And some carrots for Santa's reindeer?' Todd asked.

'Of course!' Mrs Brisbane said. 'They're working hard tonight.'

'Did you hear that, Og?' I squeaked to my friend. 'Yummy carrots?'

Og didn't answer, but I don't think frogs are very interested in carrots.

They put the food out right on the table next to us and headed for bed.

Right before she left the room, Mrs Brisbane came over to my cage. 'Remember the poem, Humphrey.'

'What poem?' I squeaked.

''Twas the night before Christmas and all through the house, not a creature was stirring, not even a . . . hamster!' Then she laughed and turned out the lights.

'That's a funny poem,' I said to Og when we were alone. '*Hamster* doesn't even rhyme with *house*.'

Og didn't seem to care about what rhymed and what didn't.

So I sat and I sat, looking at the tree.

After a while, those gingerbread ornaments looked more and more interesting to me. I like crunchy things.

'Og, I don't think it would hurt if I went over and looked at the tree, do you?' I asked my neighbour.

Og splashed around a little. I wasn't sure whether that meant 'yes' or 'no'.

A little while later, I said, 'I won't touch anything. I'll just look at the decorations.'

Og splashed a little more, but it was hard to figure out what he meant.

So I finally made a decision. I jiggled the lock-that-doesn't-lock, threw open the door and scampered out of my cage.

'I'll be right back,' I said.

The table we were on was low, so I easily slid down the leg and hurried over to the tree.

At first, I stood there and stared up at it. I'd never seen anything so glowing and glittery in my life!

Then I moved closer to look at the shiny, sparkly things.

The ornaments were fantastic! There was a tiny snowman. A jolly Santa. Lots of red and green and gold balls. Best of all, there were those gingerbread trees, stars and angels.

I scurried closer to the tree.

One of the gingerbread stars almost touched the ground.

I thought it looked delicious. I thought it wouldn't hurt if I just tasted it. Then I didn't think any more.

I raced to the tree, stood on my tippy-toes and took a bite.

Oh, my! It was delicious! So I took another bite.

'BOING-BOING!' Og said. He has a way of warning me.

But I didn't see any danger. The room was empty and surely the Brisbanes wouldn't notice a bite or two missing.

CRUNCH-CRUNCH-CRUNCH!

It was as yummy as I imagined!

MUNCH-MUNCH-MUNCH!

And there was so much of it!

'BOING-BOING-BOING!' Og twanged.

'Just a few more bites,' I squeaked back. I munched and crunched some more.

Then I heard a THUMP.

And I heard a BUMP!

I stopped munching and crunching and

looked out at the room. There was a flash of red and a dash of white.

Somebody was there!

I froze mid-crunch. Who could it be?

The red moved. The white moved. I reached up to the branch above me and pulled my feet up.

If someone was nearby, that someone might think I was an ornament.

Thank goodness, Og was as quiet as a mouse.

The red-and-white figure stood in front of the fireplace and reached up to the stockings. Then the red-and-white thing moved to the table where my cage and Og's tank sat.

Paper rattled. Something thumped and bumped. Something clinked. Something crunched.

I heard some footsteps, and then I didn't see any red and white any more.

I stayed frozen in place for a LONG-LONG-LONG time.

Even after I was sure the red-and-white figure had left, I waited and waited some more.

I have to admit, I did move when suddenly Og said, 'BOING-BOING-BOING!'

What was Og trying to say?

'BOING-BOING!' he repeated.

I thought about it. Og was so quiet while the red-and-white thing was nearby. Maybe he was trying to tell me that we were alone again.

'Og, is the coast clear?' I squeaked.

'BOING!' he replied.

Og had never let me down before, so I took a chance. I dropped from the branch and scampered across the floor towards the table.

'BOING-BOING!' Og twanged in an encouraging way.

When I got to the table, I needed a way to get back up. I was surprised to see a big pile of packages nearby that wasn't there before. I climbed them like steps up to the table and headed towards my cage.

As I hurried along, I passed by the plate for the mince pie, the glass of milk and the plate of carrots. And I noticed a strange thing.

The mince pie was gone. The glass of milk was empty. And there were no carrots!

I knew Og hadn't taken them, but who had?

I was happy to be back in the safety of my cage again. I closed the door behind me.

'What happened, Og?' I squeaked. 'Did you see who it was?'

'BOING-BOING-BOING-BOING-BOING!' Og replied. He was hopping and jumping and leaping around.

'Do you mean . . .' I paused to think. 'Do you mean it was *Santa Claus*? Here?'

Og hopped and leaped and BOING-ed some more.

'It *could* have been,' I said. 'It *might* have been. It *must* have been Santa!'

I have to say, I was disappointed that I hadn't got a better look at him.

But I was also happy that he hadn't seen me.

•ö•

'Santa came!' Todd and Jenny shouted the next morning. It was FUN-FUN-FUN to watch the family open presents and empty the stockings and laugh a lot.

While Jenny and Todd played with their presents, Mrs Brisbane came over to our table and leaned in.

'You didn't think Santa would forget you, did you?' she asked.

Then she opened my cage and slipped in a wooden object. It looked like one of those dumbbells humans use to make themselves stronger.

'Merry Christmas, Humphrey,' she said. 'Here's something to chew on.'

Jenny and Todd ran over to watch me sniff the new object.

I carefully bit into it. It was firm to the bite and a very fine thing to chew on!

'THANKS-THANKS-THANKS,' I said.

Then she gently placed a very fine plant in Og's tank and said, 'Merry Christmas, Og. This will make your house a little nicer and give you some shade.'

Og dived into his water and said, 'BOING-BOING-BOING!'

Jenny and Todd laughed every single time Og said something.

Then Mrs Brisbane announced that she had another surprise for Og and me coming soon.

Later in the day, the doorbell rang and when Mr Brisbane opened the door – guess who was there?

It was Ms Lark! And she was carrying her little keyboard with her.

'Thank you for inviting me,' she said.

'Glad to have you, Mary,' he said.

Before long, Mrs Brisbane's whole family and Ms Lark were sitting at the big dining room table. I could see them from the living room.

They ate a delicious-smelling dinner and they talked and laughed a lot.

After dinner, they gathered in the living room. Ms Lark played some songs called 'carols' on her keyboard and everybody sang. I enjoyed Ms Lark's lovely voice.

Oh, they were wonderful songs. I especially liked one about decking the halls with boughs of holly.

'Fa-la-la-la-la, la-la-la-la!'everyone sang.

I joined in. 'Fa-la-la-la-la, la-la-la-la!'

I even heard a 'BOING-BOING!'

The humans stopped singing, but Og and I were still fa-la-la-ing.

Mrs Brisbane heard us and laughed. 'Mary, I think our friends Humphrey and Og like your songs,' she said.

Ms Lark shivered. 'They're here?' she said. 'You know I'm afraid of animals.'

'Things can change,' Mrs Brisbane said. She motioned to a spot on the couch next to the table we were on. 'Why don't you come over here and watch them?'

'They're quite entertaining,' Mr Brisbane said. 'Right, Humphrey?'

'Right!' I squeaked. If the Brisbanes wanted entertainment, I was the hamster to provide it.

First I climbed up to the tippy-top of my cage. 'Watch carefully.' Then I grabbed on to my tree branch and leaped from limb to limb.

'Oh, my!' Ms Lark said.

Og hopped up and down under his plant. 'BOING-BOING-BOING!'

Jenny and Todd laughed and I think I heard Ms Lark laugh, too.

Not to be outdone, I scurried to my ladder bridge and walked across it to the other side of the cage. I climbed UP-UP-UP. This time, I hung from the top of the cage and made my way to the other side paw over paw.

'Look!' Ms Lark said. 'That's amazing!'

SPLASH! Og made a spectacular dive into the water side of his tank and began to swim.

'Oooh!' Ms Lark exclaimed.

'Now, you don't think those lovable little animals would hurt you, do you?' Mrs Brisbane said.

'May I hold Humphrey?' Jenny asked.

'Yes, but you have to be gentle,' Mrs Brisbane explained. 'He's never bitten anyone so far, but if you move too fast and frighten him, he might.'

Believe me, I wasn't about to bite Jenny!

Mrs Brisbane showed her how to hold me cupped in one hand and told her to hold her other hand a few inches above my head, like a little roof.

I felt warm and cosy.

'Can I pet him, Aunt Sue?' Todd asked.

'Yes, if you stroke his back lightly with your finger,' Mrs Brisbane told him.

Oooh, that felt so good.

'He's soft,' Todd whispered.

'How about you, Mary?' Mrs Brisbane asked.

'Sure, go ahead!' I squeaked. I wiggled my whiskers to look extra-friendly.

She reached out slowly and rubbed her finger along my back. 'Oh, yes, he is soft,' she said. 'And he's got such a cute face.'

YES-YES-YES! I had won her over!

Two days ago, she'd been screaming at the sight of me. Now she was my friend.

A new friend really is the best gift of all.

After dinner, as everyone ate cake and chatted, Mrs Brisbane said, 'This has been the most perfect Christmas, celebrating with family and good friends. That includes you, Humphrey and Og.'

'Gee-whiz, come and look out the window!' Mr Brisbane called out. He'd been peeking through the curtains, but now he opened them wide.

Outside, snow was falling, covering the lawn, the pavement and the trees. The Christmas lights twinkled merrily against the falling snow.

'Oh, it's beautiful,' Ms Lark said.

'A white Christmas!' Jenny shouted. 'We can build a snowman. And make snowflake ice cream!'

'Can you see it, Og?' I asked my neighbour.

'BOING-BOING!' Og replied.

'You know what it is? It's a winter wonderland,' I told him.

I watched the snow and thought of what my friends were doing. Simon spinning his dreidel, Holly helping her grandparents, Sophie setting up the Nativity scene.

Harry was running all over the house with his cousins, while Paul F. ran his train around the tree.

Phoebe was talking on the phone to her parents – I was sure! And I imagine Kelsey was dreaming about dancing in *The Nutcracker*.

Thomas was singing carols, while Rosie and her family were eating Christmas pudding.

Then there was Joey. He was with his dad. And he was happy.

I was happy, too. Happy to be a classroom pet and to be friends with so many GREAT-GREAT-GREAT humans and one funny frog. That's something I can celebrate every day of the year.

'FA-LA-LA-LA-LA!' I squeaked loudly. 'LA-LA-LA-LA!'

Humphrey's Merry Christmas Musings:

I wonder if I could EVER-EVER-EVER have a better holiday in my life!

Humphrey's Tips for Giving Gifts

1 Give someone a gift that they would like, not just something you like. For instance, I would not like a present that smells like stinky fish at all, but Og certainly would!

2 A handmade gift is always the best . . . unless you lose too much sleep over it.

3 The best gifts are the kind that can't be wrapped . . . like helping a friend.

4 Don't tell someone what to give you. Let them surprise you. Surprises are always fun!

5 The best time to give friends gifts is when they don't expect one.

6 It is far better to give than to receive. Giving Og a present gave me a HAPPY-HAPPY-HAPPY feeling!

7 Good things come in small packages . . . like hamsters, for instance.

8 A friend is a gift you give yourself. So I have lots of unsqueakably wonderful gifts!

9 A hug is a great gift. One size fits all and it can't be exchanged. (Although we hamsters prefer a soft stroke on the fur.)

10 If someone gives you a gift, please don't forget to squeak 'Thank you!'